Lost Midsummers

a novel of exile and friendship

By Agate Nesaule

Birch Grove Press
2018

Lost Midsummers

Nesaule, Agate (1938-)
 Lost Midsummers : A Novel of Exile and Friendship.
 415 p. cm.

ISBN-13:   978-172648828 (Paperback)
ISBN-10:   1726488225   (Paperback)

1. Female Friendship—Fiction. 2. Contemporary Women—Fiction.
3. Latvian Americans—Fiction. 4. Conflict of Generations—Fiction.
5. Self-realization in women—Fiction. 6. World War, 1939-1945—
Refugees—Latvia. I. Nesaule, Agate (1938-). II. Title.

First edition, 2018.

In celebration of the Centennial Celebration of Latvian Independence

Cover and interior design by David W. Jackson, The Orderly Pack Rat.

Published in the United States by:
Birch Grove Press
Madison, Wisconsin

Contents

Lost Midsummers

Part One

Shadows

1940s

Lost Midsummers

1

1941

The coldest winter in memory is past. Sweet grass and red clover flourish beneath skeletons of apple trees killed by icy winds. Hens cluck, brooks shimmer, and cows give milk. Bringing good luck with them, storks have returned to their nests high above churches and farms. Wild strawberries ripen on the edge of woods, and beets grow plump underground.

Russian conquerors swagger on the city streets of Latvia, but only the fragrance of evening-scented stock and newly mown grass wafts around country houses.

Velta surveys her cool, orderly kitchen in Stabules, "The Flutes," the farm her husband, Valdis, owns. She covers sweet-sour rye dough with a linen cloth, sets it to rise, and rubs glycerin and rose water into her sunburned hands. Stretching her arms high above her, she brings the palms together and places them over her heart in a position of prayer. "May I always be thankful for all I have. May I be at peace. May I be free of fear," she whispers.

Her body fills with gratitude for the flourishing vegetables and flowers in her weed-free garden, for wheat ripening in the fields, for her husband, who will be home in a few days, and for their five-year-old daughter, Alma, asleep in the barn. "May I be free of fear," she repeats, trying to rid herself of an entirely unfamiliar feeling of unease which has invaded her this evening.

Velta grew up in a Catholic orphanage, but she no longer goes to Mass. Instead she sometimes calls on Dievins, the sweet, intimately familiar God addressed by a diminutive and praised in

7

hundreds of *dainas,* ancient Latvian folksongs. Occasionally she accompanies her
husband to Lutheran services, and she always sees to it that bouquets of flowers are ready on Saturday afternoons for Valdis to take with him, to stand by the graves of his father and grandfather and talk to them.

The cemetery is next to the church, on a nearby hill where seven centuries ago ancient Latvian warriors fortified themselves against invading Germans. Witches, healers, seers, and other powerful spirits gathered there too. Velta can still feel traces of their benign presence in gentle breezes that reach her at noon. But today dark clouds roiled without bringing refreshing rain, and sharp gusts of wind slammed into birches and oaks.

Curled-up between pillows of hay in the barn, little Alma is dreaming of storks and wild geese. A simple summertime treat for children—being allowed to sleep away from the house—has calmed the five-year-old at last. Velta lulled her to sleep by telling her a story about a family of porcupines, fat and snug in their house on the other side of the hill, brewing beer and making cheese for celebrating Midsummer, which is a little more than a week away.

All day the little girl has been cranky and clingy, pulling on Velta's skirt and stepping on her heels, behavior uncharacteristic for such a good-humored, independent child. *I should have questioned her about her fears, she felt something terrifying nearby,* Velta will think later. *Children have second sight. They can sense disaster to come.*

Some danger does exist even in the countryside. People hoping to escape torture, deportation, and death by the Russians in control of cities wander the roads at night. Crazed people emerge silently from the woods. Like starved ghosts, they stand watching prosperous country houses.

Valdis would not like his wife and his daughter leaving the safety of the house for the barn, but Velta plans to tell him they did. She and her husband are partners and good friends. They always talk things over, and he depends on her common sense and resourcefulness. She respects his judgment, and so she will wedge a board against the barn door before climbing up to the loft, curling around the small body of her daughter, and pressing her face into her straight ash-blond hair.

Velta and Valdis are not a couple jaded after ten years of marriage. Valdis' name suggests someone who rules over himself and
others, but he does not rule Velta, except sometimes pleasurably in bed. She is more deferential to his wishes now than usual because of her pregnancy. The only time she has seen him cry was when she miscarried three years ago. He insists that she rest, that she let the servants do the heavy work for the next four months, and that she not jump on a horse to ride out bareback to distant fields. She obeys him or languorously promises that she will, although she likes using her strong body until it aches; she enjoys rest when it is truly earned.

Velta's robe, fine cotton sheets, and light blanket are on the scrubbed oak table. She would not think of flitting across the yard barefoot, wearing only her nightgown. She does not want the farm workers to see the outline of her bare legs or her thickened waist. Modesty forbids it, and so does her station. She was regarded with suspicion by the hired hands when she came to this farm as a seventeen-year-old bride ten-years-ago, loved by her older husband but disliked by his mother. She worked hard to earn their respect; she will not risk losing their deference or her own dignity now.

Velta fills a large mug of dark beer from the barrel Valdis has ready for Midsummer and takes a long satisfying drink. Cool liquid slides down her throat and warms her belly and groin. She sips, breathes in the fragrance of sweet peas arranged in a mug on the table, and imagines welcoming Valdis into her arms. When they are one, she feels connected to trees and fruit, earth and sky.

Mrs. Vilkacis, her closest neighbor and a mother of six, has told her that love does not last after the children come, but Velta has not found that to be true. Her body sometimes throbs with desire for her husband's physical presence, and she warms with pleasure when he touches her, just as she did when Alma was a tiny infant nursing at her breast. Shivers run up her thighs at the memory of sleeping spoon-fashion with Valdis, his calloused hand on her belly, his

9

steady breath on the back of her neck, his large solid body protecting her.

Careful of her swollen and tender breasts, Velta lifts the towel to inspect the rye dough once more. Although she employs three young women in the kitchen and fields, Velta always makes the bread herself. She loves to combine flour with water, to visualize yeast coming to life, to feel transformation begin. But today Alma's unusual demands to be held and soothed as if she were a baby have almost kept her from this meaningful task.

Humming to herself, Velta hangs her apron on a hook in the pantry and surveys her bins of sugar and flour, her jars of jam and pickles and plums still plentiful from last year although it is almost time to begin harvesting and preserving again, to move through long sun-filled days, dazed with the satisfaction of work. Wheels of cheese and a crock of butter are covered with damp cloths, and the pervasive scent of dill is everywhere. Velta will snip it and sprinkle it over cottage cheese and radishes, which she plans to serve for breakfast. She is proud that has always fed the hired hands as well as she has her own small family, and she knows that it is her hard work, intelligence, and good management which have produced this abundance for everyone who depends on Valdis and her. And she has shown her mother-in-law a thing or two.

Tying her robe tightly, Velta picks up her blanket and sheets, turns out the light, opens the kitchen door, and freezes. The stink of car exhaust and cigarette smoke assaults her before she sees the truck. Its lights and motor off, it stands ominously silent outside the gate. She can make out three men next to it. Two more may be sitting in the cab of the truck, although she cannot be sure.

Her insides lurch, and her hands go reflexively to her belly to shield it. The mug of dark beer slips and shatters on the large white stone by the steps.

Without taking her eyes off the truck, she moves back toward the safety of the kitchen. But even as she does, she is aware of futility. These men have been here for some time; they have been spying on her in her own lighted kitchen, which infuriates and terrifies her. For an instant she tries to delude herself that Valdis is among the silent watchers, that he has hitched a ride on the truck and returned earlier than expected. But she knows that is false: Valdis would never sneak up on her like this. He would stride into the yard and greet her straightforwardly. If others were watching, he would take her hand and squeeze it. Alone, he would embrace her.

Her heart pounding, Velta desperately tries to decide what to do. Run to the barn and clutch her little girl to her heart? Grab a pitchfork
to protect her? Or phone the Mayor of the nearby village and ask him to send the district police? But Valdis is the Mayor. He takes a lively interest in local as well as national politics. Pray that he will arrive in time to save her?

She can feel that these men intend harm, so it is fortuitous that he is beyond their reach. Should she stand here and wait for them to take the initiative while she, their meek quarry, trembles with fear? Should she scream and summon the hired hands asleep at the other end of the long low farmhouse? But that would rouse Alma and reveal her hiding place.

The icy anger of the men assails her even at this distance. She has to keep her little girl safe.

Velta takes a deep breath, raises her head proudly, and takes a few steps toward them.

"What do you want?" she says, without greeting.

The men are in no hurry to answer. The three in uniform are Russians, who have occupied Latvia for the past year. The other two are civilians, Latvian communists and local collaborators. The Russians look identical to Velta. Their foreignness makes it impossible for her to see them as individuals, but she recognizes the Latvians. Jurgis, a tall pock-marked man in his twenties, actually worked at Stabules two summers ago. Valdis fired him after Velta's warnings did not stop him from sticking his fingers into the pants of the women workers. The afternoon Valdis saw Jurgis try to mount a young woman weeding the flower bed, he ordered him to be gone before dark.

Jurgis leans nonchalantly on a rifle and looks Velta up and down.

11

"Where is your husband?" he demands. He raises his hand as if to strike her, but a thick voice speaking lazily in Russian halts him.

The other Latvian is the cobbler and village atheist, the only person Velta knows who does not belong even nominally to the Lutheran congregation and who boasts that he would not participate in religion, an opiate used to keep workers in line. Although not particularly devout herself, Velta respects religion. Dressed in clothes which would have been the stuff of dreams in the orphanage of her childhood, she proudly walks out the front door on her way to church on a few of the important holidays. But she feels more reverence as she sets out seedlings or lifts her eyes to the blue expanse above sheltering pines.

Like others, Velta has criticized the cobbler for mocking religion; she has said derisive things and laughed within his hearing.

The cobbler's full-face and heavy body are in a self-righteous position, but she cannot see if his nose is reddened by drink, as often it is. He looks solemn and determined, weighed down by the responsibility of exacting vengeance for his poverty and that of thousands of others.

So, these are the local supporters of the conquering barbarians from the East, Velta thinks. One of dozens of reasons she wishes Valdis were at her side is that he would laugh at this menagerie as he named aloud their motives and shortcomings.

A Russian soldier speaks self-importantly, and the cobbler translates.

"We've come to arrest the Mayor. Where is that capitalist pig?"

"He isn't home."

"We know that already, don't toy with us. Where is he?"

"Not here."

Jurgis, the former field hand, brandishes the rifle recklessly, as if it were a whip and she a recalcitrant mare. A Russian soldier steps in front of him and slaps her, hard, across the face.

This abrupt turn to violence stuns her and confirms everything she already knows. They have not come to consult with her husband about some unpleasantness in the village. They are here to hurt, punish, and kill. She has to protect her unborn child, her little girl, and her beloved husband.

She casts about frantically for something to say so that they do not hit her again. Because they have already spied into every room, they seem to accept her answer that Valdis is not home. They were not here yet when Velta took Alma to the barn.

"My husband is staying with friends, far from here." She stops herself from saying more because words flowing too easily will tip them off that she is lying. She lets them ask more questions before she adds triumphantly, "You will never find him."

Resentful, the men confer in surly voices. "We might as well take her," says the cobbler contemptuously. He does not address her directly even as he announces her doom. "Our orders are to bring them both. She's not worth much by herself."

"Go get your things," Jurgis screeches.

"You have ten minutes to pack."

"Where are you taking me?" she asks as the single bare room with barred windows in the village hall flits across her mind. The shame of being locked-up like a criminal washes over her, so that she almost blurts out, *You can't take me. I have my daughter to care for. You can't expect a five-year-old to fend for herself.*

Jurgis jeers, "Siberia, my fine lady, we're taking you and the rest of the scum who exploit workers to Siberia."

Determined to save Alma, Velta closes her mouth and gathers herself into silence.

"You heard me, cunt! Siberia, Siberia, Siberia," Jurgis mocks.

"I refuse to go," Velta brings out.

She succeeds in keeping her voice steady.

"No one's asking you," they laugh. "And you can't stay on this farm, it isn't yours anymore." The cobbler looks at the farmhouse as if it were his already. "It belongs to the people."

"No," she cries and launches her whole self past the cobbler and the soldiers, toward the woods. She struggles even after her arms

13

are restrained. She kicks, writhes, and bites, remembering not to cry out or to glance toward the barn.

A hard blow to the jaw fells her, and she feels something tear, her flesh, or the hundreds of invisible threads that bind her to these particular hills and trees, to this plentitude of peace and work.

Guilt flickers for an instant for somehow failing her daughter, her husband, and everyone else.

But, then, mercifully everything goes dark.

Jurgis says something derisive, and the others chuckle. They lift and fling Velta into the bed of the truck, and three of them, their hands already loosening their belts and trousers, get in the back with her.

There is a great slamming of doors and lowering of flaps. The motor roars into life, and the headlights come on. The truck backs up, wheels around, and assaults the white daisies and fragile red poppies lining the road.

The farmhouse remains dark and silent, although those inside are awake. Relieved that they have been spared, guilty that they have not intervened, they hold their breaths, terrified for themselves and of the future.

2

Velta wakes with a throbbing pain in her jaw; her entire body feels sore and defiled. She moistens the hem of her sleeve with spit and tries to wipe off the blood crusted around her mouth and the filth from the floor, streaked with tears on her cheeks. She manages to release the clenched muscles of her jaw, but they tighten again. She will not howl in anger and pain, she will not cry, no, she will not give them the satisfaction of knowing they have hurt her. And anyway, there is no one who can comfort or help.

She feels around on the dusty floor and finds that the three men who violated her have dumped her robe and blanket beside her. A kindness, she thinks automatically, but corrects herself. She will not be grateful for small favors from these degenerates, these rabid dogs. She will ask for nothing, she will never beg. They have flung her things next to her only because they want her alive so that they can work her to death in Siberia.

Tales of Russian brutalities she has heard all her life come back to her with horrifying vividness: young men and mere boys dragged away from home to serve in the Czar's army for twenty-five years, women and girls horse-whipped and raped, babies caught on the tips of bayonets.

She crawls to the flap of the truck, which is idling in a row with others by a railroad crossing and looks out. She is not near any station that she can recognize. In the early dawn light, soldiers shout orders she does not understand, and people are being pushed and prodded into line. A few move compliantly forward but most are holding back, dragging their feet, or stopping altogether.

Shots ring-out ahead and terrified murmurs sweep over the crowd like gusts of a storm over young birches. *They've shot a man.*

15

They've shot a woman. They've shot a child who refused to leave his mother. Through a loudspeaker an unctuous, official, voice speaks Latvian with a Russian accent, repeating unconvincingly that the shots are meant only to encourage everyone move forward.

Velta climbs over the flap of the truck, and slides to the ground. If she stays on the side of the convoy away from the crowd, she may be able to move unnoticed behind one truck to another and then run across the meadow and into the woods. Childish fears of wolves and wild boars, and more realistic ones of desperate, emaciated Germans hiding in the forest arise, but she is ready to face them. She will die if she must, rather than meekly submit.

She makes it past three trucks, only to career into Jurgis, who has come back to retrieve something.

"O-ho! What have we here!" he shouts as he seizes her by the forearms. In a moment, she is surrounded once more, though this time the men only propel her into line with others. Jurgis restrains her wrists long after she ceases struggling. Escape is impossible.

At the head of the line, guards are separating women from men, children are crying, a few adults are sobbing openly. Married people embrace, lovers cling, a young girl screams as she is pulled away from her father. The fate of children is arbitrarily decided according to lists the guards hold. So, a sixteen-year-old boy is allowed to stay with his mother, while a fatherless nine-year-old is pushed into line with men he does not know.

A Russian speaking accented Latvian repeats lies calculated to enforce order and a semblance of calm: this separation is only temporary, the men's train to Russia will be traveling right behind the women's, and everyone will be reunited in a day or two. Siberia, the real destination, is not mentioned.

"We regret we have to separate families, but we must, for the sake of everyone's privacy and modesty."

Velta sneers at the mention of modesty. If only she could wash herself, cleanse the filth between her legs and inside her body so it does not contaminate her child, she might yet live. The memory of what happened in the back of the truck will be more difficult to expunge.

16

The rising sun is cool and remote, and massing clouds threaten more rain. Velta wraps her blanket around herself to keep from shaking. Ahead of her are two women dressed in layers of sweaters and coats they have not been able to fit into their suitcases. At another time she might laugh at these clumsy figures moving stiffly, two wobbly snowmen in summer, but now she barely registers their presence. Others, awakened by sharp knocks in the middle of the night and told to pack in ten minutes, have been too stunned to bring anything to keep warm. An old woman carries a palm in a flowerpot in one hand and trails an apron with the other.

People standing near the edge of the woods start to creep across the meadow, toward the captives. A few are smug with revenge; some are merely curious. Most hope to catch a glimpse of loved ones, give them clothing and food, and say goodbye. A few are already bribing the guards.

A young mother in line ahead of Velta hands an infant to an old woman, wipes her tears angrily on the back of her hand, and turns away shame-faced yet defiant in giving up the child in order to save it. Velta thinks ruefully of her mother-in-law, who will have the pleasure of braiding Alma's hair and toweling her dry after Saturday night saunas and languorous movements in the cool pond alive with water lilies and frogs.

"Do you have children?" the guard asks Velta through a translator when she arrives at the head of the line. She shakes her head and bites her lips in order to lock in the voice that clamors to beg her enemies to send for Alma, to tell them that only she knows how to take care of her little girl, that even prison and exile are preferable to being torn apart.

But, Velta loves Alma too much, and she is too clear-sighted. She must learn to crush the guilt that torments her as violently as if she were willfully abandoning her daughter and setting off on a trip of selfish pleasure. The guards shove a form written in Russian in her face, twist her arm, and threaten to dislocate her fingers until she signs it — a declaration that she is leaving Latvia voluntarily.

They drag her to a wagon that has been used to transport livestock. It reeks of manure. The bits of ceiling and wall she glimpses through the press of women and children are filthy. The rough splintered boards scrape her knees as they heave her in.

Velta stays where they have flung her until hands reach out to lift her up and steady her. The wagon is jammed but the inhabitants seem to welcome her or at least accept her even though there is scarcely enough space to sit, let alone lie down. A foul smell assaults her, and she puts her hands over her nose and mouth. For a moment she fears that she has gone deaf or lost her mind because she cannot understand a single word until she realizes the two women nearest are speaking in Estonian.

"Don't worry, everything will be all right," a Latvian voice breaks through. "You'll be with your husband soon. The two of you will be together in a few days, they anounced that a while ago. But for now you're safe with us. This isn't so bad. Things could be a lot worse."

"I'm Latvian," Velta says, and a sad cheer goes up. She does not say that her husband is not on the men's train because putting that into words would make their separation final. A small hope still burns that he will help her escape, the way he once rescued her from the orphanage. He is brave and smart. He will save her. They have overcome dozens of difficulties in their married life. But a dark voice inside her asserts matter-of-factly that Valdis is alone now. And there is nothing one man can do against soldiers with guns.

More people are being pushed into the wagon, in spite of strangled protests about lack of air.

"How do the ignorant, uncultured Russians expect us to breathe so jammed together for a week?" A week may turn into months as the train waits to start, then dawdles or stops inexplicably in the middle of nowhere for long days.

The women in Velta's wagon agree to take turns sleeping, sitting, and standing. Those having to stand, the hardest assignment, will take their turn near a pried off plank in the back of the wagon which allows fresh air, a bit of a view, and a wall to lean against. Children, mothers with infants, and the sick will have first claims to the small sleeping area. A few children are feverish and parched already though the journey has not started yet. Everyone presses towards the door of the wagon to conceal the small pocket of space in the back.

The first night Velta stands. Her neck and shoulders ache; cramps shoot up her calves; pain encircles her ankles and stabs her feet. Her shoulders droop and her eyes come to rest on the crudely cut, excrement-smeared hole in the middle of the floor. She gags at the stench, and although she turns away quickly, dry heaves convulse her.

She considers claiming the privilege of pregnancy, but there are too many others who are worse off than she is. She will stand because it is only fair, because she is young and healthy and strong, and because she will need special consideration later, when her pregnancy is more advanced. There will be enough room when the sick die; only the strongest will survive, she thinks suddenly, and is ashamed. She must not think like that; she must not become as callous and calculating as her captors.

When her turn comes to lie down, the pain in her back and legs and groin do not vanish. She tries to fool herself that physical anguish is good because it keeps her mind from obsessively returning to the men holding her down in the back of the truck. But her spirit revolts against such specious comfort. The keepers at the orphanage used to exhort her and the other girls to be grateful for the thwack of a ruler on an open palm, the sting of twigs on bare legs, the bite of a leather strap into exposed buttocks. She will remain truthful and not delude herself. She will never agree with her jailers; she will remain herself. She will try to expunge hatred toward her captors because rage exhausts and kills.

Finally, the pain in Velta's legs subsides. She rearranges her blanket, rolls her robe into a small pillow, and hopes to sleep for four precious hours. But images of Alma, searching every corner of the farm for her, keep Velta awake. If she could rest her hand on her little girl's feverish forehead, they would soon breathe in unison and fall asleep.

Ferocious cramps attack her as well. Each time she jumps up to unclench her calves, she notes that the train is still not moving. Women grumble that since they are going nowhere their captors could at least let them outside to get water, to breathe clean air, and to look up at the stars.

In the morning, Velta forces herself to talk. Why doesn't the train move, she asks? Do the Russians think that they can fool their prisoners into being overjoyed when it finally does? Do these ignorant savages believe that we will be happy to leave our homeland simply because we have been kept waiting to start a coerced journey?

At noon, the door of the wagon slides open, several objects are handed in, and Velta hears her name called. A closely woven wool blanket and a bundle tied inside Valdis' raincoat are placed in her hands: her heavy cardigan, sheepskin boots, warmest wool dress, and some underwear.

Velta turns everything, including a pair of socks, inside out, looking for a letter or some word from Valdis. There is nothing. She cannot keep back her tears as she repacks two loaves of heavy rye bread, a jar of honey, packets of aspirin powder, a tin mug and plate, a fork and a spoon, and three spools of thread.

Heartbroken as she is, she handles every item with care. Even the thread may come in handy, although the needles have been confiscated along with everything else sharp. She feels along the rolled tightly sewn edge of the thick blanket and her fingers come to rest on something solid. A pair of dressmaker's scissors has escaped the notice of the guards. Velta knows that her chances of staying alive or taking revenge have just increased dramatically.

Gradually, it dawns on Velta that Valdis is not the one who has packed her bundle, but rather Mrs. Vilkacis, her neighbor at Burtnieki. She has gathered some of Velta's things and wrapped them in Valdis' raincoat and into her own best blanket. It is Mrs. Vilkacis who has risked arrest by sewing the scissors into the hem; she has also included a jar of clover honey for which Burtnieki is famous to remind Velta of home.

If only that meant that Valdis was safe, hidden in a shed on his mother's farm or in a dugout in the woods. Velta's heart yearns and her body aches for her husband and for her daughter. She sees Alma obsessively opening doors to rooms she searched just a few minutes ago. She hears her little girl crying, now and for years to come. How can her child grow up without her mother?

Velta puts her hands over her ears and tries to pray to the remembered sky above the pines for peace to descend on her daughter and husband, but all she sees is darkness.

Lost Midsummers

3

On the third day the train begins to move. Silent crowds have gathered along the tracks to wave goodbye. Their white handkerchiefs flutter like tethered gulls. Occasional outcries are interspersed by Lutheran hymns offered as prayers. "Dievs sveti Latviju!," God Bless Latvia, the national anthem, is taken up by a few brave voices. They are quickly silenced.

The train hurtles past blue lakes and stands of white birches, then snakes slowly across expanses of yellow grass and dry river beds after it crosses the border into Russia. Sometimes it stops at deserted stations, which are nothing more than dilapidated shacks with crude signs lettered in Cyrillic. Russian women and children materialize to barter water and cucumbers for clothing and jewelry. Occasionally a woman or child with pitying eyes takes mercy on the prisoners parched with thirst and fills a bucket without demanding payment. The water is warm, thick with algae or sand.

The train rushes on, then halts for days at a time to let pass trains full of defiant Russian soldiers on their way west to fight the Germans advancing toward Latvia. The guards grudgingly allow the prisoners to climb down, to fall prostrate at shallow puddles. Women and children lap water like parched animals and carry a few precious cups back to the train. They relieve themselves as far away from the train as possible, stretch their limbs, and lie down in the scant shade of the wagons. They crane their necks hopefully for the men's train, which does not come.

Velta is numb with shock, but she is learning. She learns how to rest the upper part of her body by pressing her buttocks and strong legs into the wall and slumping forward so her shoulders and neck go limp and pain recedes. She learns to breathe deeply, to fill her

23

whole body with clean air when she is by the missing board in the back of the wagon.

She learns to drink as much water as she can hold whenever it is available, gagging at impurities and dirt. She learns to pinch her nose shut in order to eat the coarse, stinking oats mixed with rancid sunflower oil, which the guards dole out sparingly, food that she would not have thought good enough for her horses.

She learns to conserve her strength, to stay still, and to wait. The compass of her hopes shrinks, away from freedom or comfort or joy toward enough water to slake her terrible thirst and enough food to keep alive the child she carries. Just once does she feel something close to pleasure when the women find ample water in ruts of a river bed and together they scrub the children's repeatedly dried but never washed diaper encrusted with filth. They scour the slimy floor of the wagon and its stinking hole and carry water to those too sick to move.

Afterward, turning her back on the guards, Velta washes herself. Again, and again, she douses with lukewarm water between her legs, then washes her body and hair. Coarse sand takes off the congealed dirt and oil almost as well as soap.

No one in the wagon seems real to her. These deported are from the intelegentsia, they are from the educated and prosperous classes, but they seem identical: everyone is part of suffering humanity. Nevertheless, Velta makes herself concentrate and maintain connection: she speaks to the Latvians, and she gestures back and forth with the few Estonians. She soothes feverish women and rocks whimpering children and asks nothing for herself. She believes that human attachments will outlast the diminishing supplies in everyone's bundles. But for now, the women still do not know exactly where they are being taken and what will happen to them once they get there.

They talk less because their throats are parched, and their lips cracked from lack of water. Gradually heat and dust give way to sharp wind. The nights and then the days turn cold, and still they are thirsty, and still the train moves spasmodically only.

Velta discovers that she can escape from her body altogether. That is how she lived through what happened to her in the back of the truck. She did not stay on the floor with the three copulating beasts. Oh no, she flew up to the ceiling and watched their jerking shadows from above, ecstatic to discover that she could keep herself pure by repeating, "They can do this to my body, but they cannot touch my soul."

She had not had to separate the two from each other before.

So now she looks down from the ceiling as a seven-year-old girl dies of dehydration below. More children die in the cold nights. More corpses are placed tenderly on the side of the tracks. A mother howls as she clutches the corpse of a toddler. The women have to pry off her locked fingers when the train halts beneath the endless sky.

Velta watches from above as she and other women hack at the ground with forks and spoons and bare hands. Ignoring their pleas for a shovel, the guards pace back and forth, smoking and yammering that it is a criminal offense to loan State property for private enterprise. The prisoners may be right that burying the dead is for the common good because corpses breed disease and stench, but the guards have no authorization to make an exception to the rules. Let the corpse stay behind and the train continue.

If their hearts were tender once, they no longer are. The guards have led too many train loads to Siberia carrying their own people—Russian workers, intellectuals, priests, criminals, and holy fools.

The women succeed in covering the little body with an inch or two of dirt and coarse grass, while the mother, glassy-eyed with horror, chatters about vultures and rats and starving men who will eat her little boy.

"Why do you keep them in here with you so long anyway?" a guard says. "We've told you before to throw them out as soon as they're dead." He points to the hole for excrement. "They're small enough to slide right through."

But to heave out the body of a twelve-year-old girl the guard has to call for help. Her aunt holds on as they slash at her with their rifles until she moans and loosens her grip. The girl's body lands on the incline off the tracks and rolls over, face up. Her arms and legs spread apart as if she were making angels in the snow. Although her body must remain above the earth, she seems at peace. But then a guard prods her legs wider apart, jams his rifle into the ground between them, moves his weapon up and down, and makes a coarse joke for his comrade. They laugh as they shut the doors of Velta's wagon and swing up easily into their own warm lair.

The moon rises, the stars gleam and whirl, but they are as merciless as the sun. Velta tries to ignore the sharp new pains in the small of her back and her groin. She tells herself that the moisture seeping down her legs is urine, not water or blood. She watches from above as women bend over a woman writhing in labor, sees them lift up a bloody clump with scrawny limbs and a tiny head. The women wrap the dead little thing into Velta's nightgown; the veined head wobbles and flops repulsively, like a newly hatched crow's.

Velta herself stays up near the ceiling while the women wipe someone's face, try to get someone to drink a precious cup of hoarded water, make someone lie down. The train continues into the heart of Siberia. Velta will not descend again, she will not ask what they did with the body, she will not allow herself to admit that now she is truly alone.

But when the train makes its final stop, she is forced to descend. The tracks end abruptly by a foaming river; they have come to the end of the line. Piles of logs and rocks, rusting bars, and scarred earth show where a bridge must have been attempted, then abandoned. Where are those builders now, where is the warmth of their houses, where their stores of food and fuel and dry clothes for those in the icy rain?

Perhaps because Russian temperament contains a measure of laziness along with casual cruelty, or perhaps because the land is so vast and communication so paltry, no camps girded with barbed wire await the captives. Prisoners are not separated into two groups, with those on the right to be stripped naked and gassed immediately,

26

those on the left forced to work themselves to death. No one records the precise temperature for a "scientific experiment" when the body succumbs to the cold. There are no lice-infested barracks. Indeed, there is no housing of any kind; only soggy ground that will freeze hard overnight, and the dark pines that sigh as their ice-encrusted branches splinter and strain.

The crowd of prisoners is much smaller; the guards were right about that. They can relax because their duties are at an end. How could their miserable captives escape? Where would they go with the ten-month long winter coming on? Not the thousands of miles back to Latvia or Estonia, across the frozen tundra with no roads and scarcely any human habitation, through howling blizzards and twelve-foot drifts of snow. Winter is coming to Siberia, where summer is so brief that ice never completely leaves the soil.

Stinging particles of ice invade the chill rain. Grumbling about getting wet, the guards pay no attention to the river. The mother who believes her two-year-old's corpse is being eaten by vultures and rats and starving men weaves between them howling wildly and jumps before they can stop her. They curse her and the river and their own luck in having to care for such ingrates.

As the dark water carries her away, they search out and appropriate her suitcase. Then, screaming with frustration, they beat into submission the women who have been refusing to leave the wagons because anything is better than being outside. Velta too they drag down from the ceiling and heave out onto the muddy ground.

It has been raining too long, and too much water is weighing down the branches to shelter the women and children. Their clothing is soaked clear through, their shoes and boots squelch, their lips are blue, their bodies jerk.

The women persuade Velta to put on Valdis' raincoat and to wrap herself in Mrs. Vilkacis' blanket. Velta has her scissors also, useful for self-defense and revenge, but she must discipline herself. She must not attack anyone or slash her own wrists at times when she feels Alma's desolation and Valdis' despair more intensely than

27

her own. While there is the smallest hope of being reunited with them, she must alive.

Eventually the villagers come, driven by the commands of drunken guards and their own pity and greed. They are ready to exact whatever compliance and hard work they can from these feckless strangers who have squandered their possessions for cucumbers, water, and bread. They choose only the strongest. The rest try to dig holes in the ground with their bare hands to shelter from wind and ice.

All those left outdoors die quickly. Those permitted to crouch inside the peasants' low hovels, after their daily work of felling trees and moving stones, live longer. Velta survives because her scissors, the only pair in the God-forsaken Siberian village, gain her a reputation as a fine seamstress and supplement her starvation diet.

But she is a slave.

She works brutally hard for no pay. She is beaten when she refuses. And, she is given no food when she is too sick to work. She is forbidden all choices, and she is kept from her country, her home, her husband, and her child.

She is joining millions of others all over the globe, in this century and next, who are being turned into exiles, shadows, and ghosts.

4

Alma, 1944

Were anyone to ask eight-year-old Alma, she would say that she never thinks of her mother. She would maintain that she cannot remember Velta and that she knows nothing about what happened three-years-ago, before the Germans drove the Russians out of Latvia and took possession of the country themselves. But, Alma often feels suffocated, almost as if Velta, a heavy absence, resided in her small body, compressing her lungs and blurring her vision.

Alma believes she has forgotten the Midsummer when Velta was still in Stabules, but it has left traces, like dried rose petals ground into dirt. An image of Velta, not constituting a real memory, not even revealing her mother's whole body, is all that Alma has. And this image has dimmed and shifted so much that Alma cannot be sure of the simplest details: were her mother's eyes dark blue or deep gray? Was her dress pale rose or white? Was that a wreath of daisies or a sprig of jasmine in her hair?

Sitting high on her father's shoulders on that Midsummer Eve four years ago, in love with the stars and the moon, Alma did not know that she should memorize every detail. So, all she possesses with certainty is the nape of her mother's neck, the tendrils of dark hair escaping from a tortoise shell comb, the bones fragile under sun-browned skin. Alma's mother hurries ahead, moving towards the woods where darkness reigns even at noon. And then she vanishes.

In dreams, Alma tries to catch-up with her, grasp her hand, and pull her back. She begs her mother to wait and to take her along, no matter how terrible the places they must go. But her mother does not. She disappears, condemning Alma to a lifetime of struggling to keep in tears.

This Midsummer Eve, eight-year-old Alma is waiting impatiently for her father to wake. In the barn the cows, unaccustomed to having their horns wreathed with flowers in celebration of *Jani*, nudge each other with velvety lips. In the house the young women who work on the farm have finished decorating the freshly scoured rooms with ceiling-high branches of birches and oaks. They are braiding their hair and putting on full-skirted dresses, in prints of tiny flowers. In the yard the young men gather, their white shirts gleaming, their heads held proudly high under huge crowns of braided leaves of oak. Wreaths of red clover and white daisies come to rest on the young women's glossy hair, and their hands are full of flowers. Men and women set-off together to the neighboring farm, where at dusk barrels primed with pitch will be set alight and raised on high poles. Bonfires will blaze, beer will flow, caraway cheese and *piragi,* tiny buns filled with chopped bacon and onion, will be passed around, and everyone will sing until dawn. Alma listens as their laughter recedes and their songs fade.

She shakes her father's arm in a vain attempt to rouse him. He mutters curses she can barely make out. Starving Russians should have human excrement shoved down their throats, and vainglorious Germans, who drove them out and occupy Latvia now, should all be shot. He glances at Alma without seeing her, draws up the sheet, and turns his face to the wall.

Abandoned and desolate, Alma sits down on the white stone by the kitchen door, which retains the warmth of the afternoon sun. She veers between jagged sobs and mute fury. Her father is asleep and likely to stay that way. He alone is responsible for her wretchedness. She does not think that her mother's disappearance three years ago has anything to do with her father's neglect or her own misery.

Driven by love and anxiety about Velta and the farm, Valdis returned to Stabules late at night. He had walked across marshes and through stands of trees, avoiding the main roads, and everywhere else he might encounter Russians.

He roared with pain and anger when he came to. He berated himself mercilessly for having listened to his mother that he was the one who would be deported. He should not have listened. He should have come straight back to Stabules, but instead he had slinked into a cave like a cowardly beaten dog rather than running back to protect Velta. The Russians should have taken him, not his wife and coming child. He should have fought to the death with her captors. So, let the Russians take him now.

Determined to follow Velta to Siberia, he saddled his horse. He would suffer everything she has to.

Forming a tight circle around him, his workers tried to dissuade him. Russians were still in control of bridges and roads; they enforced curfews by prison, beatings, and death. He would never find Velta. She was too far away, and it was much too late. But the Germans were advancing, and in a few days or a week they would drive the Russians out. Then Latvians will join the Germans and take revenge. Together they will invade the Kremlin, seize Stalin himself by his filthy lynx-like moustache, and force him to release the millions he is torturing. But right now, one man could do nothing. If Valdis was so set on dying, he should hang himself from a beam in the barn, rather than give the Russians the pleasure of pulling out his fingernails.

When reasoning failed, and the men were afraid to restrain their powerful employer, they plied him with drink. They would have done the same to set a shattered bone or lance an abscess. Valdis, drunk, lost his steely determination. He cursed and wept wildly. Finally, he slept.

They sent for his mother. She spoke to Valdis about Stabules and her own farm and about his father working himself into an early grave so that Valdis could inherit both. Valdis was still young, she said. His ready laugh, blond hair, and blue eyes guaranteed that he would marry again. A new wife would give him sons. Almost as an

31

afterthought, she mentioned Alma. Now that Velta was gone, Valdis must take care of his daughter.

Alma never heard her father say that she was not reason enough for him to live, but she understood it well enough.

Slowly, reluctantly Valdis allowed himself to be talked out of following Velta to Siberia. Even he could see the futility. But because a small part of him shrank in terror from the impossible task of trying to rescue her, he reproached himself cruelly. He should have given his life so that she could live. A drink or two made bearable the words he lacerated himself with; another drink made the darkness less dense. Anyway, there was no harm in taking a drink. Hundreds of *dainas* celebrated the pleasure of sweet beer and fast horses.

Valdis came out of hiding as soon as Germans marched into the village. Many Latvians welcomed the Germans as saviors from Russian brutality and more deportations. But soon the Germans too curtailed freedom and committed autrocities of their own. Latvia, like other small European countries, was merely the ground trampled as the two great powers struggled. Bitterly disappointed, Valdis resigned from public office and withdrew to the farm.

His industrious habits and sense of responsibility kept him outdoors from early morning to dusk, but dread waited for him at the end of the day. What were the Russians doing to Velta right now? Was she hungry, was she cold? Was she crying, was she longing for him? Was she dreaming of home, was she too sick to cry? He remembered how heavy her body grew with pregnancy, and how much he loved the sweet clumsiness that came with it. Velta had been convinced their coming child was a boy, and Valdis writhed with shame that he had failed to protect not only his wife but his son as well. A few gulps of vodka blurred the haunted eyes of mother and child and blotted out the implacable faces of their tormentors.

Lines of a folk song he had sung confidently at his wedding celebration ran through his head, threatening to drive him mad:

Visi ciema suni reja,
Kad es nemu ligavinu.
Visi ciema suni reja,
Kad es nemu ligavin.'

All the village dogs barked,
When I took my sweet bride.
All the village dogs barked,
When I took my sweet bride.

But, no matter how hard he tried, he could not sing the next verse. The unformed words threatened to burst the vein in his forehead. He could not whisper, let alone sing the proud lines that she need not be afraid, that with his capable hands and strong leather harness he would master his stallion, that she would always be safe with him.

Valdis did the best he could with such knowledge as he had. He put away all photographs of Velta, and he forbade people to talk in his presence about her and others deported in 1941, the Year of Terror. He held himself ramrod straight and nodded in agreement when people said life must go on. He turned away from eyes filled with compassion because they threatened to release his own dammed-up tears. If a strand of hair falling over Alma's cheek reminded him of Velta, he told her to go play outside.

But agony overpowered him at the end of the week. At noon on Saturday he washed, dressed in clean clothes, and tried to follow his usual routine. But he put off starting out for the cemetery to visit his father's grave. He was too proud to cry in front of his father, and he was ashamed to tell him that he himself was still in Stabules although the Russians had taken his wife and his son. And there was little else he wanted to talk about. Certainly not about the arrests, executions, and forced conscriptions into the army ordered by the Germans.

Valdis made himself sit down and read the paper, but his neck itched, and the letters wobbled and blurred. He could not quench his thirst; neither cold buttermilk nor warm tea helped. He doused his head with cold water once more, scrubbed his hands and neck again, but nothing worked until he harnessed the horses and set off to the neighbor who ran a still or to the general store in the next village.

This time he would buy one bottle only, have a drink or two, just enough to take the edge off, get a good night's sleep, and get up early. He would go to church and take Alma along. He would spend Sunday afternoon walking along the boundaries of the farm until he was too tired to drink.

He was ashamed of having to bargain with himself like this. Before they ripped Velta out of his arms, drinking had been as natural as breathing: beer at Midsummer, brandy at Christmas, a shot of vodka along with a handshake to seal a bargain, nothing at all most of the time. He was known as a man who took a drink to be sociable and held his liquor well at weddings and funerals.

But now he never bought just one bottle. Better have another on hand in case company came, though he himself put off anyone who hinted at a visit; a second bottle in case a farmhand was injured; then two or three more so as not to have to make another humiliating trip.

As he drove the wagon back into the yard of Stabules, Valdis felt the hills watching him. He wished the sun out of the sky so that his father could not see him, and he kept his back turned to the cemetery where his father and grandfather were buried. He cursed the bottles for clinking as he carried them indoors and lined them up against the bedroom wall. He would take them down to the basement later and lock them away. He suspected the farmhands were sneaking drinks; otherwise the bottles would not empty so fast. That they stole from him was yet another outrage, for he was a good employer, fair and generous.

Anger at the vastness of injustice assaulted him. Although fifteen years older than Velta, he had been her first and only love, as she had been his. Everyone agreed that no one and nothing could compare to the magic and intensity of first love, but those mongrel dogs, the barbarians from the East had dragged her off and were mangling her. He was bereft without her, yet people expected him to go on and work as if nothing had happened. And he did work, harder than ever, although there was no real point to it. But still they begrudged him a drink.

He had taken to sleeping in a small, narrow room next to the kitchen, away from the bedroom he had shared with Velta. Alma's cradle, which Velta had already brought down from the attic, stood next to their bed, ready for use. He could not look at it, but he was afraid to put it away because his unborn son would certainly die if he did. So, he kept the room locked. At least they knew better than to ask him for the key though he could feel his mother itching to get in there, to clean and to drive out shadows. She had never liked Velta; she had no idea at all of what he had lost.

His irritation flamed against his mother. He could have hit her, were he not certain that God himself would strike him blind the instant he lifted his hand. His mother had put the good glasses, the ones he liked to use, on the highest shelf. It was her sneaky way of reproaching and nagging. But he would show her. Spitefully he lifted down three glasses and carried them into his room. He hated to drink from a glass gummed with thumb prints and spittle. The two extras were only a precaution because this time he would have no more than two, at the most three drinks.

He drew the shades, and although everything was immaculate already, wiped the window sill and bedside table with his handkerchief. He lined up his tobacco, matches, newspapers, and packets of powdered aspirin. Not letting his mind comment, he brought in a white enamel bowl for vomit. He knew he would be deathly sick later, but he thought only of the coming hour when everything would seem possible: Velta asleep in the next room, and he himself free and easy in his body. He undressed and pulled up the linen sheets, relishing their clean smell.

His room looked like a cell, but he liked that. He knew little about monks and martyrs; they were revered by Catholics, who prayed in a language they themselves did not understand. As a young man on a horse-trading trip to Latgale, the district with many Catholics, he had slept overnight in the yard of a monastery.

35

Through a window he had glimpsed a room with nothing in it except a bed and a stand with a bowl. A crucifix and a dark garment, a coat or a robe, hung on the wall. He had wanted to go in and just sit there, but of course he had not. He felt that simply by looking he was intruding on something private and holy.

People said that nuns wore hair shirts next to their tender white skins, lashed themselves with whips, and made love to Christ as if he were their husband. Velta had told him that was not true, and Valdis had never believed it in the first place. Perhaps God came to them as a stream of light to comfort and enclose. Because they were holy women they were never alone in the dark. He drained his drink and poured himself another.

He woke on Sunday morning, sick, smelly, and ashamed. His hands shook, and his heart fluttered like a trapped sparrow. It was too late for church, and he did not want to meet Alma's expectant gaze. The thought of food nauseated him. He changed the sheets stained with vomit and ran his fingers through his hair before getting back into bed. He was pleased with himself that he had thought to provide a clean glass for his first drink of the day.

But no matter how sick he was, he got out of bed at dawn on Monday. His mother was already up, slamming doors and scolding. He stood meekly in the kitchen, staring at the floor while the tub was filled with steaming water. He kept his eyes lowered and he covered his private parts with his hands when his mother sent in Jautrite, the prettiest of the maids, to scrub his back. He understood only too well what his mother was up to. But he would never marry for the second time, no matter how she plotted. He vowed not to embarrass himself again by being seen naked like this.

Meanwhile the women threw open the windows, stripped his bed, and emptied his bowl of vomit. They dragged his mattress outdoors to air and set the sheets to soak. Alma gathered the scattered newspapers and folded them, taking a long time to line up the edges precisely. Sometimes there were photographs, published by the Germans, of people tortured to death in the basements of Cheka, the Russian secret police. Terrified that she would see a woman who resembled her mother, Alma nevertheless studied the bludgeoned bodies, dislodged eyes, and missing fingers. But all the corpses she saw were of men.

Freshly dressed, Valdis bowed formally to his mother. "I apologize," he said. Because he believed that children understood little, he did not pay attention to Alma mesmerized by the newspapers. He accepted the chamomile tea his mother shoved at him.

As his tremors began to subside, he felt light-headed and pure. He knew that an unremitting headache would assail him later and that he would have to meet bleakness directly as evening fell. But never again would he put poisonous drink into his body. Then, unable to stand the air filled with female disapproval, he pulled on his cap and went out. It was a relief to be in the open air.

"That's men for you, Alma. They do whatever they want, whenever they want, and women have no choice but to put up with it," Gran sniffed, checking the air for traces of vomit and other disgusting male bodily effusions. "But someone should do something about that father of yours." Responsibility settled on Alma's shoulders.

Gran was a wiry woman, tiny next to her tall broad-shouldered son, but she had taken a broom to Valdis once. While Alma watched, Gran had tried to smash the bottles he carried, but had succeeded only in stabbing the air and startling the horses. Valdis took the broom from her and broke the handle in two over his knee. Then he put his arm around her and gently guided her inside.

Tonight, because he had no reason to rejoice, he hardly registered the decorated doorway and the receding songs and laughter. He did not think about Alma, who was sitting on the white stone, waiting to celebrate with him their last Midsummer in Latvia.

Lost Midsummers

5

Kaija, 1944

Yellow leaves float down from maples and settle on blood-red chrysanthemums, late-blooming roses shed petals, and storks ready themselves to fly south. The sun whispers deceptively that summer will continue, but snakes find their nests, mushrooms sprout in damp woods, and rain clouds mass at the horizon. Darkness will fall early, but Ingrida has ordered that the table for lunch be set outside, in a sheltered spot near dahlias the color of bruised plums.

Annina, the maid, grumbles as she carries out chairs and heavy pitchers of apple juice and beer. Lina, the cook, lines up gold-rimmed platters for pork cutlets, potatoes, and beets; she smiles as she folds eggs into cream. People always eat with a good appetite when they are outdoors, and every emptied dish will be a tribute to her skill. The half-dozen guests at Atminas, "Memories," the Summer House in the country which Judge Karlis Veldre owns, will be generous with tips to the servants when they leave.

The Judge's wife, Ingrida, takes little interest in details of the meal, which in any case is in the hands of competent servants. She stops mid-chord in a Chopin nocturne, rises from the piano in the sitting room, and wanders into her study. But this time the subtle touches of green in the oriental carpet, the serene blues and grays of the sea in a painting by a contemporary Latvian artist, and the shelves full of her art history books fail to calm her. She turns face down a reproduction of Psyche gazing at sleeping Eros and contemplates the far end of the park-like grounds. Before leaving the room, she murmurs a quick prayer that the tanks moving inexorably towards Atminas will spare the silver saplings of birches, trees sacred to ancient Latvians and to her as well.

Upstairs Ingrida knocks lightly on her father's door, and getting no answer, tiptoes in. The windows are shut tight against drafts, and blackout drapes have been drawn to keep out the sun. Nurse Jelums is startled out of dozing. She sits up and thrusts out her palm, ordering Ingrida to stop. If it were up to Nurse Jelums, she would allow no one to come near the General, whose room and linen she keeps immaculately clean and whose body she regards as her exclusive domain. But for now, she can only delay people who wander in and wake him.

The old man is lying very still. Flesh has melted from his face, so that Ingrida inevitably sees a skull when she looks at him, but his willpower burns brightly when he is awake. Ingrida glides soundlessly to his bed. She bends over her father, puts her ear to his chest, and brushes his cheek with her lips to dissemble that she is trying to find out whether he is dead. She catches a whiff of decay under the scent of rubbing alcohol, valerian, and soap. Joy and disappointment, relief and shame burn her cheeks.

"He's better today," Nurse Jelums whispers. "His temperature is normal. He'll be up and around soon."

No one speaks the truth. The General is dying . . . and dying too slowly. Professor Ingrida Veldre, her husband Judge Veldre, and their six-year-old daughter Kaija must leave for the seacoast in a few days. They were on a list to be deported to Siberia in the Year of Terror, which claimed 15,000 Latvians out of a population of two million, and the Russians are about to take possession of Latvia again.

More than a dozen of the Veldres' friends and colleagues in Riga were arrested three years ago, as was Velta, the mistress of a nearby farm where the cook occasionally buys vegetables and *kvass,* a drink of fermented birch sap. Ingrida's heart contracted with pity when she heard there was a child left motherless. She holds on more tightly to her gawky, long-limbed daughter Kaija, the most wonderful little girl in the world.

40

Kaija was a toddler during the Russian occupation, difficult to shush when she cried from hunger, but Karlis and Ingrida saved her and themselves by hiding in the woods near Atminas until the Germans arrived. This time the Russians will deport or kill the Veldre family as soon as they drive out the Germans. They will beat and torture the General for long days and longer nights. Finally, when he does not react to their blows anymore, they will drag him outside, prop him upright, tie his broken fingers and arms behind him, and shoot him.

Karlis has secured passage for three on what may well be the last ship leaving Latvia. Much as they do not want to go to Germany, they must because other countries are not accepting refugees. Karlis is vaguely reassuring when Ingrida questions him. Is one of the boarding passes for her father, with six-year-old Kaija admitted gratis, or are they only for husband, wife, and child? Everything will resolve itself, Karlis murmurs and pats Ingrida's shoulder. Anxiety chokes her. To transport the General to the harbor in Liepaja, more than a hundred kilometers away, and onto a ship is impossible; it is equally impossible to leave him behind.

More than anything Ingrida wants her father to live; she prays desperately to God and all his angels that he recovers. But she also prays to Death, a bejeweled skeleton dressed in black velvet, to come quickly. Death will embrace her father, kiss him on the mouth, wrap him tenderly in his cape, and carry him away. But Death has too many other responsibilities now: for soldiers and suicides, for the crippled and crazed, and for innocents soon to be murdered.

Ingrida wants to be with her father when he dies. She wants to wipe his brow and tell him that none of his mistakes matter. She alone can assure him that her dead mother has forgiven him for being unfaithful and that she still loves him as tenderly as she did when they were first married. But the General does not admit that he is dying, and Ingrida is not supposed to know, let alone speak of his infidelities.

Ingrida's younger sister Astra, dead of TB at seventeen, and their mother have already come to the cloud-obscured gate in heaven, beyond lilies and ferns, to welcome him. They motion to

41

him to climb the steep incline, walk through the gate into the light, and merge with them.

But the General does nothing. He does not open his arms to welcome death; he does not sit up and get out of bed.

It is Ingrida's responsibility to see to it that her father is cared for to the very last, that his body is dressed in his uniform, and that his
medals are pinned to his chest. It is much too late for a funeral befitting his station, but his body must be buried, safe from wild animals and from marauding soldiers who will dig it up and display his head on a pole.

Ingrida wills him to die, even as she believes the earth will split open if she says out loud that she wants her father dead. Karlis thinks that Ingrida is a womanly woman with only tender and noble feelings; he is certain that she loves him more than she does her father. He would be shocked if she suggested that they risk the life of their daughter Kaija in order to stay with the old man.

But Ingrida loves both her father and her husband. Her father praised her intelligence, encouraged her study of art history, and successfully opposed her mothfer, who did not believe in higher education for women. He faced down stodgy old professors and used his considerable influence to secure a position at the University of Latvia for her. Her husband understood her aspirations, and he did not stand in the way of her Professorship. He is also the object of all her romantic feelings and more realistic wifely love.

Ingrida might bring herself to leave Atminas if her father slipped into a coma which was certain to be his last, and she has mentioned this possibility to Nurse Jelums. What would it take for the nurse to keep him comfortable and to see to it that his body is buried? But Nurse Jelums insists that the General is getting better and will be up soon. She says that he will live for many years and that she cannot accept responsibility for him for so small a consideration as Ingrida's jewelry and some of the General's personal effects. She does her best to make Ingrida feel guilty. She murmurs that the General will be wild with grief when he learns that his only daughter has abandoned him. His heart is strong and therefore he will live on for a long time as a grieving and lonely invalid. Only the spacious rooms and familiar garden of the Veldres' Summer House, where he has spent the last three years, can comfort him. Nurse Jelums says she must have a deed to this property if she is to stay with the General.

Ingrida would sign anything, but the house is not hers to give; it belongs to Judge Veldre, as it did to his father before him. Karlis would never agree to Nurse Jelums' demands. He believes that he and the thousands of other Latvians who are now forced to flee will return to their homeland in a matter of months, or at most a year. The war will end. Hitler will be in chains. Stalin will be exposed as the monster he is. Roosevelt and Churchill are champions of democracy, and therefore they will see to it that Russian troops withdraw immediately from the three Baltic countries, whose sovereignty they have violated, and whose people they have deported and murdered. Latvia will be independent again when the war ends.

Ingrida might be able to speak frankly with her husband if they still made love. In their intimate moments, he recites love poems and whispers that he adores her. But they have scarcely been together like that since the Year of Terror, in spite of the fact that they both would like to have more children.

Karlis wants a son, and Ingrida wants another daughter. Kaija deserves a little sister like Astra, whom Ingrida cherished and protected all through childhood and adolescence. But Ingrida's desire dies when she thinks of being a pregnant refugee. She will have to stifle screams while giving birth in a bomb shelter or hovel; she cannot simultaneously carry a suitcase, hold onto Kaija, and protect a baby. A baby will not survive homelessness, cold, and disease.

Ingrida and Karlis are civilized people, and they are exquisitely polite to each other. He does not try to manipulate her or arouse her passion; he would never force himself on her. A slight shake of her head keeps him on his side of their bed. They have too much self-discipline to participate in the frenzy to create life in the face of death, which overpowers others in wartime. But they are also too reserved to discuss the cold tension between them.

The General stirs, opens his almost colorless eyes, and fixes them on Ingrida.

"Don't leave me," he says. "Promise me you will not leave me."

"Yes," Ingrida whispers.

"Say it again, more clearly this time," he demands.

"I promise that I will not leave you, Father."

"You are a good daughter," the General says and drifts off again.

Ingrida walks to the window and moves aside the blackout curtain.

Her guests are gathered in the garden below for what may well be their last meal at the Summer House. Women in crepe de chine and silk dresses have taken their seats; men in elegant light jackets stand smoking and talking. Their fear of the advancing Russians and their grief about having to abandon their homes and their lives are not evident.

Seemingly oblivious to the concerns of adults, Kaija, her blond hair escaping her braids, is in the swing, propelling herself higher and higher. But her eyes are on the front door, anxiously watching for her mother.

A photographer is setting-up his tripod.

On her way down the stairs, Ingrida puts on a pleasant expression to match those of her guests. The men bow, kiss her hand, and pull out her chair; the women continue making charming conversation. She touches her husband's hand lightly as she takes her seat next to him; he moves just a little closer to her. Kaija runs to her parents, leans against their knees, and smiles. Everyone looks in the direction of the road leading away from Atminas. The photographer signals for silence and takes their picture.

6

1945

The war seems to be over. Rain falls on smoldering ruins, and water washes recent wounds in the earth. People are afraid to crawl out from basements and holes in the ground; only tanks and jeeps disrupt the stunned silence of German villages. Blackened trees stand bare, but here and there a single branch of forsythia flares bright yellow.

Karlis Veldre is among the first to emerge. As evening falls, he coaxes Ingrida to weave between bundles and sleeping bodies, to climb up a ladder and out of the air-raid shelter. Seven-year-old Kaija is outside already, sheltered from rain by a tarp in a cart fashioned from rough boards and cast-off bicycle wheels. Karlis grasps Ingrida with one hand, the cart with the other, and begins the ten-kilometer walk to a camp he has heard is run by Americans. He must save his small family from the Russians who occupy this part of Germany. The only hope lies with the Americans, who have a reputation t for treating civilians well.

The road is muddy, and stars and the moon are obliterated by black rain. But the cart is light and easy to pull. The Veldres have abandoned most of their possessions as too heavy for overcrowded trains and long treks on foot: some they have traded for food; the rest they have lost to thieving civilians and looting soldiers. They still have a single album of photographs, two of Ingrida's art history books, and a few items of clothing . . . all precious reminders of their former life.

Ingrida is numb as she trudges along, but fresh air, steady movement, and imminent danger begin to wake her. She moves to the other side of the cart, places her hand next to her husband's, and adds her strength to his. Love and protectiveness surge up in her for Kaija, whom she, sunk in grief and guilt herself, has mostly ignored for the seven months since leaving Latvia. Ingrida knows the little girl has experienced too many wartime horrors without her mother's full attention. She vows to make it up to her. She will give up her life if she must in order to save Kaija from seeing more Russian savages rape women and girls.

When Ingrida and Karlis come to a manor house without lights, she prays to God to pass it safely, as fervently as she once did for her father's recovery. A dozen Russian soldiers are stationed there, but no one seems to be on sentry duty on this rain-drenched night. She prays again when they come to the farm where the farmer sometimes let his vicious dog off the chain. But the dog has been killed and eaten during the last months of the war or he has been shot by the Russians. At any rate he is no longer waiting at the roadside, ready to lunge. Ingrida prays for endurance and strength to help her husband and to save her child.

And she believes God hears her. They are not captured on the way, the camp is indeed run by Americans, and the Veldres are admitted to it at dawn.

In the safety of the displaced persons' camp, Ingrida comes fully back to life. To Karlis she is a water lily opening white petal by white petal; she is the sun warming and soothing the wounded earth for Kaija. It is a miracle: Karlis' wife and Kaija's mother is back.

Ingrida holds Kaija's hand until she falls asleep; she comforts her when she wakes screaming from nightmares about wounded horses, dismembered limbs, and women writhing under grunting soldiers. To help Kaija forget, Ingrida tells fairy tales of princesses, castles, jewels, and frogs as well as stories of lovers and great artists. Her voice transports them to Riga, Prague, Paris, and London.

Ingrida makes quick small sketches to illustrate her tales, and she encourages Kaija to draw solid houses and ripe fruit on the dwindling number of blank pages in her sketchbook. Somehow Ingrida procures a packet of graph paper, which keeps Kaija entranced for hours as she creates geometric patterns and intricate mazes.

Kaija remembers kissing her Grandfather's feverish cheek before leaving the Summer House, but she learns not to ask her parents about him. Ingrida flinches and looks away when she does, and Karlis steps in quickly to assure his daughter that all is as it should be.

"Grandfather died before we left the Summer House; he is snug in a deep grave lined with branches of pine and spruce," Kaija's father says.

"Safe as houses," he adds when Kaija looks doubtful. "Russian soldiers will not find his body, and I will see to it that a fitting memorial is erected as soon as we are back in Latvia."

The small family luxuriates in their safety. They believe their truthful answers about their politics and wartime residences have satisfied American officials during repeated interrogations. Not only have the Veldres been admitted to the camp, but they have also not been ordered to leave, as some others—Nazi supporters, criminals, or disruptive people— have. Above all, bombs no longer wake them in the night and soldiers do not threaten them during the day.

When people are sorted according to nationality, the family is moved from their corner in a Quonset hut. The four barracks designated for Latvians are a great improvement. Wood floors instead of bare soil are underfoot, the solid roofs do not leak, and shattered glass has been replaced in the windows. Two and three families crowd into the largest rooms, but blankets, tarps, and cardboard provide privacy or the illusion of it. The Veldres savor every small comfort.

In addition, everyone has the delight of running into a former acquaintance or neighbor and of speaking in Latvian. Judge Karlis

Veldre is elected to the governing board of the camp, and he urges the few malcontens to stop making envious comments about the Ukrainians, who have been allocated six stately apartment buildings near the front gate, and to work for the common good of Latvians by helping to establish a school, a congregation, and a program of cultural and athletic activities.

Reliable news of what is going on in the world is difficult to come by: newspapers are not available, no one has a radio, and telephones are silent. Germans in the nearby villages and farms may know more but leaving the camp to fraternize with them is forbidden. They are said to be hostile, and who can blame them? Foreigners are occupying buildings from which they have been evicted; strangers from nations that fought against Germany are getting fed twice a day in the displaced persons' camp while local residents are scouring the fields for overlooked carrots and potatoes.

No one wants to stay in the camp for long, but for now there is nowhere to go. The future is unknowable. When will Russian troops withdraw from Latvia, Lithuania, Estonia, and other countries they have occupied? Where will the money for tickets home come from? Germans or Americans are paying for transportation for Jewish people who want to go to Israel, but it is unlikely that Russians will give a single kopek to atone for their atrocities against citizens of the Baltic States. Is Hitler really dead? Is Stalin still alive? When will the two be tried for their war crimes?

Kaija wants to go back to the Summer House, whose rooms and gardens she recreates in her head before going to sleep. But something warns her not to pester her parents about a definite date.

For adults, wariness colors the hope for a happy ending. Stalin is devious and murderous; Churchill and Roosevelt are naïve and uninformed about his crimes. He may trick them into giving up too much territory and power. But no one expects outright betrayal by the West. When Kaija hears a man proclaim that Latvia will be handed over to the Russians for good, Ingrida shushes her. She tells Kaija to ignore things she overhears and does not understand. Rumors disappoint if the good they predict does not come to pass, and they terrify needlessly with the bad. Perhaps everything will still be well.

Judge Veldre tells his countrymen to pay attention only to facts and hard evidence. He says the same when a rumor surfaces that in another camp Ukrainian and Russian women have been dragged by the hair, men have been beaten senseless, and children have been flung like chunks of meat into trucks. All have been forcibly taken back to their countries, which are now in the hands of Russian communists. Only the corpses of those who managed to slit their wrists or hang themselves were left behind.

Karlis maintains a stance of manly confidence and courage in public and is gentle in private as he pleads with Ingrida not to undertake too much. He is afraid that despair will seize her again and she will once more be inaccessible to him and Kaija.

But Ingrida is full of energy. She takes regular turns in the communal kitchen to help the women who know how to cook and in the store room to guard dried peas and ground corn, the main ingredients of the monotonous, inadequate meals. Thieves, some Latvians among them, generally look for better things to steal, but hordes of fat rats tear viciously into boxes and sacks at night. As a member of the Rat Patrol, Ingrida leaves killing the rats to others, but she learns to set traps and to use a cudgel and a whistle to drive them off. The organizer of the nightly watches, a forest manager in Latvia, is impressed by her courage.

Ingrida has never had to scrub floors, but she gets down on her hands and knees, watches other women, and after a few false starts imitates them successfully. Someone finds a cache of old newspapers in the communal dining area, and Ingrida and the women wash and polish every window with them in the Latvian barracks. Ingrida basks in the emerging transparency and light.

She is radiant when asked to do anything requiring her professional knowledge, anything even slightly reminiscent of her former life as an art history professor. Pastor Saulcere, a young Lutheran minister, organizes a group of men to knock down walls between rooms and to build benches to create a space suitable for church services. He consults Ingrida repeatedly about proper

49

proportions and placement of the altar, pulpit, and seats. They have detailed discussions about which decorations would be most meaningful to people who have been through too much during the war. One young man after another holds a rickety ladder so that Ingrida can participate in painting the walls.

The minister and other non-smokers pool their allocations of Camels and Lucky Strikes, which they could have used to trade for food, and the increasingly successful black marketers bring back paint from surrounding German villages. There is white, black, and some sky blue similar to that found in paintings in churches and cathedrals. The dingy ceiling and scuffed walls are slowly transformed.

After her duties are over, Ingrida runs laughing to Kaija, scoops her up, kisses her thin cheeks, and twirls her around. She asks Kaija to help her cut out ornate capitals and graceful lower-case letters from brown wrapping paper, to be used as guides for inscriptions. The two sit side-by-side, their heads bent, concentrating on their work.

"A beautiful mother and beautiful daughter, happy because they are working together," a young man says as he imitates Kaija absorbed in her task, her small tongue sticking out between her lips.

Kaija looks on as her mother paints the first line of the national anthem, "Dievs, sveti Latviju!" above the altar. A few lines from the Psalms and the New Testament go on the walls. With the bit of paint remaining, Ingrida draws the stylized images of the sun and stars which Latvians have used since ancient times. A temporary space in a barracks camp far from home takes on a serene, timeless quality for the displaced.

"We did it!" Ingrida says, wiping sweat from her face.

Everyone applauds, and she laughs and takes a bow.

She grasps Kaija's hand and together they raise their arms in victory.

"We *both* did it," she says, and they bow again to more applause.

Young veterans in the camp talk to Ingrida without their usual reserve. They admit they miss parents and sweethearts they had to leave behind in Latvia, describe their less horrifying wartime experiences, take comfort in her undivided attention, and bask in her affection. One young man writes her a poem, another brings her a bouquet of wild anemones, and a third confesses shyly that she is always in his thoughts. She accepts these tokens respectfully and gently discourages more. Young men different from others—those without wives and girlfriends, more spiritual, more aesthetic, more sensitive—were drawn to Ingrida when she lectured at the University of Latvia, and she treats everyone here with equal acceptance and tact.

"Latvians have had to go into exile before in our long and complicated history. And we must learn from them," Judge Veldre says at a general meeting of Latvians. "Our great poet Rainis continued writing while he was in exile inSwitzerland, and his wife, the poet Aspazija helped him every day. From them and other exiles we know that preserving our language and culture is paramount. Exercising creativity is important too. We can be proud that, like Latvians in other camps, we have founded a grade school and high school and now we have a beautiful space for church services."

Children have missed a great deal during the war and must catch up. Adults agree that they must be given plenty of homework, so they have no time to brood on their terrifying memories. They must be taught that although they and their parents have lost their possessions, homes, and countries, no one can take away what they know. Children can carry knowledge with them wherever they go in their lifetime.

There are no salaries for teachers, of course, but Ingrida is glad to be among those who have the opportunity to do useful work. Books, pens, and blackboards are not available at first, though eventually a few supplies arrive. Learning in the early days in the camps consists of teachers saying what they remember and students writing down and memorizing their words.

Ingrida has lectured on art history at the University of Latvia, but she is determined to engage young children and high school students alike. She tells them about countries, wars, and political intrigues; she describes patrons of art, ingredients of available paints, and lack of heat in castles and hovels; nude models, rich patrons, the unconventional lives of artists; and the interplay of shadow and light. She sees to it that her students think and have the words to express their thoughts about details of what they see; she encourages them to ask about anything that puzzles them in the reproductions she holds up in her book of Renaissance art. The cover is damaged and smeared with mud left by the boots of Russian soldiers, but the pages are intact. She turns and displays each page with something approaching reverence.

Her students learn that creativity is more important than social status and living conditions and that art can reveal and nourish the soul. They learn to put into precise words what they see, isolate what they admire or dislike, and ask about what they do not understand. Such active discussion and the equality it implies with students are unusual. A few of the more conventional teachers grumble about her methods, but she is much admired by others, and she inspires a life-long love of art in many of her students. Kaija shushes others to pay attention when her mother is praised.

"That Mrs. Veldre is amazing. A professor *and* a woman," one of Ingrida's coleagues remarks, and Kaija grins with pride.

On Sundays, the only day of the week when school is not in session, the Veldres attend services in the new church and listen to Pastor Saulcere's sermons about peace and hope. When the camp gates are opened later in the afternoon, they join others for long walks. Everyone is warned to stay in groups, to avoid farm yards and cultivated fields so as not to provoke the local residents, and to stand shoulder to shoulder if confronted by mad dogs or vicious wild pigs which are common in this part of Germany. But in spite of such dangers, almost everyone takes the brief opportunity to touch a living tree, dangle bare feet in a brook, smell wood violets and wild phlox, and look for mushrooms.

This Sunday Ingrida has to choose. Much as she enjoys these outings with Karlis and Kaija, she has promised to return *Madame Bovary* to the library, which consists of two carefully catalogued and assiduously guarded boxes of books temporarily loaned by camp residents. Ingrida has read it before, but she wants to savor every page before giving up the small leather-bound volume published in France. The list of people waiting for it is long, and its owner may withdraw it any time to trade for food, so it is now or never.

Karlis encourages her to stay behind. He spreads out a blanket for her in a spot protected from wind and promises he will not get distracted by discussions of problems in the camp but will keep a close eye on Kaija.

In order to protect Kaija from anxiety, they whisper in German about the barbed wire fence being patched and reinforced. Men younger than forty-five have been ordered to build the new sections and repair the old. But why? Germans are not pressing to get in, and most people in the camp do not want to leave its safety.

Kaija carries a small basket made of willow branches, the product of one of the many after-school activities for children. Mostly Latvian intelligentsia fled the country in 1944, so there are more than enough people to teach academic subjects, and accomplished farmers, craftsmen, seamstresses, and knitters have myriad skills to teach as well. Kaija declares that she will fill her new basket with mushrooms, kisses her mother goodbye, and pulls on her father's hand to get going.

Ingrida passes fully into an imaginary world in France, far from barracks and barbed wire fences, so she is startled when a shadow falls over the thin pages of her novel. Reluctantly she abandons Emma Bovary at a performance of Lucia di Lammermoor and looks up. A tall woman, holding a large box open on top and one side, has taken a position between Ingrida and the sun.

"Hello," the woman says, which tells Ingrida nothing. She could be any nationality, even Latvian. By now everyone in the camp says, hi, okay, and hello with an American intonation.

"What are you reading?" the woman asks in German, then French.

When Ingrida, unwilling to be interrupted, does not reply, the woman bends down and taps the title.

"Which is your favorite part?" she asks. "I wager it's not Doctor Flaubert amputating that suppurating leg," she says. She grimaces and saws the air.

"Actually, I'm thinking about clothes. Like Emma, I want beautiful clothes," Ingrida laughs.

"I *am* Emma, as Flaubert said. Well, so am I. I would give anything for a ball gown," the woman agrees.

"And for a ball to go to," Ingrida says as she marks her place with a dried anemone and closes the book.

Here is someone who may have similar tastes to her own. Ingrida moves over and pats the place next to her on the blanket.

The two women continue speaking in French, a language less weighted with recent experiences than Russian or German.

"Happy to meet you," the woman says after she sits down.

"I am Alexandra Boyenko. I am Ukrainian. Definitely, not Russian," she adds.

Everyone in Europe who has survived the horrors of the last decades is lucky, but every Ukrainian is a living miracle. Ukrainians have suffered more than others because of Stalin's premeditated mass murder of eight million by starvation in the early 1930s. They have seen skeletal people chew on stones, feces, and their own fingers. They have been transported through eerily silent woods where every living creature has been devoured and through villages full of desiccated and mutilated corpses, straight into firestorms and slavery as forced laborers in Germany.

No longer squinting into the sun, Ingrida can see the woman's strikingly beautiful features, her straight slender nose, smooth white skin, and high cheekbones. Her luxuriant black hair is restrained by a rough strip of burlap and her eyes look haunted.

"What about this box then?" Ingrida asks quickly.

"It's a model for a stage set, for Mother Courage or for Comedy of Errors. I can't finish it because I can't decide what to do. I have enough willing actors and plenty of people eager to help with staging, makeup, and costumes, but which play should we put on? Is it better to laugh and be distracted or should we watch Mother Courage, look at war directly once more, and talk about what happened to us?"

"Better to be distracted. Better to try to forget. Reminders will drive us mad."

"I am not sure about that," Alexandra says. "But here, take a look."

She hands the box to Ingrida. "It's a lot like the one I made when I was a slave of the Nazis."

The three-sided box is constructed from sticks, cardboard, and brown wrapping paper. Artfully arranged twigs suggest a tree, either damaged by cannon shots or temporarily bent by heavy rain. A cart for the clever twins to hide behind or for Mother Courage to pull stands to one side.

"We had to package explosives in Germany for twelve, thirteen hours a day, and the Nazis made us guard them at night too. They gave me a cudgel and told me to kill anyone who broke in. One woman and one cudgel to protect a warehouse stuffed with war supplies! They said they would shoot me if I fell asleep. At first, I thought, good, let them, it will be a relief to be dead and out of everything. But then I realized that I was letting them win. So I had to figure out how to stay awake, exhausted as I was.

"A lot of mice lived in that warehouse. I screeched and jumped around when I saw the first few, but that's just what's expected of us women. Soon, I started thinking about what I could do with what I had. I saved crumbs from my ration of moldy hard bread and made friends with one mouse, then two. Eventually I found Raisa. She was exceptionally intelligent. A lovely, graceful, intelligent mouse. She learned to follow my commands, to walk, to stand still on her tiny hind legs, to look up at me, to bow, to dance, to go away, and to return when I called. I built her a stage similar to this box, just larger, with whatever I could find or steal.

"I was an actress in the Ukraine but directing was a revelation. I can see why men go from acting to directing. There is nothing as satisfying as imagining and creating a world which did not exist before. Even for a single performance. It got so I could hardly wait to go on guard duty, and I wrote the script on other nights. I spoke all the dialogue, and the mice performed appropriate actions. I found a partner worthy of Raisa and trained him, and the supporting actors were learning fast."

Alexandra falls silent.

"So what happened? Did you put on a full performance? Did others get to see it? Or did the Nazis destroy everything?" Ingrida whispers.

"No. But it *was* a great conflagration because Americans bombed the factory. Those of us who survived were transported to the next place, to clean and mend uniforms of dead Germans."

"Do you think Raisa escaped? Did some of the other mice?" Ingrida offers tentatively, though she knows the answer.

"No," Alexandra says. "No, they did not."

The two women contemplate a tiny theater lit by candle-stubs in the middle of a vast floor in a dark warehouse full of bullets and grenades ready to explode.

"Might they have put on a performance anyway before they died, maybe when you were not with them?"

"No."

But then to Ingrida's surprise and relief, Alexandra laughs. "That's just Communist propaganda that there are great concerts by symphony orchestras without conductors and magnificent buildings without architects. I do hope the surviving mice danced as I taught them," she adds.

"I *am* sorry."

After a long pause, Ingrida asks, "Was it worth doing even so?" "It was. Thank you for asking. I can see you understand creativity. It can save us, if only temporarily. I can see we'll be friends," Alexandra smiles and squeezes Ingrida's hand.

Friendship develops quickly between the two women. They talk, laugh, read to each other, and exchange clothes. They try to ignore ominous signs. The high reinforced barbed wire fence extends around the entire camp. No one, including black marketeers, can slip out quietly at dusk. Many nights the noise of a convoy of trucks idling in the near distance wakes restless sleepers. A hundred or so soldiers arrive and pitch tents on the edge of the woods facing the gate of the camp. These turn out to be Americans, but Lithuanians on the Firewood Brigade, who gather fallen branches and saw up rotting trunks for heating and cooking, report seeing another, possibly a Russian army encampment deep inside the forest.

When Karlis holds Ingrida in his arms, she thinks of Alexandra, who has no one to protect her. May she be safe and unafraid, Ingrida prays. Kaija is told to stay close to her parents, except for school and group activities.

One afternoon, American soldiers with guns station themselves at regular intervals outside the double fence. Others line up by the gate. They do not engage in friendly exchanges with the camp residents, as they normally do. Instead they keep their eyes focused on distant points, anxiously pleading for answers to urgent questions. Eventually the voices of the displaced drop to whispers, and then they too fall silent.

Far away trucks start up, pulsing and whining. Wheels rumble and motors roar as they advance on the camp. Some Americans order the inhabitants back to their dwellings; others hold the gate wide open for the Russians.

Dozens of Red Army trucks roar into the camp without slowing. They screech to a halt in front of the Ukrainian buildings. Russian soldiers leap from the covered beds of the trucks, where they have been hiding. Guns at the ready, they shout, "Repatriation!," "Father Stalin!," and "Mother Russia!"

They are slowed down at Alexandra's building. Brave inhabitants, with Alexandra probably among them, have blocked the doors. Ingrida prays aloud that Alexandra will be safe, that the Russians will not gain entry. But the delay is brief because no one has heavy furniture or many possessions for a real barricade.

"Alexandra!" Ingrida cries out. She ignores Kaija's hand seeking hers.

Ingrida believes she sees Alexandra dragged to a truck although she cannot be sure what is happening in the roiling upheaval.

Ingrida screems Alexandra's name again, and Kaija is helpless. She cannot spot Alexandra either, nor can she comfort her mother.

Ingrida's voice joins the great chorus of anguish. Shouts of resistance to certain imprisonment, torture, and death in Soviet occupied territories. Pleas for help from the Americans. Cries of pain as guns strike unprotected flesh and as fists land on the faces of women and children. Moans from people half-conscious being dragged face down over stone and cement. Terrified whimpers from children who see people bleeding from jaggedly cut wrists or hanging by the neck in the dust-choked attics of the Ukrainian apartment buildings. Screams of despair as children and parents are pulled apart again. Murmurs of reproach to the Americans who have betrayed all refugees, displaced persons, and exiles by not intervening. Futile pleas from Kaija for her mother's attention.

American soldiers watch, but do not stop the Russians as they carry out their brutal assault. Most Americans are numb with shock. Some simply cannot believe that people would rather die than return home just because their home is in Soviet territory and where they would be subject to their law. Some try to convince themselves that what they are witnessing is acceptable because at the Yalta Peace Conference, Roosevelt and Churchill granted Stalin the *right* to repatriate "by force if necessary" those he believes belong to him. Some will later successfully protest to General Eisenhower that this horror does not fit into any definition of military action and is morally repugnant.

Finally, the trucks are jammed full of Ukrainians as well as a few Poles, Hungarians, and Russians mixed-in accidentally. Satisfied that they have done their duty to Stalin at one more camp, the Russian soldiers take up a song. But the great chorus of anguish overpowers these banal sounds and continues to reverberate.

For several nights after the assault, Ingrida stations herself near the empty Ukrainian buildings. She scrutinizes the doors and windows for Alexandra as if waiting to attend the opening performance of "Mother Courage." She does not react when Karlis passes his hand in front of her eyes.

Karlis' wife and Kaija's mother is gone. In their place is a woman who cannot contain this final terror and grief. Having basked in the attention of her mother, Kaija has an unbearably sharp sense of what she has lost.

The shooting has stopped, and the treaties have been signed, but the war *is not* over yet. Like a large ugly stone cast into a quiet lake, it creates ever-widening black ripples which lap at the feet of survivors.

Lost Midsummers

Part Two

Girlfriends

1950s

Lost Midsummers

7

1950

Alma quickly pinned her father's dark work clothes on the line so that they would shield from view her own scrubbed and much mended underwear. She stepped back and surveyed the clean laundry, enjoying her brief triumph over disorder and dirt. If only a stiff breeze would spring-up and disperse the sticky humidity, she would not have to spend the evening getting her father's thick work shirts dry with an iron. Maybe he would smile and thank her instead of looking past her, as he usually did when she handed them to him. Maybe her slip would even have that evanescent fragrance which only wind and sun and grass impart.

Nothing dried satisfactorily up here on the tiny second-floor balcony, but anything left outdoors on the street level would disappear in five minutes, and the heavily shaded back yard was dank again with rubbish and mold.

When Alma and her father, Valdis, arrived in this slum neighborhood in Indianapolis, Indiana, from the displaced persons' camps in Germany a month ago, she had done her best to change that. By making sweeping and raking motions to overcome the language barrier, she had managed to borrow tools from the landlord, who would be astonished by such a request from anyone, let alone a fourteen-year-old girl. She had gathered piles of trash, pulled-up stubborn thistles struggling for light near the alley, and raked away years of debris. She was thrilled as she watched fire consume filth.

But, the Americans who crowded into the three dilapidated buildings on Park Avenue near 24th Street, along with the Latvian immigrants, two and three families to every two-bedroom apartment, continued to toss cigarette butts, bread wrappers, and soggy bags of garbage into the yard, not bothering to dump them into the rusted barrels that served as incinerators.

The landlord shrugged when Alma handed him a one-sentence long note of complaint, which she had painstakingly composed with the help of a dictionary.

"What do you expect? They're hillbillies from Kentucky," he said.

Alma did not know enough English to ask him what that meant. She studied the language every day by herself, but she was a long way from having the confidence to try any of the strange, non-phonetic pronunciations out loud.

She turned her considerable energies next to the bathroom and hallway which she and her father shared with a family with three small children. She muttered about lazy Americans as she battled scum, dirty diapers, and pubic hair. Did they not know how important cleanliness was to Latvians, people who had been driven from large sparkling-clean homes by the Russians, who had sheltered in rubble in Germany during the war, and who had been forced to live in bug-infested barracks in displaced persons' camps afterwards?

She assumed, mistakenly as it turned out, that the American family would follow her example as she made the floor and bathtub gleam for her father. Not that Valdis noticed much when he returned from the grimy tool factory, which he would be happy to trade for much heavier work out in the open air.

Alma wished she were older than fourteen so that she could get a real job and earn real money to help him. Pastor Gottman, whom people suspected of sponsoring Latvians from the DP camps for the sole reason of increasing the size of his dwindling American congregation, had said he would find an American lady who might pay as much as twenty-five cents an hour for housework, but so far he had been too busy getting menial jobs for the adults. If only she were older, the landlord would take her seriously and provide her with brushes and paint. Fake marble fireplaces and large sun porches in front were reminders of the modest elegance of Park Avenue in the 1020s, and Alma had a lot of ideas how to improve the room she shared with her father. Painting the dirty walls would also be preferable to sitting around and worrying about having to start as a freshman at Shortridge High School in September.

A door shut on the ground level below Alma, and the tall girl who had arrived the night before stepped outside. Head bent and hands over her face, she stood still for a minute.

Then, to Alma's surprised approval, she squared her shoulders, looked around, and began picking up crumpled Wonder Bread wrappers and empty Campbell's soup cans.

Catching sight of Alma, she called out with forced cheerfulness in Latvian, "Good morning, neighbor."

"Morning," Alma replied grudgingly. People expected her to be friends with this skinny girl with long braids, whose name was Kaija, because she, too, was a Latvian, newly arrived from the camps, and because her rich parents had had a summer house not too far from Alma's father's farm.

Anyone could tell Kaija was a baby. Though taller than Alma, Kaija was twelve at most, and on top of that, a sissy. Last night, at the dinner Alma had helped prepare to welcome the new arrivals, Kaija had been teary-eyed and dazed, as if still seasick from nine stormy days on a troop transport between Bremenhafen and New York. She looked as if she had been crying just now, too.

Alma was sure that a girl like that had nothing to cry about. Kaija had been flanked by two parents: her father, Judge Veldre, a tall and distinguished man, had courteously stepped aside to let his daughter precede him up the front steps; and, her mother, a professor of art history, had held onto her elbow. Mrs. Veldre, dressed in high heels and a badly worn elegant black wool suit, had been perspiring in the Indiana heat, but she had stayed glued to her daughter's side all evening. She had livened-up only when she greeted Pastor Saulcere. They had evidently worked together in schools and congregations in the camps. But, she had not spoken another word

65

after he left to settle a family dispute in one of the other three buildings.

In any case, parents like Kaija's dispelled every worry their children had, tucked them into bed, and sat with them until they fell asleep, while Alma had been taking care of herself and her father ever since they left Latvia when she was eight.

"Please excuse me for troubling you, Miss Alma, but would you consider doing me a favor?" Kaija asked in formal Latvian. "I need to find a store that sells food. I must buy coffee for my mother and a few other things, too."

"Kroger's isn't far, but coffee is expensive," Alma volunteered. Mrs. Veldre must be a wasteful woman if she was ready to squander on coffee the $20 Pastor Gottman loaned every newly arrived family until their first payday. Latvians mostly had to do without caffeine and alcohol during the war, and for the life of her, Alma did not see why they could not continue that way. But, they longed for coffee and cream in delicate china cups and for French cognac in heavy crystal decanters like the ones they had had to abandon when fleeing Latvia. And they aspired to approximating these luxuries for their guests, if not for themselves. Alma, too, had recurrent daydreams about cupboards filled with staples and delicacies, but she had made-up her mind that she would not become dependent on anything that could easily be taken away by war, or any other disaster.

"Please tell me how to get to Kroger's. Coffee might cheer-up my mother."

The tremor in Kaija's voice and the familiar need to take care of a parent prevented Alma from delivering a lecture on self-discipline vs. self-indulgence.

"You'll never find it on your own. I'll go with you," Alma was surprised to hear herself offer. Well, she had done so only because the new girl would be cheated by the clerk who always took more than was owed from palms offering unfamiliar coins and bills. Alma would not allow any Latvian to be cheated.

"Thank you, you're very kind. My mother will be delighted to meet you."

Alma's plain broad face broke into a surprised smile at the compliment, and the news that Kaija's mother would be happy to meet her.

"What's she so sad about then?" Alma asked an hour later, when the two girls had settled down on the front steps of the apartment building, the only place where private conversation was possible.

Kaija had made and served the coffee, and the unaccustomed caffeine was making Alma talkative. She would have to be careful not to blurt out that she had been shocked to see slender, pretty Mrs. Veldre still in bed, reading, at ten in the morning. The open suitcases and dirty windows made their room seem even more cramped than it was.

"Mmm, delicious," Mrs. Veldre had murmured after taking a sip. "Thank you, darlings, so thoughtful of you." She had picked-up her book again before the girls were out the door.

"She's disappointed," Kaija said. "She thought we'd finally have a nice place to live after five years in the DP camps, and that we'd have a bit of help when we got here. You know, that there would be American ladies like the ones described in letters to Germany, who welcomed Latvians with food and clothes, helped them find good jobs, and drove them to English classes. But Pastor Gottman told my mother last night she'll have to wash floors in an insurance office and that if we don't repay his $20 in thirty days, we'll have to start paying him 10% interest. I wonder how he explained all that to other Latvians the minute they stepped-off the train in Indianapolis, before he found that nice Mrs. Krumins to translate for him."

"What did your father say?" Alma asked.

"That Pastor Gottman has fulfilled his contractual obligations: he has found jobs and a place to live and that the "kind" of jobs and apartments was never specified. My father has to start in a metal works on Monday himself. But none of that's any comfort to my mother."

"My father was disappointed too," Alma sighed. "But we mustn't say anything. If we complain, the Americans will think that we're not grateful."

"But can't we be grateful and disappointed at the same time? Besides, all Americans aren't alike. America is bigger than this," Kaija gestured excitedly, "and other Americans are kinder. Just because we don't like this run-down building doesn't mean we aren't glad to be in the United States. Just because we wish that Latvia were free of Russians so we could go home, doesn't mean that we're not thankful to be out of the camps."

This assault of logic made Alma's head spin. Kaija's father, the Judge, must have taught her to this.

"Never mind," Alma snapped. "Just don't complain where anyone can hear you. You have to sign an oath that you've forgotten everything about Latvia if you want to become a United States citizen. That's what Pastor Gottman told Mrs. Krumins."

"That can't be right. No one can forget home just like that." Then, instead of responding to Alma's irritation, Kaija changed the subject. "Anyway, I'm happy you're here, Almin. Thank you for taking me to Kroger's and for borrowing Mrs. Krumins' coffee pot."

Almin, Kaija had said. Alma could not remember the last time someone had called her by that sweet diminutive. Yet Kaija had said it so easily that the affection it implied seemed natural and almost deserved.

"That's all right, Kaijin," Alma said, blushing.

"Hurry up, darlings," Mrs. Veldre urged. "Pastor Gottman said he'd drop you off at the swimming pool in Broad Ripple. You can have an exciting ride in a private car and get cooled off afterwards. Isn't that exciting?"

Mrs. Veldre opened her small coin purse and carefully counted out seventy-two cents, enough to cover the twenty-five-cent admission to the pool and the eleven-cent bus ride back for each girl. Mrs. Veldre might be nervous about being inspected for a job, but she was astoundingly generous with Pastor Gottman's twenty dollars. Well, she could afford to be, Alma thought. The Veldre family had not spent a single night in Pastor Gottman's house. They would not have to pay him the shocking sum of a hundred dollars for every week there, which he charged for accommodations. Alma had heard that a small house in this neighborhood cost only thirty times that.

In the chlorine-saturated dim dressing room, Alma locked herself into a toilet stall to change into her suit, a faded navy one-piece which covered her shoulders and upper chest, like a tightly fitting sleeveless blouse rather than a revealing slip. Kaija stayed out in the open as she put on a little flowered cotton two-piece, with ruffles and bows, which was clearly home-made too but suitable for a much younger child.

The girls stepped out into the blinding light, at first almost tripping over people baking in the sun. Hundreds of deeply tanned or burned-to-blistering bodies lay everywhere except for a small strip of shade near the shallow end of the pool. Carrying their rolled-up clothes, Kaija and Alma moved cautiously to avoid stepping on the edge of a blanket or rudely passing too close to someone's face.

"Look," Kaija whispered as she pointed to a tall, silver-haired woman. The woman's richly oiled skin, tanned almost chestnut brown, glowed against her iridescent white two-piece bathing suit, which she wore confidently in spite of her thickened waist. The woman raised her firm arms above her head, interlaced her fingers, and stretched. Then she poured some clear liquid into her palm and rubbed it into her shapely legs, which made them shine even more.

69

"She's older than my mother, and she's out here enjoying herself," Kaija said. "That's what I'm going to do when I'm her age. Oh, if only my mother could be here."

"That woman is half-naked. I'm surprised her husband lets her," Alma said.

"Maybe she doesn't have one."

The woman, aware of the girls' eyes on her, looked-up and smiled.

Embarrassed, Kaija and Alma busied themselves finding a place to spread out an old army blanket Mrs. Veldre had pressed on them.

"Let's get farther away from them," Alma said, motioning to a group of teenage boys scuffling near a water fountain. Kaija obediently moved the blanket a few feet before Alma picked it up and carried it all the way to the chain link fence.

They settled down comfortably. A slight breeze ruffled Alma's light brown, recently sheared-off hair, and the water glistened cool and green and blue. The girls grinned at each other.

"Perfect," Alma sighed, "I could sit here all day."

"It is nice," Kaija agreed. "But let's do go in."

"What about our clothes? Someone will steal them."

"They'll be all right. That woman knows they're ours, and we can keep an eye on them if we stay at this end. We won't be in the water very long. It's too crowded to swim properly anyway," Kaija urged.

Kaija and Alma seated themselves on the rough cement edge and dangled their legs in water. Reflected light danced on their shoulders and arms as they readied themselves.

And then they were in it. Cool liquid enfolded them, caressed their bodies, lifted and held them. Yielding to its welcome, they closed their eyes and turned their faces towards the sun.

Suddenly Alma was in a mass of roiling, straining, and twisting bodies. Hands clamped onto her arms and waist, palms pushed and held her face below water, legs tried and failed and tried again to hook around hers.

Alma went under but then managed to rise and catch her breath. Half a dozen adolescent boys surrounded Kaija as well, who was gasping for air. The boys' eyes were narrow with excitement and spite. Their hysterical, high-pitched squeals reminded Alma of pigs at her father's farm.

Alma hit and scrabbled until she could brace herself against the side of the pool, as Kaija's head came up briefly only to be pushed down again. A mysterious directive, one of the few pieces of advice Alma's father had ever given, came back to her.

"Aim between the legs and kick hard," she shouted in Latvian. Kaija's terrified face bobbed up once more, but her limbs looked paralyzed.

Alma tried her best to follow her own advice. Her legs were muscular and strong, but the boys pushed against her, retreated, and closed in again. Water cushioned the impact when she did connect.

A fat boy, his eyes red-rimmed by chlorine, shouted into Alma's face, "I love you, I love you." Alma's stomach turned over with revulsion even as she realized that she had actually understood a spoken sentence in English. His mouth strained towards hers. His fingers pushed into her thigh, pinching her and probing her pants for an opening.

Alma planted her foot against his groin and ground into it until he yelped and let go. Kaija was slammed against the ledge in the midst of the attacking pack.

"Kick," Alma yelled again, but too many hands gripped her.

Three sharp blasts from a whistle cut through the grunts and shouts. The boys' hands loosened and then withdrew. A muscular young man, as handsome as a statue in one of Kaija's mother's precious art history books, was running towards them. The silver-haired woman was on her feet too, motioning and scolding. She pointed at the boys, and the young man shouted and blew his whistle again.

The boys backed off, swimming nonchalantly in different directions.

Alma cowered next to Kaija, grateful that everyone else seemed to be ignoring them. They climbed out, and stood up,

71

steadying each other. Without saying a word, they gathered their possessions, which were blessedly untouched, and made their way into the dressing room. The fat boy watched them go.

Alma was surprised that Kaija did not burst into tears, but dressed quietly and deliberately, taking great care with her clumsy lace-up shoes and the dozens of tiny buttons on her short polka-dotted dress. Alma's irrational anger that Kaija had not freed herself evaporated in the dismal silence. What was the use of reproaching her? It would just make both of them feel more ashamed.

Kaija wrung out and rolled up her bathing suit before turning to Alma. "I'm trying to figure out what to do. They'll catch us if we run across the park to the bus stop. That fat boy and the other hooligans are out there waiting for us."

"I don't know," Alma said. She was relieved that Kaija did not expect her to come up with a solution. Neither girl mentioned phone calls or rides. All the adults were at work, they would be angry at the girls for getting into trouble, and no one had a car or a phone anyway.

Alma surveyed the nearly empty dressing room, found her small notebook of English words and phrases in her dress pocket, and started paging through it.

The silver-haired woman, who had followed them in, stepped naked out of the shower and reached for a rose-colored towel. She draped it loosely around her shoulders, not bothering to cover her private parts first. Alma stared at her, open-mouthed.

Kaija grabbed Alma's notebook of English words, flicked through it, and strode up to the woman.

"Auto to autobus? Please," Kaija said. She pointed to the Park Avenue address.

The woman looked puzzled, said something that sounded like an apology and turned away, but Kaija persisted. The woman shrugged into a loose cotton shift and checked her reflection in the mirror while Kaija continued miming and talking.

"Please. Auto to autobus? Please."

Alma's cheeks burned with embarrassment at Kaija's clumsy English and with admiration for her daring.

"Please," Kaija repeated.

Understanding lit up the woman's face, and she held out her hand for the address.

"Of course, I'll give you a ride," she smiled. "I'll take you all the way home in my car. Auto to Park Avenue, not to autobus," she added to make sure the girls understood.

During the ride, the woman asked, "Where are you girls from? When did you come here?"

Kaija looked confused, then bobbed forward repeatedly as if courtesying to show her gratitude.

The woman asked more questions, but Alma hardly noticed these failed attempts at communication. A dull ache was spreading from Alma's pelvis, across her belly, and up her back. In front of the apartment house on Park Avenue, she could not force her face into a smile, and she almost screamed as she stepped from the car and murmured a thank you. Pain seized her and would not let go, and irritation against Kaija flamed-up despite herself.

"I suppose now you'll run and tell Daddy and Mommy what happened," Alma said. Were Kaija the one in pain, Judge Veldre would help her up the stairs and Mrs. Veldre, murmuring endearments, would find aspirin and a hot water bottle. In an unwanted flash of memory, Alma saw her father Valdis unclenching her fingers, as if her desperate attempt to hold on were as insubstantial as a spider's web and as annoying as the whining of a mosquito.

Ignoring Alma's hostility, Kaija considered her assertion.

"No, I'm not going to tell. There isn't any point. They can't do anything about it. And they're too sad already about losing their parents and home. . . ."

"I know," Alma cut off the rest of the list. She wished Kaija would go to her own room instead of hovering. But Kaija was asking Alma what hurt, offering to rinse out her swimsuit, and bustling around to make chamomile tea. Alma felt she would die if she did not get away by herself and into the bathroom.

She locked the door behind her and collapsed on the toilet seat. The pain was threatening to cut her into two, and at first she concentrated simply on not crying out. Then slowly and fearfully, she began to examine her underclothes and her body.

She heard tentative taps, which gave way to hard knocks, twisting of the door handle, and finally to pounding. Angry American voices demanding to use the bathroom mingled with Kaija's mild questions whether Alma was all right. A vicious kick made the door shudder, steps pounded down the stairs, and a car screeched out of the alley.

"They're gone," Kaija said. "Let me in."

Alma looked desperately at her blood-speckled skirt.

"No. I can't. I don't want anyone to see," she said. Her voice was trembling with embarrassment.

"Well, you can't stay in there forever," Kaija said practically. "You might as well let me help you before the Americans get back. I think they said something about calling the police if you don't let them use the bathroom."

Alma opened the door an inch or two. "I'm hurt, down there," she motioned. Her face burned with shame.

Kaija looked unsurprised as she picked up Alma's bloodied underwear and turned on the taps.

"Don't worry, you won't bleed to death," she said. "Go ahead and wash yourself while everyone is gone. It will be all right, Almin. My mother is gone so I can get some of the things she uses. A girl on the ship from Germany told me that all girls get this when they're old enough."

"Why?" Alma could hardly pronounce the single word.

"I don't know, it's just the way it is. It'll end in a couple of days. My mother asked me to buy Kotex for her when we went to the store, but she'd be embarrassed if I questioned her what it's for. I bet she won't even notice when I start to bleed. She'll be in bed, reading or staring into space. Oh, sorry, I shouldn't have said that."

"I hate everything," Alma said as Kaija helped her into bed. "This day, this street, America, everything."

"Oh no, not America, Almin, never America. Wasn't that lady who gave us a ride nice? So glamorous and independent and

74

driving her own car. I loved the way she issued orders to that young man at the pool."

"Yes, and smoking. Shameful for a woman."

Kaija changed the subject. "Mrs. Krumins said we can go downtown with her, to L. S. Ayres. It's the best department store in Indianapolis. That will make you feel better. We still have the $.22 my mother gave us for the bus ride back from Broad Ripple, so we won't have to walk thirty blocks."

"We can go shopping on Saturday like all the Americans."

Lost Midsummers

8

In the 1950s, Sundays were still family days for Americans, and stores and restaurants remained closed.

No one in the buildings on Park Avenue went to work, and all the Latvians dutifully trooped off to Pastor Gottman's Lutheran church on Walnut and 11th Street to listen to his sermons, though only Mrs. Krumins knew enough English to understand them. After lunch people wrote letters, read, napped, or tried to keep up the European tradition of going for long Sunday afternoon walks.

In the evenings everyone gathered in Mrs. Krumins' place, which consisted of a kitchen and a large enclosed back porch, to share meals, laugh about the puzzling behavior of Americans, and congratulate each other on small successes. Even Alma's father Valdis, having no room of his own to retreat to for solitary drinking, listened appreciatively to often repeated stories about arrogant Nazis tricked by clever Latvians and about Russian officers too uncultured to know the difference between a toilet and sink.

Mrs. Krumins, her face swollen and streaked with calamine lotion, made gentle fun of herself for mistaking poison ivy for a benign roadside plant which grew in Latvia. She had put a few of the toxic broad leaves on her nose to prevent sunburn, and she was far more miserable than she let on.

Mistakes more embarrassing and humiliations more painful were not admitted to anyone, but group laughter took out the sting of the less severe. Mrs. Krumins described a talk she had given at one of the club meetings that American ladies were always having, probably because they had nothing to do and nowhere to go in their high heels and white gloves. Someone had asked her about her folks, and Mrs. Krumins, knowing only terms like family and relatives, had answered that foxes lived in caves, hibernated during the winter, stole chickens from farm yards and devoured them live, bones, feathers, and all. The ladies had stared open-mouthed. Mrs. Krumins had inadvertently confirmed their prejudices against foreigners and had failed in her mission to enlighten the ladies that most Latvians were well educated and had had much more comfortable lives at home than in the United States.

Old Mrs. Jansons got everyone laughing too with her story about being fired on her first day of work. The American lady whose house she was cleaning had shelled a handful of almonds and popped the nuts into her own mouth. Mrs. Jansons, who spoke no English, took this as a demonstration of what she was expected to do. Musing about the peculiar things Americans considered suitable for lunch, she had nevertheless eaten the whole pound of nuts the lady wanted to put into a cake. Pastor Gottman had to whisk Mrs. Jansons away and deliver another Latvian woman as a replacement.

This Sunday night the jokes were more forced than usual, and soon everyone turned to their real concerns. Mrs. Krumins summarized once more Pastor Gottman's stern sermon against ingratitude. He had not bothered with a biblical text but had exhorted his congregation to give up their obstinate clinging to their own language and their failure to assimilate to America.

They had sat through the sermon as passively as they always did, but the meeting in the church basement afterward had turned stormy as soon as Mrs. Krumins started translating. In a ringing voice, Pastor Gottman had repeated that Latvians had no right to hold religious services in a foreign language, that he was deeply disappointed in them for asking, and that they were ungrateful to him and to the United States for getting them out of the camps. They were flying in the face of every American principle, and they were contradicting the firmly established concept that America was a melting pot. He had singled out Pastor Saulcere, who had offered to conduct the services in Latvian for free, for special condemnation. Mrs. Lapsa had interrupted and said that she wanted to understand what was being said when her sons Ojars and Laimonis professed their faith at their confirmation, and Mr. Berzins had impulsively declared that Pastor Gottman was trying to prevent everyone from praying the Lord's Prayer, which Jesus himself had not said in English.

Pastor Gottman lost his temper and threatened to have them deported, while Judge Veldre tried to calm the situation by assuring him that everyone would still pay church dues and attend services in English. But Pastor Gottman was beyond compromise. Red-faced and perspiring, he shouted that he could report them to the FBI for engaging in un-American activities. When people did not appear sufficiently cowed even by this, Pastor Gottman took out his big white handkerchief, said they had deeply hurt him, and made a show of wiping his eyes. Pastor Saulcere immediately urged compassion, forgiveness, and reconciliation, but everyone else laughed at the handkerchief and the tears as ridiculous for a grown-up man.

"Gottman can go to hell," Valdis said hotly. "He's making lots of money off us now, but we'll sponsor other Latvians ourselves."

"Will he report us to the FBI?" Mrs. Berzins worried.

"Can he deport us?" Mr. Liepins asked. "What are we going to do?"

Everyone looked to Pastor Saulcere and to JudgeVeldre for answers.

"See what I mean?" Alma whispered to Kaija. "They listen to your father, but no one pays attention to mine."

Valdis, handsome in a clean white shirt and sharply-creased slacks, was entirely sober this evening. Kaija felt a rush of guilt for the deference shown to her father; she wished she could somehow make up for it to Alma. That Valdis' had been rich and Stabules a model farm did not matter to the men who had attended the University in Latvia and still wore their visored fraternity hats and colorful ribbons to private gatherings. They had subtle ways of showing that they did not consider other men to be their equals.

"God will protect us and give us strength to preserve the language of our fathers," Pastor Saulcere said confidently. "The Godless Russians occupying our dear homeland will not triumph. But since they've forbidden Latvian language in the schools, it is the duty of those of us in exile to preserve our language and our culture."

"People cannot be deported for praying," Judge Veldre said. "I believe that the Bill of Rights, which is attached to the Constitution of the United States, offers legal protection for religious freedom. And the precedent of Milwaukee may be relevant here also."

Dozens of Latvians had made a perilous escape from Mississippi to Milwaukee. Plantation owners in the south had turned to the DP camps to replace their African American workers who had courageously made their way north. Latvians had lived in cabins originally occupied by slaves, done back-breaking work in cotton fields, and been threatened with imprisonment, beatings, and death if they attempted to leave.

A Latvian woman who had married an American diplomat and had lived in the United States since the 1920s had carried out a daring rescue. She had rented a bus and made clandestine trips to bring her countrymen north. Kaija daydreamed that she too would perform courageous and selfless deeds after she learned how to be a brilliant physician or a world-famous writer.

"As far as I know," Judge Veldre said, "not a single Latvian in Milwaukee has been arrested or deported for disobeying a sponsor."

"Let us have faith in God. He helped us survive the First World War when we were children," Pastor Saulcere said, "and he saved us when forty thousand of our friends and relatives were deported in 1941 and 1949. He protected us from bombs and guns and tanks. In his great mercy he has brought us here, to freedom. He'll help us as we found our Latvian Lutheran congregation."

"And an Indianapolis Latvian Association," Judge Veldre added.

Kaija and Alma were paying rapt attention to future plans when Mrs. Lapsa tugged on Kaija's sleeve.

"Come on, you lazy girls," she whispered, "let the men do the talking. I need help in the kitchen."

"You two don't know how lucky you are," she bristled as she set Kaija to chopping cabbage and Alma to peeling potatoes. "You don't have to work and worry like the adults. You two have nothing to do except waltz off to school and chatter nonsense with your friends. You didn't see the First War, and you've already forgotten the Second. Oh, it's easy to be young!"

Ojars, Mrs. Lapsa's 16-year-old son, had followed Kaija into the kitchen.

"Skaista ir jauniba,
Ta nenaks vairs . . . "
"Youth is beautiful,
It won't return . . ."

He sang mockingly until his mother ordered him to the other room, to listen to the wisdom of men.

She turned to Kaija next. "So where is your mother?" she asked. "Is she too fine to give us a hand? Is her nose up in the air so high again that it's pushing clouds?"

Kaija blushed dark red.

The Latvians on Park Street treated Mrs. Veldre with respect because she was the daughter of a general and the wife of a judge, but they mostly ignored her academic and professional achievements. She did not try to make herself popular either. She had not entered into the spirited discussions about purchasing a modest bungalow on 25th Street and Central Avenue, which might be suitable for a Community Center. She had only remarked that it was too early to pledge monthly contributions for the mortgage when no one had the money for an individual apartment, let alone for a house of their own. People sitting near her had whispered that she did not value Latvian culture and that she was selfish, an unforgivable failing in a woman.

Mrs. Veldre looked bored when women talked about cooking or showed off bargains they had found in Kresge's Five and Dime, and she refused to participate in gossip, the basis of most conversations. She admired Pastor Saulcere and referred to him as "a true person of the soul," but she did not condemn Pastor Izaks as unpatriotic and politically suspect. The latter had announced that he would stay in Pastor Gottman's congregation and he tried to dissuade other Latvians from establishing an authentically Latvian congregation. Mrs. Veldre had discriminating taste in clothes, but she refused to criticize another woman's inadvertently ridiculous outfit. If a young man's drunken episode was the subject of discussion, she remarked, "That's below comment," and left the room.

Kaija wanted to defend her mother, but she did not know how to stand up to adult disapproval. She was ashamed of herself whenever she remained silent. She wished she could eloquently explain her mother's behavior and ask for extra consideration. Nobody could imagine what her mother was really like; nobody knew what Kaija had lost when her mother changed. But Kaija had been repeatedly admonished that anything concerning family should remain within that family. And she probably would not find the right words anyway.

"Don't pay any attention to Mrs. Lapsa, Kaijin," Alma whispered. "She's just envious because your mother is beautiful and because Pastor Saulcere likes talking to her. My father said just the other day that many Latvians have the same flaw—envy."

"I'm going to make it up to my mother," Kaija whispered back. "I'll take her home soon."

But the girls knew that returning to Latvia was unlikely. More Latvians were being deported to Siberia, more Russians were being brought in to take over their land, homes, and possessions, and the United States was not going to provoke the Stalin by protesting.

Alma adjusted the white collar on her navy-blue dress, which with a black pinafore over it had been her school uniform in the camps, and laced her white tennis shoes, which looked dingy in spite of the pains she had taken to cover the scuffs and worn spots with chalk. The dress was even shorter on her than last year, but it would have to do. She put on her best cheerful smile as she bid goodbye to her father, who surprised her by patting her shoulder and wishing her good luck.

At least she did not have to walk the twenty-one blocks to Shortridge High School alone because the Cross-eyed Twins, Mrs. Lapsa's two sons, were coming too. They were neither cross-eyed nor twins, but that's what Alma called them behind their back. She had no use for either of them. Laimonis played the accordion beautifully, but he was fatter and lazier than a real man should be. Ojars, on the other hand, was tall and skinny as a broom handle, but Alma despised him for sneaking cigarettes in the back yard and for acting as if the five hairs sprouting on his upper lip constituted the world's handsomest moustache and turned him into Valentino.

But the boys might provide some help when she was attacked with fists and sticks, as she fully expected to be. After the incident at the swimming pool, Alma had concluded that Americans were exactly like Germans. The latter had yelled "Verfluchte Auslander," damned foreigner, and pelted her with stones on the rare occasions she had ventured outside the gates of camps. She had wanted to curse and beat them, but she knew she would be overpowered, so she had run instead.

Still, being attacked outright was preferable to being shamed. After the war, before they were admitted to a camp, Alma and her father had wandered the dark, rubble-filled streets, hoping to find something to eat. Her mouth had filled with saliva when she saw a family sharing bread and laughing behind brightly lit windows. Eventually she had found a bowl of boiled peas set outside a front gate by some kind, generous soul. The food had already touched her father's and her lips when they realized that a clump of human excrement was hidden beneath the thin layer of peas. Alma had since learned that French housewives used this trick regularly to humiliate starving German prisoners of war, but she still gagged when she remembered her defiled hands and her father's shame-tormented face.

Near 30th Street, another Latvian girl joined the trio from Park Avenue. Brigita was fat and flouncy, with eyeglasses thick as milk bottles, but her brown and white saddle shoes and tiny zippered white purse announced that she was more American than anyone. Brigita had hardly said "Good morning," before she launched into a

83

detailed account of the horrors awaiting the Latvians and of the ostracism she had heroically endured the previous spring when she had been the only foreigner at Shortridge High School. Everyone had stared, and no one had spoken to her until some of the darker-skinned students had taken pity on her and invited her to walk with them. Taunts of "nigger-lover" and "Jew" had followed her down the long hallways after that.

"If I've learned anything, it's that you have to act and dress exactly like the white kids and you have to stay away from Negroes," Brigita counseled. "Your dress is too short, Alma," she pointed out.

Alma's heart contracted with worry and unexpected tenderness. Kaija's dress was even shorter, she did not have saddle shoes, and she was likely to befriend anyone who greeted her as she walked to Public School 45 by herself. Kaija's English was better than everyone's except Mrs. Krumins,' she had a smile that could melt the heart, and she could write "judge" and "professor" before the names of two parents on all forms she had to fill out, but Alma still wished she could be there to look out for her. Had Alma known that God could be addressed anytime, anywhere, and on any subject, she would have said a little prayer for Kaija and maybe even for herself. But she believed he could be called upon only on Sundays and only in formal prayers from which every selfish personal desire had been excised.

Brigita melted away as soon as she pointed out the principal's office in the huge, light-yellow brick building, but no one taunted, tripped, or hit the Latvians. After some general bewilderment, Miss Fritz, the German teacher, was summoned to communicate in a language all the newcomers knew.

Alma felt assaulted by questions. Who were they? Why hadn't their parents come to school with them? Were their parents irresponsible? Didn't their parents love them? Why were the Latvians here instead of in their own country where they belonged? Were Latvians fascists because they had fought against the Russians during World War II? Were they communists because Latvia was now part of the Soviet Union? And why did they insist on calling themselves Latvians when their country no longer existed?

"Ask them, are their parents Latvian too?" Miss White, the guidance counselor, prodded Miss Fritz.

You idiot, Alma wanted to shout. What else could they be? Zulu, Chinese, Eskimo? Who was this Miss White anyway, who talked in a whispery little girl voice and kept her knees and ankles clamped together as if she had to pee?

Eventually the new Latvian students were given slips of paper with room numbers and class times and sent out into the wide corridors to find their way. Other students watched but did not interfere.

Alma's head ached with the effort, but she could not even make out the subject of the first class. The second was a little better though. The math problems on the board were easy, much simpler than those she had had to do in the camps, and she could actually follow some of the teacher's explanations. She felt almost confident when she found the cafeteria.

Standing in line was already familiar from the camps, and Mrs. Krumins had explained that she was to pick up a tray, select lunch from the items displayed, and then pay the lady at the end. Alma had plenty of money because her father had shocked her by giving her much more than she had asked for. She picked out canned green beans, mashed potatoes, fried chicken, and a square of red Jell-O topped by a dollop of mayonnaise. Her spirits soared as she looked at the good and plentiful food, at the huge clean windows letting in sunlight, and at other students laughing and talking.

She congratulated herself for noticing that the tables were segregated: only white boys at some, white girls at others, and black students of both sexes at the one farthest away. She headed for the nearest half-empty table of white girls.

There was a collective intake of breath as she sat down. In less than a minute, the girls had picked up their trays and moved to other tables, leaving Alma in isolation. Her face was burning, but she shivered as if she had been doused with ice water. Even the shiny

85

red square of Jell-O had lost its appeal. She felt her tears rising and threatening to fall.

But no, she was too proud to cry in front of these people. She would not do it if they beat her black and blue. She would not let them know they had hurt her even if they bludgeoned her beyond recognition, like the Latvians tortured to death by the Russians. She shook her head, trying to rid herself of images in newspaper photographs she had memorized while her father slept.

"All alone, are you, Miss Stuck-up?" Ojars asked as he sat down on the bench and slid over, too close to her.

"Not anymore," Alma sniffed.

Suddenly she was flooded with good will. How kind the Latvians were. How could she have disliked a single one? She would call the Cross-Eyed Twins by their proper names from now on, she would ignore Ojars' silly moustache, and she would not make any of the smart remarks she had thought-up about the ridiculous white plastic pouch that Brigita called a purse. She would not put any effort into making friends with silly American girls. They had no idea what life was like; the only thing they had to worry about was which shoulder their circle pins belonged on and whether their twin sweater sets matched their skirts. She would stay with her own people, she vowed, as she smiled to welcome Brigita to the Latvian table.

At 3:15, Alma was at the bus-stop where Mrs. Rank, her new employer, had told her to wait. Just this morning, Alma had anticipated being picked-up by a rich woman in a new and expensive car. Other students would assume she had a mother who loved her so much that she could not wait for her to arrive home. They would all envy her. But now, Alma did not glance at her American classmates straggling out of the building to see if they noticed. She reminded herself that she did not care what they thought.

"Come here, Alma," a woman called loudly as she motioned to Alma. She wore a smart black and white striped blouse, and a small black hat wobbled above her tightly permed hair.

"I am Mrs. Rank. Get in, Alma," she ordered.

When Alma hesitated, the woman cupped her hands around her mouth as if that would keep others from overhearing the shameful information she was about to impart. "I'm the one whose house you'll clean. What language do you speak anyway?"

"You see, Alma, there are a hundred different countries in the world," Mrs. Rank explained while Alma got into the car silently. "People in different countries speak different languages, and they also have different names. Mr. Rank knows which languages and which names belong to more than a dozen countries."

Who was this Mr. Rank, who probably knew fewer people from foreign countries than Alma and her father had encountered in Europe? Was he some very old relative who had to be venerated, Alma wondered. Latvian women did not call their husbands Mister.

Inside Mrs. Rank's kitchen, in one of the mansions on Meridian Street, Alma tied a large red and white checked apron over her school dress. She would bring her shabby cotton skirt and blouse to change into next time.

Mrs. Rank spoke to her as slowly as if she were retarded, but at least Alma understood that she was to start cleaning on the outside and work backwards: from the front steps to the "foyer," to the "reception room," the dining room, Mr. Rank's study, and the "powder room". She should leave the parts of the house that the family actually lived in for later. Alma thought this was exactly the wrong way to go about it; she had glimpsed unwashed dishes and unmade beds farther into the interior. She wished she had spoken up about the sequence of cleaning or corrected Mrs. Rank's assumption that she did not know there were many countries and many different names.

Still, it was good to work outside, if only briefly, on a warm and sunny September afternoon. Red leaves floated down from maples, and yellow leaves shaped like small fans danced on a tree Alma had never seen before and could not name. Mounds of bronze and dark red chrysanthemums lined the long drive, and purple and white flowers, whose name she did not know either, spilled over the edges of two great cement urns. Nevertheless, being out in the natural world was comforting, almost as if she were back in Stabules. Someday she too would live in a house like this on Meridian Street, surrounded by trees and flowers, instead of on Park Avenue with its rundown buildings and compacted soil.

She dreaded going inside because of a large Siamese cat she had glimpsed earlier. He had stared at her coldly while she stood still, afraid to move. Finally, he raised his tail and turned his back on her, rudely exposing his bottom. She would have to be on guard that he did not sneak up. She could endure it if he merely came close, but she could not keep from crying out if he rubbed against her legs or leapt on her. She would scream. Then she would lose her job and the afternoon's pay.

Alma had not always been afraid of cats. She had loved Varonitis, Little Hero, the sleek black cat with a white diamond on his forehead who lived in the barn in Stabules and went confidently about his business of hunting mice and baby birds. She had been scolded more than once for setting out saucers of milk and for letting him sleep on her bed. He purred loudly, grinding with his little windmill as Latvians called it, whenever she stroked his white belly. He gazed thoughtfully at her to let her know that he understood her every word. At other times, he waited for her outside and trotted companionably at her side when she went to scatter grain for chickens or to pull up carrots in the vegetable garden. He had run away from her only once, but that was when she tried to put a doll's dress on him in order to amuse two girls who lived on a neighboring farm. She didn't blame him; she knew she had insulted him. She had humbly apologized for not respecting his dignity, and eventually he had forgiven her.

He was the last pet she could remember. No cats or dogs had accompanied the carts of refugees on their way to the seashore. What had happened to them all, Alma wondered now. Had their owners left them with neighbors who would care for them, had they abandoned them, or had they quietly put them to death? She remembered German shepherd dogs, but these wolf-like creatures were not pets. Their purpose was to terrify people as the Nazis went on their rounds. But she had not seen other breeds of dogs or any cats at all once she and her father arrived in Germany. Had they all starved to death because there was not enough food for people, let alone animals? Had they been killed in air-raids or eaten by the starving? She had heard of people eating horses and rats, but surely not pets. But maybe she had simply not noticed; she could not recall a single bird singing during the war either.

The first cat she remembered seeing after the war was in a camp, when she was nine. It was painfully thin, with striped gray and black fur matted from living in the wild, its eyes sadder than any she could imagine. She had spoken to it reassuringly, and she had put out her hand to coax it to her, but it had backed away. When she hurried outside again with a little powdered milk dissolved in water in the lid of a jar, he had disappeared.

She saw him a day or two later, splayed against a fence. Someone had fashioned a crude cross of branches and lashed the cat's legs to it with barbed wire, in a crude parody of Christ crucified. The cat's head drooped, and at first, she assumed he was dead. But when she bent down, she saw that he was still breathing. He tried to raise his eyes to meet hers but could not.

She spoke soothingly as she untwisted the wire. She could feel how much he hurt, and she worked with frantic haste, letting the barbs scratch her hands. Specks of rust mingled with drops of her blood and his, and she knew she should not be doing this. Germs would get into her cuts and hurt animals could lash out as mercilessly as people. But she could not stop. She had to undo what some war-crazed man or band of cruel orphans had done.

The cat stirred his back legs weakly once she got them free, but his head continued to loll from side to side. She used her small body to prop up his so that it would not sag and drive the barbs deeper into his flesh.

When she had freed the last leg, she cradled him in her arms. Her heart swelled with joy as she felt him gathering strength. Suddenly he let out a terrible sound, something between an agonized moan and furious yowl, squirmed around, and dug into her. He sank his claws into her arms and neck, trying to get at her throat. It took her a moment to realize what was happening: he was attacking her as if she were his tormentor instead of his savior. She used all her strength to push him away, but he buried his nails in her clothes and flesh.

Eventually her screams brought out people from the barracks, and a long time seemed to pass before her father detached the torture-crazed animal from her. He lifted her in his arms, and out of the corner of her eye, she saw other men holding open a sack while the cat heaved and writhed against their efforts to stuff him in. And then she was indoors, on the nearest bunk bed, as women hurried to remove her clothes and boil water fetched from the distant pump. They washed her wounds with rough brown soap, and someone produced a bottle of precious hydrogen peroxide, which stung and bubbled over her wounds. Someone else smeared her face and throat and hands with a black pitch-like salve. It was the best they could do, with no hospital or doctor available.

She was lucky. She did not die. The cat must not have been rabid, and she did not get blood poisoning or lock-jaw from the rusted wire either. Some months later, a young woman who owned a hand mirror offered her a look, and Alma saw that most of the scars stretching across her neck and face were already faded, like strands of pale yarn, except for a purple half-moon on her throat.

She began to encounter cats regularly in Indianapolis. They seemed to have infinite freedom to roam. She memorized which houses they lived in, and she crossed the street to avoid them. A fat orange cat, probably sensing her fear, had leapt on her just a week ago. It had taken every bit of her courage not to die right there. She had jerked him off her waist and kicked and pushed and stamped her until he ran off.

Mrs. Rank's Siamese cat stayed hidden while Alma vacuumed, but he slid in through a tiny door designed for his exclusive use, as soon as she entered the kitchen. Alma was almost relieved that he was out in plain sight so that he could not sneak up on her. She spread out her arms on the counter between herself and the cat, and she widened her stance to make her body appear powerful and large.

The cat watched as she sliced cheese and set it on round crackers in preparation for something Mrs. Rank called "cock's tales." Ordinarily Alma would have puzzled over a party given for the purpose of telling stories about roosters, but she had to concentrate on the cat. For now, he showed no interest in the food, but that would change as soon as she started stirring dried onion soup into sour cream, which was a new food popular with Americans. He must be as ravenously hungry as she was, though pride and honesty forbade her to sneak so much as a sliver of cheese into her mouth.

The cat was pacing restlessly. Keeping his cold blue eyes on her, he looped along the wall and edged closer to her. She would be the one blamed if cat hairs fell into the "dip" or if he upset the bowl of cream. And how could she complete the tasks Mrs. Rank had set for her if she had to stay alert for the coming attack? She was desperate to do well. Mrs. Rank would notice what a good worker she was and would begin to like her, maybe even love her.

The cat was near enough to attack.

She drew herself up to her full height, twisted her face into a horrifying grimace, raised her arms, and screeched.

"Oh, my God," Mrs. Rank said as she stepped through the door. "What's wrong with you, Alma? Don't you see you're terrifying the poor thing?"

Clouds of perfume, which Alma would later learn was called Joy, wafted around Mrs. Rank. Her midnight blue taffeta skirt billowed, her open-toed heels clicked, and a silver bracelet with dozens of tiny objects attached to it tinkled around her wrist.

"Don't be frightened, sweetheart. It's all right. I'm here to protect you. Alma is a bad girl," she cooed as she knelt down.

"Stay right there, Alma," she hissed over her shoulder.

Bad girl. Alma wanted to explain and to apologize, but she did not know the right words in English and she could not have said them even if she did. Her pay, her job, and her foolish hopes that

91

Mrs. Rank would appreciate her work and come to like or love her—all was lost.

Mrs. Rank stayed on her knees, letting the cat lick her face. After an eternity, she lifted the cat, cradled it against her breasts, and carried it through the door to the family rooms.

As soon as she returned, she started giving Alma instructions on how to arrange cooked shrimp on lettuce leaves.

Alma understood that she was not fired after all.

Mrs. Rank rummaged in her dresser for a pair of used nylons and a garter belt and stood over Alma while she put them on.

"I am deeply regretful for to alarm cats," Alma brought out. She could not keep her voice from trembling, but she did not cry. Alma was proud that she had kept her foolish hopes for affection hidden.

Mrs. Rank was urging Alma to hurry, but she stopped mid-motion and looked at her. Something like compassion crossed her carefully made up face. She took Alma by the hand, led her to the dresser, and gently pushed her down in front of the mirror. To Alma's great surprise, she started brushing her hair.

As Mrs. Rank counted the strokes, Alma began to relax. She leaned back and closed her eyes to fully experience each touch. Mrs. Rank did not know the proper way to clean a house or to discipline a cat and she had called Alma a bad girl, but here she was, lovingly brushing Alma's hair.

As her scalp almost rose with pleasure to meet Mrs. Rank's brush, Alma allowed herself to daydream once more. Mrs. Rank would gently correct Alma's English, she would tell her what to do to succeed in school, she would teach her womanly secrets that other girls learned from their mothers, and she would come to value Alma and depend on her.

"Ninety-eight, ninety-nine, and one hundred," Mrs. Rank concluded.

"And do something about that nose of yours," Mrs. Rank said.

"It's shiny," she whispered when Alma looked confused. Mrs. Rank acted as embarrassed as if she were pointing to blood on Alma's skirt.

Mrs. Rank dabbed at Alma's nose with a pink powder puff. She tapped some powder into an envelope, added a wad of cotton wool, and handed it to Alma.

"You must use this every day, without fail," she advised. "And you should do a hundred strokes each night too."

She applied some carrot-colored lipstick to Alma's narrow lips, wiped it off, picked up a dark red one, and used that.

"This one doesn't help much either," she sighed. "But you do look nice, Alma," she added.

Alma hardly registered the compliment. An ache that she would never be good enough pierced her heart and remained there after the party was over and Alma had learned what cocktails meant. Mrs. Rank had unexpectedly given her eleven cents extra to cover the bus ride to Park Avenue, and Mr. Rank had winked and slipped her a quarter, a whole hour's pay, for a job well done.

None of that made Alma happy until she was out of the house and noticed the luxurious fragrance coming from the purple and white flowers in the large urns. She was glad she had asked Mrs. Rank their name. Petunias. And the name of the tree with the fan-like leaves was a gingko.

"Petunias. Gingko. I like the smell of petunias and the leaves of the gingko," Alma practiced as she walked down the long drive to the dark street and on to the bus stop.

Lost Midsummers

9

After returning from Shortridge High School and their part-time jobs, Alma and Kaija usually did their homework together. At a round claw-footed table, which Alma had persuaded her father to buy on the installment plan at the used furniture store on Sixteenth Street, they quizzed each other on vocabulary lists, tried to understand the how and why of footnotes, and if Valdis was not home, discussed the day's events frankly. They did not speak about the war or the camps.

Urged on by Kaija, Alma too read everything and anything: the Indianapolis Star occasionally purchased by the adults, Superman comic books offered by 18-year-old Ojars, novels and poetry in Latvian belonging to Pastor Saulcere, copies of the *Silver Screen* thoroughly studied by Mrs. Krumins, and stacks of books in English the girls brought back weekly from the Public Library. Alma disapproved of Kaija wasting money on occasional copies of *Modern Romance* and *True Confessions*, but she avidly read those too.

Tonight, Alma had to tell Mrs. Veldre that Valdis was unwell and that Kaija could not study in their room. Alma was relieved when Mrs. Veldre invited her in and did not inquire more closely.

"It's nice that you girls can spend the evening studying," Mrs. Veldre said. "I always loved school too. Oh, what I wouldn't give to be a student again!"

On her way out she added, "Please forgive me, Alma, for abandoning you alone in our home. But I cannot be late for washing floors."

Alma was too respectful to sit down at Judge Veldre's battered desk, which nevertheless dominated the beds and kitchen appliances in the former living room. In the small attached sun porch

Mrs. Veldre had contrived a space of her own with nails, clothes lines, blankets, and the back of a wardrobe—a method for creating privacy perfected in barracks in the camps.

A photograph of Astra, Mrs. Veldre's younger sister, holding white lilies in impossibly thin hands, was propped up on a crate covered with a paisley wool scarf next to the narrow bed, and a thin volume titled *Mother Courage* lay on her pillow. Unframed photographs shared the area crammed with books, sketches, and notes. Mrs. Veldre and Astra as school girls in white-collared dark uniforms and black pinafores, holding hands under the Laima Clock, near Brivibas Piemineklis , the Monument to Freedom, in the center of Riga. Judge and Mrs. Veldre with friends on the way to the opera, the women in bias-cut satin dresses and piquant little hats light as butterfly wings, the men in tuxedos, high-collared shirts, and white vests and gloves. Mrs.Veldre smiling as she guided five-year-old Kaija's hands on piano keys. Mrs. Veldre's sister Astra in her coffin, surrounded by tall vases of white peonies and early roses, with light pouring over her through an open window. Kaija, Judge and Mrs. Veldre, and their friends outside, at a table set with fine china and platters of food. "The last gathering Atminas, October 1944," Mrs. Veldre had written on the back.

Alma remembered a maroon leather album with gold tassels on a high shelf in Stabules, but try as hard as she could, she did not remember any of the photographs. Had she forgotten them or had her father forbidden her to look? It was no use asking him. If he had hidden the album in the farm house to await their return, it had long ago been defiled by the filthy fingers of Russians in illegal possession of Stabules. If he had carried it with him into exile, it had turned into ash in the air raid that destroyed the rest of their belongings.

A photograph lay face down, a little apart from Mrs. Veldre's other photos. A white rose, like those women made in the camps of crepe paper and wire to beautify dismal corners of cramped rooms, had been placed on top of it. Knowing it was private, Alma nevertheless picked up the photo and turned it over. A stern old man, a row of medals across his chest, looked contemptuously at Alma.

"Remember me," the inscription across the lower corner ordered. This must be the General, who even in death guaranteed respect for Kaija's family.

Hearing Kaija's steps, Alma hastily put down the photo and laid the rose on top.

"Were you looking at Astra's death portrait?" Kaija asked. "My mother looks at it too. She was probably staring at it when you came in. I bet she didn't ask you a single question about school or what you had to do at Mrs. Rank's today."

For the life of her, Alma could not understand why Kaija minded. Being questioned by adults usually meant having to tell some inanely cheerful half-truth.

"I don't blame her," Alma said. "That picture is beautiful. Astra looks like an angel. And I love the one of you and your parents in the garden."

"Why?" Kaija demanded.

"Your mother and your father together. All of you good-looking and happy."

"Happy for the last time," Kaija lashed out. "I wish she'd put those photos awaay. She cries whenever she talks about Astra dying, and I hate it when she looks at herself in those silk dresses before she goes to work."

"But we all have to work," Alma said mildly.

"No and no, a thousand times no," Kaija cried. "It's different for her. You don't know her. You don't know how different she used to be."

Ready to argue, Alma stopped on seeing Kaija's stricken face.

"You just don't understand. Nobody does," Kaija whispered.

Alma had learned from her father's conduct rather than verbal instruction that questions should not be asked about painful subjects and what happened inside families was stricktly private. Alma would not embarrass her friend by prying.

"Tell you what," Kaija said after a few minutes. "I have a plan. Let's study till our brains smoke and get on the Honor Roll at Shortridge this semester."

One of the many things Alma loved about Kaija was that she never stayed sad or angry. Kaija blushed and cried much too easily, of course, but then she would blow her nose, put on a sunny smile, and go on to something else.

"I couldn't," Alma said. "The only A I ever got was in math."

"Of course, you could. All anyone has to do to get an A is study. It's easy."

Easy for you, Alma thought.

"This is how we'll do it, Almin. We'll study for three hours every night during the week and if we need to do more we'll get up early on Sundays. We'll get good grades, graduate with big honors, and get scholarships to Indiana University. You'll go to the Bloomington campus first, but then I'll come, and we'll share a room, only much nicer than this."

"Yes, we'll have diplomas and then we'll get good, steady jobs," Alma cried, carried away by Kaija's enthusiasm. American diplomas were essential. Without them, well-educated immigrants labored in slaughterhouses and cleaned toilets.

"That's what all the boys want too. Go to Purdue, become an engineer, marry an industrious wife, have two children, make a lot of money, buy a house, and stay put."

"Sounds good to me."

"But don't you want more than that, Almin? Like living in Paris and New York, or reading every book in the Indianapolis Public Library, or being the muse for a ravishingly handsome man who writes poetry? He'll have to be American or Italian because Latvians can't devote themselves to art right now. I want to learn everything. No one can take away your knowledge when another war comes."

"Yes, but you can't make money doing that."

"Sure, you can," Kaija declared. "Take doctors, for instance. When there's war, they can remove bullets and bandage wounds. When there's exile, they can serve as hospital orderlies or work in insane asylums. My father knows a Latvian doctor who is working in a madhouse in Kentucky right now while he studies to get certified again. Only the degrees of lawyers and judges are useless in a new country, so I'll probably study medicine myself."

Alma looked doubtful. At Career Day for juniors, Miss White had said that doctors were unbelievably brilliant and that they studied so much that ordinary people could not even begin to imagine it. Kaija was probably smart enough though. Kaija had gotten a "genius level" score on her I.Q. test, which even Mrs. Veldre had been excited about, and she had been transferred into college preparatory classes.

"I can try, but I'll never get more than a C in English," Alma sighed. Poems were difficult enough to understand, let alone to reduce to précis, which all students were regularly required to write. In addition, Miss Donovan, Alma's English teacher, assigned compositions about subjects that were impossible for immigrants: where did you go on your summer vacation, which American President did you admire when you were in first grade, and which of your aunts is the best candidate for "The Most Unforgettable Character I Ever Met" in *Readers' Digest*.

"We've got to write 'a process theme' for next week," she sighed. "I can't even think what about. Miss Donovan is mad at me already because I said a lot of aunts had been killed in the war or remained in their own countries. She said that I had talked back to her in front of the class, and that she had never seen a student as rude as me, but that I should describe how my mother cooks at Thanksgiving. But I'm not about to tell her that you and I do cooking and housework, and I am *not* going to write about cray-fishing."

Latvians trapped the tiny dark creatures in Fall Creek, boiled them in water seasoned with salt and dill, and spent whole evenings socializing and nibbling and sucking. Otherwise only black Americans ate what they caught in the muddy water.

"In that case, why don't you write about something you haven't done but would like to?" Kaija suggested.

A room in which Alma and her father had briefly found shelter at the end of the war came back to her. Russian soldiers had evidently not been in it because the floor was not covered with vomit and feces. Instead, tall graceful windows without glass looked out

99

on an overgrown garden, and a grand piano, its strings broken, and its lid scarred by falling plaster, stood on a low platform, but otherwise the room was empty. Valdis shoved aside debris and Alma cleared away shattered glass to make a space to lie down. Waiting for sleep that refused to come, Alma used her coat-sleeve to polish a small area directly in front of her face. The intricately laid parquet floor was only nicked here and there, and she saw that work and care could rescue it from dirt and bring back its original beauty.

Alma sometimes cheered herself up by imagining how she would restore this room. Maybe Kaija had seen rooms like this during the war too, because she nodded as soon as Alma mentioned a few details.

"I'd like to clear out that room. I could make the house really nice to live in too," Alma said.

"Oh? And how would you do that?" Kaija asked. "What equipment would you need? What would you do first? What is the logical order of proceeding after that?"

"I'd need a broom handle or a thick sturdy branch. I'd attach buckets at each end and balance it on my shoulders. That way I could carry two at the same time; otherwise it would take too long. A hammer and a chisel to break up debris into pieces that I can lift. A place to dump everything, but not in the garden because I want to clear out and replant that. Not in a ditch across the street because I never want to see rubble again. I'd inspect the foundation to see if it was solid, and if it was, I'd replace glass, oil window frames, repair the sashes, and polish the floor."

Someone else would have to restring and tune the piano, while Alma positioned a couch upholstered in dark blue velvet, graceful lamps, and mahogany tables and chairs. These would be shaped like the tiny furniture she had envied in a rich German girl's doll house.

"So, write it down, just like that, Almin. Don't think about Miss Donovan reading it, imagine that only I will. And don't worry about making mistakes in spelling. If you can't think of the right word, just put it down in Latvian and look it up later. Read it aloud to see where you need commas or periods. After you correct everything, all you have to do is copy it over. And hurrah! You're done."

Miss Donovan, perspiring in her tent-like gray dress, lumbered around the room, handing back papers. Alma had to rein in her excitement when only hers remained in the teacher's hands. Miss Donovan usually praised the writer and then read the best composition aloud.

"I want to see you, Alma, right after class," Miss Donovan said. "The rest of you are dismissed."

Miss Donovan was frowning, but Alma still expected praise.

"You copied this, Alma," Miss Donovan said angrily. "There's no way you could have written this by yourself. You cheated."

"I did not," Alma said, but she felt herself blush. She had looked up words—sill, parquet, hammer, and sash—in her Latvian/English dictionary. But that could not be cheating because Miss Donovan repeatedly told the class to look up and learn words they did not know in order to improve their vocabularies. Kaija had read Alma's theme, but she had not made any changes. She had only pointed to a few commas that Alma might want to reconsider, and then she had pronounced the theme excellent.

Miss Donovan had lectured to her class of sixteen-year-olds about the criminal nature of plagiarism before. Failing to footnote, she said, was the academic equivalent of murder because it denied immortality to writers, which consisted of their names being properly acknowledged in student papers. Copying something was stealing and it foretold a life of crime: first you handed in something that was not yours, and then you went on to joy-riding and shoplifting. Pretty soon you were a juvenile delinquent, hand-cuffed and on your way to jail.

"We're going to the Principal's office right now, Alma. You better get ready for what Mr. Broaden has to say."

The basement of the city jail, to which Alma had accompanied Mrs. Krumins to pay a fine for drunk driving by one of the disillusioned veterans on Park Avenue, flashed before Alma's eyes.

Mr. Broaden's office was nothing like prison, but to Alma he looked grim enough to be a jailor. Tall and very thin, with a striking resemblance to President Lincoln, he neither smiled nor told jokes like the Vice Principal did at all-school assemblies.

Alma cringed because Miss White, the guidance counselor, was in the room too. Miss Donovan had already ruined Alma's reputation by telling these people about her.

"I know for a fact Alma copied because she's a trouble-maker," Miss Donovan said. "She talked back to me in front of the class. She said people's aunts are dead or in other cou tries. And she flat out refused to write about cooking a turkey, which I know a girl like her can handle."

"Let's leave that aside for the moment," Mr. Broaden said. "You're here because you believe she cheated."

"Yes, that's right," Miss White spoke up. "And I have the proof, Mr. Broaden," she added, flourishing a booklet that looked vaguely familiar. "Her I.Q. is only 60. She doesn't even know how to think."

Alma remembered marking answers in a similar pamphlet during the first week of her freshman year when she knew little English.

"Did you copy, Alma? Or did you write the paper yourself?" the Principal asked. "Now is the time to tell the truth."

"I wrote it myself," Alma said firmly. To her great relief, she did not blush.

"How are you doing in you other subjects, Alma?" he asked.

"She's keeping up in Math and Consumer Ed, of course," Miss White said before Alma had a chance to answer. "I've recommended she take Introduction to Business next semester. I'm doing my best to see that she isn't a burden on society."

"Sounds to me like she can think then," Mr. Broaden remarked.

"But that doesn't mean anything," Miss White bristled. "Retarded people often have unusual gifts, especially in music and math."

"Just a minute, not so fast. We're not talking about retarded people here. You just said Alma is keeping up in other subjects."

"Yes, but that's because she's an over-achiever," Miss White explained. "Under-achievers are more common, but the opposite condition is not unknown."

Mr. Broaden turned to Miss Donovan.

"And what do you have to add?" he asked.

"Just that she is sneaky. She copied from a book or a magazine, but she cleverly put a few commas in the wrong places, so I would think it was her work."

Mr. Broaden gazed out the window before he rose to pronounce judgment.

"If you don't mind, ladies, let me summarize what we have. We have your accusation, and we have Alma's statement that she wrote the paper herself. You have also expressed the opinion that she is too stupid to have written the paper herself and too clever because she covered her tracks with commas. But you have presented no evidence. I will only believe that Alma cheated if you find the book she copied from and you show me which words on which page match hers exactly. But until then I will take her word for it that she wrote this herself. It certainly reads like her work. She knows that you need hard work and courage to restore damage caused by war."

"But . . . "

"I'm sure you will agree that innocent until proven guilty is a basic American principle? It's what I fought for in the war, and it's what other Americans died for. It applies in the criminal justice system, and it should apply to people accused by Senator Joe McCarthy. But by God, I'll see to it that it applies in Shortridge High School."

"But . . . but . . . ," Miss White sputtered.

103

"If you say so, Sir," Miss Donovan said sullenly.

"You may go now, Alma. I'm sorry you were put through this," Mr. Broaden said, escorting her to the door and courteously opening it.

Alma wanted to kiss his hand. In her experience, men did not apologize. In addition, Mr. Broaden had just announced a principle that was surely one of the best things about America.

Alma was opening her locker when Miss Donovan caught up with her.

"Don't think you're getting away with this, Alma, because you're not," she panted. "I'll find the book you copied from, even if it takes me the rest of my life. Then I'll flunk you in the course, and you'll lose your high school diploma. You just wait."

Latvians in America celebrate Thanksgiving in November with their fellow citizens; but, they also celebrate their ancient day of thanks when trees are in their autumn glory, and fruit and vegetables are still ripening in orchards and fields. Religious or not, every Latvian on Park Avenue went to the rented church on 22nd Street for *Plaujas Diena,* Reaping Day. Most had been city dwellers, but they had spent childhood summers in the country and missed an intimate connection to nature.

Kaija sat with head bowed, waiting for the first prayer to end. She knew God was not listening. She had seen only darkness and a vast indifference when she prayed during air raids and when her mother wept. She disliked herself for conforming outwardly. She wished she were brave enough to refuse to attend church. But even Alma had been outraged when Kaija tried to tell her she did not believe in God. Alma had maintained that Kaija did not know her own mind, that people who did not believe in God were wicked, and that she could never be friends with an atheist. Kaija thought that faith was a mysterious state of being which others had but which she repeatedly did not achieve although she concentrated as hard as she could.

Everyone looked up as Pastor Saulcere began his sermon. He did not try to evoke fields of golden grain and trees weighed down with fruit for his listeners who worked indoors, deplored tube tomatoes and tasteless apples, and gravitated to the banks of Fall Creek as the only bit of the natural world within reach. Instead he spoke of other reasons for thanksgiving. Exile was bitter, he said, but everyone here had been spared while Nazis imprisoned and murdered thousands, and Russians tortured, deported, and shot thousands more. The two great atheist mass-murderers of the Twentieth Century, Stalin and Hitler, had not succeeded in mudering the people worshipping God in this sanctuary. No one was awakened by terrifying knocks in the middle of the night; everyone had daily bread to eat and a safe place to sleep. The beautiful generosity of America would continue to shield them until Latvia was free and they could go home again.

Alma snapped her mind shut the instant Pastor Saulcere mentioned deportations. She had heard more than enough about people dying of thirst in cattle-cars and being worked to death in frozen forests. She did not want to learn a single additional detail. She refused to feel anything for the thousands lost; she would not allow those starving multitudes to take over her mind. She succeeded in visualizing the sun-warmed stone near the kitchen door at Stabules and she kept her attention fixed on it. By the time she stood up with others to pray for the sacred soil of Latvia, now trampled and despoiled by invaders, she was impervious to words like Siberia, starvation, thirst, and torture.

After the service, Alma and Kaija lingered on the front steps of the apartment building. Both girls took great comfort in their first experience of real friendship. They had been too young in Latvia to form lasting attachments with rarely visiting playmates. In Germany children who seemed like friends after a terrifying night together in a bomb shelter inevitably left the following morning. Later tentative friendships ended as people were moved from one displaced

105

persons' camp to another or emigrated to Britain, Canada, Australia, and finally the United States.

"Can Miss Donovan find that book?" Alma half-whispered.

"Of course not," Kaija declared. "It doesn't exist. You wrote that theme yourself."

"But what if someone else said exactly the same thing, in exactly the same words, and I don't know it?" Alma persisted.

"That won't happen," Kaija said. "A coincidence like that cannot happen in a million years. It's statistically impossible. It's not logical."

Alma was grateful for once for Kaija's worship of logic, which included pumelling Alma with Latin phrases and pointing out mistakes in reasoning, which could be identified by putting what people said into a form of three sentences called syllogisms.

"But it's all over now, Almin, isn't it?" Kaija asked, trying to cheer up Alma.

"Yes and no. I didn't get punished, but Miss Donovan hates me, and I'm in English for dummies. Mr. Broaden said it would be better for me to be out of her class, and there was nowhere else to put me."

"They can't do that," Kaija was incensed. "You didn't do anything wrong. You have to be in college prep. It'll ruin everything if you're not. We're going to share a room in Bloomington. Remember?"

"Oh, Kaija, that's just dreaming. You know we'll never have the money to go."

"But we will. Some kind American will notice how hard we study and he'll help us. Maybe we'll get scholarships. Or we'll win one of those contests about why we like Spam meat or Prell shampoo, in fifty words or less, and get five hundred dollars. We'll work. We'll save. There's got to be a way. Amerfica is the land of opportunity," Kaija insisted. "What about going to Mr. Broaden again and asking him to move you to another class?"

"You know I can't. Only parents can do that. That's what the Americans do, the mothers go if it's not too bad, and the fathers if it is."

Both girls fell silent at the clear impossibility of getting Alma's father to intervene. Valdis would not want to take a day off from work, and he would be angry that Alma had made a mess of the little that was expected of her. His English was clumsy, and he might have a drink before confronting American authorities.

"Cheer up, Kaijin," Alma said. "It doesn't matter. I don't need their stupid college prep. I'll figure out something else. I don't like studying all the time anyway. I'm not brilliant like you."

Kaija grinned. She loved hearing that she was smart.

"Anyway, I'm not going to give them the satisfaction of knowing they've hurt me," Alma said defiantly. "Sated or starving, hold your head high, just like the proverb says."

She wanted Kaija to reassure her that Miss Donovan did not have the legal power to confiscate her high school diploma, but Mrs. Veldre motioned through the window, and Kaija jumped up. Alma heard their soft voices, a duet of mother and daughter talking gently together, as she passed the closed door to the Veldres' room. She put on a determined smile before she opened her own door and called out a cheerful greeting to her father.

Lost Midsummers

10

1954

The Three Handsome Brothers from Louisville arrived regularly on Friday nights in order to spend their weekends in Indianapolis. Americans did not socialize with Latvians, and it was a common practice for Latvians of all ages to travel long distances to visit with each other.

The brothers were young and energetic. They pulled up in their battered yellow-and-brown Nash in front of the buildings on 24th Street and Park Avenue and raced upstairs, laughing and rough-housing. They did not care that it was almost midnight or that the floors that they would sleep on were hard. Invariably convivial, they loved to stay up late, talking and singing.

The brothers appeared at every event held at the first Latvian Community House. They wore wreathed silver rings of a design which immediately proclaimed them as Latvian and open-necked white shirts with the sleeves pushed up, long before that became fashionable. Their dark hair, their tanned faces glowing with good health, and their solidarity were thrilling. They seemed ready for anything, and in this they were intoxicatingly different from the staid Latvian boys of Indianapolis, who aspired only to graduate from Purdue and become engineers.

The brothers were all good-looking in a lanky kind of way, but Ivars, the youngest, was so beautiful that even married women found it impossible not to stare. Ivars' vigorous yet fluid movements exuded sexual confidence; his moody dark eyes and soft-looking lips invited female solicitude. The fact that he was expected to be successful at whatever he chose to do increased his appeal.

Alma fell in love the first time she saw Ivars. Her body vibrated in his presence; she had to sit on her hands to keep from secretly touching the back of his jacket. She recited his virtues, real and imagined, to Kaija, and his face floated above her as she fell asleep. But during the day she worried that he was too good for her. Thirty years ago in Latvia, his father had been the president of Letonia, the fanciest fraternity, and he had gone on to serve in the Italian embassy. His mother was a renowned beauty belonging to the best sorority, whom the young men at the University of Latvia had nicknamed Greta Garbo. Still, if Ivars would only look at Alma, he would realize that fate had brought him to her. He would marry her, she would take good care of him, they would have two sons, and they would live happily ever after. If he rejected her, she would never love anyone else. She would live her life in sad but dignified singleness.

Like many Latvians, Alma believed that first love was fated and everlasting. The love story of her father Valdis and her mother Velta was Alma's great treasure. It was a translucent piece of amber the color of light honey, which she polished in secret. It was the talisman that would determine her life and guide her to lasting happiness.

Every detail of Alma's parents' meeting was vivid to her, though she could not remember who had told her. Her father never spoke of her mother, her grandmother in Latvia did not conceal her dislike of Velta, and Jautrite, the liveliest of the farm workers who had taken care of Alma after her mother disappeared, would not have spun stories of Valdis' first love while she fluttered around him herself. Maybe Alma's mother had talked of the great love. Alma would be furious if anyone suggested that she had made up her parents' love story.

In Latvia, the days were cool and blue at Midsummer, the nights white and fragrant, and hard work gave way naturally to pleasure and rest. So Valdis, tall and blond and powerful on his white stallion, was surprised to see a peasant girl still raking hay at dusk. The kerchief restraining her hair and her unbleached linen blouse gleamed in the shadowy meadow as she moved efficiently among haystacks.

Valdis felt the enjoyment of work in his own body as he watched the girl raking, until he noticed that she was barefoot. He could not see any cuts from the stubble, but he felt them as if his own instep were being pierced. Anger welled up in him against the neighbor who had sent this girl, surely no more than seventeen years old, into the field without any shoes and who kept her out alone and working so late in the day.

The girl set down an armful of hay, rested her rake, and wiped her forehead. Her face was turned away from Valdis, towards the last light of the sun. He was not sure whether he heard or only imagined the girl's voice because he too knew the words of the song.

> "Saulit' tecej tecedama
> Es paliku paena.
> Nava savas mamulinas
> Kas iecela saulite."

> The sun moved unrelentingly,
> I was left in half-shade.
> I do not have my dear mother
> To lift me into the sun.

Latvia had once been full of orphans because mothers died in childbirth and fathers were killed in wars. It still was, and Valdis was a practical man. Yet the girl's voice, as light and as pure as a lark's, touched his heart. He swallowed his tears, which were not of pity, and waited for her to become aware of his presence.

When she finally looked at him, he took off his hat and bowed as well as he could from high on his horse. Then, disliking himself for towering over her while paying his respects, he dismounted, and bowed deeply again. Though neither spoke, their souls recognized each other.

111

Within a week, Valdis had found out the girl's name and the orphanage which had hired her out to his neighbor. He told his mother that he was in love. In spite of being past thirty, he had never been in love with anyone else, nor would he be. From now on his mother could stop pointing out young women of property to him. Money, prestige, land, and family connections were nothing compared to Velta.

He wrote two formal letters of honorable intent: one to the nuns who ran the orphanage and one to Velta. Only after the expected denial arrived from the nuns, who refused to allow marriage to a Lutheran, did he resort ever so briefly to secret letters, go-betweens, and whispered meetings. One night when clouds hid the moon, with his swift horses he carried Velta away from the orphanage.

He arranged the wedding at the Lutheran church on the hill bordering Stabules as well as the three day long sumptuous celebration afterwards. Velta refused his offer of lace veils and silk gowns, and she did not put on the heavy necklace of silver and amber Valdis gave her until after their wedding night. Dressed in the same simple white shift she had worn for her first communion, she carried white roses, which scented the dark aisles and damp ante-chambers of the church. Not a single angry word passed between the lovers once they were joined in body, mind, and soul.

Alma and Kaija watched as couples waltzed to accordion music of songs popular in Latvia in the 1920s and 1930s. The small dance floor had once been the living and dining room of the modest-sized bungalow which was the Latvian Community House now. A Latvian flag, its cream-colored and dark red panels recalling blood on the unbleached wool cape of the hero who died protecting Latvia from German invaders, was displayed in the place of honor, next to the Stars and Stripes. The same colors, off-white and dark red, were repeated in the candles and roses on the mantle-piece.

The 18th of November was Latvian Independence Day, and though the Latvians had enjoyed only two decades of self-determination between the First and Second World Wars, the day continued to be celebrated. Apple cakes, beautifully decorated tortes, and platters of small colorful open-faced sandwiches competed for space on a narrow table, and the fragrance of good coffee wafted up to the two girls on the dark staircase.

"We Latvians really know how to set a table," Alma remarked. "I don't know why anyone would want to go to an American party."

"I do," Kaija said.

"Why?" Alma asked. She was afraid that Kaija would announce that she had accepted an invitation to an upcoming American sock hop or other event.

Alma believed Kaija was very popular. She had overheard remarks that Kaija was "cute" and "had personality," two elusive but highly-prized qualities at Shortridge High School. Kaija had been asked to join a girls' club, to go to a slumber party, and to run for sophomore class secretary, while no one ever called Alma on Pastor Saulcere's telephone, which served the whole Latvian community on Park Avenue.

Kaija had trained herself not to complain, so Alma did not know that her friend often felt as painfully alone at school as she had that first day when the American girls left her sitting in isolation in the cafeteria. Unlike Alma, however, Kaija could not bring herself to dismiss her American classmates as irrelevant. She tried to be appropriately dressed in spite of having very few clothes, while Alma was likely to show-up in a stretched out, black and brown checkered skirt cast off by Mrs. Rank, topped by a green polka-dotted blouse, which Mrs. Krumins had received in a CARE package ten-years-ago in Germany.

Kaija sometimes suggested that at least some of Alma's skirts and blouses or shoes and purses should match, and she brought home discounted and damaged items from her part-time job at the Indiana Merchandising Company, a wholesale house for cosmetics and toiletries. This evening the heads of both girls were wreathed in

113

curls, the result of a "Which Twin has the Toni?" home permanent and of restless sleep on tightly wound rings of hair tacked down with bobby-pins.

"Why *would* someone go to the Americans?" Alma persisted.

"Well, for starters, we wouldn't be wall-flowers there. We might not dance every dance, but someone would ask us once or twice."

"Maybe they'd ask you. I don't care, but they don't even talk to me. But why doesn't anyone dance with us here? What's wrong with us?" Alma moaned.

"Nothing is wrong with *us*. There just aren't enough boys. There are thirty-three Latvian girls but only twenty-four boys my age in Indianapolis, and twenty-eight girls and seventeen boys your age. If you like, I can give you the exact figures for all the other ages too."

This information was the result of Kaija's bungled conversation with Pastor Saulcere. She had wanted to ask him something else entirely, something about others having faith in God and the courage that flowed from it. But once she was alone with him in the room which served as his bedroom and kitchen as well as the office for the Latvian Lutheran Congregation, she had lost her nerve and blurted out a ridiculous question about the scarcity of boys. He had obligingly looked through the church register for her. Later she had completed her research by secret study of her father's records of the Indianapolis Latvian Association.

"It's not the shortage of boys I mind. It's the injustice," Kaija went on. "The boys get to choose who dances and when, and all we can do is say yes. If we say no, we are told that we are stuck-up, with our noses up in the air and tripping over our own feet."

"But that's the natural order of things."

"And who decided that? Some old man with scraggly whiskers who wanted to have the first pick of young women. I'm not going to sit around waiting like this forever. I'll do the asking myself, as soon as I get out of Indianapolis. I'll dance with everybody, fat, thin, young, old, married and not," Kaija laughed.

114

Alma was about to condemn this plan as immodest when the three Handsome Brothers entered the room. But she saw only Ivars. Coatless, with snowflakes in his wavy black hair and with his white shirt gleaming under a dark blue jacket, he paused by the door, smiling, ready to enjoy himself.

"Look, Kaija, look, there he is. Oh, I hope he didn't catch a cold, he should have worn a coat, he doesn't even have a hat, I would have seen to it that he was warm. Do you think he'll dance? With whom? Do you think he'll ask me? Or will he ask that awful Dzintra? Why does he always dance with her? It's not fair. She gets to dance with him every week at folk-dancing practice. What do you think he'll do?"

Alma fired questions at Kaija to tamp down her worry that with her plain face, wiry body, and dull—though tonight very curly—hair, she could not compete. Dzintra was willowy, with cheekbones so high, eyes so blue, and hair so blond that she could have adorned posters as an ideal of Latvian womanhood. She was soft-spoken and sweetly provocative, and she had additional unfair advantages. At twenty-one, she was the exact contemporary of Ivars; she had had a lot more time than seventeen-year-old Alma to acquire sophistication and self-confidence.

Ivars nodded pleasantly at Dzintra and started across the room.

"Oh, my God, he's coming towards us, Kaija. He's coming here. He's going to ask me. Oh, my God, Kaija." Alma's heart beat with trepidation and joy.

Alma was half-way on her feet when Ivars stopped in front of the two friends. He bowed slightly to Kaija and stretched out his hand. And Kaija, Alma's best friend and the only person in the whole world who knew how much Alma loved him, placed her hand in his and went off without so much as a backward glance.

Alma's cheeks burned. Had Ivars seen that she had started to stand up? Had others noticed that he had rejected her? Why could she not make herself invisible?

In the middle of the floor, Kaija and Ivars were moving perfectly in step. Their faces were radiant, and their eyes locked.

115

The only reason Alma did not die right there and then was that Dzintra looked put out and was trying hard to appear nonchalant by pretending to yawn.

Alma's thoughts leapt from a single waltz to life-long marriage and two successful sons. Ivars would choose Kaija, who by now was a slender and graceful young woman instead of the skinny overgrown child of three years ago. Kaija was pretty, Kaija was smart, and Kaija had highly respected parents. Ivars would fall in love and marry Kaija, and Alma would lose them both.

Ojars yanked on Alma's arm to get her attention. She stood-up reluctantly and let him propel her onto the floor. His hair, in spite of being profusely oiled, stood up in a Woody Woodpecker cockscomb, and his breath smelled of Sen-Sen and beer. Alma concentrated on keeping her feet out of his way instead of paying attention to his account of how much money he made at his construction job and how cleverly he had bargained for his used red Pontiac convertible.

When the music stopped, Ojars deposited Alma back on the stair step, while Ivars and Kaija stayed in the middle of the floor, absorbed in conversation. They were obviously going to dance again. Ivars' older brothers were standing near the food, smoking and joking, instead of doing anything to rectify the shortage of male dancing partners. Desire, jealousy, anger, and disappointment were so jumbled in Alma's mind that she could not have said what she felt. Finally, the second dance ended, and the music died away as Ojars' roly-poly brother Laimonis set down his accordion. Ivars escorted Kaija back to her seat on the stairs.

"Thank you, Kaija," he said. "It was a great pleasure to dance with you."

Alma turned away, too hurt to speak.

"Did Ojars step on your feet, Almin? Do you think he has been drinking? Or, was it all right dancing with him?" Kaija finally broke the silence. "Aren't you going to speak to me?" she asked when Alma remained sullenly silent.

"It was awful. Kaija, how could you?" Alma burst out.

116

"How could I what? Dance with Ivars? Is that what you mean?"

"Yes, of course. What else could I mean?"

"I danced with him because he asked me. It's exactly like I said earlier: the boys get to decide, and we can't really say no. You had to dance with Ojars, I had to dance with Ivars, and Dzintra was cross because no one asked her. I did not go up to Ivars and pull him to the middle of the floor."

Kaija knew she was being disingenuous. She had made it sound as if she were reluctantly doing what was expected, when in fact she had enjoyed herself very much. She had loved how graceful she had felt under Ivars' self-assured guidance, and she had liked talking to him. Instead of asserting, as many Latvians did, that American culture was inferior to Latvian and then not listening to a word said in contradiction, Ivars had asked her good questions about writers she studied in her Advanced Literature class, and he had told her that he wrote poems. He had offered to let her read some of his and to lend her a new anthology of Latvian poetry just published in Sweden, which he had gone to a great deal of trouble to obtain.

"You like Ivars, don't you?" Alma said.

"Well . . . I don't know . . . ."

Alma had first claim, Kaija reminded herself sternly. Alma was her friend, Alma had no mother, Alma's father drank too much, and Alma loved Ivars, so it was only fair that Kaija give him up. She resolved to repeat "I do not like him," ten times every night before she went to sleep.

"I think he's interesting, but I don't think I actually *like* him," Kaija said. It sounded false, and she had no idea what she would do if he asked her to dance again.

But Ivars went outside with his two brothers, either to cool off or to take a swallow of vodka from a pocket-sized flask, and he danced only with Dzintra after that. It was all too much for Alma.

"Let's leave," she urged. "I don't want to be here when everyone starts teasing him that he's in love with Dzintra and congratulating him on their upcoming wedding."

117

"I don't want to see that either," Kaija agreed. The friends found their coats and left as another lilting waltz started behind them.

The coming of spring changed everything. The bedraggled lilac bush in the back yard was leafing out, and Park Avenue was abuzz. The romance between Ivars and Dzintra, which had flourished during the gray Indiana winter, was over. Alma could stop declaring that she would shut herself up in a cloister on the day that Ivars married, and Kaija could stop reminding her that Lutherans did not have nuns. Alma could now turn her attention to pondering whether to continue hating Dzintra for keeping Ivars entangled or to condemn her for breaking his heart. Dzintra was getting married. Her husband-to-be was an American, a prosperous businessman from Chicago, who had singled her out from other key-punch operators at the Polk Dairy Company. He was a dozen years older than she, which might have been overlooked because of his wealth, but the older generation was unanimous in condemnation. Being rich could not make up for being American. By becoming the first young Latvian woman to marry an American, Dzintra had broken her parents' hearts, betrayed the entire exile community, and failed in her duty to Latvia.

The few Latvians from Park Avenue who had been invited staunchly refused to attend the wedding, so Alma could not find out whether Dzintra's parents had boycotted the ceremony too. All she knew was that they had spent the night before the wedding receiving condolences in Mrs. Krumins' apartment, and they had been dressed entirely in black, as if in deepest mourning, when they departed the next day.

Ivars was given space to suffer and to dramatize himself. He was routinely offered beer and shots of vodka, and he was allowed to make nihilistic comments without being contradicted by positive platitudes more characteristic of Latvians. If he got surly, he was jollied along; if he fell down, he was helped up. For the rest of his life he would be indulged if, late at night, he got maudlin about his first love. But he was also expected to shut Dzintra away in a special chamber of his heart, to marry someone else, and to settle down.

Alma saw her chance, and she began preparing for marriage to Ivars as if it were a certainty. She would complete the commercial program at Shortridge, graduate with respectable grades, take some courses at the Indiana Business College, and get a good job in an office. Then, one by one, she would accumulate china plates with gold rims and engraved silver forks from L.S. Ayres. She would save up for a woodcarving of the skyline of Riga and a large green ceramic vase, items made by Latvian artists, she had seen at the Song Festival in Chicago. Others might call her ideas antiquated, but without a mother to teach her or a father who helped her pay, Alma set about acquiring a dowry, which she fervently hoped would be followed by acquiring Ivars himself.

Kaija's brief flares of excitement differed from Alma's steadfast devotion. Her crush on Ojars bypassed her "genius" brain completely. He was attractive simply because he was there.

Ojars had had a hard time meeting the high standards in the schools Latvians established in the DP camps, and after a single miserable semester at Shortridge, he had quit to work on a construction crew. His darling dimples were supplemented by newly developed rippling muscles and narrow hips, and his dazzling red Pontiac convertible, bought for the relatively high wages a strong young man could command for manual labor, had been the first car in the Latvian community. Kaija forgot that she had laughed at him because he could not get the point of algebra and because he maintained that Indians still roamed the Wild West, stopping buses

119

and cars with bows and arrows and scalping businessmen in gray flannel suits.

Once the excitement over Dzintra's marriage had died down, Ojars became the main target of gossip. He stayed out late at bars, and sometimes he did not come home at all. He was rumored to have an American girlfriend, a divorced woman with two children, who was wily and possessive and obviously far more experienced than he. Nevertheless, Kaija usually happened to be by the window when screeching brakes, blaring radio, and clouds of cigarette smoke announced that Ojars had returned to Park Avenue. As he pounded up the stairs, she was on her way down more often than mere chance could explain.

One hot summer evening, Kaija drew Alma into the bathroom. She locked the door and leaned against it to make doubly sure of privacy.

"Do I look any different?" she demanded. She lifted up her blond hair, which now fell in graceful waves rather than snarling and frizzing.

"Notice anything?"

Alma shook her head.

"Look again," Kaija insisted. "More carefully this time, Alma."

"Well, maybe you are a little flushed," Alma ventured.

"Good. Anything else?" Kaija turned back to the mirror.

Alma leaned forward and peered.

"No. That's all I can see," she said.

"Me too," Kaija sighed. "I cannot believe I'm not completely changed."

"But why should you be?"

"Because I've been kissed, Alma, kissed by Ojars. Just now, in the stairwell."

"Oh, Kaija. How could you?" Alma demanded. A kiss might be just a kiss in a song, but it was a lot more than that to Alma. Her mother's purity and her father's steadfast devotion leading to the happiest union in the history of the world did not allow for stolen kisses with shady nobodies in dark hallways. The word "slut" rose to Alma's lips, but she managed to swallow it.

"I wanted to find out what kissing feels like," Kaija said.

"You shouldn't . . . you must not . . . you should never . . . you're disgusting."

Kaija's eyes filled with tears. Why did Kaija always fasten on the one-word Alma wished she had not said?

"All right, all right, I'm sorry. I meant Ojars is disgusting, not you," Alma amended. "Kissing is for married people."

"That's not true," Kaija's voice was shaky but firm. "Stewart Granger kissed Deborah Kerr in *King Solomon's Mines,* and they weren't married. They didn't even like each other."

Alma wished that Kaija would not bring up the scene in the hammock, which had left her strangely excited as well. She would put her fingers into her ears and close her eyes if Kaija started reciting logical fallacies and pointing out which one Alma had committed this time.

But Kaija only looked dreamy, "Kissing is nice, Almin, it really is. You'll like it when Ivars kisses you. He will, you know. I never thought Ojars would kiss me, but he did. Several times. Ojars is going to take me for a ride in his convertible."

"You shouldn't...Ojars is terrible...that convertible of his is a disgrace...it's parked overnight in front of the house of a divorced woman...under no circumstances should you...Ivars would never...."

"Oh, wouldn't he?" Kaija interrupted.

"Of course, he wouldn't. Ivars is different in every possible way from silly boys like Ojars. I've known Ivars for two years, and so I know everything there is to know about him. He is reserved, he has beautiful manners, and he will always behave like a gentleman. So what could go wrong for any girl he chose?"

Lost Midsummers

11

Kaija was too loyal to put it into words, but Shortridge High School became an easier place to be after Alma graduated and enrolled in the Indiana Business College. Snickering did not erupt, as it had when the two girls absent-mindedly clutched each other by the hand, which was fine for girlfriends in Europe, but not here. Kaija liked striding along without Alma glued to her side. She did not have to encourage and explain; she could accept without apology the few invitations that came her way; and she did not feel vaguely guilty about her academic successes.

The friends still saw each other regularly in the evenings. Kaija was too anxious about her academic future to notice growing differences between them, which would have been obvious to someone else.

One evening she talked Alma into seeing *The Moon is Blue*, a movie which had been released without the usual code of moral approval because in it the word "virgin" was actually said out loud. People stood in long lines even on week nights at the Esquire Theater near 30th Street to witness this shocking event.

Kaija might as well have stayed home because her mind began to race as soon as the screen lit up. Why was she sitting in a movie theater instead of studying? She should be catching up on her school work. She should write the first draft of her research paper about euthanasia for Advanced Composition, she should revise a poem for a contest for high school students sponsored by *The Atlantic Monthly*, and she should write up her last chemistry experiment. She was an irresponsible creature driven by curiosity and pleasure. She was wasting her time and ruining her life.

That other movie theaters and drive-in restaurants like the Tee Pee and Knobby's were full of high school students made no difference to Kaija. Others did not have to perform perfectly on everything. If they did not win one of the very few scholarships available, their parents could pay for them to go to college.

Kaija kept her anxieties to herself because no one understood. Alma, satisfied with her courses at the Indiana Business School, did not see the point of going to university. Kaija's mother was unperturbed when Kaija tried to tell her she was terrified that she would fail to win a scholarship. The infusion of government money into education, which made student loans, work study, and various grants and scholarships possible, was still in the future, but Mrs. Veldre expected Kaija to attend Indiana University as a matter of course. Kaija had been certified by an I.Q. test as intelligent. The rest was simply dedication and hard work.

The ever-present joke that girls went to college only to get their Mrs. degrees was not funny to Kaija. She believed that Indiana University would transform her life. It would allow her to leave behind the apartment near 38th Street, to which her parents had recently moved. A vast improvement over the single room on Park Avenue, it was nevertheless permeated with her mother's sadness. Kaija had failed to accommodate herself to that persistent gloom. She had even composed poems because Ivars had told her that writing about sad things helped him appear outwardly happy. But Kaija's melancholy rhymed verses about weeping rain and moaning trees had brought no relief.

At Indiana University, Kaija would make friends to whom she could reveal her real self, she would learn something important in every class, she would earn her medical degree, and she would be an American success. Her mother would not wash another floor after Kaija graduated. In fact, Mrs. Veldre would not have to work at all. Kaija would buy her all the things—books, concerts, trips to museums, elegant clothes—which would make her happy.

Final credits were flashing on the screen when Kaija came back to herself.

"What did you think of the movie, Alma?" she asked to cover her inattention.

"It *was* sort of funny," Alma admitted reluctantly. "But people are right. That word shouldn't be used."

"Not even as in the Virgin Mary?"

One of Kaija's most dismal experiences during her first year at Public School 45 had been portraying the Virgin Mary in a Christmas play. Her teachers had insisted she take the role because she towered over other seventh-grade girls and because she had braids. It had been supremely embarrassing to walk across the stage and coo to a rag-doll, while three robe-clad Wise Men, their heads wrapped in dish towels and their faces smeared with soot, tried to get her to laugh and make a shamble of the whole production.

"That's different. That is religion," Alma said firmly.

"Well then, what about medicine? Could a girl tell a doctor she was no longer a virgin?"

The question embarrassed Alma. Kaija wished she was at home, sorting out logical arguments for and against euthanasia for her term paper instead of harassing her friend.

"How many pages do you have to study for Business Principles tonight, Alma?" Kaija asked, changing the subject.

Each friend described her assignments and deadlines in considerable detail.

Kaija had made a new friend, Stella Harris, one of the most popular girls at Shortridge. They walked together from one class to the next, and Kaija sat with Stella's friends at lunch. Under Stella's sponsorship, the other girls accepted her readily. They were remarkably incurious about Kaija's experience of war and camps; they knew nothing about poverty or about life in exile communities. Sometimes their wrong assumptions and lack of interest made Kaija angry, but most of the time she was glad she did not have to reveal anything. Compared to her tight friendship with Alma, the frequent laughter and uncomplicated conversation of American girls were a relief.

Kaija knew that she could not have gotten through the previous four years without Alma's loyalty and friendship. Alma alone understood how frightening and humiliating America could be; only with Alma could she share her constant longing to be in Latvia. The two girls had been through a lot together, and Kaija believed they would be best friends forever.

On a late afternoon in September, Kaija finished a long after-school tutorial with Miss Justin and headed to her locker. The Latin teacher had picked Kaija to beat the Catholics in the Indiana State Latin Contest, which she said was unfairly rigged against students from public schools. Latin was not a foreign language to Catholics, Miss Justin maintained, because they sneaked in extra practice every Sunday at Mass; they also spoke in Latin when they went into those dark confession booths and whispered together with their Italian-looking priests. It was up to Kaija to demonstrate that the clear light of reason could triumph over medieval superstition and that American Protestant virtues could best the foreign irrationalities of Rome.

Having concentrated hard for two hours, Kaija was dazed as she started down the deserted hallway. Numbers on lockers and doors were indistinguishable already, but a few slanting rays of the sun still illuminated the landing below the huge westward facing windows above the front entrance.

Kaija stepped into the light, and suddenly she was flooded with happiness. In spite of trembling and blushing, in spite of being riddled with anxiety, she was all right. She had pleased Miss Justin, she was doing well in all her subjects, and she was saving money from her job at the Indiana Merchandising Company. If she continued getting straight A's, she had a good chance of a scholarship. Then, instead of two or more years of saving every penny from monotonous jobs, she could go to Indiana University the same year she graduated. Her American girlfriends treated her now as if she belonged, and new friends, only more intellectual, would include her at the University.

Something shimmered at the far end of the hallway, and it took Kaija a moment to recognize Stella coming toward her. Stella's blond short hair tanned slender arms, and sleeveless yellow cotton dress gleamed between shadows.

"It's getting late," Stella said, "but I'm going to see you again, Kaija." Stella's face radiated kindness and love.

"See you too," Kaija whispered.

And then Stella was past her, the shadows closed behind her, and she was gone.

Kaija wanted to shout Stella's name; she wanted to run after her and drag her back into the light. For in that instant when Stella had been within an arm's reach, Kaija had had an irrational but certain intuition that Stella was going to die.

Shocked and guilty that she had not stopped her friend, Kaija struggled to regain her composure.

Of course, Stella would not die; it was absurd to think she would. That fleeting insight had no validity; it could not have any effect. To believe without any evidence that something terrible would happen was irrational. Her eyes had tricked her; she was simply more tired than she realized. It would have been supremely embarrassing to scream for Stella to stop. If she had grabbed Stella, what could she have said to her? She would have made an embarrassing scene, that's all.

Determined to forget her terrifying intuition, Kaija collected her belongings at her locker and hurried out of the building.

But as she walked home, she remembered other experiences. This was not the first time she had foreseen that something would happen before it actually did. In Germany during the war, when she was seven, she had known exactly what she would find before she looked down into a ditch and saw a dismembered human arm. She had also had a vivid dream of three blinded black horses rearing and screaming, so that she recognized them rather than merely saw them the next day in a bombed-out railroad station. She had been frightened by these premonitions and remembering them confused her now.

Stella did die. She fell into a coma that evening, was rushed to the Methodist Hospital, and was diagnosed, too late, with diabetes. Doctors and nurses tried their best, but they could not save her. Kind and intelligent Stella was dead before she had had anything like a full life.

Kaija's grief was made unbearable by unrelenting questions and self-blame. How and why had she known Stella would die? There was, there had to be a rational explanation. Could she have saved her friend? She should have insisted on walking home with Stella; she should have stayed overnight with her. Worse, had her inexplicable knowledge caused Stella's death? And what had happened to the essence of Stella?

Kaija did not believe in a heaven to which the souls of the dead ascended. Instead of a comforting belief in an afterlife, she knew the sky was an empty space, which was disturbed by British and American planes dropping bombs meant to kill her. God did not exist. She had prayed for the air raids to stop; she had prayed for her mother to stop crying and speak to her. But God had not answered. Kaija felt she was a total outside when she stood up with others in church confessing their faith in the resurrection of the body and in eternal life. Her integrity kept her from whispering the actual words, but she condemned herself as a hypocrite for conforming outwardly.

But if God and heaven did not exist, where did Stella's liveliness and good humor go? Stella's radiance and goodness could not simply disappear without a trace, or could they? Kaija's recent intuitive foreknowledge threatened her hard-won reliance on science and reason, both of which she found deeply comforting. If she could not rely on logic, she would have to face it that only chance ruled a chaotic world.

There was no one Kaija could talk to. Even Pastor Saulcere, who knew a lot about Christianity and other religions, would doubt her experience. If she told him about her foreknowledge of Stella's death, he would suspect that she had stumbled into some ridiculous superstition, like fortune-telling, Ouija boards, and ghosts. Worse, he would think she was lying. He would ask her if she believed in God, and she would have to confess that she did not. Pastor Saulcere would be disappointed in her, and he would certainly tell her mother. They had a close friendship which rested on their interest in artistic and spiritual matters. Kaija's father would be upset too, and everyone would conclude that she was a bad person.

For once, Kaija did not care whether she had the right clothes as she entered the Flanner and Buchanan Funeral Home, a few blocks from the swimming pool in Broad Ripple where she and Alma had had their terrifying first experience of America. Dressed in her mother's worn black wool suit, its waist narrowed by hidden safety pins, Kaija stopped at the foot of Stella's white and gold coffin. She set down her bouquet of tiny white roses, touched the lid, and concentrated as hard as she could. She wished she could see into the closed casket. She passionately wanted to reach Stella before her essence dissipated into nothing.

Feeling ridiculous speaking to a dead person, Kaija nevertheless formed silent questions. Why did you die, my sweet and beloved friend? What did you mean when you said you would see me again? What are you trying to teach me?

Kaija felt she was getting close to Stella's spirit or soul or whatever it was that she was trying to contact through white wood and gold leaf when one of Stella's friends touched her elbow. The girls drew Kaija into their small bereft circle, and the moment when she had come close to understanding something essential passed. Later she blamed herself that she had almost experienced something like faith. But instead of entering the transcendent world behind this one she had allowed herself to be distracted.

In the following weeks, Kaija formulated a convoluted explanation. Stella had died at seventeen, and Kaija's Aunt Astra, the sister whom Mrs. Veldre mourned but Kaija had never known, had been the same age when she died. Astra meant star, and Stella meant star, so their names were really the same. One name had triggered the other, and one death had caused Kaija to imagine the other. From there she had tangled herself up with portents and mysteries. This explanation would fall apart if Kaija examined it too closely, but it would have to do. She resolved to try to forget this disturbing experience, as she had done with others like it.

12

1956

Kaija had not been granted United States citizenship along with her parents, as younger children automatically were. She had been over sixteen and therefore presumed to have a choice, which she could not responsibly exercise, however, until she turned eighteen. She would have to go through the intiminating process by herself.

Worried about missing so much as one hour of school, Kaija tried to change her obligatory appointments to the late afternoon.

"Just who do you think you are?" the courthouse secretary demanded. She sounded shocked, as if Kaija had asked her to forge a passport or cash a check guaranteed to bounce. "Everyone else shows up when they're ordered, and they all have full-time jobs, young lady. You better get serious about this."

But Kaija did take the opportunity for citizenship seriously. If she failed, she believed she could be separated from her parents and deported to back Germany or even Russian-occupied Latvia. She had watched her parents as they worried and studied and quizzed each other for months. Her mother had been afraid she would be fired if she asked for time off work, but when she finally brought herself to ask, her boss had congratulated her. Kaija's father, on the other hand, struggled with ethical dilemmas. How could he swear that he had given up every last shred of loyalty to Latvia when he wanted to return there as soon as the Russians were driven out? But what if at that very moment his labor was required for the welfare of the United States? Even at his age, he would gladly carry a gun to defend America, he would donate money, and he would make other sacrifices, but what if a war broke out between Latvia and the United States? Mrs. Veldre, who had no hope of returning home, pointed out that tiny Latvia, about half the size of Indiana, was not going to start a war with the United States. Judge Veldre conceded she might be right, but Russians could forcibly induct young Latvians into their army and send them to invade America. He could not fire a gun at another Latvian.

During Kaija's first interview in the massive gray Post Office building on Pennsylvania Avenue, a stern clerk asked whether she was a member of the Communist Party or another organization planning to overthrow the government of the United States, and she could swear with a clear conscience that she was not. In quick succession, she had to add a column of figures, to calculate 33% of $179, to name two Senators and two Congressmen from Indiana, and to identify passages from the Declaration of Independence and the Constitution.

How did that dummy Ojars, whose kisses now made her burn with embarrassment, pass a test like this, she wondered. Did the people from the Kentucky hills on Park Avenue know the answers? But they had been born here, and that made all the difference. Every one of them could aspire to being President of the United States, which naturalized citizens could not.

Kaija mouth was so dry with anxiety that she had trouble pronouncing her name at the next appointment. The basement at the City Jail did not resemble the bloody cells of the KGB in Riga, but her legs trembled anyway because police had the power to arrest and imprison.

On June 14, the Day of Mourning for Latvians deported to Siberia, speakers inevitably referred to Russian chambers of torture. American policemen were different, of course, but Kaija was afraid of all men in uniform.

A bored policeman at the entry waved her into a room with half a dozen others waiting to be fingerprinted and photographed. Only one woman, a weary platinum blonde in her forties, was present. Her skimpy summer dress and open-toed spike heels were inadequate for the deep chill of the building, and her handcuffs made her look furtive and guilty.

"Move your tush," a policeman said. He kept his hand on her buttocks as she climbed the low podium with exaggerated slowness. She turned and looked past the photographer and the camera, directly into Kaija's heart.

Kaija dropped her eyes. This woman acted as if the two of them had something in common simply because they were both female. Kaija wished she could announce loudly that she was here only to get her photo taken for her citizenship certificate; she was not a criminal. She shared nothing with this defeated creature, and she never would.

"Step up here, stand straight, and don't grin," the photographer ordered. Grinning was the last thing Kaija would do. Her photograph and fingerprints would be stored forever in government files, along with those of traitors, criminals, and perverts. She would be among the first to be rounded up if fanatics—communists, fascists, or some crazed religious group—seized power. With an effort, she forced herself to stop imagining disaster. If no one came forward to denounce her, and if nothing incriminating was discovered in the interview she had last week, she would not have to stand in the line marked "Aliens only" every January at the Post Office, in order to register for the coming year.

The seal above the podium, the line of flags, the hard-wooden benches, and the absence of flowers and other details which could be construed as feminine made the room chosen for the citizenship ceremony forbiddingly solemn. Men in dark suits and women in somber dresses waited in silence to be naturalized.

Kaija could not figure out the nationality of two strikingly handsome men who sat down next to her. Their gray silk suits fit her vague notions of Italian opera singers on holiday or Spanish flamenco dancers on their day off, but she would have to hear their language to try to place them.

The judge directed everyone to stand and recite the Pledge of Allegiance. Eventually Kaija was called to the front of the room, where she raised her hand, said "I do" to the judge's questions, and signed a document.

This was it. She was a citizen of the United States of America. But the elation she had expected did not come.

"You are now going to participate in a celebration," the judge announced after everyone had been sworn. "The Indianapolis chapter of the Daughters of the American Revolution has gone to a great deal of trouble to prepare a party for you."

"Cake and wine," the man next to Kaija winked.

"Impossible," his companion laughed. "We're not in Italy, my friend. There is no wine in Indiana. They only have Mogen David, and you have to go to church to get that."

A dozen women in substantial hats and Queen Mum shoes walked through the massive doors. They carried a cardboard box the size of a baby's coffin, partially covered with a crocheted red, white, and blue doily.

"Our chapter has paid for gifts, so that each of you will have a memento of this, the most important day of your lives," their leader announced. "In return, we ask that you treat our gift with the respect it deserves. You should assign it a special place of honor in your living room and use it daily to teach patriotism to your children."

The women folded the doily as ceremoniously as if it had been a flag draped over the body of a fallen soldier and began to pass out American flags. Made of flimsy paper, attached to handles less substantial than Popsicle sticks, they reminded Kaija of the small checkered black and white flags advertising the Indianapolis Speedway, which were routinely given out as consolation prizes at Riverside Amusement Park. One would have to insert the tiny flag pole into a raw potato to make it stand upright, but the thin wood would probably break. Her parents must have received similar flags, and under no circumstances would they have disrespectfully thrown them into the trash. But they did not display them next to the white and blood-red Latvian flag in its amber-studded polished wood and silver base on her father's desk.

"No wine," and "no cake," the men teased Kaija as she slipped her flag into her purse.

She wanted to feel something about her changed status, but neither her father's final commitment to absolute loyalty to the United States, nor her mother's continuing regrets about bountiful tables under blossoming apple trees in Latvia surfaced. She wished briefly that she was going to the University of Latvia in Riga: her mother would be there to offer advice about courses and professors; her father would provide financial backing and the advantages of family sponsorship. That could not happen now, and she must stop regretting it. But her future in America, whose rich promise she regularly preached to Alma, produced no real feeling either.

She had been wrong to expect a meaningful ritual. As she did almost every day, she reminded herself sharply to be rational and to think positively. She had in fact felt truly accepted in America last week, and she had been elated. On Honors Day at Shortridge, as the Principal announced that she was the recipient of the Jonas Salk Scholarship, her surroundings had gained a sharp and beautiful clarity. Her trembling stopped, and her anxiety vanished as father stood up and bowed to her. Later, after returning from work, her mother kissed her on both cheeks.

At Honors Day, Kaija had been so pleased by applause that she had not heard the mild grumbling behind her. What were those teachers thinking when they gave a $1,000 pre-med scholarship to a girl, especially one who could not be very smart because she was only going to Indiana University rather than to a prestigious Eastern school?

Such pettiness could not touch her, even had she heard it. How wonderful America was! How lucky she was to be here! Where else in the world would an immigrant be given such opportunities, which would be reserved for native-born citizens in other countries? She had received so much generous help in her classes at Shortridge as well. She loved her teachers, the intellectual single women and the few dedicated married men who had taught her so patiently and so well. And they had chosen her to receive this largesse.

135

Kaija was happy and young and female, and it did not occur to her that the last characteristic might present problems. The bleached blonde at the City Jail might think life was hard for women, but Kaija was sure she would succeed if she maintained straight A's.

13

Alma stomped back and forth on the smudged linoleum in the waiting room of the Greyhound Bus Station. She had not mastered the art of clicking along smartly in high heels, but otherwise she was the very image of efficient secretaries in movies. Her tightly buttoned white nylon blouse and severe navy-blue suit proclaimed her status and her achievements. Her job description and pay might be those of a bank teller, but in actuality she did exactly the same work as the male accountants. She was simultaneously proud and embarrassed to have a respectable job at the same bank which older Latvian women cleaned at night.

But where was Kaija? Why was she not here so the two friends could spend some time together? Irritability could not mask Alma's panic. Life without Kaija was going to be awful. Alma would have no one to talk to, she could not confide anything private to anyone else, and she would have nowhere to escape to when her father was unwell. Attending social events would be terrible. She would look ridiculous sitting alone on the steps at the Latvian Community House. She would have to stay home for the rest of her life because she would never make another friend like Kaija.

"You're late, Kaija. How could you? It's the last time we'll be together," Alma said mournfully as Kaija entered, dragging her mother's suitcase.

Alma thought her despair was obvious and should be the center of attention, but Kaija rattled on about the contents of the suitcase: her stsarched and beautifully ironed blouses wrapped in tissue paper, two new lambswool sweaters, and three new skirts, including a frivolous version of kilts worn by Scottish heroes defending their homes in misty Highlands. She congratulated herself

137

for wisely skipping other items considered essential for coeds: white knee socks, itchy Black Watch plaid Bermuda shorts, brown leather loafers with ugly slots for shiny pennies, and pink nylon baby doll pajamas. Instead Kaija had tucked into a warm flannel   nightgown gifts from her parents: a dark amber pendant shaped like a tear from her mother and a framed photo of the Monument to Freedom in the center of Riga from her father.

"We're parting forever, and all you care about are clothes." Alma was close to tears.

Instead of contradicting these unfair and untrue words, Kaija said nothing. Both girls had said goodbye too often to regard leave-taking as insignificant. They had said goodbye to other children befriended briefly in bomb shelters and to classmates dispersing from displaced persons camps. Neither girl had a friend whom she had known since early childhood. Their stricken faces contrasted with those of others in the Greyhound station parting more casually.

"I'm sorry, Almin. But I had to wait for a taxi." Kaija tried to keep self-importance from her voice. Taxis, like long distance phone calls, were for emergencies only.

Kaija saw no one she knew waiting to board the bus to Bloomington. Stella's friends were off to Eastern girls' schools, and students of more modest means were being driven to Bloomington by fathers trying to act manly and by frankly tearful mothers.

"Oh, well, I'll get a seat by the window," Kaija shrugged.

Alma's heart contracted with worry. Kaija was going to be alone in a scary and difficult place. Alma no longer thought Kaija had an easy time of it just because she had a mother; she knew Kaija would not have comforting or frequent visits from her parents.

"I'll write, Almin, and I'll come home as soon as I can."

Kaija did not repeat her earlier invitation to Alma to visit, and Alma could not bring herself to remind her. Kaija would make fancy new friends; she would go to football games, dances, and dates; she would decide Alma was boring.

Kaija interrupted Alma's gloomy thoughts.

"I'll really miss you, Almin," she said. She sounded close to crying.

"Don't start sniffling," Alma tried to joke.

"We'll always be best friends, Almin. Won't we?" Kaija asked.

Gratitude flooded Alma. Kaija could just come out and say what really mattered while Alma was too proud to show it when she was hurt.

Alma grabbed Kaija's suitcase, side-stepped the bus driver's half-hearted gesture to help, and settled it into the baggage compartment. She reached out to shake hands, but Kaija hugged her and held on. Kaija was crying openly now, which embarrassed and pleased Alma.

"Go on then," Alma urged. "Everything will be fine, Kaijin. Remember you're smarter than they are. You'll do just fine. You'll see."

Kaija climbed onto the bus and reappeared at a window.

The two friends continued waving even after the bus made an abrupt turn towards Highway 37 and they could no longer see each other.

Kaija wiped her eyes with a lace-trimmed handkerchief, a gift from the store of dozens of items Alma had crocheted, embroidered, and knitted in preparation for her dream marriage to Ivars. She blew her nose, stuffed the damp small square of cloth into her purse, and told herself to cheer up.

"I apologize for disturbing you but are you Latvian?" a male voice asked in English. "I heard you saying goodbye to your friend," he added in Latvian.

Kaija looked up to see a tall young man, with sun-bleached hair, gray eyes, and a serious expression. An encounter with another Latvian was always happy coincidence, and a handsome man her age whom she had never seen before was fabulous. Why had the Latvian grape-vine not informed her that he existed?

"It must be nice to live in Indianapolis, with other Latvians. By the way, I'm Maris Zalums from Lafayette. Are you from the Latvian *kolkhoz*?" he used the joking nickname for Park Avenue as a collective farm.

He has beautiful coloring, Kaija thought, without being aware how closely it resembled hers. His skin was tan and without imperfections, and shadows played around his high cheekbones. His hands looked competent and strong, which must mean that he was manly, but his long fingers and beautiful oval nails suggested that he was also sensitive and intelligent. Perhaps he was a poet or a musician? At six feet, he was as tall as Kaija, maybe an inch taller. She hoped he had not seen that she, a sophisticated university student, had been crying.

"You live in Lafayette, and you're not going to Purdue?" she asked. Had he announced that he was flying his own plane to Paris, she could not have been more surprised.

"But I don't want to be an engineer. I want to be a doctor."

"Me too."

After a slight pause, Maris said, "That's great, we'll be in the same classes then. It's a very good profession. Don't you agree?"

"Oh yes, I do. Please, sit down," Kaija motioned to the empty seat next to her. She was ready to discuss medicine, chemistry, and the scientific method, while her mind jumped back and forth between the enchanting coincidence of meeting a *Latvian* boy who would be in her classes and the possibility of kissing him. Maris' lips were full and a little bruised looking. What would it be like to touch them, very gently, with her own? What would she feel when he kissed her back, tenderly at first, but then more decisively? She hoped they would be more than intellectual friends.

Russet ivy clung to limestone walls, a few yellow leaves drifted down to pale autumn crocuses, and small purple cyclamens pushed up through creepers and vines. The pre-war buildings of the University looked solid enough to survive the coming winter and the loss of all this poignant loveliness. The Quonset huts which were used as emergency classrooms to accommodate veterans of World War II were not visible from Kirkland Avenue.

At the Women's Quad, Head Resident Martha Smith embarked on an apology as soon as she had greeted Kaija. People in the Housing Office had made every effort, but they had been unable to find a suitable match for a roommate and had had to assign Kaija to a tiny single room, next to the broom closet, in Sycamore Hall in the Women's Quad. Kaija would have to face life alone, which was a disaster.

Kaija had been singled-out as different once more, but this time she did not mind. She had achieved many things by herself, and she was pleased to have a room of her own. The entire broad windowsill was hers for arranging books she would buy with her bountiful scholarship money. She could study all night, with no roommate to complain that the light bothered her. She would not have to consider anyone else's preferences when she attended performances, plays, and free lectures. Harry Belafonte, W.H. Auden, and Robert Graves would be coming to campus, and she planned to see and hear all three. She would get to know girls in other rooms, but she would allow only Maris Zalums to interrupt her studies.

Kaija was impatient for classes to start. Indiana University was the best of all possible places because reason and justice ruled here. Kaija believed that professors ignored poverty, religion, class, race, sex, foreignness, and eccentricity; all of them judged their students by their work alone.

Shocked squeals in the hallway interrupted Kaija's high-minded musing. A sophomore named Grace was terrifying half a dozen freshmen girls about the upcoming physical required of all students. That one of the doctors at the Health Center smelled of gin was the least of it. Other doctors asked embarrassing questions about hymens and swollen breasts and menstrual cramps; they ordered girls to take off everything, panties included, and stand in front of a camera.

"Camera? Don't you mean an x-ray machine?" Kaija asked.

"No, I do not," Grace said firmly. "Of course, they have to take chest x-rays if you have a positive skin test for Tb, and that's ok with me. But I'm talking about photos. You have to throw out your chest and hold your breath, and you don't even have your bra on! They claim they're doing scientific posture studies. Ha! Dirty old men, they'll never convince me it's for science," Grace laughed.

"But it has to be done if it is for science," Kaija said passioonately. Whether named in any one of the fourlanguages she knew— *zinatne, Wissenschaft, science,* or *scientia*, there was nothing she respected more.

14

Chemistry for Pre-Med Students was Kaija's favorite class during her sophomore year. She loved everything about it: the sturdy tables, glistening test tubes, huge windows, and the small comforting communities formed by friendship or chance in the lecture hall. Best of all, she and Maris sat next to each other.

Professor Waxman lectured in a soft monotone regardless of whether his subject was an important event in the history of science, a medical mystery to be solved in the future, or rows of complex formulas. So rarely did he seek eye contact even during his occasional digressions into advice for young doctors that Maris and Kaija joked that if an A-bomb irradiated his students, he would finish his exactly-timed lecture and leave the room with only a slight suspicion that something was different.

But Professor Waxman was not always so remote. To the terror of his graduate assistants, he dropped in unannounced to the labs, where he answered questions, demonstrated shortcuts, and praised good work. In this more informal setting he asked students for their names and engaged them in speculation about theories or alternate solutions to well-known problems.

"You've got a first-class mind, young lady," he had said to Kaija. "Tell me your name again."

Usually Kaija was first to arrive for his weekly lecture. She tried to use the time to review the assignment, but all too often she drifted into her favorite game. Eyes closed, she imagined Maris coming towards her. She counted his steps and willed him to hurry, but she did not look at him until he sat down next to her. Then, at exactly the same moment, they looked at each other and touched fingertips.

Kaija knew that Maris liked her. They did not hug or hold hands in public, but he was possibly even in love with her. That he was not more demonstrative had bothered Kaija until he gave her Donne's "A Valediction: Forbidding Mourning," copied from a textbook in his beautiful firm hand. She was flattered that he expected her to figure out a poem which his English professor had spent an entire class period explicating. Kaija had labored over it until she understood that their love was so refined that it expanded "like gold to airy thinness beat" when they were separated; they were lovers so exalted above all others that they did not cry or sigh when they were apart because they were always connected; like the legs of a twin compass they "yearned and harkened" after each other as they roamed far apart and "grew erect" when they were reunited. She overlooked the part about the woman being "the fixed foot" which stayed firmly at home.

At other times she entered her favorite daydream while waiting for Maris. She and Maris rode side by side on powerful bay stallions. They were like two brothers heading toward battle in a Latvian folk-song:

> Div dujinas gaisa skreja
> abas screja dudodamas.
> Div balini kara jaja,
> abi jaja domadami.

> Two doves flew in the air,
> Cooing as they flew.
> Two brothers rode to war,
> Pondering as they rode.

The brothers were ambivalent about leaving their beloved farm, but Kaija and Maris had a clear sense of purpose. They moved across vast battle-grounds, but they were not soldiers out to kill and to maim. They came to heal instead. The meadow was strewn with severed limbs, mutilated corpses, abandoned weapons, and smoldering fires; the earth itself, scarred by trenches and mines, was weeping.

On the edge of pine woods, in a white tent, which shuddered with every gust of wind, they stood shoulder to shoulder. They stanched blood, set splintered bones, changed filthy dressings, cooled burning fevers, and murmured comfort and courage and hope. They did not stop to admire each other's competence, but they were aware of it, always.

Maris lifted a strand of Kaija's hair to his lips before he rode off to help starving and sick children in another camp. Kaija wiped sweat and blood from the forehead of a soldier, not much more than boy, who lay dying next to a young woman nursing a baby.

Late at night, under the stars, Maris and Kaija were reunited. She massaged his tired shoulders, and he stroked the back of her neck with his competent, slightly rough hands. His breath came more quickly as he unfastened a restraining clip, and her hair tumbled down like Brittomart's.

Stop it, Kaija told herself when Maris arrived. His thigh brushed hers, she opened her eyes, their fingertips touched, and their hands came to rest next to each other. Happy that he was near her, Kaija lost herself in Doctor Waxman's lecture.

Girl Talk, a series of presentations arranged by the Dean of Woman, absorbed Kaija as completely as daydreams and chemistry. Designed to teach young women about Life, the talks took place in the dorm after the doors were locked at night. Men were permitted to enter only the living room and only during the day, but an exception was made for learned speakers.

Tonight, an affable bearded psychologist offered a shy confession. He was unable to sleep because innocent men, wrongfully convicted of rape, were sitting in prisons throughout the United States. Girls had led them on: they had flirted and kissed and petted, and then changed their minds and cried rape. These girls were as responsible for the unjust prison sentences as the men's

145

mothers, who had scarred their sons by being simultaneously seductive and rejecting.

"Rape is a highly problematic concept in the first place because no one can thread a moving needle," the psychologist asserted.

Kaija's vocal chords tightened painfully. At age seven she had seen Russian soldiers in Berlin rape women and girls only a few years older. Women had not flirted, petted, and then changed their minds. They had avoided eye contact and hidden in dark corners; they had cried, writhed, and fought to get away. But they were overpowered, either by a gang or by a single soldier with a gun at the woman's throat.

Kaija identified the psychologist's reference to the moving needle as a false analogy and faulty logic and felt momentarily better. Many women, Kaija included, found that moving a needle was in fact an effective way to engage a thread.

She had a brief fantasy about pointing out this discrepancy, which she would follow with astute questions and thus cast doubt on every one of the professor's assertions about rape. But her mouth was dry and her lips were glued shut. Who was she to challenge a famous professor who had spent years studying his subject? No one would believe her if she told what she had seen. She would be ostracized, just as the raped women and girls in Berlin had been.

The psychologist was saying that men "who exposed themselves" would never, ever rape. These mild shy perverts had only a naive, touching desire to show off their private parts. All they wanted was astonished admiration from women. These men should be treated with kindness because they had suffered psychological torture when they were children: their mothers were frigid, lesbians, prostitutes, or all three. These timid gentle males would never do more than open their pants and just stand there, humbly waiting for applause. Under no circumstances would they ever "harm" a woman.

"Young ladies, you don't appreciate how privileged you are to be at Indiana University, where information is being courageously sifted and winnowed in order to arrive at truth, in spite of the ignorant Yahoos and Babbits in the rest of the state. You can walk right by the Kinsey Institute on Human Sexuality, where exciting research is being conducted even at night by dedicated, highly trained professionals."

Flattered to be treated like grown-ups who could handle hard truths, complex issues, and objective scientific findings, the girls were listening with rapt attention. Kaija stood up. Trying to ignore disapproving glances, she stepped over a dozen legs and tiptoed out. She could not possibly stay: she would be furious with herself if she did not speak up and ineffective if she did.

As was her habit, she turned on her radio for the evening news. She had been elated months earlier when Hungarian freedom fighters took over the streets of Budapest. She was too stunned to cry when the Soviet sickle and hammer came down on Hungary even harder than before. But no one on Campus talked about these events, though perhaps she did not know the right people. By now there was hardly a reference to the Hungarian Revolution on the news, yet Kaija could not stop her obsessive practice of listening for it.

But tonight, there was a story. Hungarian students, thirty boys and six girls, would be coming to the Indiana University campus in a few weeks. Kaija had been wrong: people *did* care about the young idealists who had risked so much and who had been crushed so completely in rising up against the Soviet Union. It did not occur to her to wonder whether tax money, foundation support, or private funds were making their arrival possible. She had been furious when the West failed to help the Hungarians, but she was happy that at least something was being done for a few Hungarian students now.

The next morning two American girls from Crown Point, with whom Kaija had gotten to be friends and with whom she shared the tiny "vanity room," a cubicle with mirror and sink, were told they had to move. Four girls from other rooms would have to go to another dorm as well, but Kaija would have to stay. The semester was well underway, and they were upset by the arbitrary decision, but they did not protest. They were nice girls, it was the 1950s, and

147

they were in Indiana, where rebellion was unthinkable, and not for girls only.

Maybe the Dean of Women had considered how to teach the six Hungarian girls the hundreds of intricate rules and prohibitions governing American womanhood in the 1950s and realized that a hundred hours of Girl Talk would not be enough. Housing the Hungarians in close proximity to another foreigner might help though.

Kaija was from Europe, which made her and the Hungarians practically identical, and she was presumably fully assimilated because she had been in the United States for six years. She had declined to join a sorority, so the Hungarians could live next door to her without having to go through the bizarre rituals of rushing, black-balling, and pledging.

Kaija spoke English with a barely perceptible accent, and she had enough of the right clothes to play the part of an American coed. She had only failed to modulate her voice to the endearing half-whisper of a breathless child—which many young women did so easily it seemed natural— but that had not counted against her before.

Yet she had been reminded once again she was a stranger and a foreigner, different from everyone else, and therefore deserving isolation, this time in a kind of displaced persons' mini-camp. Her recently acquired friends said goodbye, and although they all vowed to get together, Kaija knew that given the realities of dorm life, with dining room meals and with strict curfews for girls, her fragile friendship with them was finished.

She resolved to study in the library rather than in her room, to go home on weekends, and to avoid the Hungarians. She would respect and admire their courage from afar, but she would not get mixed up with them. If the Head Resident told her again that going to Indianapolis more often than at Thanksgiving and Christmas signified "a failure to adjust," she would hint then that it was not her fault.

But on the day the Hungarians were to arrive, Kaija woke strangely excited. She looked into the three rooms, which the maids had finished putting in order the day before. She liked the freshly painted light green walls, the tightly drawn surplus army blankets over starched white sheets, and the spotless brown linoleum floors. The smell of bleach, ammonia, and furniture polish lingered in the air, and the immaculately clean panes and bare window sills contrasted sharply with gentle sunlight glinting through ivy and yellowing leaves. The rooms were immaculate but coldly impersonal.

How would the Hungarian girls, arriving in this strange place, know that someone understood and cared? What would they eat if they arrived late at night, after the dining room closed? Who would encourage them during the first days of classes, which were bound to be intimidating? What would allay their longing for home, likely to be rawer than Kaija's dreams of the Summer House? She knew what it was like to arrive in a foreign country.

No one had told her what was expected of her in regard to the Hungarians, but it was up to her to do something. She would rise to the occasion, just this once. Electrical appliances and refrigerators were not allowed in dorm rooms; just to make popcorn or to use an iron everyone had to go to the small utility room at the end of the hall. There were no dishes, though each room was supplied with two plain glass vases for the red roses boys were supposed to bring unless the girls were absolute social failures. To welcome the Hungarians with a real meal was out of the question, and wine or liquor in a dorm room was grounds for expulsion from the University.

Kaija walked downtown, and after much consideration, bought a shallow wood bowl, a wild extravagance. She chose apples, pears, and oranges in a tiny grocery, and blazing red gladioli, the last before frost. The vivid flowers and fruit on the stark window sills transformed the rooms into something peaceful yet festive.

Kaija sat down on the rough wool blanket folded at the foot of a bed and looked at the late afternoon sun caressing plump fruit and graceful blossoms. To her surprise she felt tears rising to her eyes. How serene the Hungarian girls would find this after all they had been through, how safe to return here from the Quonset huts, where they would have their intensive English language and American history and government classes.

She waited for her tears to recede, wiped her eyes, and told herself to stop being so maudlin. Then she washed her face, powdered her nose, and headed to the dining room, where as Chairman of the Scholarship Committee, she would supervise other girls during Quiet Hour, the sixty minutes set aside five days a week for undisturbed studying or napping.

15

Three apple cores, a half-eaten pear, spills of powder, and strands of black hair were in the white porcelain sink when Kaija returned from her afternoon classes. Wadded up Kleenex littered the floor, and a pair of lace-trimmed panties, not too clean, was draped over the doorknob to the room of two of the Hungarian girls.

Kaija sighed. Magda and Kati had probably not understood that they were expected to clean up after themselves. They had arrived late, and their classes had started early, so they must not have read the regulations posted by the bathroom mirror. Maids did change the sheets and clean the rooms once a week, but in preparation for their arrival, all clothes and shoes had to be in the closets, and every surface had to be clear except the tops of bureaus.

Kaija gritted her teeth and started wiping the edge of the sink. She would do this one thing more, and then that really was it. She was not going to be identified with the Hungarians; she had done more than enough by welcoming them. She refused to be a foreigner forever.

A muffled sound, as of someone crying in the other room, startled her. She knocked gently, and after some snuffling and nose-blowing, Magda opened the door. Her huge blue eyes were barely visible through wreaths of cigarette smoke.

"What are you doing here?" Kaija asked. "Aren't you supposed to be in class?"

"I guess so, but I could not push me. Maybe, if I like, I'll go tomorrow," Magda said in lightly-accented English.

If she liked? Kaija stared at her. She had cut class once or twice herself, but guilt had prevented her from enjoying it, and she would never, ever cut an entire day, especially not at the beginning of a course. The University strongly discouraged such behavior,

151

going so far as to subtract half a credit for each class missed at the start of the semester and on the days before spring vacation and Homecoming. But let someone else explain all that to Magda; it was not Kaija's responsibility.

"Did you find the dining room all right, Magda? Have you had your lunch?"

"I went an hour ago, but they said I was too late for breakfast, and I didn't have a meal ticket for lunch. I was hungry, but they refused to feed me."

"Well, the hours for breakfast are . . . ."

Suddenly Magda grabbed her, kissed her on both cheeks, and held on tightly. Kaija tried to keep her own arms stiffly at her side, but Magda's enthusiasm was so genuine and her hug so warm that she found herself hugging back. She had to stoop awkwardly because Magda, who was considerably shorter, clung to her like a child.

"I can see right away that you are kind," Magda said. "I would have fainted without the fruits, and my spirits were weak until I look at your beautiful flowers. I have eaten all the apples."

Kaija motioned with her eyes and Magda, understanding, dropped the cores in the wastebasket. Then she took Kaija's hands and studied her face.

"Yes, I can see that we are going to be very good, very special friends. We look alike, no? You have high cheekbones and large eyes, just like me! Eyes are windows into soul. Yours are gray, of course, and you're very tall, but otherwise, yes, we're like sisters. Same mother, different fathers. Mothers are most important for girls," she announced confidently, thus contradicting the received wisdom of Kaija's professors and the snickering Freudian allusions of her classmates.

Flattered by being compared to beautiful Magda, Kaija impulsively decided to give her a good impression of America by taking her for a hamburger and fries at the diner across the street. Kaija studied Magda's white skin and large blue eyes beneath swollen lids, while Magda wolfed down French fries, smoked, and gestured with the self-confidence of a diva. Did Kaija really resemble her?

Kaija was beguiled by the few similarities which Magda had isolated or perhaps invented because in most ways they were strikingly different. Magda's wavy short black hair was in an Italian urchin's cut, lately popularized by Sophia Loren, while Kaija's blond bob was under Grace Kelly-like control, almost never falling over her eye like Veronica Lake's. Her small breasts and slender body failed to live up to the standard of the day for breasts-waist-hips, which was 34-24-34, while Magda's exceeded that in all the right directions, 36-24-35. Kaija learned these statistics right away because the first of many things Magda borrowed was a tape measure, in order to make sure that she would be a success.

But their mutual recognition had deeper roots. Like other exiles, they were drawn to each other because they could sense well-hidden past terror and present grief. Kaija felt something intimately familiar in Magda, as if she were the sister she had never had, or the intimate confidante Aunt Astra would have been had she lived. This friendship was going to be different from Kaija's more superficial relationships with American girls.

By the end of the first week, the shared phone by the tiny sink started ringing, almost as if Magda had sent out waves of pheromones, which the fraternity boys picked up by invisible sensors located in the empty spaces around their brains. Boys whom Magda had never met or heard of called with offers to buy her cokes and coffee or to take her on moonlit hayrides and darkened movie theaters. There were so many that Magda started jotting their names on the wall by the phone, which the maids, grim-faced, scrubbed off.

"Many men are crazy in love with me, many are suffering because I am too busy for them," Magda bubbled. "I am very popular."

"You certainly are," Kaija agreed.

"I would tell you everything that is happening in my life," Magda said as she applied mascara, "but soon you will have a very romantic, very passionate love affair yourself, and then you will not want to hear about my boring little sex . . . I mean my love life."

Little did Magda know how much Kaija wanted to hear exactly that. Kaija had no real information about women's sex lives. She did not know a word for "sex" or "sexy" in Latvian, her mother labeled all intimate matters "below comment," and Alma flushed dark red and turned righteous if Kaija only alluded to the subject. Women's sex lives were barely implied in the novels Kaija had read, and they were not explicit even in *True Confessions* or *Modern Romance*, which Kaija had studied during her adolescence.

No one talked about sex honestly in the dorm either. Pure, like Ivory soap was advertised to be, 99.4% of the girls on campus were supposedly virgins. At pajama parties after Saturday night dates, girls reported the things boys had tried to pull, and they boasted about how ingeniously they themselves had drawn the line. They had kept their virtue intact, while the abashed boys remained hopeful enough to take them out again the following week.

Kaija daydreamed that Maris would kiss her as passionately as she wanted him to. She would kiss him right back, and she would never offer up for general discussion anything that happened between them. She had imagined kissing him the first time she had talked to him. Usually he kissed her lightly on the cheek, like a brother instead of a lover, but tonight he had kissed her ardently on the darkened bus between Indianapolis and Bloomington. He had whispered her name in a smoky, hoarse voice before he drew back from her. But he shook her hand coolly when they parted in the midst of embracing couples in front of her dorm.

Thuds and shouts from Magda's room interrupted Kaija reliving the kisses on the bus. She knocked, opened the door cautiously, and ducked to avoid a flying pillow aimed at Kati, Magda's roommate. The floor was littered with newspapers, underwear, belts, orange peels, crumpled letters, an open can of talcum powder, a hastily wrapped used Kotex, and piles of dirty and clean clothes jumbled together. The closet, which Kati and Magda shared, stood empty on Magda's side except for a scuffed brown leather jacket, a sable coat, and a few shoes missing their mates.

Magda had little appreciation of her own considerable intelligence, and she attributed her good though occasionally unidiomatic English to the imitative talents of her mother, who as an opera singer had had to mimic strange sounds in foreign languages. The other Hungarian girls were not nearly as fluent, so that in spite of good will and patience, Kaija did not always understand them right away.

"Shame and punish," Kati brought out between delicate little sobs. "Punish and shame."

Prepared to take time, Kaija sat down on the bed.

"Shame?" she asked.

Kati searched through the debris on the floor and produced a crumpled letter signed by the Head Resident. The maids had complained that the room had not been readied for cleaning the last two times, that they had not been able to get near the beds to change the sheets, and that they had observed dangerous germ and disease-breeding objects lying about on the floor. Like Kati, Kaija blushed with embarrassment.

Magda pawed around in the rubble, pulled out a respectable flannel nightgown, and flung it at Kati, who let out a wail.

"Stop that, Magda," Kaija ordered. "Can't you see how upset Kati is?"

"Good. I will stop now because I am finished. Her area is ready for inspection by military police."

The floor on Kati's side was clear, except for the few items that Magda had let fly. Kati's books and cosmetics were on her bureau in a pathetically straight line. Magda sat triumphant in the midst of chaos.

"Shame and punish, punish and shame," Magda mimicked as she lit a Pall Mall. "If they want to clean, let them clean. Nazis, fascists, KGB bullies, Stalin's bottom-lickers, uncultured Russians, narrow-minded petit bourgeois." For all Kaija knew, she would have added, "a nation of shop-keepers," had she not been interrupted by

Head Resident Martha Smith, who entered after a perfunctory tap on the door.

"How are you doing, girls? Good, good, it looks like you're making progress. You're half done, just keep at it," she said without fully appreciating the location and extent of the remaining disorder. "Let's go now, choo, choo, choo. I think I can, I think I can," she chanted as she picked up a pair of grubby socks. "Altogether now, choo . . . ."

When no one joined in, Martha Smith, Head Resident and Ph.D. candidate in education, paused to explain. "That's 'The Little Red Engine Who Could,' but you girls from 'Over There' wouldn't know that. It's an American story."

Perched on her unmade bed, Magda watched Martha through wreaths of cigarette smoke.

"Come on, Magda, you've got to put your shoulder to the wheel too. See how nicely Kati has picked up that blouse? See how neatly she is sliding it over the hanger? See how prettily her clothes are hanging in the closet, all facing the same way? Look, let me demonstrate. See how one end of the hanger goes into each shoulder of the blouse? See how I smooth it out and button the top button?"

Martha spoke very slowly and very loudly, as if she were dealing with a half-deaf, not too bright child.

"Now, some things are dirty, and some are clean. We will make one pile here for the clean, another for the dirty. After you hang up all the clean, you must sort the dirty into white, dark, colored, machine wash, hand-wash, dry-clean . . ."

"Where do I put half-dirty?" Magda asked eagerly.

"With dirty."

"Oh, thank you, thank you. Where the half-white?" Magda smiled enchantingly and pointed to a pair of black and white animal print Capri pants. "With white?"

"No, with colored."

"Oh, thank you, thank you, you have explained your American social system very well. Half-dirty is dirty, and half-white is colored, not white. What about machine wash, hand wash, or dry clean?"

156

Martha started to answer, but stopped, realizing that Magda was making fun of her. She jerked the cigarette from Magda's hand, stubbed it out, forced a pair of white silk panties, clearly dirty and hand-wash, into her palm, and closed her fingers around them, one by one. She seized Magda's upper arm and pushed her forward until she deposited the stockings in a new pile.

"Ouch! Let me go! You are hurting me very much!" Magda yelled, as Martha, abashed, came to herself. She wiped her hands on her khaki Bermudas and looked down, embarrassed. Magda rubbed her plump white upper arm, where red marks announcing bruises were clearly visible. Her eyes filled with tears.

"I'm sorry. I don't know what came over me," Martha whispered, close to tears herself. Magda stared at her until she dropped her eyes.

"I'm sorry, please excuse me," Martha said as she backed out of the room.

In the silence that followed, Kati broke first. Keeping her eyes downcast, she gathered Magda's clothes and swiftly sorted them, while Kaija fished out Magda's books and papers. Magda relit her cigarette and sullenly rubbed her arm. Finally, she sighed elaborately, rewrapped the dirty Kotex, dropped it into the wastebasket, and started gathering her cosmetics and brushes.

"You are a good friend to me, Kaija," she said when the room looked presentable. "Thank you for helping me."

"You have to do this yourself next time, Magda," Kaija said. "Otherwise there will be real trouble."

"From that woman?" Magda laughed, "Oh, no. She will not bother me, she is crazy in love with me."

"In love with you? What are you talking about?"

"Did you see how she looks at me? Did you see how she cannot let me go, even when I cry? She likes to hurt me a little, not too much."

"That's not love," Kaija said, nervous about contradicting a startling theory convincingly presented.

"That woman is studying to be a professor, so she can teach big girls how to teach other girls, but what does she do? She pulls

157

on ugly pants, she buckles her leather belt, she laces up men's shoes, she locks up girls at night, she likes to punish when we don't come to her at ten-thirty. She cannot keep from touching, she wants me to submit, she feels great shame, she is in conflict, she blushes, she says sorry, she runs away. She cannot help it, she is in love with me."

Kaija failed to change Magda's mind, especially after a dainty bouquet of pink carnations arrived the following day. Magda tore up Martha's note of apology, put the flowers in the vase provided for homages from boys, and displayed it on the window sill as proof of her popularity.

Inevitably, chaos returned. The next week Magda grudgingly picked up a few of the items she routinely dropped on the floor, but only after Kaija pleaded with her to be nice to Kati. After Kati herself complained to the Head Resident, Magda refused to put away so much as a chiffon scarf. Kati stayed for a few days in the rooms of the other Hungarian girls, inconveniencing them just enough to make them angry with Magda too. She moved on to the worn leather couch in the TV lounge, where surrounded by a few clothes and books, she sat wrapped in a blanket like a lost refugee child. The maids ostentatiously avoided Magda's side of the room as if it were filled with land-mines. Martha Smith did not reappear, and if there were more written warnings, Magda did not show them to Kaija.

16

Alma held her head high and hoped her disappointment did not show. Kaija had arrived on the very last bus from Bloomington on Friday, she had spent the entire Saturday helping her mother, and she had just announced that she would leave first thing on Sunday morning because she had to study. But instead of finding seats away from others so that they could have a real talk, Kaija had plunked herself down next to a Mr. and Mrs. Zalums and their son Maris, a family recently arrived in Indianapolis. She was in animated conversation with them; in fact, she was leaning towards them so much that her shoulder touched Maris.

Alma seethed with resentment. Kaija could chatter with the Zalums family another time, but now the two friends were not using theirchance to talk. The Chicago Latvian Men's Choir was coming on to the stage at the new Latvian Center on the far north side of Indianapolis.

Alma yanked on Kaija's elbow. "Let's go to Mrs. Lapsa's later," she said. "She's giving a party."

Kaija turned around, startled. "I haven't been invited," she whispered.

Kaija was turning into a real snob at that Indiana University of hers, Alma huffed to herself. Mrs. Lapsa was a social inferior to Judge and Mrs. Veldre; she would be flattered if Kaija visited her.

"That doesn't matter. We can just go," Alma said.

"I'd rather not."

"Please," Alma said, angry at having to plead. "I don't ask you for much." Alma sounded pathetic.

"I don't want to, Alma. I don't want to run into Ojars."

If that was not ridiculous, Alma did not know what was. Kaija had kissed Ojars, she had gone for rides in that stupid convertible of his, and now she was acting as if she was too good for him and everybody else who did not go to Indiana University.

"Ivars is going to be there," Alma said.

Kaija groaned. "Oh, all right then, but let's not stay."

Mrs. Lapsa's home, which she shared with her lover Edgars and her two grown sons, was in one of the living rooms with a small sun porch attached on 24th Street and Park Avenue. Most Latvians had moved away from the area as soon as they could afford something better. Unlike other immigrants, they settled in various locations throughout the city rather than making one neighborhood their own. Alma and her father lived farther north, near 34th Street, at an address that would have been almost acceptable at Shortridge High School.

Alma paused on Mrs. Lapsa's threshold and craned her neck. Where was Ivars?

A dozen or so men sprawled on three beds, which had been pushed against walls. Guttering candles gave the only light, and the air was thick with cigarette smoke. The table was littered with glasses, ashtrays, and half-empty bottles of vodka. The smell of beer was overpowering.

Alma nudged Kaija happily; she had spotted Ivars. In her opinion, he was more sober and more respectable than everyone else present.

Kaija knew that the other men, older than Ivars, were veterans of World War II. Most had been wounded; some had been prisoners of war; all were separated from sweethearts, wives, and families left behind in Latvia. Against international law, which forbid occupying powers to draft the occupied into the armed forces, Germans had forced young Latvian men into the army. With the love of Latvia foremost in their hearts, they had fought on the German side to save their homeland from Russians. All had been on the losing side of the war.

These veterans were defensive and secretive. It was impossible to explain the complexities of Latvian history to Americans. Refusal of military service would have meant imprisonment or worse, but that did not keep them from being labeled fascists now.

Too old to enter into the American educational system to resume schooling interrupted more than a decade ago, the men saw themselves as doomed by history and fate. Because status in the exile community was determined by professional positions years ago in Latvia, they were not held in high regard there either, as were Judge Veldre and others. Their pain and rage erupted in occasional drunken rants, threats of suicide, and car crashes.

"I don't like this, Alma," Kaija said. "I want to leave."

"Half an hour, I promise," Alma whispered, embarrassed because everyone had heard Kaija.

Resting on an elbow, with his long legs outstretched, Ivars reclined on one of the beds. He raised his hand in a languid greeting.

"I'm sorry that we don't have Seven-Up," Mrs. Lapsa said as she pulled up the elastic of her off-the-shoulder blouse. "I won't insult such fine ladies as you by vodka or beer." She did not rise to welcome the newcomers.

"This is a scandal," someone declared facetiously. "The first duty of a hostess is to provide Seven-Up for all distinguished guests, especially for those who deign to visit us from the great University of Indiana."

"And the second duty is to provide a throne for a lofty personage like Miss Veldre and Alma, her lady-in-waiting," another laughed.

"Thrones won't be necessary," Ivars said amiably. "Someone can sit on my lap."

Alma wished she could do so.

"We'll make do," Mrs. Lapsa giggled. "Let's all move closer together on this bed." She scooted over and rested her head on Ivars' shoulder.

161

"This is nice," she sighed. "Let's squeeze a little closer."

Before anyone could understand what was happening, Mrs. Lapsa was off the bed and bent over backwards. Arms flailing, her high heels scraping the floor, she scrabbled frantically to right herself. Edgars, her lover, had jerked her up and away from Ivars.

"I'll show you squeezing together," he spat as he held her down. "You forget where you belong, woman. Your place is under me, remember?"

He bent over her, and his mouth dug into hers.

"How do you like that, woman? Had enough?" he taunted.

"No, no, kiss me again," someone called out, in cruel parody of Mrs. Lapsa's high-pitched voice. Ivars smiled enigmatically.

Edgars rammed his tongue between Mrs. Lapsa's lips.

"Satisfied?" he challenged as he pushed her away.

Mrs. Lapsa landed hard on the edge of the bed. She laughed insincerely as she pulled up her blouse again, which had slipped low enough to reveal her bra. Shame and pride alternated in her expression. Finally, like a ruffled hen released by a maddened rooster, she settled herself placidly at Edgars' side.

"I'm going," Kaija said. Alma looked yearningly at Ivars as she backed out of the room.

The friends ran down the stairs and into the night. They were half way to the bus stop on Central Avenue before they spoke.

"That Mrs. Lapsa," Alma spat. "She is such a slut. How can she let Edgars kiss her like that, in front of all his friends?"

"She couldn't help it. He forced himself on her. It wasn't her fault, Alma."

"Yes, it was. She was asking for it."

"She looked a little drunk, but she didn't . . . ."

"That's no excuse."

"Maybe not. But Edgars is the one who humiliated her. He's the one who made her feel ashamed. I can't stand him. Or his friends. I was scared they would grab us next."

"That's mean, Kaija. Latvian men would never do that. They're just having a few drinks on a Saturday night. Lots of men do. It's normal."

162

Kaija knew that she should be compassionate because the men at Mrs. Lapsa's had survived terrible experiences and they had lost everything important to them. But she had felt their hostility, and she was angry.

Alma continued railing at Mrs. Lapsa. "She should have better sense. She should have stood up to welcome us. She's the mother of two grown sons, and she's living with a veteran who isn't her husband. She's the hostess. She was crawling all over Ivars. Somebody had to do something."

"Then your precious Ivars should have. He's not a suckling babe in his mother's arms. He should have stood up and given you his seat, and he should have told Edgars to cut it out."

"Don't you dare criticize Ivars. Mrs. Lapsa started it."

"That's just stupid, Alma," Kaija snapped. She had never spoken contemptuously to Alma before.

"I'm sorry, Alma. I'm not saying what I mean," she amended. "I think the whole thing was between the men, but Mrs. Lapsa happened to be there and they took it out on her. They hate us because we have a future, and they don't. That isn't quite right either, but it's the best I can do. I don't know how to explain what happened, but I want to learn."

"How? By studying twenty-four hours a day at your precious Indiana University? You don't have time for your friends as it is. You expect me to stand up and salute whenever you mention that place."

"That's not true," Kaija cried.

"Yes, it is. You've changed so completely I don't recognize you. I don't know who you are anymore."

Hearing the hurt beneath Alma's anger, Kaija said gently, "I'm sorry, Almin. I'm just confused because the rules are different every place I go. There are the staid wholesome Latvian boys at the Community Center and the angry men at 24th and Park, there are the nice American girls in my dorm and the fraternity boys crazy for sex like a pack of hounds after Magda, there are the Hungarians and the Latvians and the Americans . . ."

"Don't you worry about the Hungarians. They'll take care of themselves," Alma exploded. "They're getting a free education and everything else handed to them on a silver platter."

Kaija sighed. Defending the Hungarians would make the disagreement worse.

The friends did not linger by the brightly lit windows of a house they had often admired before. Alma liked its plush furniture and rooms spacious enough to accommodate a husband and children, and Kaija coveted a window seat like the one with rose-colored cushions between walls lined with books.

Neither girl remarked on the house tonight. Instead they stepped on the squares of light reflected from the windows and hurried on. From a distance they looked like two friends companionably making their way towards the bus stop on Central Avenue, but Kaija sensed their friendship was in danger. She was always the one who intuited feelings, smoothed things over, and apologized even when it was not her fault. But she had to make Alma feel better now.

"Anyway, I'm sorry. I'll come to Indianapolis again. Soon, Almin," she said.

Alma gave her a sullen look.

"Next weekend, if you like," Kaija offered before remembering that she had promised to go with Magda to a party the Hungarian men were organizing in the recreation room of their dorm.

Alma was not mollified. "I don't know. You're not moving back to Indianapolis for the summer, you're not coming to celebrate Midsummer Eve, and you don't spend time with me when you're here. What in the world is the matter with you?"

"I have a job in the library for the summer, but I *can* be here Saturday after next. I'd like to do something with you."

"The week *after* next? You're putting it off already. But all right," Alma agreed.

"There won't be a party then that meets with your approval, but we can always go shopping."

164

17

Kaija hoped that Alma and Magda would come to like each other if they did something enjoyable together, but the future of the threesome did not look promising.

As they passed through the revolving front door of L.S. Ayres and entered its dim interior and vast halls, Alma and Kaija fell silent. The chaos and crowding in the displaced persons camps was eight years in the past, but the high ceilings and wide aisles still seemed almost sacred to the two friends. Near the locked glass jewelry cases, the fragrance of heavy old perfumes—Shalimar, Joy, and Chanel Nineteen—enveloped them.

Magda charged ahead, Alma moved as slowly as possible, and Kaija dithered. She did not want to abandon Alma even as she tried to keep up with Magda.

At the jewelry counter, Alma stopped altogether. "Aren't these beautiful, Kaijin? Which one would you choose if you could have absolutely anything in the world?" she asked in Latvian, pointedly excluding Magda. She gestured towards the diamond engagement rings and strands of pearls on black velvet.

Magda scanned the rings, wrinkled her nose, and headed for the escalator. "Let's go look at sweaters and shoes," she commanded.

Alma bent over the pearls. She was not enthralled by them, but she did not want a co-worker from the bank to see her in the company of Magda. Instead of a ladylike skirt, nylons, heels, and gloves, which by now even Alma considered essential for trips downtown, Magda was wearing a pointed bra, a tight short-sleeved black sweater with a hole near the armpit, leopard print toreador pants, and scuffed backless high heels on bare feet.

165

As the escalator lifted the three above the vast hall full of women speaking in subdued reverential tones and bowing in front of objects, Kaija made another doomed attempt to bring Magda and Alma together.

"Don't you just love this store?" she said. "That's the first revolving door and escalator I've ever seen." She held on tightly, as if she expected the escalator to speed up and willfully trip her.

"Didn't you have escalators in Latvia?" Magda asked astonished.

"Of course, we did," Alma blazed. "We had everything in Latvia because our homeland was a perfect place. Latvia was the most advanced country in Europe, with the highest literacy rate. I remember riding on an escalator in Riga." Turning her back on Magda, she added in Latvian, "But you were only six when you left, Kaijin. Isn't that so, Little One?"

"Hundreds of escalators in Budapest," Magda said dismissively. "Revolving doors too. And this shop is nothing compared to what they have in Moscow. I went to Moscow all the time when my father was conducting. The Soviet leaders adored him and his orchestra. They took us to marvelous stores for Party members only."

Alma drew in a horrified breath. "Is your father a Communist? Are you?"

"Of course not," Magda gave Alma a pitying look for her ignorance. "Papi fell from grace because he is a great patriot. He was for a free Hungary. He hates the Russians; he is revolted by all totalitarian regimes. He conducted the singing of the national anthem as Soviet tanks rolled down the streets of Budapest. He was at the radio station when students pleaded desperately for help from the West. And now he and my mother are in danger because I have escaped. I am a democrat."

Instead of being impressed, Alma only sniffed until they straightened it out between them that Magda meant a lower case "d" and that she might consider joining the Republican Party when she was very rich and very old. Alma insisted that Magda should act

166

now because the Republicans, especially Vice President Nixon, were "tough on Communism."

Magda made little farting noises with her lips. She shrugged when Kaija gave her a pleading look.

The sweaters on the second floor briefly united Alma and Magda. Pure white, creamy beige, navy, and black lamb's wool, they were displayed on headless busts of mannequins strung high above shelves holding modest stacks in a few additional colors. The most expensive, of unusual design, or made of cashmere were kept out of reach behind the counter. Even Magda did not have the nerve to ask the saleswoman to spread out the sweaters, one at a time, on the counter so that they could examine them. The clerks would do that only for someone likely to buy, and even then, touching was discouraged.

"Lovely," Alma murmured, and Magda nodded in agreement and smiled.

But this moment of near intimacy made Kaija uneasy too. She shifted from foot to foot while Magda and Alma played the which-one-would-you-buy-if-you-could game. Any second now Magda might say something which revealed that she knew more about Kaija after a few months than Alma did after eight years. Magda might point to a dark red sweater and say it was exactly like the one Kaija kept on the highest shelf in her closet, and Alma would be hurt because they used to know each other's possessions as well as their own. She would demand to know when Kaija had bought it, where she had gotten the money for cashmere, and why she had spent it so frivolously.

Maris had bought Kaija her first and only cashmere sweater. She did not choose it herself. He gestured for the saleswoman to take it from the high glass case and spread it out in front of him, which she obligingly did. A beautiful dark red, it had a deep v-neck and a rounded Peter Pan collar, that contradiction of sexiness and innocence typical of the fashions of the 1950s. The woman held her arms protectively around the sweater as she offered it to Maris to feel, effectively barring Kaija from participating in the transaction.

Maris and Kaija stood facing her, the sides of their thighs touching. He turned to Kaija, brushed a strand of her ash blond hair away from her forehead and gently looped it behind her ear.

"All right, Kaijin?" he asked.

A shiver went through her.

She nodded, unable to look away from him or to speak.

Without taking his serious gaze from her face, he gave the sales clerk a handful of bills. Kaija could feel his presence on the skin of her entire body. The muscles in his thigh contracted, and his hand brushed hers as he shoved the change into his pocket. He worked long hours for his money, waiting on tables for fraternity boys, but he did not count the change.

Later in the dorm, with the door locked, Kaija opened the sealed package, unfolded the tissue paper, and slipped the warm wool over her size 32B breasts. The sweater was blood-red, not cranberry at all as the saleswoman had called it. The words "blood red" pulsed through her. She ran her hands over her arms and breasts covered by the soft material. Then she took the sweater off, folded it in tissue paper again, and put it away in her closet.

She did not wear it in Indianapolis because Alma and even her mother, were she to notice, would insist she return it. The rules were firm. Anything over $10 was too expensive to accept from a boy without taking on an implied, never explicitly-stated obligation. An item of clothing was entirely taboo, especially one which touched both breasts and hinted at prior sexual and therefore shameful contact with the giver. How but by wandering fingers and grasping hands could a boy know the size required? Because the girls in Kaija's dorm had similar rules about sexual transaction, obligation, and disgrace, she said that she had had the sweater for ages, whenever they commented how "cute" it was.

Kaija's mother and the girls were right in one way, of course. Maris and Kaija vibrated to each other, though their relationship was different from what others might imagine. Their intimacy was shy and very sweet. Sitting side by side in the living room of Kaija's dorm, they obeyed the rule that a couple should have at least three feet on the floor at all times. Under the watchful eyes of the

Housemother and other girls, only their hands locked. On the few occasions when they were alone, they kissed, gently at first and then more urgently. Maris' lips were warm and firm. Some nights Kaija parted from him with her face just this side of bruising, while the rest of her pulsing body remained untouched.

Maris did not own a car, and he was too busy studying to run around with other boys from whom he might have borrowed one, which is one reason they never did more than kiss. But in the language of the day, he also "respected" Kaija. She had stayed overnight at Maris' house once. They met at midnight in the dark living room, while his parents were asleep upstairs. They kissed breathlessly, wildly, moaning with surprise and desire. But after about an hour they drew back from each other, hugged, and returned to their respective bedrooms.

Kaija had not told anyone she was in love with Maris. Although he was Latvian and perfectly presentable, her parents would disapprove of the powerful attraction between the two, which might distract her from her education. Bright, respectful, well-mannered, handsome in an unobtrusive way, an inch taller than Kaija, a hard worker, and a good student on his way to becoming a doctor, Maris would also be condemned by Alma if she knew that Kaija intensely desired him.

"I'm bored," Magda interrupted Alma's detailed explanation why a beige sweater would be the best investment. "I want to see shoes."

On the next floor, Magda dismissed the black patent leather Mary Janes, which had captivated Alma.

"Suitable for very small boys only," she scoffed. "I know a film director in Budapest, very brilliant, very famous, very influential, who dressed me up in a sailor's blouse and short pants, with white knee socks. I looked like a dear little boy. He made me wear shoes like that. He put a straw hat on me, like so," she demonstrated by moving Alma's respectable navy boater to a wild angle over her left eye. "Then he turned my face towards the shadows, away from him. He entered me, excuse me, how do you

169

say, entertained himself at my back. You understand of course that he did everything but."

Twenty-one-and-never-been-kissed, Alma was confused enough by the event, but Magda's excellent English inevitably turned obscure whenever she referred to sex. In the intensive English language courses Magda was taking, sexual terminology did not come up. And Kaija did not know enough terms in English to effectively consult a gynecologist or to ask Magda a pointed question. The words for women's intimate body parts were a mystery to her in Latvian, her mother tongue, as well.

Alma had evidently gotten Magda's drift because she blushed. Why, oh why, Kaija moaned to herself, had she brought Magda with her to Indianapolis? And why was she inflicting this excursion with Magda on Alma, her oldest and most loyal friend?

It was exciting to go with Magda, of course. Magda loved chunky imitation garnet earrings, white linen suits with tight skirts and jackets worn right next to the skin rather than over blouses as everyone else wore them, satin underwear, stiletto heels, and ballerina flats made by Capezio to go with full skirts for the European waif look lately popularized by Pier Angeli and Audrey Hepburn. She was teaching Kaija to love them too, instead of the pastel twin sweater sets and plain blouses favored by girls in the dorm.

Magda had the power to transform. Kaija was skinny and unhappy because she wore size 9 shoes and because at 5'11" she towered over most boys. She treasured Magda's pronouncements.

"All shapes of women are beautiful," Magda would say. "Female bodies are much more sensibly designed than male, with nothing dangling or puffing up, and real men *adore* real women." To Magda, they were women, not girls. Their bodies were wonderful, only the bras and shoes were wrong. Magda would laugh, turn things upside down, and imply that Indiana rules were ridiculous and did not apply anywhere else in the world even as she half-heartedly tried to follow them.

"I'll faint if I don't have a cigarette and something to drink." Magda looked at Alma challengingly.

"All right," Alma agreed, and Kaija relaxed.

But the good feeling lasted only until they were seated in a booth in the East Washington Sweet Shop. Magda leaned forward, propped her breasts on the table, and winked at the waiter, a handsome middle-aged black man, who set down their sodas and presented straws with flourish befitting a magician. Kaija tensed. She knew exactly what would come next. Alma would say that Magda should not flirt with him because blacks were inferior to whites, Kaija would sanctimoniously point out that all men were created equal, Magda would call Alma a fascist, and Alma would call her a Godless communist. Kaija resolved to keep her two friends in separate compartments in the future, as she did everything else in her life.

Lost Midsummers

18

In spite of Magda's parents being state-supported artists, she had not had proper dental care in Hungary. Maybe she had been terrified of drills; maybe she had eaten sweets, smoked cigarettes, and ignored directions to brush. In any case, Magda's stained, and cavity-marred front teeth were her one less than lovely feature.

Magda whimpered that she would die because only sadists became dentists and enjoyed inflicting pain. She wanted to skip her appointment, but Kaija insisted and walked her to the office of Doctor Payne, one of the dentists in Bloomington who had volunteered his services for the Hungarians.

Magda returned in high spirits, however, in spite of her swollen upper lip.

"I have had a big adventure," she announced.

"Did it hurt?" Kaija asked.

"Yes, it did, but I don't mean that. My teeth have oh-so-many problems, but they are very fine teeth, and he will fix them very nicely. But I learned something very interesting about myself from this Dentist Payne. I am the most passionate woman he has ever had! I mean as a patient, of course. Can you imagine this, Kaija? He explained to me how men can tell. If a woman starts to breathe fast when her mouth is packed with cotton, that is Number One sign. Number Two, if her neck and breasts blush in her décolletage. Number Three, if she shivers and gets . . . duck . . . goose dots when her mouth is rinsed. Just think, I have all, One, Two, and Three Signs. He showed me exactly where I am most responsive."

"Where? How?" Kaija practically shouted.

"First with water, then with his fingers, and then with his tongue."

"He kissed you?"

"Yes, yes, but it was more than that. He helped me to understand more about myself and how to receive pleasure in my life."

"He put his tongue in your mouth and you let him?" Kaija screeched. She had told Magda that it was up to the girl draw the line and to see to it that a couple kept three feet on the floor.

"But of course, he put his fingers in, he is a dentist."

"Oh, Magda," Kaija let out a snort of laughter in spite of herself. She imagined a fat little dentist, drill in hand, advancing on Magda. But what had happened, exactly?

"Were you scared, Magda?"

"No, no. He is a nice man, but very, very old. He must be forty, maybe fifty. And his wife is ancient because she has glasses and wrinkles and white hair. He has a picture of her on his desk."

"That's good," Kaija said. That he was married meant it would not go very far.

"I like him because he is so . . . so like a father . . . or grandfather. He has a nice big stomach, and his pants are down to here," Magda motioned towards her crotch. "He pressed himself against me like so, and he put it in my lap, the stomach I mean, and it growled there quietly and peacefully all the time. That is typical of a very old man."

"Magda, you must not have anything to do with him. He is not nice," Kaija declared, thus excluding Doctor Payne from the all-purpose positive label of the 1950s. "He is dangerous and irresponsible. He tried to seduce you, and that was very wrong of him. You are a young girl, without your parents, alone in a foreign country. You deserve male protection. I'm worried about you, Magda."

"I can take care of myself," Magda said confidently. "But you are very kind to worry, Kaija, you are my good and dear friend. You are my only friend in this terrible place. Anyway, I did push him away when all his particles got hard."

174

Perhaps she was translating directly from Hungarian, but Kaija understood what she meant. She could not have phrased it more precisely herself.

"Magda, you should not see him again. You must ask for a different dentist."

"But he is a very good dentist, and he will fix my teeth with diligence. He is a Man of Science."

"You must tell the Dean of Women what happened," Kaija said. "Or at least tell the Head Resident."

But they both knew that was futile. The Dean would blame Magda for letting it all get out of hand in the first place, and Head Resident Martha Smith would feel vindicated and smug.

"I know," Kaija said brightly. "Switch dentists with one of the Hungarian boys."

"But I *like* Dr. Payne. I started to cry when it hurt, and he wiped my face with his big handkerchief. He said he can give me pills—aspirin pills, sleeping pills, wake-up pills, happy pills—any pills I want. He is a very, very kind man. He likes me. He is most interested in my future."

"At least, don't let him give you another Novocain shot. That's what confused you in the first place."

Fraternity house punch and Novocain were rumored to be the two great aphrodisiacs, even as salt-peter was supposedly being secretly stirred into milk throughout the state of Indiana to suppress the sex drives of college students and prison inmates.

"Oh, but I loved that shot."

"Magda, I'll go with you and I'll sit right next to you while he drills. When is your next appointment?"

A vague look appeared on Magda's face, and she started leafing through a dictionary she had been using as a doorstop. Kaija knew there was no point in persisting. Magda would continue to see Doctor Payne and he would make her flawlessly beautiful.

175

Jerry Locksmith had presented himself to Magda while she was having a Coke at the Regulator.

"What were you doing in the Regulator? Isn't that a bar? Don't you have a class at four o'clock?" Kaija asked, alarmed.

"Yes, but they were talking about the Louisiana Purchase, and I could not listen. Imagine, buying a whole country and all the people in it for money, like a basket of eggs in a shop. At least they shouldn't tell everyone the price. It's vulgar to talk about money. The professor gave me a very big headache."

"But, Magda, you'll flunk out if you keep cutting."

Magda had started out at the head of her class but was falling behind because she overslept, did not do her homework, and told the teachers she was bored.

"Weren't you afraid someone would see you in the Regulator? A lot of professors go there for martinis."

"I don't go for the alcohol, Kaija. I have spirits enough myself, thank you very much. And the coffee is terrible. But it's more cosmopolitan there, and I like the people because most are alive. I don't mean the professors in their old tweed jackets with shoe leather on the elbows. They drop their eyes when I look at them. Maybe they don't like women, maybe they're scared of me, who knows? But stone-cutters and real artists go to the Regulator too."

The mixture of class and sex felt explosive to Kaija. Recently there had been several drunken brawls between the young men who worked in the limestone quarries surrounding Bloomington and college boys looking for sex and liquor in working class bars.

Jerry Locksmith had introduced himself to Magda as an artist first and a photographer second, guessed her breast-waist-hip measurements almost to the inch, told her things about the planes and angles of her face that she would never have learned by herself, and expressed surprise that she was not a professional model. He had offered to show her his etchings, and she had accompanied him to his studio in the stone-cutters' part of town. He had photographed

176

her in many artistic poses and promised to make prints, so she could begin building her portfolio.

"And imagine, all this is for free, Kaija!"

"Take your picture? Make you a model? Show you his etchings? Oh, Magda, that line is a come-on! He was actually asking you whether you'd go all the way with him."

"You can get a portrait of yourself too, Kaija," Magda offered. "I have made all the arrangements. Very elegant, very professional, very well done."

"I don't think . . . ."

"You'll need them for your scholarships and for jobs. I told him you are my good and special friend."

All applications did indeed require photos, so that no prospective employer or scholarship committee was ever in doubt about a candidate's sex or race.

Kaija picked up the phone book. Being listed implied respectability, but the entry "J. Locksmith" said nothing about photography or art.

"That's because he's just getting started," Magda explained. "He's in his studio by appointment only. He will wait for you on Friday, at four o'clock."

It was strictly against the rules for a female student to enter the room or apartment of a man not her father or brother, but surely visiting a male professional was different? Otherwise hundreds of young women would die of appendicitis and thousands more would face life with teeth without braces. Women professionals were so invisible they seemed not to exist. But did it follow that it was all right to visit a part-time photographer who offered to show off his etchings?

"Listen, Kaija. Maris will have a birthday, and you will have to give him a gift. Jerry will take your picture, and you will buy a frame. You will give Maris your portrait, he will put it on his bureau, and everyone will know you exist. Or you can give him a very small picture of yourself to carry close to his heart or near his . . . . Never mind, Maris is crazy in love with you," she concluded.

177

Magda had met Maris only briefly, and he had endeared himself even more to Kaija by not groaning and clutching his private parts, as other boys did when Magda walked by. Magda knew nothing about him, but her "crazy in love with you" convinced Kaija. She could handle Jerry Locksmith a lot better than Magda had old Dr. Payne.

19

Kaija was not so confident when she arrived at the address Magda had given her. A Laundromat occupied the lower level of a large shabby building with rickety stairs clinging to the outside. But a newly painted red door, certainly the first and only one in Bloomington, maybe even in the entire state of Indiana, gleamed above. A sign with vaguely Chinese-looking black calligraphy announced that "Jerry Locksmith, Artist and Photographer" lived above.

Kaija looked around to make sure that no one was watching, took a deep breath, and ascended.

A very tall, powerful, sleepy man answered her knock. Dressed in paint-stained faded jeans and a white undershirt, which revealed muscular shoulders and arms covered with thick curly black hair, he seemed to fill the entire doorway. He ran his hands through his hair and massaged his temples while inspecting her.

"Mr. Locksmith, please."

"You're looking at him."

Kaija peered past him into the interior, where an easel, sketches, and paintings were spread out in a mostly empty white space. Cameras and spotlights were set up at the other end of the gleaming wood floor.

"*You* are Mr. Locksmith?" She had imagined an old man with a grumbling stomach.

"*Jerry* Locksmith. You're Magda's friend. Come in, come in. I really *was* waiting for you. I'll just wash up a bit. Have a cup of tea. Special order herbal all right? It's much better than Lipton."

He poured some bitter lukewarm tea into an ugly brown dragon-encrusted mug, handed it to her, and disappeared behind sheets billowing from ceiling-high clothes lines. She could hear running water, a flushing toilet, and more water. Kaija tried to pretend she did not hear these private sounds, just as she would have if she were waiting for someone sitting across from her to finish a phone conversation. But she was keenly aware of Jerry's activities as she studied photos of various dark-haired, big-breasted women, semi-nude and nude.

Kaija was relieved that Magda did not appear among these, nor was she in another series which featured fully-clothed women on bicycles. Most of were of a slender silver-blonde, thoughtful-looking young woman pedaling away from the photographer, ever larger distances separating them as she followed her own path.

Moody landscapes were displayed above a platform holding a mattress with a tightly drawn white bedspread and immaculate pillows. Either Jerry Locksmith had stopped to make the bed when she knocked, or he slept so gingerly he did not rumple anything.

Kaija was thrilled to be in the studio of a real artist, of course, yet something was not quite right. Maybe it was that his living quarters were so tidy, which did not fit the myth of the unconventional genius bursting with creative male energy about which she had learned in Art Appreciation. Even the paint tubes on his worktable, an oversize door set on sawhorses, were lined up in straight rows.

Jerry was all business when he returned. He motioned Kaija to sit, commended her for wearing her dark red cashmere sweater, which he said would make a terrific contrast to her oval face, and ordered her to smile and then to "look soulful" while he arranged lamps and tested cameras.

"But that sweater has its limits, honey," he sighed. "These poses will be all right for the toothless old guys who want to hire you, but otherwise bare shoulders are a must. You want some pictures for your boyfriend, don't you? The lucky sod. Let's do something snappier. And something for yourself too, to look at when you're old. There aren't many young women with your shining intelligence."

Kaija glowed with pleasure. Here was an artist, an American, and a man at least seven years older than she, and he spoke to her as if she were his equal. Even more important, he had recognized her intelligence, which she relied on, but which most people ignored.

Jerry reached into a drawer in the platform under his bed and pulled out a large piece of blue velvet.

"If you drape this right, it'll look just like a formal," he said as he accompanied her into his immaculately clean all-white bathroom. He motioned to a large glass jar holding cotton balls.

"You might need a few of these," he said casually as he lifted the lid.

Kaija turned away to hide the blush spreading over her neck and chest. He had gauged accurately the size of her breasts and had guessed that she needed help.

Kaija tried to feel grateful that Jerry was so matter-of-fact, indeed so professional, as she locked the bathroom door. She maneuvered three cotton balls under each breast and adjusted the square of velvet. She might as well inspect the bathroom while she waited for her blush to subside.

A small print of the silver-blonde, ethereal young woman on the bicycle was taped to the lower corner of the mirror. She must be Jerry's all-important first love, though she looked as if she needed no one at all. Kaija wished she were equally self-confident instead of worried about Jerry's opinion of her.

She could not resist opening the mirrored cabinet. At first she noticed nothing interesting except that the combs and brushes looked very expensive. Several bottles of medicine told her nothing beyond the fact that they contained neither aspirin nor Alka-Seltzer.

But taped to the inside of the door of the medicine cabinet was a poem clipped from a book or magazine. The last line, "I burst inside you like a screaming rocket," stunned her. By every standard she had been taught in her English classes it was a badly *written* poem, but someone had actually dared to speak in a way she assumed was very explicit about sex, and furthermore someone else had dared publish it—all at a time when professors bragged how daring they were if they owned a single copy of the unexpurgated edition of *Lady Chatterley's Lover* smuggled into the United States from France.

"Terrific," Jerry said when she took her seat under the glaring lights, "but you could go lower." Afraid of dislodging the cotton balls, Kaija moved her bra a sixteenth of an inch.

"Lower," Jerry said while focusing the camera. "Lower, and lower yet," he motioned. "We want some good cheesecake here."

Finally, he sighed, stepped in front of the camera, and began adjusting the blue velvet. Kaija held her breath and hoped that would keep her nipples from popping out and cotton balls spilling all over the floor.

Jerry put his hands, their backs covered with black hair, on her upper chest and stroked her collar-bone with his thumbs.

"Don't worry. I'm just cooling you down, baby," he said as his hands moved lower. "I want to make sure this won't show," he said placing his palms on the bright flush in her décolletage. Magda had told her that was sign Number Two, but Jerry had probably always known that.

"There, all cool and collected again," Jerry said as he raised his hands to her cheeks, lifted her face to his, and kissed her. This was so surprising that Kaija forgot to close her eyes, and for the first time she noticed long narrow scars on the inside of both his wrists.

"What happened to you?" she blurted.

"A troop transfer in Korea that got out of hand," he shrugged dismissively. He stuck his hands into the back pockets of his already tight jeans.

The kiss had traveled like electricity through her body, searing her nipples, and threatening to topple her from the high stool on which she perched. The room took on a kind of fuzzy other-worldliness in which she could move only very slowly and think hardly at all. She was in a state like that of sex-dazed ducks who waddle into the paths of speeding cars every spring.

Jerry was back behind his tripod as if nothing had happened. Shouldn't he say something after such a significant action? Would he ask her for a date? Did he want to be her boyfriend? Was he beginning to fall in love with her? But he only peered into his camera and clicked away.

"Neat," he said finally, using the current term of high approbation. "I think I've captured your intensity and your intelligence. And the repressed passion too, but that won't last, the repression, that is. Stay right there."

He disappeared into the bathroom again. Kaija could hear the door of the medicine cabinet slamming and water running, but no flushing.

He returned smiling and very animated.

"Now tell me, Kaija, just what are you going to do with those brains of yours?"

"I'm going to be a doctor. Surgeon probably."

He whistled. "Really? You? A doctor? I have to hand it to you, honey. You've got guts. Ever read Emma Goldman?"

Kaija had not heard of her or of any other woman intellectual except Simone de Beauvoir, and that was because she was Sartre's girlfriend and the word "existentialism" floated through conversations in the Student Union.

"No," she said.

"Then you should. She was the most important woman of her day, an anarchist, a revolutionary, and an advocate of free love. She had a terrific way of putting things. She said she wouldn't join any revolution that didn't allow her to dance."

He spoke with approval instead of implying that she was not a normal woman.

"My father . . . er . . . my old man has that quotation on the wall in his studio. He's an artist too, very successful as a matter of fact. He's in the decadent East, but not in the Village, not even in New York. He's no Jackson Pollock. My mother is a DAR, he met her at the West Chester Country Club. He's got a studio in Andrew Wyeth country, lots of stone fences, good fences make good neighbors."

The allusion to Robert Frost's "Mending Wall" was the only item Kaija could have identified correctly on a multiple-choice test.

When she said nothing, Jerry started bombarding her with questions. How did she plan to rebel against "the System?" Did she think that the suburbs, with their "little boxes made out of ticky-tacky" were ugly or did she long to live in a house with a white picket fence? Was she reading Kerouac, Ayn Rand, or both? Had any of her friends gone "on the road?" Where would she go if given the chance?

"Nowhere. I'm staying right here. I want to get my education."

"Good," he nodded approvingly. "Don't buy into that self-indulgence and irresponsibility of the Beats, that's all it is, believe me."

Kaija was disconcerted again. She had expected that an artist would approve of unconventional behavior.

"Would you like to take your bra off now?" Jerry asked as casually as if he were offering her another cup of his bitter lukewarm tea.

"No," she said firmly, though she did not succeed in mimicking the outrage of girls in her dorm.

"That's too bad. But all is not lost, you're basically a brains and legs girl anyway. This will be much better."

He produced a pair of fishnet stockings attached to a pair of short black satin shorts.

"Put this on," he ordered.

Kaija obediently retreated to the bathroom and took off her garter belt, stockings, and slip. Easing into Jerry's theatrical garment, she learned to pull one stocking part way up before starting on the other. She marveled at not having to deal with clumsy hooks and snaps. In the days before pantyhose, Jerry's strange contraption felt wonderfully liberating. She rearranged the cotton balls in her bra and checked her reflection in the mirror.

She had no idea why she was going along with Jerry's costume changes instead of declaring that she was insulted and storming out. She had experienced war, she had read and admired Wilfred Owen and other World War I poets in her English class, and Jerry had been scarred by war, but Kaija did not see a unifying meaning between these disparate facts.

Obeying orders from male professionals partially explained her compliance, but mostly, she was curious. Here was a man— older, bigger, more muscular, and sexier than the man with the eye-patch in the Hathaway shirt ads—talking to her as if she were a sophisticated adult. What would he say and do next? If only his paints were not lined up so straight, everything would be perfect.

Kaija's mother talked about great artists but not bourgeois painters of limited talent, with long lines of wealthy and conservative backers behind them, who only gave the appearance of rebellion. Kaija knew that Van Gogh continued to paint obsessively when no one bought his paintings, but she had no idea that other artists engaged in self-promotion, advertising, and marketing. Nor had she noticed that Jerry's moody watercolors were identical with each other rather than subtly varied like Monet's haystacks and water lilies.

"You're a very curious person, Kaija, very interesting," Jerry murmured. "Curious in the most basic sense too. I heard you open that bathroom cabinet."

Kaija blushed below her décolletage. But Jerry was not comparing her to American girls and finding her lacking. He did not seem to hold her to any standard of good behavior.

"It's all right," he laughed. "I liked you doing that. I would've done it myself. Want to come to a party with me at Clayton Eschelman's place tonight? He's a poet."

"No. I can't. I'm sorry."

"Ah yes, the boyfriend. I forgot about him. You could come without telling him, but you'd probably feel guilty."

"Yes, I would," Kaija said, although she had not thought of Maris except once, when Jerry mentioned photos for the boyfriend.

"Terrific legs, Kaija, really great. Glance back at me over your shoulder. Look at me as if you want me to make a pass. That's right. Better than the famous photo of Betty Grable in her white one-piece swimsuit. Let's do some Marlene Dietrich shots next."

Jerry handed Kaija a top-hat and cane. "Turn around. Bend over. Step up there."

185

When Kaija came to herself, more or less, she was standing on top of the table. Jerry's camera was pointing up at her crotch, and his hand was on her inner thigh. The voice of male authority had systematically guided her into this ridiculous position.

"Drop those panties," Jerry said.

Kaija jerked her legs together. She would break her ankle if she jumped in her high heels. She squatted, then slithered down gracelessly. How had she gotten herself into this ridiculous position when Magda had posed for Jerry with no problems? What had Kaija done to be humiliated like this?

She slammed and locked the bathroom door behind her, pulled her sweater and skirt over Jerry's stockings and shorts combo, and stuffed her underwear into her coat pockets. She stood for a moment, shifting the cotton balls from hand to hand. Finally, she flushed them down the toilet. She had to get out of here before it overflowed, or something more dreadful happened.

"Please excuse me," Kaija said politely, "I must go." She kept her voice steady while she prayed silently to no one, "Please, please, let me get past him without being stopped. Please let me not get attacked, raped, murdered, decapitated, hacked into pieces, stuffed into bureau drawers, flushed down the toilet. Please."

"It was nice to meet you, Jerry," she smiled to appease him.

"You can give that stuff you're wearing to Magda," he said. "But I expect you'll be back yourself."

"Maybe," Kaija said.

"No means maybe, maybe means yes," Jerry laughed. "I'll have your prints ready next week, Kaija. But come back anytime. I'll be here when it gets too boring for you out there," he called after her.

"Fat chance," Kaija muttered when her feet were safely on the sidewalk.

Back at the dorm, she marched straight into Magda's room. She was angry with her, though not sure why.

"How'd it go?" Magda asked without glancing up from *Photoplay*, her favorite movie magazine.

"Oh, I don't know," Kaija replied sullenly.

Magda looked at her. "Oh, Kaija, I can see you're upset. He must have asked you to take off your clothes."

"Yes, he did," she exploded. "Why didn't you warn me? Why did you let me go? Why didn't you stop me? Why . . . ."

"Because you wanted to," Magda said simply.

"Don't be angry with me, Kaija," Magda said, jumping up to hug her. "Did anything really terrible happen?"

Kaija could not explain exactly what *had* happened. She had liked Jerry kissing her, but she did not want to learn that he had kissed Magda too and made extravagant declarations of love to her because she was so very beautiful.

"Oh . . . nothing."

"Did he ask you to drop your panties while you were on top of that table?"

"Oh, yes. Yes, he did." Magda asked questions which others would not dare to hint at.

"And you're the one who's always lecturing about three feet on the ground," Magda laughed.

"Please, Magda, be serious. It was so awkward . . . so . . . so terribly embarrassing."

"Yes, of course. But how can we ever learn anything otherwise? Didn't you find it fascinating?"

Kaija could not deny that she had.

"There, I knew you would. Jerry really appreciates women."

Magda was the only person who spoke as if women had some kind of group identity. Kaija believed that Magda called women "we" rather than "they" because her English was not yet perfect.

"Curiosity about women is very sexy in a man, as is self-confidence. Anyway, why not give a man a little pleasure? Artists have to have inspiration. A famous Hungarian painter I know is still painting women's breasts and bottoms, and he's over eighty. He asked my mother to show him her navel at a reception for the Pope."

"Did you read that screaming rocket poem, Magda?"

"Yes," Magda blew out a string of tiny smoke rings, gazed thoughtfully into the darkness outside, and produced a literary evaluation contradicting Kaija's. "A very bad poem, I think. Beautifully *written*, of course, but the writer has no experience. A man isn't a screaming rocket inside a woman. There just isn't enough room for all that zooming and screeching."

20

Usually everyone slept late, but the Saturday following Kaija's encounter with Jerry, she was propelled out of bed by doors slamming and people running. A dozen girls in baby doll pajamas were out on the sidewalk below her window.

"You can't be here without any clothes," Martha Smith hissed. "Get back. Now."

She flapped her arms as if shooing chickens.

"There's nothing to see. Get inside this minute. Get. Hurry up, or I'll have every one of you in front of the Student Disciplinary Board. This is an order."

Martha advanced on them, but even so, the girls could not have retreated more slowly.

A van backed up, and a uniformed driver opened the back doors. A few minutes later, two policemen carried out a stretcher. From the casual, even careless way they handled it and by the blanket covering the face, Kaija could tell that it held no one alive. A girl in the dorm—someone who went to classes, worried about clothes, and daydreamed about love, just like Kaija—was now nothing more than a corpse lashed to canvas and wood. Like Stella, Kaija's friend who had died four years ago, another girl had died in a time of peace, not war.

The name of the dead girl was Grace.

She was a senior majoring in music. Although rich enough to join any sorority, she had chosen to be GDI, a God Damned Independent, as Kaija and the few others who did not belong to "Greek" organizations were called.

Given to dressing in black turtlenecks and full skirts, Grace wore her long hair loose and straight. Sometimes she pinned it up, and then she looked otherworldly, a Rossetti beauty with black

189

tendrils framing a pale oval face and green eyes, who had been incongruously set down in the American Midwest in the 1950s.

Martha Smith had called Grace "maladjusted" when she tried to talk Kaija into joining a sorority. Sororities and fraternities had to maintain a C average, and competition for the best grades was keen, at least among sororities. Girls who had not glanced at Kaija earlier were eager to have her on their premises because of her straight A's. Kaija did not have the money that belonging to a sorority required, and she had seen the tears, threats of suicide, and withdrawals from school of girls who were black-balled, and she had hardened her heart against the whole system.

Grace laughed when she called the doctors at the Health Center dirty old men. Had Magda not arrived to conveniently take on the role of scapegoat, Grace would have been labeled the Scarlet Woman of the Women's Quad.

Rumors had circulated earlier that Grace, at age fifteen, had run off with her boyfriend to get married in Kentucky, where girls of twelve were supposedly married off to toothless old men of seventy and forced to produce one baby after another in isolated mountain cabins. But Grace's mother had followed the lovers to a motel and rescued her daughter.

The boyfriend existed all right. Grace's mother had not intimidated him enough to stay away. He roared up to the Women's Quad, jumped off his motorcycle, ran a comb through his ducktail, and shouted up at Grace's window. She ran down the stairs, flew into his arms, and laughed as he whirled her around. The spurs of his boots jangled as he kicked the starter and whisked her away.

Otherwise, Grace was solitary. She spent most of her time practicing her flute in the old Music Hall behind the Women's Quad. Whenever lonely sounds speaking of immense distances and remote mountains floated through open windows, Kaija imagined that Grace was the one playing.

Kaija had wanted to run straight to Maris one night as she watched Grace and her boyfriend in the circle of lamplight. The tips of Grace's fingers rested lightly on his; she seemed to float as he slowly turned her with him. Kaija did not think then of her as a little

190

girl who had trudged dutifully to ballet lessons and learned to stand painfully on her toes. Grace seemed enchanted, her sleek voluptuous body like a black swan's in some long-forgotten fairy tale. She stepped closer to the boy, and he rested his chin on top of her head. He pinned her arms to her sides and held her, his totally willing captive. They swayed together for a long time. It was languorous and very beautiful.

Kaija did not trust herself to put this image into words at what was, in effect, a wake for Grace. It would mean that she saw beauty in behavior which had led Grace to her terrible death. For Grace had not died in some *Liebestodt,* committing suicide because of love. Nor had he killed her because he "loved her too much" to let her go on living without him, a seductive poisonous romantic notion endorsed by trashy novels. Grace's death was sordid.

"A-b-o-r-t-i-o-n," a girl who had seen her corpse whispered. The dreaded word spelled out, like d-i-v-o-r-c-e before children. Terror, nakedness, blood, and shame.

"Did she do it herself?"
"Did someone else?"
"Coat hanger, needle, or crocheting hook?"
"Hot baths or steep stairs?"
"Vodka or gin?"
"Jumping off tables?"
"Running uphill?"
"Bicycling?"
"Skating?"
"Falling down stairs?"
"Did she do it herself?"
"Who did it then?"
"Doctor or nurse?"
"Some back alley hack?"
"Maybe her boyfriend?"
"He wouldn't dare."
"Wouldn't know how."

But wouldn't he? The horror of the boyfriend pushing a coat-hanger between Grace's legs silenced everyone.

"He is the one who brought her back to the dorm."
"Where is he now?"
"He's run away."
"Hope that they find him."
"Put him in jail."
"That won't bring her back."
"Where did she go?"
"I wonder to whom?"
"Who does things like that?"

Silence to this, but Kaija wanted to know.

"Really, where *did* she go?"
"That doctor on Kirkland who gives out shots?"
"That dentist with tablets?"
"That Brown County quack?"
"Who finally found her?" Kaija asked
"Grace's mother called, and Martha Smith checked."
"She saw Grace was dead."
"Face down on the floor."
"Curled in a ball."
"In pools of blood."
"Her hands smeared with blood."
"Blood on her legs."
"Blood in her hair."
"Naked herself."
"Her feet blue and cold."
"Hair over her face."
"Must've wanted to hide."
"Must've known she'd been bad."
"Must've been sorry."
"Must've been scared."
"She was alone."
"She was so alone."

Sex was compelling and beautiful and deadly. What had happened to Grace could happen to anyone.

For a week or so the girls were gentle with each other. They spoke less and listened to replies to "How are you?" But then, so slowly as to be imperceptible, they withdrew from each other and turned back to the boys and men in their lives. The girls might be scared, they might be ashamed of what they had done in the dark, but at least their boyfriends knew the truth about them.

Lost Midsummers

21

Magda wedged her toes apart with chunks of a sanitary napkin and began applying Fire and Ice nail polish. She turned up "Heartbreak Hotel" on the radio when Kaija suggested that she change into a skirt and blouse for dinner.

Magda regularly ignored the dress code. She went to dinner wearing slacks and with her hair in pin curls, which was permitted only on Saturday mornings. She did not bother to squeeze herself into the required church-going dress or prim suit for lunch on Sundays, and she wore heels on weekdays when loafers or saddle-shoes were in order. But she turned into a combination of sharp trial lawyer and tear-stained Oliver Twist holding out an empty bowl whenever anyone tried to reprimand her.

"Yes, but *why* won't you give me breakfast just because I'm wearing my robe? I have a nightgown under here, see? I'm more covered up than you. American girls go out on dates in dresses without straps, their breasts pop out for boys to see. Moreover, you do not have a legal right to cancel my meal ticket. But why, oh why, do you refuse to feed me? Why do you want me to starve? As a child in war-torn Europe I was so emaciated I almost died, and now you deny me food here, in America, in peace and prosperity."

Kaija was taken aback by her boldness, but secretly she sided with her. Who were they to tell Magda how to dress? They had no idea who Magda was or what she had done. Magda had not cowered in fear when Russians killed three thousand of her countrymen during the Hungarian Revolution. Wearing a striped jersey, she had stood on tanks and helped raise the Hungarian flag. Women as well as men had been mesmerized by her radiant beauty. They had not snickered then about dark hair curling in her armpit, as the girls in the dorm did.

195

Magda had shared danger with unshaven, hollow-eyed young men in scuffed leather jackets and black turtlenecks. Following defeat, they had traveled towards the border, moving cautiously only at dusk, hiding under bridges and in ruined barns. She had made love with doomed revolutionaries behind rough barricades; she had slept entwined with world-weary poets in fragrant hay while sharp hail hammered on the roofs of barns. It was nobody's business what Magda wore, though Kaija did wonder what Magda had done to get her sable coat.

Kaija hungered to learn about love and revolution, about the inevitable defeat and the loss of freedom and hope. But Magda talked very little about the past. She was a hero no longer. She had risked everything, but her side was defeated. Now she was an undistinguished immigrant from some unnamed country which was part of the Soviet Union. Like Kaija, she could not go home again. But in order to survive in the female world of the dorms, Magda could not speak the truth.

"We were comrades only," she would say. "We fought to reclaim our dear native country from totalitarian communism. I would never go all the way, believe me."

Despite such sanitizing postscripts, by now Magda's virginity seemed as fictional as Doris Day's. The other girls called her a slut out loud rather than whispering it behind her back, and Kaija blushed to imagine what the fraternity boys said. She suspected that Magda's name and phone number, which she shared, were scribbled above urinals in men's rooms all over the campus.

"Tell those dumb fraternity boys to get lost, Magda. Why don't you spend more time with the Hungarians?" Kaija asked. "Why are they the only men you don't you find romantic?"

Kaija adored the Hungarians. They were intelligent, moody, given to abstract talk about the absurdity of life and the logic of suicide. They were only in their early twenties, but Kaija, barely out of the teens herself, thought of them as fully adult men who understood politics and lived with disillusionment. If they felt vulnerable as they tried to make their way in a foreign country, they kept their fears and nightmares to themselves.

The Hungarians were serious about studying, but they also danced well, and they knew waltzes, polkas, and tangos, which were no longer popular among Americans. They were confident in their masculinity the way American boys were not; not one of them, even if a foot shorter, hesitated to ask Kaija to dance or to go for a walk. Like young Latvians, they sometimes drank too much, but Kaija was familiar with that, and she liked their company.

"I don't find the Hungarians sexy because I *know* them, Kaija. They are my dear friends and fellow freedom fighters," Magda intoned.

"Don't you think you should be more careful or stay in more at night?"

"I *am* careful, Kaija. I am in fact very *discriminating*. I choose *whom* I see. The girls are *inferring* something which I am not *implying*. See, I stayed awake in my English class today. You better worry about what's-her-name instead."

"Who?"

"That boring friend of yours, the one with the flat face and frizzy hair. You know, the one with the fascist politics." Magda was pretending she had forgotten Alma's name, and Kaija would not validate this unfair description of her friend by supplying it.

"*Whom* are you talking about?" Kaija asked, imitating Magda's exaggerated emphasis.

"Alma, of course."

"Alma is not a fascist."

"Republican then. Plus, she believes men have the right to do what they like. She waits on her father from his knees to head. She'll worship the first man who looks at her; she'll crawl on stones if her husband orders because she thinks marriage is Happy Ending. She's the one you should warn to be careful. I have excellent judgment, Kaija. I know what's for fun and what's dangerous."

Magda's prediction had a ring of truth. Kaija doubted that Alma and Ivars would be happy forever, so she changed the subject abruptly.

"I'll be back late, Magda. I have study hall."

Kaija had spent the afternoon making posters. "Get all A's this semester!" "Make the Honor Roll!" they exhorted.

As Chairman of the Scholarship Committee of her dorm, Kaija supervised the cramming sessions which took place after hours during midterms and finals. Considered fully trustworthy, she had been given a key to the Tudor-style building that housed the dining hall. She would take attendance, shush whisperers, and lock up at midnight. Afterward she was expected go to the side door of her dorm, ring the bell, and wait in the deserted courtyard for Head Resident Martha Smith to let her in. To simply give a key to the dorm to someone as responsible as Kaija was out of the question.

Girls who missed the 10:30 lock-up on school nights and 12:30 on weekends had to use this remote door too. Martha Smith took her time answering, making the miscreants wait and worry before she let them in and handed out late slips. Three of these pink forms meant an obligatory appearance before a Student Disciplinary Board and possible expulsion from the University. Kaija had worried that Magda would be hauled in front of this Board, but after one or two false starts she seemed to have mastered getting back on time.

Another door in Kaija's dorm, much closer to the dining room, was never used after dark. A whole mystique attached to this door and to the electrical wires running from a light switch to a fixture above. Rumor had it that these wires snaked secretly all the way through the building and into Martha Smith's remote bedroom. Opening this door after hours would trip a loud warning bell and a flashing red light. One girl claimed she had actually seen such a light while she waited for Martha to write out her pink slip. Electricity was dangerous and mysterious, liks sex.

The campus was kept "romantically dark" at night. Although nervous rumors about frightening encounters circulated occasionally, no one demanded additional lights because the University was assumed to be a safe haven. On weekend nights girls were supposed to be on dates and therefore under male protection, or they were expected to stay in decent seclusion in their rooms if no one had asked them out. Women students going about alone or

198

in pairs to movies, restaurants, or the Student Union on date nights were so rare as to cause stares and harrassing comments.

The boys seemed to disappear after hours as well. Sometimes male voices singing "The Sweetheart of Sigma Chi" or "I Love You Truly" rose out of the tree and shrub-filled darkness in the center of the Women's Quad. For brief moments the songs caressed everyone, but then they focused to a girl newly "pinned" to a fraternity boy and lingered there before they receded, faded, and died. Though free to roam all night at will, the "college men" and "nice boys" seemed to vanish then too. Their joyful exuberance, drunken shouts, and angry scuffles did not permeate the confines of the Women's Quad.

Night and silence reigned, though the dark was never really empty. Other, more dangerous men were out there, somewhere. They sharpened knives, checked ropes and knots, hid ghoulish faces behind masks, drew on rubber gloves. Devious and murderous, they could slither down walls, pounce in alleys, muffle pleas for help, and do the unspeakable. Girl Talk had also informed the young women of their dark natures: deep down they supposedly longed for sordid encounters, and they could unwittingly force men to act out their worst compulsions.

Kaija was not thinking of these things as she walked across the courtyard filled with trees and shrubs, the corners shadowy with rustling ivy. Two or three lamp-posts, placed at considerable distance from each other, held only dim single bulbs, but the diamond-pattern panes of the huge windows of the dining room blazed with lights.

Armed with sign-up sheets to record arrival and departure times so that no girl would sneak off for an hour of kissing with her boyfriend, Kaija clattered down the broad stairs. In spite of her posters, fewer than a dozen girls had bothered to come. Only the brains and a few others desperate to get off academic probation were spread throughout the huge room. These included Slavena Jones, whom Kaija was determined to ignore.

Kaija set out her books, opened her notes on John Stuart Mill's *On Liberty,* and tried to concentrate. But soon her eyes closed, and she was with Maris in the rain. He took both of her hands, kissed the palms, and drew them inside his rain-coat and onto his nipples, erect from excitement and the chilly night air. The branches of lilacs were bare, but the air was full of fragrance. Mixed up with this memory of Maris was the faint, not entirely unwelcome imprint of Jerry's hands on her collarbones.

Kaija turned to her notes, but her mind wandered. How had Harriet Taylor, mentioned ever so briefly in the Introduction to *On Liberty*, found the opportunity to carry on with the great philosopher while married to another man? How had she dared? According to Kaija's history text, the Victorian Period had been the Dark Ages for women; fortunately, everyone had come a very long way since then.

Something shimmered just outside Kaija's line of vision. Was she getting one of her rare migraine headaches? That would be a disaster at the start of exams. But she sensed neither the tightness nor the rising nausea which preceded these attacks. In fact, although she had a vague feeling she was being watched, she felt particularly well.

Her uneasiness was Slavena Jones' fault. Oh no, not again, Kaija groaned as Slavena grinned foolishly, moistened her lips, and flicked her tongue. Because of a childhood illness or accident, Slavena wore a wig, a horrid artifact with white cotton backing and rusty threads showing through thin matted hairs. Bouffant shiny wigs as an essential fashion accessory had not reached southern Indiana yet. Slavena's dingy white blouse and shapeless pilled cardigan showed that she had long ago given up all hope of being pretty.

Ordinarily Kaija would feel sympathy for someone so pathetic, but Slavena had pestered her one time too many. Smiling hopefully, Slavena used to slide into the seat next to her at dinner or walk into her room without knocking. Phrases like "as Europeans we both agree" and "as our common European background makes inevitable" punctuated her chatter. Kaija was outraged. How dare Slavena assume an affinity between them? Slavena had been born in the United States; her mother was Russian, but that did not count as European. Because of their brutality, rapes, vandalism, and filthy toilet habits, after the war Russians were regarded as uncultured barbarians by Europeans. Kaija would die of embarrassment if someone confused her with a Russian.

Slavena opened Kaija's books, fingered her clothes, and polished her few pieces of costume jewelry, which she moistened with spittle. When Kaija, disgusted, washed her necklace later, she noticed that her imitation garnet pin was missing. She could not believe at first that Slavena had taken it. Why would she when she so badly wanted to be friends? It required a real effort for Kaija to confront her.

Slavena denied possession, and Kaija became so enraged she wanted to take off a shoe and beat her about the ears. Although the enforced proximity in the dorms could produce surprisingly intensive feelings, Kaija was shocked by her rage.

In a cold judgmental voice, she threatened Slavena with every authority she could think: the Head Resident; the Dean of Women; parents; newspaper reporters; the police; and, the Student Disciplinary Board. Slavena looked so defeated when she handed back the pin and two pairs of missing cotton panties that Kaija almost regretted terrifying her. But when Slavena produced the amber pendant Kaija's mother had given her, Kaija was furious all over.

They had not spoken since, yet here was Slavena again, grinning and lolling her tongue. She need not think that she could keep Kaija on edge. Kaija would show her that an industrious Latvian would triumph over a lazy Russian every time. She made up her mind to concentrate, and the flickering movements off to her side subsided.

Kaija came back to her surroundings as other students were gathering books, signing out, and drifting away. It was 12:20, ten minutes to closing time. Only Slavena, tongue between parted lips, was still absorbed in her work. She looked like a little girl trying to do her best.

Kaija walked to the window and cranked it open. Light from the dining room illumined the immediate area, but corners and ivied walls remained shadowy. Suddenly she felt exposed. Anyone outside could see that she was almost alone in the otherwise deserted building. She craned her neck to make sure no one was in the courtyard, but either the window-screen prevented her from having a full view or it was empty.

Clouds scudded across the moon, a branch tapped against glass on the other side, and something stirred, rhythmical and slow. Kaija jumped as a branch or a trailing vine loosened by wind flicked away.

"Want me to wait? I'll walk back with you," Slavena offered.

"No. You go on. I'm not ready." Kaija made a show of studying her sign-up sheets.

"Please. I'd like to walk with you," Slavena said meekly.

If Kaija let her, Slavena would be on her doorstep again, like a scrawny mewing cat. Kaija refused to have that, especially since she wondered now whether Slavena's school-girl crush was not better explained by Magda's, "crazy in love with you."

"I have other things to do," Kaija said importantly.

Slavena's expectant smile collapsed, and Kaija hardened her heart once more against the girl who was even more an outsider than she was. She turned her back while Slavena tiptoed out.

Slowly, like well-defined lines and distinct shapes rising through clear liquid to reveal the image in a developing photograph, everything coalesced. Kaija's brain clicked on to alert. Instead of daydreaming about Maris and the scent of lilacs and fretting about Slavena's pathetic attempts at friendship, she should have paid attention. A man was masturbating right next to the window.

Kaija's body language must have signaled that she had finally seen him because he turned sideways, forcing her to have a full view.

Kaija froze. The rapes she had seen during the war were part of her paralysis, but this sordid threat was enough by itself. He was forcing this repulsive intimate interaction on her. Her heart pounded, obliterating every other sound.

Frantically she scanned information from Girl Talk: this timid stranger would not hurt her; he would be grateful for her attention; he would go away if she was nice. If she told him that she was impressed by his naked organ, he would leave.

But cutting-edge scientific knowledge did not triumph so easily. Kaija's imagination shifted into high gear in direct contradiction to Girl Talk. She saw a knife slashing her face, a nylon stocking tightening around her throat, and repulsive hands forcing apart her legs. Kaija, who wanted to be a doctor and to dispel ignorance, was failing her first real test.

She had to say something. If she did not, she could not hope to bring the light of reason to matters of life and death. She would never convince an ignorant mother that her child must be vaccinated or that the throat of a choking man had to be cut open to save his life. She would not be able to live with herself if she abandoned scientific knowledge.

She gathered all her will power and leaned towards the screen.

"You out there," she said, pleased that her voice did not shake. "You can go home now. I've seen it."

No reply.

"I've seen it, you can go home," she repeated.

She knew she should add, "It's very impressive," or some other compliment because he must be waiting for that, but her vocal chords refused to announce this lie. Maybe that was just as well. Any compliment would sound mocking.

"Thank you," she nodded in the general direction of the man and cranked the window shut.

She would give him ten minutes to zip his pants and leave. There was no other exit except where he had stationed himself, and that very spot was tainted.

But her fears kept rising: he had been watching and plotting for hours, he knew a lot more about her than she did about him, he might not leave, and he might have an accomplice. No matter how hard she tried, she could not believe that he was a vulnerable, timid soul whom she had to flatter and pity.

Be rational, she told herself. The worst that could happen would be that he exposed himself again. She knew she could keep herself from throwing up by resolutely thinking of something else, as she had done the day she had to dissect the eye of a pig in biology class. Later she had summoned her will power, turned aside her face, and efficiently cleaned up the vomit of a male classmate.

Judging that enough time had passed, she picked up her books, locked the dining room, and strode decisively to the switch. The bulbs in the stairwell went off too, and she began to grope her way up. The very faint light through the stained-glass panels above the doors assured her that she would soon be outside.

But as she took the next step, she careened into something solid and alive. He was here, in the stairwell, blocking her path. For a moment she lost control of her limbs altogether. Then, sensing that he was holding onto the banister too, she veered abruptly to her left rather than grappling with him face to face as he must have expected. She bent down as he flailed for her higher up, slipped under his arm, bounded up the rest of the steps, and threw herself against the door. To her elation, it yielded. If she could get into her dorm, she would be safe.

But rage succeeded terror. She did not have a key to the front door or to the nearest door either. No one had trusted her; no one had cared enough about her to give it to her. The stupid rules would allow him to kill her while Martha Smith followed her usual practice of punishing late comers by dawdling before she opened up.

The door slammed as, trying to regain his advantage, he grabbed her from behind. He was taller and more powerful than she. His arm shot across her throat, and she felt herself being jerked back against him. Information from Girl Talk and her own intuition vied with each other as she frantically tried to decide what to do: should she fight and try to get away, which would make him angrier and "excite him more," or should she be nice to him, flatter him, "treat him as a person?"

Intuition won over cutting-edge research. She squirmed, struggled, scratched, writhed, and kicked. When all that failed, she bit as hard as she could into the pale hairy flesh of his arm.

The man cursed and loosened his grip slightly. She bit down harder, craving to draw blood, to sever muscle and nerve. She was trying to keep her teeth clamped together as he flung her from him.

She righted herself against a tree and turned to face him. Nothing up to this point had come as close to undoing her.

He was faceless.

She could not make out a nose or lips, only cruel slits for eyes. Here was the phantom killer of all nightmares. Even as she slowly realized he was wearing a woman's stocking for a mask, her terror increased. Whose stocking was it? What had he done to the woman who had worn it? Where did he bury the women he killed?

Holding the length of another nylon stocking as a noose, he advanced on her. There was no way she could win. She had no place to run, and he was not human. He was pure evil; he could and would do what he wanted. A growling chant, rhythmic and terrifying, rose from behind his mask.

Kaija could just make out his muffled words. "You bitch, you bitch, you fucking bitch, who do you think you are, trying to humiliate me like that? How dare you say, thanks, I've seen it? You bitch, you bitch, you fucking bitch . . . . "

And then, as if there were no end to horror, she felt something move to her right. The monster was not alone; his vile accomplices were with him. Kaija tried to summon an image of her mother and prepared herself to die.

A hand other than his touched her arm.

"You, mister, you get away from her," Magda hissed. "I've called the police."

Magda's small strong hand closed on Kaija's, her other arm went around her waist, and she half-pulled, half-carried Kaija to the side door with the red light and the alarm. The man started after them.

"Get away from here, you stinking pervert, you filthy old man, the police will beat you until you're black, they'll hang you, they'll fry your particles in the electric chair, you devil criminal, you!" Magda spat.

Neither flashing lights nor warning bells erupted as Kaija entered through the forbidden door, which Magda had propped open with a hairbrush. Magda deftly removed the brush, pulled the door closed, pushed Kaija down to sit on the stairs, and put her hand over Kaija's mouth to indicate she should not speak. They clutched each other until Kaija's trembling slowed.

Magda motioned once more for Kaija to be quiet, propped open the door, and peeked out. Seeing the courtyard empty for good, she glided out. She returned with Kaija's scattered books and papers, secured the door, and ushered her up the stairs.

With a warm blanket around her and two pills from Doctor Payne inside her, Kaija was finally able to speak.

"Thank you, Magda. Thank you for helping me." No Head Resident summoned by lights and bells had appeared even now. "How did you manage to open that door?"

Magda rummaged in her purse and pulled out a piece of bent wire. "With this. It's better than a key. I use it all the time."

This extremely serious infraction of the rules did not register on Kaija.

"Thank you, dear Magda, thank you," she said effusively. "You are so brave. You took a great risk coming out. He would've killed me if you hadn't come. You are a good friend."

"Shush, Kaija, you'd do the same for me. And anyway, I didn't come out, I was just coming home."

"Oh, Magda," Kaija said, but she was in no state to explain that it was very wrong to stay out past hours and to pick locks like a criminal.

Magda blew her nose, lit two cigarettes, and passed one to Kaija. Only then did Kaija realize Magda had been crying. Magda had been terrified, just like her.

"That man is terrible, very, very dangerous," she said, her voice trembling. "I saw him once before, beating his slimy eggs and peering into a window. He hates women. He'd kill us all if he could."

Magda's evaluation made more sense than all the theories Kaija had been taught. Intuition was more effective than Kaija's beloved science.

"The police . . . ?" Kaija began.

"Oh, I only said that to scare him. We can't call the police." Magda wiped her eyes and started to laugh. "Imagine, here is a very dangerous man, he wants to kill us, but we can't call the police because Martha will give us pink slips. He will murder a woman one day very soon, maybe he has already, but they will expel us if we say so. There was a man like him in Budapest, right after the war. He raped many young girls before they caught him. He tied their hands with barbed wire, and he cut crosses into their breasts and bellies. That's why they arrested him, because his hands were scarred. He claimed he was a holy man with stigmata. My mother told me all about it."

Kaija felt a prick of envy that Magda could discuss such essential subjects with her mother, but Doctor Payne's pills were carrying her off.

"The Head Resident . . . my attendance sheets . . . ," she murmured.

"Don't worry about it," Magda said.

By the time Kaija woke, Magda had informed Martha Smith that Kaija had a bladder infection but would stagger out of bed to do her duty, and the Head Resident had remembered that there were no bathrooms near the dining hall. Considering the sparse attendance, canceling the cramming sessions was judged no great loss, and Martha Smith herself took down Kaija's posters about straight A's and Honor Rolls. Kaija stayed in her room, grateful, for once, to be locked-in at night.

Lost Midsummers

22

Professor Waxman strode into the Chemistry lecture hall together with Maris, patted him on the shoulder, and climbed the steps to the lectern. Kaija smiled in welcome, but Maris only nodded and sat down in a seat across the aisle. He did not look at her again.

Kaija felt as if he had slapped her. She did not expect Maris to hug her or hold her hand, but this Monday morning she especially needed him to acknowledge, if ever so subtly, their last time together. A second fabulous kissing session had taken place between them in Maris' parents' dark living room on Saturday night, and they had once more parted chastely. They had not referred to their passionate time together on Sunday morning or Sunday night. They had in fact not touched until Maris' father dropped her off at her dorm. Then Maris had walked her to the door, kissed her palms, and held on to them as if he wanted their hands to grow together.

Kaija regretted greeting him enthusiastically just now. She wished she had acted equally remote and kept her dignity. She put her hands over her burning cheeks, trying to cool them.

But the established habits of a good student are useful. After a few minutes she focused her attention on Professor Waxman, who was well launched into one of his regular asides on the life of the doctor.

"It is impossible for the doctor to succeed all by himself. His parents, if they are comfortably middle class, or better yet wealthy, will have to make great sacrifices for his education. The doctor's wife—and hopefully he will choose a girl who will not insist on having babies right away—must also make her contribution. It is her responsibility to keep him well fed and undistracted by domestic worries. As his helpmate she must also contribute to family income by typing and other skills until he finishes his education and has a well-established practice. But now let's get back to the formulas from last week."

Kaija made an effort to concentrate on the chains of letters and numbers on the board. She glanced surreptitiously at Maris. Was he worrying about the same thing? His parents' income did not begin to approach middle class; they could never support him in medical school. Like her parents, they worried about being homeless again when they were too old to work.

After class, Maris fell easily into step with Kaija. Without speaking, they walked to the River Jordan, the creek winding through the campus, where they usually separated until Friday night. Maris looked pre-occupied, his eyes already on his dorm and away from Kaija.

"Aren't you going to say anything?" she blurted.

"About what?"

His cool tone infuriated her. Had he not yearned to sit next to her, with his shoulder brushing against hers? Did he not know that she was upset because Professor Waxman had said a doctor needed rich parents, plus a wife? Maris had not been very solicitous after the pervert had attacked her, and he did not worry about her grades as much as she did. But how dare he look as if they had never kissed, let alone kissed like that? Why did she have to be the one to bring up something that concerned them both? Kaija's anger turned easily against Maris rather than against any shadowy larger causes of her distress.

"Oh, not a damn thing, we don't have to talk about a Goddamn thing," she bristled. Profanity, never part of her vocabulary to begin with, had been taboo ever since boys had had to say all the girls' lines containing the word "damn" when they read aloud a modern play in English class at Shortridge.

Maris stopped, suddenly attentive. "What's the matter, Kaijin?" he asked softly.

Kaija glared at him, her cheeks flaming.

"Dearest, loveliest, my beloved Kaija, do you mean I should say something about us?"

These few words were all it took for Kaija's feelings to change. No wonder she adored him, he was so sensitive, so respectful, and so quick to understand what was important to her. She would always love him, no matter what. In the background, violins and cellos swelled into a popular song of the day.

Blow me a kiss from across the room
Say I look nice when I'm not
Touch my hair as you pass my chair
Little things mean a lot . . . .

He was so nice to her, and she was so unfair to be angry. He did not insist on a showdown with her parents but was giving them time to come to appreciate his good qualities. Unlike other boys, he did not smile ironically and hint that she was a lesbian when she told him she could not see him because she had promised to do something with Magda. Plus, she knew that he loved her. He had told her so Saturday night.

"Yes, Kaijin, you're right, we do need to talk."

He smoothed back her hair, held her face between his hands, and kissed her, in broad daylight, in the middle of the campus, with hundreds of students around them changing classes. With an effort, he let her go.

"Damn it, Kaija, I think we should get married."

He said it with anger, the words tearing out of him.

"And the sooner the better," he added in a tone of resignation.

When they had first met, they had both announced blithely that they would stay single until they were through medical school and established in their respective practices. Yet a great sadness descended on Kaija now because he was not overjoyed about being married to her.

Maris' face lit up. "Professor Waxman told me he'd help me get into any medical school I want, Kaijin."

For the second time this morning, Kaija felt as if she had been slapped. Envy and a sense of injustice silenced her. Maris had good grades but she had straight A's, Professor Waxman read aloud answers from her exams, he had used her experiment as a model of excellence, and he had told her she had a first class mind. But she was not sure that he actually knew who she was, in spite of having asked once to raise her hand.

"Congratulations, I'm happy for you," Kaija brought out.

"I know I'll do well in Medical School, Kaijin, and I'll make very good money afterwards. I offer you myself and my life. And you know I'll always love you."

These generous gifts were not enough.

"But what about me?"

"I'll take excellent care of you." Maris rushed on, misunderstanding her question. "I'll work hard. I'll help your parents too, with whatever they need when they're old. And of course I'll always do the very best for our children."

The powerful stallions of Kaija's daydreams reared up and galloped away, the white tents on the edge of the battle-field collapsed, and the excitement of working shoulder to shoulder vanished. Kaija could not let that happen. She could not.

"But what about my degree?"

"I just told you, you don't have to worry, Kaijin. I'll take the responsibility. You'll be able to stay home, enjoy life, do whatever you want."

Photos from the *Indianapolis Star* of heavily oiled, deeply tanned doctors' wives holding up tennis rackets and grinning at benefit balls gave way to the real-life image of pallid Mrs. Roy Schenker, who lived across the street from Kaija's parents. Her hair in pin curls, her fat body straining against the seams of her house dress, she edged the grass of her tiny front yard with hand-shears. In the late afternoons she sat on her front porch, eating Hostess Twinkies and watching the street, not even looking at her women's magazines. She bustled inside when she spotted her husband's Studebaker rounding the corner.

Kaija knew she would not turn into her, at least not right away. At first she and Maris would have martinis in frosted glasses while he talked about his day and she searched for a tactful way to suggest a different diagnosis for one of his patients. She would pretend to be happy because she loved him; she would not want him to feel guilty because she had given up her dreams.

"We should marry soon, Kaija. Now, if possible," Maris was saying, "I don't think it's good for us to wait. I'm not sure I *can* wait, and I would never, ever want to hurt you."

Maris smiled for the first time. "Please, Kaijin, say yes. Yes, you'll marry me."

"No."

"What?" His smile faded.

"I said no."

"But why? Don't you love me?"

Kaija could not explain, though she loved him with all her heart.

"I see, Kaija, you *don't* love me. You don't appreciate what I'm offering." His voice had taken on an edge of anger and hurt. "I'm willing to marry you even though I haven't lived myself yet. I haven't done any of the exciting things . . . . "

"What exciting things?" She had refused him, but she was furious that he thought anything could be more exciting than marrying her.

"Lots of things. I've never been to Paris, climbed the Alps, ridden on a camel, or swum the Hellespont . . . ."

"Oh, for heaven's sake, of all the adolescent . . . ," Kaija began.

"Or known other women."

"Other women? Oh, I see, other women! That's just what you'd like, to get me pregnant and locked up in the house. Then, while I'm nursing a baby, you'd . . . ."

"No, I would not, Kaija. You're being hysterical. I just told you I'm willing to give everything up for you. If I give you my word I'll be faithful to you, I will be."

"Oh, very nice, good for you. And I'm supposed to be grateful? I should be overjoyed when people call me the Doc's Wife or Mrs. Maris and talk to me as if I didn't know an artery from an appendix? Well, I'm not going to pick up socks and iron your shirts. You can go whistle. I'm going to be a doctor myself."

213

Maris was angry as well. "Never mind, you aren't going to be Mrs. Maris Zalums, I wouldn't think of inconveniencing you. I didn't know you were so selfish, you're an egoist of the first rank. I see I've made a huge mistake."

"Selfish? Me?" She was stunned. She had told him her first duty was to her parents because the war had robbed them of the chance to have other children. But he was distorting her motives as if she were his enemy. And how dare he say that it was selfish to heal the wounded and feed the starving?

"I am *not* selfish. You don't understand the first thing about me. You never did," she blazed.

"Oh yes, I do. You're selfish, and you're competitive," Maris shot back. "Always trying to outdo everyone with your straight A's."

His hostility shocked her. She wanted only to do the very best she was capable of rather than triumph over others, but he saw her as vain and greedy because she worked hard. He had hidden his resentment of her successes so well that she had assumed he was pleased when she excelled. Yet all the time he had envied her. He had been thinking mean thoughts and storing up hostile remarks while pretending to admire and love her.

She was disappointed in him but also hurt and ashamed. That he did not treasure her because she was unlovable. He did not love her, just as her mother did not. No one had ever given her a fraction of the ridiculous attention the fraternity boys used to give Magda. Kaija felt clumsy and ugly, as if her very body had suddenly changed. She turned and ran so he would not see her tears.

23

At first, Magda listened attentively to Kaija when she talked about Maris. He had tried to speak to Kaija after their fight, but they had argued again, more bitterly this time. They had hurled cruel, untrue words at each other, which could not be unsaid. Worse, he had taken up with Rachel, a plain, hard-smoking biology major "with a reputation."

'I really loved him," Kaija said tearfully as she handed Magda the shy romantic verses she had written about kisses in the rain and embraces under flaming autumn trees. She had planned to show them to Maris when the right moment came but was glad now that she had not. At least he could not gloat that she was abjectly, pathetically in love with him. At least she had kept her dignity.

Magda took a long time to read the poems. Kaija tried to look unconcerned when her friend finished, flipped through them, and read some for the second time. She steeled herself for the verdict. It did not matter that literary criticism was not Magda's strong point. Magda had misjudged the "screaming rocket" poem in Jerry's bathroom, yet Kaija relied on her evaluation now.

Finally, Magda set the poems down and lit a cigarette.

"Your poems are marvelous, and you are a genius," she declared. "First you will be a doctor, and you will make a lot of money, like doctors do for some strange reason in this country, and after that you will be a writer and have a famous salon for poets and artists. I will come every time I can." Without having heard of Gertrude Stein or her advice about what every writer needed, Magda had given Kaija praise, praise, and more praise.

"A salon? Here? In Bloomington? Or, in Indianapolis?" Kaija knew that being called a genius at poetry was excessive, but she loved Magda for saying so.

"Oh no, Indianapolis is too provincial," Magda laughed. "Maybe New York, but I think the West Coast. That's where everything is happening now. In Hollywood probably."

"A writer's salon in Hollywood?" Kaija could hardly conceal her disappointment at this glaring mistake from sophisticated Magda. Did Magda not know that the crude commercialism of movie producers had posed a grave danger to the artistic integrity of William Faulkner? Or that the false glitter of Tinsel town had threatened to destroy what was left of the talent of F. Scott Fitzgerald?

"Yes, yes, Hollywood, Kaija. I'm going there very soon. It is most urgent I see Elvis."

"Elvis Presley?" Even if Kaija could be persuaded to go to Hollywood, she would want to meet Laurence Olivier, Elia Kazan, or Arthur Miller. She had paid close attention in her Freshman English class to an essay which explained that clear and absolute distinctions existed between high, low, and middle-brow culture.

Actually, Kaija liked Elvis' music. Ironing layers of starched petticoats, which young women wore under full, circle-cut skirts and over slim hips lashed in by girdles and garter belts, Kaija had been far more likely to hum, "Don't Be Cruel" than, "Exultate, Jubilate," while getting ready to see Maris. She turned dewy-eyed every time she heard "Love Me Tender." But she considered these to be temporary aberrations. Her taste would evolve naturally and soon she would listen only to classical music, as her parents did. Kaija laughed at the ignorant politicians and radio commentators who claimed that Elvis's music was a Soviet plot to subvert American morality and "Negro music propagated to destroy the culture of the white man," but that was the extent of her loyalty. Elvis was an uneducated Southern boy, with tacky and even vulgar taste, who could never be part of the intelligentsia to which Kaija aspired.

"Why him, Magda, of all people?"

216

"I cannot help it. He has such energy . . . he is so alive . . . so very now . . . his eyes . . . his lips . . . . Anyway, it is most necessary I meet him."

"And then what?"

"Get to know him, as you say."

"But that's just it, Magda. You won't get anywhere near him. He's surrounded by hundreds of screaming girls everywhere he goes. Do you plan to write your telephone number in lipstick on his white Cadillac convertible and hope that out of dozens you are the one he calls?"

"I am not worried about other women, Kaija. I hope I can hold my own in that respect. I will sit in the first row. Silly girls can throw their underpants at him, but he will see only me. I will look into his eyes, he will look into mine, and he will know that I am the one."

Magda turned sideways, raised her bosom, dropped her left shoulder, and gave Kaija a look of such smoldering sensuality that it would have set Kaija's map of the world on fire had she not been standing in front of it.

"What about his bodyguards?"

"Oh, I'll think of something. They're only men, after all," Magda laughed.

"Would you sleep with one of his bodyguards in order to get near him?" It was now or never for specific information.

"Of course not," Magda looked as primly shocked as anyone in the Women's Quad. "I am interested in Elvis only."

"Well then, will you sleep with Elvis?"

Instead of a straight yes or no, Magda murmured, "The experience of a lifetime . . . rapture divine . . . ecstasy extreme."

"But you'll get married first?" In the words of a popular song, love and marriage, love and marriage, went together like a horse and carriage.

"Oh, no. He may ask me, of course, because everyone says he is nice. He probably *will* ask me because I know he can appreciate a real woman. But I'll say no, even to him. I will break his heart."

"But why? Why go to all that trouble if you aren't going to marry him?"

"Because I know about marriage to famous men. My mother cried about the young sopranos sucking my father's fingers and the cellists showing him their underpants as they sawed away. If Mami hadn't had her career and her own lovers, she would have slit her wrists."

"Your *mother* has lovers?" Aware that she sounded naïve, Kaija added hastily, "I didn't realize your parents were divorced."

"No, no, my parents are married, they just don't live together. After a week together, they argue, they shout, they slam doors, and they go off in different directions."

Magda spoke matter-of-factly of behavior that shocked as it intrigued: married people living separately, unmarried women tempting married men, and married women taking lovers. Americans said they did not do such things, and Latvians did not do them. In the glorious 1920s and 1930s, during Latvian independence, women had received University degrees and entered the professions; one or two might have had an erotic adventure then. But in America in the 1950s, married Latvian women had no time for romantic self-indulgence. In addition to holding menial jobs, they were exquisitely attentive to husbands and children, kept immaculate homes, cooked elaborate meals, gave generous presents even if a step from going hungry themselves, provided delicacies for social events at community centers and churches, and participated in demonstrations to remind the world that Latvia was encircled by barbed wire and overrun by Russian tanks.

"Woman is the soul of the home," was a commonplace in the Latvian community and Kaija expected she would be transformed into a perfect house-spirit herself even as she continued to perform daring feats of surgery, travel to India to help victims of war and famine and attend medical conferences in Vienna and Paris.

Magda yawned and stretched. "Of course, I could have a child with Elvis. But I don't think so. I don't want children."

Kaija tried to absorb this yet more scandalous admission. She had never heard a woman say that she did not want children. Only an abnormal or deranged woman would speak like that.

"Of course, I hope you meet Elvis and all that, Magda, but terrible things happen to girls in Hollywood while they're waiting to be discovered. Not everyone is spotted right away sipping a soda in Schwab's Drug Store, like Lana Turner. White slave traders are lurking everywhere, and the casting couch is very dangerous," Kaija declared grandly.

"Then why don't you come with me, Kaija? Here, did you read this?" Magda waved a movie magazine. "Otto Preminger is looking for an unknown to play Joan of Arc. It's a wonderful role for an actress. It's not quite right for me, but you'd be perfect. Your figure is just right for a virgin, you can smile in a spiritual way, and your eyes water easily, which is good for a saint. Your legs will look great in armor. I don't suppose they will make you walk around dressed in heavy metal, do you? No, they'll probably wrap you in aluminum foil. You will kneel and kiss a cross. This is how you will look when they burn you at the stake." Magda rolled her eyes heavenward, made a horrific grimace, and whipped her head frantically from side to side.

"Oh, Magda, I don't have a snowball's chance in hell of being Joan of Arc. That's just another come-on, like those drawings of women on matchbook covers. 'Draw me,' they say, and when you do, a pushy salesman comes to your door and won't leave until you buy two hundred dollars' worth of art lessons from a correspondence school."

"But this is *The Silver Screen*, Kaija. *Someone* is going to get that role, so why not you? You will be a Star."

"I don't want to be a Star, I want to be a Doctor, and I don't want to leave Indiana University." Kaija clung to her classes and scholarships as if they were branches above a rushing river.

"At least think about it, Kaija. I'm going to Hollywood, as soon as I get the money. I'm only sitting in these boring courses till then."

"Speaking of courses, I have to study."

219

"Oh, go out and have some fun for once," Magda urged. "Maris isn't sitting in his dorm crying, so why should you? He is not good enough to shine your shoes," she added loyally.

Kaija changed her mind about studying when she saw Maris and Rachel sharing a cigarette on the front steps of the library. She veered around, crossed the street, and marched downtown and straight into the Regulator.

She was amazed how easy it was to break the rules. Although she did not look a day over seventeen in the mirror above the bar, let alone the required twenty-one, the bartender set a beer in front of her.

Jerry Locksmith strode in half-an-hour later, almost as if they had arranged to meet. Even larger and darker than Kaija remembered, he loomed over her as her second beer was beginning to make glasses and mugs on the periphery of her vision wobble.

"Well, well, look who's here, Miss Brain Surgeon herself," Jerry rubbed his hands. "Waiting for that lucky boyfriend of yours?"

"No."

"What then, slumming? Seeing how the other half lives?"

Kaija said nothing.

"Won't answer? Now, that's fascinating. I'll tell you what happened. Straight Arrow and you had a fight. He went off in one direction, you in the other. Never mind, Gorgeous, he's a real jerk. He shouldn't let you out of his sight. I wouldn't."

Kaija nodded agreement to that and accepted Jerry's offer to pay for her beer and buy her a martini.

"Let's have a real drink, baby. And then I'll get you out of this Den of Iniquity. A nice girl like you doesn't belong in a dump like this."

Kaija believed drinking held no surprises. In fact she considered herself to be a sophisticated European in this respect.

Without getting the least bit befuddled, she had sipped the single ceremonial glass of wine allotted to ladies at countless Latvian celebrations.

She had also kept her wits about her as she escorted her giggling former suitemates from Crown Point past the lions in front of the Art Museum. In Chicago women were allowed to drink at eighteen while men had to wait until twenty-one. The three girls had consumed a daiquiri each in the Berghoff Restaurant, while Kaija walked steadily while her companions careened or pretended to. But then she had not thrown down two beers followed by two martinis, on an empty stomach, in a state of jealousy, anger, and hurt.

Through the unaccustomed haze, Jerry began to seem like the world's most perceptive man. He knew that Maris and she had had a fight, he disapproved completely of Maris hanging out—and with such unseemly haste too!—with Rachel, and he understood that Maris was only trying to show Kaija that he did not care, although he did, very much in fact.

Well, if Maris thought she was going to mope around, he had another thing coming.

Fragments from a song, which must have been from the 1920s rather than the 1950s, drummed in Kaija's head:

Ashes to ashes, dust to dust,
The springs in my mattress ain't gonna rust.
Serve Maris right, whatever she did.

When Kaija was more or less in possession of her wits again, Jerry was handing her two aspirins and talking about the Philistines he encountered at art shows.

"In Indiana the public response to art is dismal. You'll come with me to my next opening and I'll show you what I mean. They only say three things, 'Gee, that doesn't look like a tree to me,' 'I could do better than that,' and 'I don't know anything about art, but I know what I like.'"

"Your paintings are very subtle, Jerry," Kaija murmured while trying to figure out where she was and how she had gotten here.

She was wearing one of Jerry's white t-shirts and smelling of vomit and expensive soap. Her hair was wet from a recent shower, it was dark outside, and she was in what seemed to be Jerry's bed.

"Oh, my God," she cried, "what time is it?"

"Ten thirty. I thought you'd sleep forever."

"But I have to be at the Quad. They're locking doors right now."

Kaija jumped out of bed, then jumped back in. The t-shirt did cover her, but just barely. There was an aching soreness between her legs and a few small drops of blood on the bottom sheet.

"Too late now," Jerry said. "You'll have to stay the night."

"But the pink slips . . . ."

"No one will miss you. Did you sign out for the evening?"

"No, I had no idea I'd be gone for so long. But they have bed checks. They'll come into my room . . . they'll shine the flashlight . . . I'll be kicked out of school . . . it will kill my parents . . . this is the end of my life."

"They only do bed checks every six weeks. But if that worries you, I'll call Magda. She'll make a dummy with pillows."

He knew more about circumventing dorm procedures than she did. Relieved that he was taking charge, Kaija pulled a sheet over her face and lay still.

Jerry laughed. "And by the way, Miss Passion Flower, it's more like the beginning of your life. Don't worry, no one will look whether you're actually in bed. Martha Smith will just put her head in the door and carry on to the next room. They all trust you because you're such a good girl. But wow, there's fire under that ice," he murmured, kissing the top of her head. "I'm half in love with you already."

Slowly but inexorably, it all came back to Kaija: the way Jerry had half pushed, half carried her up the stairs. He had held her head while she threw up on his immaculate living room floor, stripped her naked, and guided her into the shower.

Scrubbing in the hospital-like cubicle, she had imagined that she was getting ready to perform a daring feat of surgery, until Jerry, stark naked, stepped into the shower with her. As delicately as a knight offering a lady a lily, he handed her a toothbrush, then soaped her back while she cleaned her teeth. She could feel his velvety penis brushing against her buttocks, nuzzling then prodding.

"You'd be so easy to love," Jerry whispered.

With water snaking down their bodies, he kissed her neck, then her mouth. Her nipples brushed against him, the slight abrasion exciting rather than unpleasant. Jerry knelt down and kissed her between the legs, tentatively at first, then more insistently as his tongue found Doctor Payne's spot.

Pretending that Maris was finally kissing her without restraints, Kaija shut her eyes. But it was no good. Jerry's hairy body was too powerful, and his penis too real for any imaginary substitution.

Like Little Red Riding Hood going into the woods to meet the Big Bad Wolf, Kaija opened her eyes and began to move into Jerry's practiced rhythm.

"Trust me," Jerry murmured as he met her steady gaze.

He knew the essential 1950s male motto, belatedly though he had said it.

Kaija's head pounded and her eyes burned in the bright morning sun. Besides asking her to trust him, what had Jerry done to prevent her from getting pregnant? She could not recall a single thing.

The cup of coffee in her hands shook. Absolute stillness paralyzed the grassy field behind the Student Union. How could she have done something so stupid, so shameful, and so horribly dangerous? Sex had killed Grace, but Kaija had not remembered her at all. She could never tell anyone what she had done.

But was last night all there really was to love and to sex? If so, why did everyone conspire to keep secret something so simple and so evanescent?

Instead of feeling an everlasting bond with Jerry because he was her first lover, she had wanted to get away from him when she woke, and she felt completely separate from him now.

She would laugh, she really would, if only it was not so sad.

24

It was the last Midsummer to be celebrated on the shrub and mosquito rich banks of Fall Creek. The Indianapolis Police, responding to complaints about poor people from the Kentucky hills, black people from rural Mississippi, and foreigners from who knows where, had announced they would start issuing tickets after July Fourth to anyone building a fire, drinking a beer, or playing an instrument.

Jani or Midsummer, coming a few days after summer solstice, fell between the hard work of planting and harvesting. Alma felt in her body that it was a celebration of fertility and growth, and she did not try to mask its pagan origins by calling it St. John's Eve or claiming that it honored John the Baptist as some Latvians did. As far as she was concerned, *Jani* had nothing to do with religion. Lutheranism had been the major denomination in Latvia before the Godless communists fouled the altars and locked up the churches. But for centuries before that at Midsummer, Christ on the cross had languished alone above dark altars, while magic silver blossoms appeared on ferns to lovers in dark forests during the short white night.

This evening at Fall Creek men were standing a little apart from women, and the two groups were challenging each other in song. Alma was thrilled by this clear and absolute division of the sexes. Even during the subdued, make-do celebrations of Midsummer in the DP camps, she had loved it when men and women separated and then, each group secure in and proud of their solidarity, teased the other with songs. The moment when their voices finally united in harmony had touched her deeply. She had felt an elation verging on giddiness, as if she were dizzy from drinking fermented birch sap or seeing drooping seedlings revive in dry hot soil after being watered.

In early spring, the farmhands at Stabules doused the young women workers with water, and in turn they were ambushed and soaked themselves, all to the accompaniment of a great deal of laughing and shrieking. Alma's breathing had quickened, and her body had tingled. She could not wait to grow up so that she herself would be pursued with intent, rather than being splashed accidentally from a bucket aimed at someone else.

Alma would have to spend this Midsummer Eve with older women and married couples because Kaija was in Bloomington. Classes were over, but Kaija maintained that her job at the library and long reading lists for the coming semester kept her away from Indianapolis. She had not come to the Captive Nations demonstration at the Circle Monument on June 14th, in which almost every adult Latvian, Lithuanian, and Estonian had participated. Kaija was failing in her duty to Latvia. Alma was convinced that, accompanied by that slut Magda, Kaija was at some American cocktail party right now.

Though surrounded by other men, Ivars was alone this evening. His brothers were not at his side, and no girlfriend was desperately trying to hold onto him. All the young women were with young men, and Ivars' brothers and their wives were celebrating Midsummer in Chicago. Unwilling to encounter Dzintra, his first love, in her married happiness, Ivars had stayed behind.

He took a long swallow of beer and nodded casually in Alma's direction.

Her heart leapt. She could see that he needed someone to sympathize with him, to dispell his gloomy thoughts, and to lighten his solitude.

A delighted smile transformed her plain face. Her wreath of blue bachelors' buttons and white clover helped Ivars overlook her freckles and clumsily styled hair. He noticed for the first time that her figure was very good, lithe yet womanly, in a tight bodice and full-skirt of blue material with tiny white daisies. In the twilight her pale hazel eyes were almost deep enough to get lost in.

226

Ivars set down his beer, strode over, and knelt in front of her. In a parody of a serious suitor, he clasped his hand over his heart.

"Kur tu augi, daila meita,
Ka es tevi neredzeju?
Where did you grow up, you lovely girl,
That I didn't see you?"

Alma understood this for the playful flattery it was, but Ivars was a singing to her, and he was calling her lovely. Ivars, the handsomest of the Three Handsome Brothers, her first and only love, was kneeling at her feet.

"Vai tu augi pie maminas,
Vai maminas purina?

Did you grow up with your mother,
Or inside her hope chest?"

Alma's exultation was beyond words. Ivars had intuited that she longed for her mother; he understood her deepest feelings.

Alma play-acted as was expected, but her reply came from her heart.

"Es uzaugu pie maminas,
Ne maminas purina.
Baltam diegu zekitemi,
Sarkanami kurpitem.

I grew up with my mother,
Not in her hope chest,
Wearing fine white thread stockings,
And little red shoes.

Alma had a good voice, a rich mezzo soprano, which Ivars found soothing.

He stood up laughing and brushed his knees. "But really, Alma, where *did* you grow up?" He sounded sincerely interested.

227

Like most exiles, Alma had ready a single sentence for the complex interplay between the personal and political.

"Eight years in Latvia, in the district of Vidzeme; five in Germany, in DP camps in the British Zone; and eight in Indianapolis," Alma said.

She knew Ivars would understand the implications of each phrase the way no American could.

"Thirteen years in Riga; four in camps run by the Americans; two as a slave in the cotton fields of Mississippi; and then an escape to Louisville and to freedom," Ivars said.

He offered her his arm although he doubted that she would accompany him into the woods at midnight. He would not be able to convince her, as he had other women, that just because no one had ever seen ferns bloom with magical silver blossoms was not reason enough not to go look. He could tell that Alma had *tikums.*

Tikums, praised in hundreds of *dainas,* the ancient four-line Latvian verses, and by his mother, was more than virtue or sexual purity. It encompassed industry, integrity, thriftiness, good sense, self-confidence, and pride. Maternal power and centuries of Latvian tradition descended on Ivars and eclipsed his own desire for feminine charm and compliance.

"Will you do me the honor?" he asked and motioned to the clearing where couples were twirling to Latvian dance music from the 1920s and 1930s, interspersed with German cabaret songs like "Lili Marlene," only with anti-Russian and anti-German sentiments added.

"Mes sitisim to utainos,
Pec tam tos zili pelekos . . . ."

We'll beat the lice-infested ones
The blue gray uniforms as well . . . ."

A violin, an accordion, and a *kokle,* a zither-like instrument, lilted as sweetly as at country dances in Latvia. Only the broken beer bottles, used condoms, and disintegrating cigarette butts reminded

228

everyone that the green meadows, pure rivers, and white birches of Latvia were far away.

Ivars and Alma danced every dance together, and they sat side by side during breaks. They ate some *Janusiers*, the creamy caraway cheese made especially for Midsummer, but they drank little of the abundantly available beer. Ivars seemed oblivious to the fact that dancing exclusively with one woman was tantamount to a public declaration of love.

But everyone else commented on the pairing. Ivars was smitten, Alma had caught him, and a wedding would be celebrated soon. Alma was a good young woman and a good daughter to her unhappy father, and she deserved a good husband. She would calm Ivars down and keep him from running around and drinking. That Alma had not saved her own father from drink was not mentioned.

Alma felt beautiful and cherished in Ivars' arms, and she moved more gracefully than she ever had. She knew he had devoted himself like this to other women, only to ignore them later, but she did not worry. Let him believe he was master of the situation; she had more than enough willpower for them both.

The fragrance of wilting clover from Alma's wreath mingled with the scent of mock orange spilling over the crumbling foundation of an abandoned cabin. The scented air and soft darkness unbroken by city lights were intoxicating. Ivars was as tall as her father; their straight backs and masterful postures were practically identical. But Ivars' movements were fluid instead of tightly controlled, and his dark coloring was in stark contrast to Valdis' blond hair and blue eyes. Alma did not see any similarities between the two men.

Near midnight Ivars retrieved his crown of oak leaves. He set it on his head, took Alma by the hand, and suggested half-heartedly that they stroll into the woods. He would show her how silvery sprays of blossoms exploded above dark matted mounds of ferns.

Alma yearned to go. He reminded her of a thrilling proud animal: a stallion who could not be broken by any man, a Centaur in one of Mrs. Veldre's books, or a prince turned into an elk by a magician. But she shook her head no.

She had waited too long for Ivars, and she would accept nothing less than marriage. She mastered her own strong desires, and she resisted the seductive lines echoing in her head from a poem by Goethe, which Latvians loved to quote, that it was a woman's fate to love and to suffer. Alma would guard her wreath of flowers, that ancient symbol of virginity. She would not allow anyone, not even Ivars, to crush it or fling it carelessly into swirling rapids.

"All right, Alma, in that case I'll take you home," Ivars said. He had expected her to refuse the woods.

The accordion player abandoned the music of Europe for a medley of Elvis Presley hits. Delighted, the youngest couples began to gyrate and the oldest to boo. It was time to leave.

"I don't like that vulgar American stuff," Alma and Ivars said almost simultaneously.

Their departure was duly noted. They were now a couple.

25

At the end of a routine meeting of the governing board of the Latvian Community House, Ivars announced that he was engaged. Alma was far more emotional as she told the news to every Latvian she encountered. That was as it should be: it was properly feminine to be excited about love and marriage. The wedding was set for Saturday on Labor Day weekend so that it could be celebrated for three days and three nights, as it would have been in Latvia. Guests would come from cities in the Midwest and from as far away as New York. Even Kaija had promised to abandon Indiana University in order to attend.

Only Latvians would be invited. Ivars and Alma took it for granted that Americans would stare at customs strange to them, taste the unfamiliar food gingerly, and require constant translating and reassuring. She would not invite Mr. and Mrs. Rank, who had been kind to her during the four years of high school that she worked for them, and she did not show off the ring Ivars had given her to her co-workers at the bank. She was proud of it, but she believed the women would think the ancient silver design weird and the large piece of amber inferior to the tiny diamonds, ugly little chips of broken glass in paltry settings, which they strove for. They would expect to be asked to the wedding, which was out of the question.

Alma and Ivars had been too old when they arrived in the United States to try to pass as Americans. Only their rightful place among Latvians mattered. And Latvians were pleased. Alma's marriage to Ivars would benefit the entire exile community. The couple would work together to expose Stalin's crimes against humanity—as great and greater than those of Hitler, though mostly unknown in the United States—and to drive the Russians out of Latvia. They would raise their children to be good Latvians.

231

Alma was already settling into her wifely role. She clucked when Ivars accepted a drink, distracted him when he was about to take a swig, and urged him to leave parties long before they actually did. No one paid attention to such fussing by women, and certainly no one expected the men to obey. A man is not a mouse.

Alma felt honored to look after Ivars. She exchanged sympathetic glances with married women as she coaxed him to get up from the table. She waited patiently when on their way-out people surrounded them and went on talking by the door and then by the car. Any goodbye could be the final one. But she also sensed that drinking would never be as important to Ivars as it was to her father. And what else could possibly come between them?

When Ivars finally started the car, Alma did not curl up next to him or rest her head on his shoulder. Back straight and hands folded, she sat close to her door. Occasionally she held up her ring so they both could see light radiate through the amber which was the color of dark honey.

Ivars parked in front of the duplex that Alma shared with her father and with two other Latvian men she cooked and cleaned for. At the front door, he gave her a brotherly kiss on the cheek. He did not press for sexual privileges, which she, her face taking on a high color, would refuse. They both knew that nothing much would happen between them before they were married. Ivars hardly thought of her as he headed off to his room, which he rented from a Latvian family. He was fond of their company, and he stayed up late talking with them.

If there was a Latvian social event the following evening, he picked Alma up and took her there. Otherwise they saw little of each other, newly engaged though they were. Ivars spent weekend mornings at the Jordan Institute of Art, wandered through the city to study buildings and make sketches, or sat in the Public Library trying to write poems. Alma snatched minutes from tending to her father and their two boarders to plan the wedding and take care of hundreds of details.

Ivars and Alma believed they were as intimate as any two people could be. The relatively few times when they were alone together, they gossiped about friends and acquaintances, recounted happy memories from Latvia, and laughed over funny incidents during the first years in America.

Alma was uneasy when Ivars criticized Latvians. He said they all talked about their homeland as a rural paradise. But only Riga, nicknamed the Paris of the North, had been a vibrant, sophisticated city, full of writers, musicians, and artists. Alma learned not to be embarrassed when Ivars expressed startlingly different opinions from others.

Through him Alma came to know every building designed by the great architect Eisenstein on Elizabete Street, where Ivars had lived until he was twelve. She could picture the larger than life size stone figures which decorated the roof lines. The faces of the sculptures of women were anguished because they foresaw the coming horrors of the Twentieth Century. Ivars' minute descriptions of their agony made Alma uncomfortable, but eventually he changed the subject or paused long enough so that she could ask him about something else.

Ivars listened attentively as she named the flowers and trees and crops of her father's farm Stabules, which brought back his own sun-drenched summers. His parents had followed the Latvian custom of sending children out of Riga to the countryside for fresh air during the long sunny days. He could almost hear the voices of his brothers rising above gentle hills as Alma talked.

But a few weeks before the wedding, as Ivars escorted Alma to her front door, they had an argument so fierce it stunned them.

It began with Ivars saying that his father was increasingly frail and Alma reassuring him that, unlike her own father, whose real trouble she did not put into words, he would live to a ripe old age. She hinted that because Valdis had no one to take care of him, he might move in with them sometime after they were married.

"Your father can come live with us on the day of the wedding for all I care," Ivars said.

Pleased as she was that the matter was so easily settled, a cloud passed across her sunny skies. Did Ivars not want some privacy with her, a few months of hungry passion and sweet satisfied desire? Did he not have shy secret fantasies of their wedding night as she did? But she pushed these questions aside. Ivars was reserved, and he always behaved like a gentleman, so of course he could not speak about such things. She was lucky to be engaged to a man so ready to honor her wishes about her father. It did not, could not mean that her did not love her.

"But I hope you understand, Alma, that your father can live with us for the time being only," Ivars continued. "I'm going to do what everyone in my family wants and stay in Indianapolis for the next couple of years. But my brothers are getting more settled, and they'll be able to take care of my parents soon. I can start living my real life then."

"But we don't have to wait. We can look for a house before that. It can be quite run down, but we can fix it up. As long as it has three bedrooms . . . ."

"After my parents move in with one of my brothers, I'm out of here. Goodbye, Indianapolis! No more engineering, no more wasting my best years."

He had her attention now. "What do you mean, wasting your best years? You've got a good job with good pay and you work in an office with air-conditioning. My father would love to sit in a clean room instead of standing on his feet all day in front of a greasy machine. And your father . . . ."

"I know, Alma. Spare me the details. I know about the terrible jobs the older men have. But I'm talking about me. Damn it, listen to me, Alma." He raised his voice to her, which he had not done before.

"But you got a nice raise as soon as you said we were engaged," Alma persisted. "Your boss didn't scold you for getting married. He didn't say you'd disappointed him by picking an inconvenient time, the way mine did. Your boss likes you, you told me that yourself."

"I don't care, I want . . . ."

"How can you not care? You're not going to be reprimanded when I get pregnant."

Alma had watched the teller with the biggest breasts of all the women employees in her bank being pinched, whistled at, and pressured for dates by every male employee and every travelling salesman, only to see her fired the morning she announced she would marry the man who worked next to her. Alma blamed the woman for leading men on, but she felt uneasy about her own job when she thought of her.

"Your boss will give you a raise when I hava a baby. And you say you don't care?"

"I want an entirely different life, Alma. I'm bored to death by engineering. I don't like the dull weekends either, drinking beer at the Latvian Center and listening while everyone tells the same old jokes and brags about houses and cars."

He was so wrong that Alma did not know where to begin: weekends at the Latvian Center were not dull, being bored was for spoiled rich Americans, and money to earn and houses to buy were privileges to be grateful for.

She tried once more to tell him her dreams. "We'll look for an old house. We'll work on it side by side . . ."

"I'll stick to my job for two or three years, Alma, and then I'm going to Taliesin," Ivars interrupted.

"And what may this Taliesin be?" she asked sarcastically.

"Damn it, Alma, I've told you before, but you don't listen. You're not interested in anything aestetic, you don't care about creativity or the life of the spirit. Taliesin is a school, for architects."

"What? You want to go school? At your age? You said you didn't like your courses the first time. It's ridiculous. What would you say if I announced that I want to be an opera singer and spend our savings on voice lessons? It's preposterous . . ."

Inarticulate fury tightened her throat. Let him say what he wanted to; she would not listen.

But then a phrase, "communal living," snagged her attention. She had heard it before when he made her look at a book about houses no sensible person would live in.

"At Mr. Frank Lloyd Wright's Taliesin, students and their wives live communally," Ivars explained.

235

He must be deranged. He was planning to drag her and her children to some God-forsaken collective farm, a *kolkhoz;* he wanted to give her possessions to greedy strangers too lazy to work themselves. And he was calling the demagogue who had misled him "Mister."

"That Wright of yours is a Communist. He's made a collective farm like the ones Russians force people into. I can't believe you'd have anything to do with anyone like that."

Ivars had fallen in love with some crazy American notion of exaggerated equality; he had forgotten what Russians had done in the Baltic countries. A total of one hundred forty thousand Latvians had been deported by now and their farms turned into collectives. Russian workers were brought in to replace them and to destroy Latvian language and identity. People from all three Baltic countries were dying in Siberia this minute, while Russian bureaucrats, those fat oily tomcats, smacked their lips and called their slaves "comrade." A vein began to throb in Alma's forehead.

"You're hysterical, Alma. I hate the way you and other Latvians jump to conclusions. You make everything political because you're too lazy to make distinctions. There is simply no similarity between forced and voluntary communal . . . ," Ivars began.

Alma's whole self contracted in fury. He was a stranger to her, and a dangerous one at that.

"You're a damned leftist, that's what you are. You sound like a Communist, like a traitor to Latvia," she spat.

It was the worst that could be said of anyone, ever.

No one would blame him if he struck her; he had never been called such vile names. With an effort, he stayed his hand.

Alma's words skittered from the serious to the ridiculous. Why, she had never worn anything red, not so much as a scarf or a scrap of ribbon, after Russians seized Latvia, nor would she, not until the Soviet Union collapsed, which would not happen in her lifetime. Every honorable man had a duty to work against Communism rather than support sneaky leftist sewer rats bent on destroying the United States from within. She refused to live in a displaced persons' camp again or to wander homeless and unwelcome everywhere. Taliesin was in the wilds of Wisconsin and in the Southwest, which was a desert; no one lived there but wild Indians. Good God, Latvians did not do such things.

But even as she railed, a small terrified voice inside her clamored for attention. She would die if he left her; she would lose him just as she had lost everyone and everything. Men could and would do what they wanted; there was no stopping them. Her grandmother and her father had taught her that.

"There you go again, making everything political, Alma. I can't stand it," Ivars shouted. "I'm not in love with you, I never have been."

He turned his back and strode to his car. In spite of the oppressive heat and humidity, he rolled up the window to shut himself away from her. He would not explain or justify himself; her accusations were too enormous. He, who loved Latvia with all his heart, who pined for his homeland every day, who would willingly die for Latvia, had been called a traitor. Alma had gone too far, she really had. He need not marry her now.

To hell with Alma and the wedding. Let her complain to the old women she gossiped with, as if she were an ancient crone already. Let all the old hens cluck in chorus. Let Alma keep his ring; let her undo all the arrangements. He didn't care; it had nothing to do with him.

He only hoped she would not tell anyone the reason for the breakup. Latvians would avoid him if they suspected he was a leftist; they would ostracize him if they heard that he was a Communist. They would say that where there was smoke there was fire, and they would line up side by side with Alma. She was probably on the phone right now, yammering away, complaining about him to everyone in Indianapolis.

At least she would not call his parents because long distance was still used only in cases of death or disfigurement. But his mother would find out anyway. She would be upset because she feared gossip about her family. She would remark mildly that Alma would have taken better care of him than all the pretty girls he had danced with. Underneath, though, she would be pleased. She liked having him, her favorite, for herself.

But his father was another matter. He would blame Ivars alone. Ivars' resentment against Alma flared at the thought of his father. Why did people call her an industrious little orphan girl when she was a grown woman with a father living? Why did they constantly praise her, as if she were the only one who did her duty? How had she managed to secure such an enviable reputation?

The trouble was that his father had such old-fashioned ideas about women. He would demand that Ivars act like a man, not a boy, and the duty of a man was to behave honorably towards women. He would say that Ivars had given his word and that he must stand by it. He would ask Ivars whether he had taken advantage of Alma sexually. The very thought of having to speak of such matters with his father made Ivars blush.

Ivars could stand up to his father's anger, but not to his abject terror. He had seen his father tremble at a knock on the door after dark, and he had watched as his father tried to master his fears that the Russians had arrived to bludgeon, the Germans to execute, the Americans to deport. That his father was loyal to the United States made no difference. Guilt or innocence was irrelevant, his father maintained. Governments could and did persecute anyone they chose. Only naive Americans believed that it did not matter how they voted. Secret records were being kept on everyone, including those who failed to vote.

Others would call his father paranoid, but Ivars did not feel the truth of it. What if the old man was right? It would kill him to hear that his son was politically suspect. Regardless of what Ivars had shouted at Alma, everything *was* political.

And it was time he got married. His brothers were married, all the Latvian women his age were wives and mothers, and all the younger ones had boyfriends. He alone had kept dancing too long. It was essential he marry a Latvian; an American was unthinkable. Dzintra, his first love, was still ostracized for daring to marry an American. He would have to make it up with Alma somehow.

He pulled over to the side of the road and stared at a clump of dusty willows. His brief elation at being free had evanesced. He wished he had not told Alma that he did not love her. She would overlook everything but that.

A simple apology would not fix it. His mind wandered to his poems, stored in a locked suitcase under his bed, where he also kept his sketches of buildings and statues.

He had written poems of ecstasy when he was in love with Dzintra; he had poured his grief into them when she married. They had flowed effortlessly, almost as if he were an instrument in the hands of a master musician. He only had to sharpen an image here or change a word there, and they were perfect. But no strong current of words had passed through him for Alma.

An image of Kaija gazing at him admiringly while he talked about poetry flashed before his eyes. He would never be able to talk to Alma like that. Alma did not understand how much he wanted to be a poet, which he imagined as part performer, part seer. But the Russians would never allow his poems to be published in Latvia, and Latvians in exile had little time and no resources to support poets. But he could not feel words in English deeply enough to write for Americans.

For a split second Ivars imagined flipping through his notebooks, copying-out lines written for Dzintra and, with eyes averted, handing them to Alma. But he respected creativity too much to allow the temptation to form fully. He would conform outwardly, but he would keep his inner life pure. He would marry, but he would not let Alma into his heart and his soul.

Ivars reached into his back pocket for the fifty dollars he always carried with him because a war could start any minute, an A-bomb could destroy Chicago or New York, a crazy Communist or a Nazi demagogue could seize power. He resented having to squander part of this money on Alma now.

He drove into the tiny parking lot of the flower shop across from the Methodist Hospital which Latvians frequented on their way to Floral Park Cemetery. Inside the dim space, he ordered a dozen red roses. He hunted among the yellowed enclosure cards for one with the word "love" on it so he need do no more than sign it. He slipped the card into the white oblong box with black letters, where the roses lay enshrouded in tissue paper. That should do it.

Part Three

Love and Consequences

1960-1980s

Lost Midsummers

26

Kaija was surprised at first that Jerry—an American, an Artist, a Korean War Hero, a Rich Boy, and an Older Man—had meekly turned into a Boyfriend. But Jerry assumed, as naively as any co-ed, that because they had Done It, they were now a couple.

He dutifully called her every Tuesday night for weekend dates, and he escorted her to and paid for concerts, plays, and dances. In addition, he showed her another side of sanitized Bloomington, one she had not known existed. Kaija and Jerry drank sour wine in attic rooms filled with artists, musicians, writers, and others who only talked about what they were going to write and paint. In the dim light of candles stuck in straw-covered bottles of sour Chianti, everyone sounded profound.

Jerry moved easily in these circles, but he also endorsed Togetherness, a term coined by women's magazines to describe the perfect marriage, and he insisted that he and Kaija spend a lot of time alone with each other. They ate huge meals of roast beef and fried pork chops in diners frequented by stone-cutters, and they walked in the wooded hills of Brown County, which were mostly deserted except during the high colors of fall. They made love on cold damp leaves because Jerry found the remote danger of interruption exciting. In D. H. Lawrence's *Sons and Lovers*, one of Jerry's sacred texts, Paul had made love to Clara outdoors and crushed her red carnations beneath her. Kaija had ruled out other thrills by stubbornly insisting they talk about birth control, which meant that Jerry now grudgingly wore a condom.

Afterwards they stopped in Nashville for steaming cups of pale sour coffee and thick honey-glazed ham sandwiches. Or they drove the narrow back roads leading towards Indianapolis, going into shabby taverns for beer, trying to find the one in which on his final American tour Dylan Thomas had drunk faculty members of the English Department under the table.

It serves Maris right, Kaija thought when Jerry told his friends that they were 'getting serious' instead of just 'going together.' But in spite of Jerry's flattering curiosity and attention, she felt obscurely trapped.

Jerry listened as she unburdened herself of anxieties about deadlines, grades, scholarships, and jobs.

"Why kick against the pricks, Kaija?" he said when she was finished. "Why make things so hard on yourself? Change your major. You don't know all those dead languages for nothing."

The only dead language Kaija knew was Latin. She hoped that he was not be consigning Latvian, which had survived centuries of foreign repression, to some linguistic cemetery.

"Go to the English Department and see what they'll do for you," Jerry urged. "They must be short of students in Medieval or Renaissance. Or, go to Comparative Lit, they'll love you over there."

"But I'm in Pre-Med."

"You'll do great in the arts, Kaija, you have excellent taste," Jerry declared, no doubt recalling her praise of his watercolors and her satisfying compliance in other matters. "Cultural affairs are your forte. With a degree in English, you can lead Great Book discussions, host visiting poets, do all that sort of thing once you're married. Or get a teaching license. You can always fall back on that."

"But I want to be a doctor."

"And that's another thing. Why are you so obsessed with that?"

Maris had called her goal selfish, so Kaija began by explaining her duty to her parents.

"You have so much to learn, Kaija baby. That's their problem. If they wanted more kids, they should've adopted them."

Kaija caught a glimpse of the chasm between Jerry and her. Adoption might be an option for the rich people and commercially successful artists among whom he had grown up, it might be an answer for solidly middle-class Americans, but it was out of the question for people like her parents, who held low paying jobs, lived in a small apartment, and spoke accented English. They would speak in their own language to any child they took care of, and they could never provide a financially stable, well-equipped home administered by a cheerful housewife. No adoption agency would give them a child even if they were not past child-bearing age. But like other glaring realities about immigrant life, this was impossible to explain to Americans.

Despite Jerry's wealthy family and his graceful flattery about the positions her parents had held in Latvia, Kaija did not want to introduce them. The minute he left, her father would start the Latvian Mantra: Latvians should remember that Latvian culture was superior to American; Latvians should put their loyalty and trust in each other; Latvians should marry Latvians; and Latvians should raise their children to be Latvians. Latvians in exile were responsible for the survival of Latvian language and culture, which Russians were systematically destroying in Latvia, so Latvians should organize Song Festivals, attend Latvian churches, and support worthwhile Latvian cultural events. Latvians should fight Godless communism, organize protest marches during Captive Nations Week, and at other times, Latvians should work unceasingly for an independent Latvia. And, Latvians should return to the sacred soil of their fatherland as soon as the Russians were driven out.

Kaija's mother would look sad and her father would speak sternly of duty, but both would expect her to disentangle herself from Jerry. For their sake as well as Alma's, Kaija had evaded close friendships with American girls in high school.

"Be rational, Kaija," Jerry went on. "Let's talk about that Med School plan of yours. How many women doctors do you actually know?"

"Lots," Kaija snapped. Women doctors and women dentists had cared for her in Latvia and in the DP camps.

"So, where do you think you'll practice? Do you expect some famous research hospital to hire you? Or that the Great Unwashed will come to you for pills and shots? Don't kid yourself, Kaija," Jerry went on mercilessly. "No one ever went broke

245

underestimating the stupidity of the American public. Face the facts. Everyone prefers guys to gals, whites to blacks, WASPs to foreigners. Girls only go to college to get their Mrs. degrees."

Seeing Kaija's hurt expression, Jerry whispered, "I'm crazy about you, baby. You'll get your Mrs. Degree from me, if you're very, very good." He smiled ironically to show he was above middle-class, Midwestern conventions like marriage, but the words remained said.

On a cold Saturday morning Kaija found herself lying half-nude and shivering on Jerry's white enamel table. She refused to take off her panties but she had given in otherwise to his pressure to pose nude for him.

Jerry chattered happily as he sketched, while Kaija seethed with resentment. She could not read, she could not study, and her arm was going to sleep. Being a muse might be exciting if one could inspire from afar, but being a model was uncomfortable and boring.

Four months into the love affair with the great artist, Kaija wanted out. Jerry's insistence that they spend a lot of time together interfered with her studies, and she hated their constant bickering about sex. She regularly resolved not to sleep with him because she could not stand the anxiety and guilt which followed. But she gave in more often than not, for the sake of sweet peace, for Jerry's words of love, and because of her body's startling desires. Sometimes she believed him that she had no right to say no because he tried so hard to please her. At other times she longed for oblivion as he moved above her.

Afterwards, back in her dorm she scrubbed until her skin tingled. She felt like her real self again only after she had put on clean clothes and straightened her room. She vowed not to sleep with Jerry, to put an end to disorder and chaos, and to begin a life of disciplined solitude. But after a week or so she gave in to Jerry's pleas.

Jerry's calm assumption that he would marry her terrified her. It might be a shortcut to upper middle-class America, but then she would be Jerry's wife rather than her real self. Early in their relationship she had fantasized about resting her hand languidly on a window sill to show off an engagement or a wedding ring, as Lydia Bennett had in *Pride and Prejudice*. But shallow bouncy Lydia, hurriedly married-off at fifteen, had only disappointment and gossip to look forward to.

Kaija had lost interest in hurting Maris by flaunting Jerry's devotion. She had seen Maris' stricken face as she stood surrounded by Jerry's friends during an intermission of *La Boheme*, with Jerry's hands possessively on her waist. Another time Maris had nodded to her through the plate glass window at the Dandale, the only fancy supper club in Bloomington, as Jerry fed her a piece of his steak. She had felt sad, not triumphant at all.

"Jerry?" Kaija began. "Don't you think we're seeing too much of each other? Maybe . . . ."

"No, baby, I do not. I've written to my parents that we're getting serious. I'm taking you home, so they can meet you."

"Oh? But I wish you'd asked me first, Jerry. I'm very busy right now, what with papers to write and my job at the library, and . . ."

"Then make the time, Kaija. Boy oh boy, my Mom will blow her stack."

Jerry's relationship with his parents was more convoluted than hers. She simply kept her parents ignorant of anything that would upset them, and she did not ask for their sympathy and help when things went wrong. Jerry, on the other hand, tried to get his parents to see his point of view. He gave them full details of what he called his Bohemianism and then worried that his father would disinherit him.

"Your mother will blow her stack? Why, Jerry?"

"I'm afraid she's a bit xenophobic," Jerry laughed. "Believe it or not, she still belongs to the Daughters of American Revolution, in this day and age, years after Eleanor Roosevelt showed them up for their bigotry toward Marian Anderson. But she's so darn bullheaded." His voice was full of affection and pride. He would not really like it if his mother suddenly saw she was a racist and joined the NAACP.

"Tell me more about your mother," Kaija said to gain time to absorb this. If Jerry's mother disliked strangers and foreigners, Kaija was the very person to upset her.

"Let's see. She's always after me to get married," Jerry laughed. "She keeps pointing out the nice girls at the Country Club, daughters and nieces of friends of hers, and nagging me to call them."

The wind probably whistled between the ears of these rich girls, but Kaija did not like being compared to them. She would not go to meet Jerry's parents if someone put thumbscrews on her.

"I've got to take a shower," she said jumping up. Maybe hot water would start her period. "What? Right now? I'm not done with you, Kaija. We're discussing something important here. I'm offering you a chance to meet my parents," Jerry said.

"Hell, no," she snapped, surprising Jerry and herself. "Don't think you can parade me in front of them like some prize sheep you've won at a fair. I'm not going where everyone stares at me, mispronounces my name, picks on my accent, and tells me that Latvia no longer exists because on their map that part of Europe is the Soviet Union." Never mind that she would have to join an order of cloistered nuns pledged to silence to avoid such comments.

"I can't believe you could be so insensitive, Jerry," she plunged on. "I wouldn't go East with you if you were the last man in the State of Indiana."

She was violating all the rules for breaking up, which called for writing a "Dear John" letter to soothe the boy's feelings, returning his presents, having a last poignant date, and sniffling when "I'm walking behind you on your wedding day" came on the radio. But freedom was within her grasp.

She felt pleased with herself as she locked the bathroom door and turned on the shower. Only the crotch of her panties, as purely white as before, worried her. Jerry's thick white towels remained unstained as well.

248

When she came out fully dressed, Jerry was stretched out on his bed, a glass of clear liquid in his hand.

"May I trouble you, Kaija, to get me that bottle of Miltown? On the second shelf in the medicine cabinet? And would you please be so kind as to refill this?" he asked with elaborate politeness. He gulped two or three tablets, washing them down with vodka.

"Don't do that, Jerry," Kaija said. The danger of mixing alcohol and tranquillizers was generally unknown before the death of Marilyn Monroe; but, Kaija had questioned him about his pills when she was eager to learn everything about him. "No more than one every six hours," she pointed out.

Jerry adjusted his pillows and patted the place next to him. "Come here, Kaija baby. I'll fall asleep soon, and then you can go, happy on your own as always, while I stay here and battle my demons alone."

The self-pity in his voice outraged her. She had just wasted the entire morning modeling for him when what she wanted to do was study.

"Never mind, Gorgeous," Jerry gave her a world-weary smile. "I know you don't care about me. You don't care that I suffer. You locked the bathroom door against me, and you've never done that before. Remember how we made love in there the first time?" He shook out another pill.

"Jerry, please, don't. You're going to get sick. You could die if you take too many."

"Maybe that's what you want. But I won't take another if you stay."

His behavior repulsed yet drew her. Did she really have so much power over a man that he would risk death because of her? Did he love her more than he did himself? It had also been drummed into her that desperately unhappy men should never be left to drink alone. Anxious to get away, she sat down.

Jerry's face was gray, his forehead beaded with sweat. Kaija perched on the edge of the bed, ready to slip away as soon as he dozed off.

"This is nice," Jerry smiled contentedly. "Talk to me, Kaija. You never talk to me."

Kaija's mind went blank at this half-order, half-plea. Her hand brushed against the raised scar on his wrist.

Ordinarily too polite to probe for painful memories, Kaija blurted, "Did you get this in Korea, Jerry? What was it like over there? What happened to you? Were you wounded?"

"Korea?" Jerry held up both wrists and laughed bitterly. "You want to hear about me, big hero John Wayne, in Korea? Other guys have the real war wounds. I cut these babies myself."

"Why?"

"Seemed like a good idea at the time. I'll be damned if I can explain it now."

"Try, Jerry."

"Just one of the things you girls make us do. Let's see, it was Karen . . . no, it was Nancy . . . no, it was what's her name . . . was it Slavena?"

He was beginning to slur. Was he talking about Slavena, that pathetic half-Russian? Kaija did not know anyone named Karen, and the only Nancy she could think of was a sad middle-aged woman with a pronounced limp, a waitress at Nick's English Hut, the graduate student bar on Kirkland Avenue. Men milled around Nancy at closing time, competing with each other to take her home.

"I don't mean Karen. I mean Nancy, yes, of course, Nancy. Nancy is very generous, very giving. I'll tell you a secret," Jerry giggled. "She's got a wooden leg. She lets you take it off before . . you know, before you do anything . . . . very sexy, don't you see. She couldn't leave if she wanted . . . women in Korea . . . kneeling in front of us . . . animals . . . Slavena begs for it . . . bald as a baby . . . doggy style . . . blind-folded . . . anything we wanted . . . American girls don't. . . D. H. Lawrence . . . modern women don't surrender. . . but Slavena. . . ."

"What are you talking about?" Kaija demanded.

"Foreigners," Jerry brought out firmly.

She felt nauseous. Had Jerry seized Nancy's wooden leg and held it away from her as she begged for it? Had he yanked off

Slavena's wretched wig and pushed her face down into his lap? Or had he mounted Korean women from behind and called them dogs?

Kaija leaned over and inspected him. Drops of saliva glistened in his beard, but his eyes were closed and he was breathing regularly. He would be all right. She had believed that this pathetic person was a sophisticated man who would teach her about art and life in America. He had said he loved her. Animals and foreigners, he had said.

She need not see him again. She would not feel guilty; she refused to pity him. He was unmanly. The men she respected did not talk about sex, let alone blubber about taking off wooden legs and mounting women like dogs. If Jerry's behavior had something to do with the aftermath of war, she was not prepared to take it on.

She tiptoed away from the bed and, just in case he died, looked around for anything that could incriminate her. Finding nothing, she flew down the stairs and ran, elated to be free.

Lost Midsummers

27

But on an overcast day in June, Kaija was on her way to meet Jerry's parents. His white Lincoln convertible, with the top up to keep out fumes and grime, zoomed along the Pennsylvania Turnpike.

"By the way, Kaija, I've brought a hostess gift for you to give to Mother. It's in the back seat, in that silver box with the pink ribbon. Just hand it to her nicely. And don't call her Marge, no one, not even her frends do that."

"Any other instructions for the foreigner from somewhere over there? Should I study Emily Post?"

Jerry's jaw tightened, and Kaija softened her remarks. "Don't worry, Jerry, I'll behave. Aren't these hills nice?"

She had hardly noticed the landscape. She was concentrating her whole self on her period starting. In a few short months she had ruined her life. She had gotten a much-dreaded B in Biology, and she had lost one of her three scholarships as result. Having no mentor to advise her otherwise, she believed that this single failure meant that she would never get another scholarship or be admitted to medical school, so she had changed her major to English.

To top it off, she had gotten herself pregnant.

She was wild with shame and regret.

Kaija had not consulted her mother about being pregnant. Her mother would only cry, scream, and then retreat into silence. Kaija would get neither sympathy nor useful advice from her. Alma would berate Kaija, and she too would have no idea what to do. In any case, Kaija had already shamed and lacerated herself more than her mother or Alma ever could.

But Jerry's mother, a well-connected and well-informed American woman, especially one who would not want her son to marry a foreigner, might know what to do. To get any help Kaija would have to tell Jerry she was pregnant, and he in turn would have to ask his mother for advice. Kaija was too frightened and ashamed so speak to her directly.

Jerry's mother was waiting for them on the porch of a remodeled farm house in West Chester, Pennsylvania.

"So glad you're finally here, Gerald," she said, embracing him. She kissed him on both cheeks, too close to the mouth Kaija thought.

Marge was a beautiful woman, with flawless skin and blond hair in an elegant French twist. Slender and very tall, she was able to look Kaija squarely in the eye. She did just that, nodded coolly, and stepped adroitly between Kaija and her son.

"Did you have a good trip, Gerald? You must be tired after driving all those miles. Have you had your lunch, Gerald? Did you bring me that book about British royalty from the Rare Books Collection? There's something exciting in there that I want to show you, Gerald."

Uncertain what to do, Kaija unobtrusively set down the box of expensive soaps Jerry had bought for her to present to his mother.

They were in a huge kitchen which, with the exception of appliances in newly fashionable avocado, was meant to suggest uninterrupted historical continuity. Blackened pots and rusted iron tools hung above a stone fireplace, old cutlery and faded plates were displayed on a wall, and a crude wood box, shaped like a pig-trough, held magazines and newspapers. Marge's headquarters were at a massive oak table in the alcove where she probably received homage from visitors and supervised the Czechoslovakian maid and the black gardener.

Kaija tried to disparage Marge's white suit with navy piping, her white and navy polka dot blouse, and matching white heels with navy trim. They were incongruous in the artificially rustic setting, but their neat precision made Kaija feel dowdy. She wished she had worn something better than a sleeveless light blue dress and scuffed brown sandals.

"This is Kaija, Mother."

"So, I gathered. I'm surprised her mother allowed her to come. I may be hopelessly old-fashioned, Gerald," Marge said with tinkling laughter meant to suggest the opposite, "but in my day, mothers corresponded first, before girls were allowed to travel clear across the country and stay in the homes of young men."

Kaija knew instantly she could expect no help from her. Marge would advise Jerry on how disentangle himself, of course, ande she would not give Kaija a thought.

"Well, Kaija is here now, and I for one am very pleased," Jerry said loyally.

"Anything you say, Gerald. But in that case, you'd better tell me her name again."

"Kaija," Kaija said.

"Ah, yes, I see, Kay."

"No, Kaija."

"Key."

"Kaija. It's a beautiful name, Mother. It means 'Sea Gull.'"

"Really? A bird's name for a girl? How very odd."

"Kaija," Kaija said.

"All right if I call her Kay, Gerald?"

Jerry grabbed Kaija's hand to keep her from bolting.

"Kaija," he said firmly.

"Oh, all right. I'm sorry, Gerald. Kaija, Kaija, of course, Kaija. I've put her in the small guest room, the one just past mine. I'll have Marcus carry up her things."

"All right if I show Kaija around, Mother? Want to take a walk, Kaija?"

"Remember, Gerald, drinks at seven, dinner at eight."

Three blessed hours out in the open air before Kaija would have to face open disapproval again.

"Sorry about that," Jerry said, "she gets like that sometimes. She'll come around."

"Of all the rude . . ."

"She can't help it, Kaija. Things are pretty rough for her."

"Oh yes?" Kaija's disappointment erupted as anger. What could be rough for that pampered, useless, polka-dotted woman? She would not last a day if she had to work for a living.

"So, what does she do all day?" Kaija asked.

"Runs the house."

"Oh, really? And what do the gardener and maid do while she does that?"

"They require a great deal of supervision. She has lots of details to see to."

"Oh, yes, of course," Kaija threw caution to the winds. "It must be hard to teach the maid to curtsy. My mother's boss has the same problem. He has to make sure she gets up from scrubbing the floor and bows to every insurance salesman who crosses the threshold."

Jerry, embarrassed or unwilling to argue, said nothing.

"For God's sake, Jerry, what does she *do*? It can't take her sixteen-hours-a-day to put on makeup and order the servants about."

"All right. She does genealogy."

"What's that?" Kaija knew nothing of this common preoccupation of older Americans.

"She's hoping to pounce on a famous ancestor," Kaija said as soon as Jerry had explained. "I bet she hides any evidence of a peasant or a prostitute."

"Not much chance of that. She's traced our ancestors all the way back, from the Mayflower to Richard III himself."

"Really? A king with a name like Locksmith?"

"That's my father's name. She's doing her own family."

"So why is that important? How does knowing you're descended from Richard III change who you are?"

"How many generations do your parents go back to, Kaija?" Jerry asked, trying to smooth things over. "What about your ancestors?"

Kaija saw again the chasm between immigrants and Americans she had glimpsed before. Latvian immigrants did not have time for hobbies like genealogy, and all records were in Latvia, sealed forever behind the Iron Curtain. Anything impressive in them would be dismissed as irrelevant in America anyway.

What was she doing in this place, with these people? She had been a fool to fantasize that Jerry's mother would help or that Jerry could offer solace. Kaija was too odd, too much an outsider to be Marge's daughter-in-law or Jerry's wife.

If the very worst happened, that is, if Jerry had to marry her, he would look down on her too. He might enjoy shocking his parents at first, but he would return to his senses. Kaija was more likely to get respect and affection in a prison for bad girls or in a home for unwed mothers, both of which were vivid from Girl Talk.

"Let's go see Dad. You'll like him," Jerry promised. "And you'll love his studio. He paints there, night and day."

They started across a meadow, towards a gray stone building with a two-story high tower.

"I don't think we should interrupt him, Jerry." Kaija did not want to face another bruising encounter.

"Oh, come on. I want him to meet you."

Jerry kissed Kaija's wrist absent-mindedly, and his affectionate gesture calmed her a little.

She was in one of the loveliest places she had ever seen. Wild pink roses tumbled over a low stone wall, and the fragrance of clover and mint filled the air. Being married to Jerry might not be so bad. His father must be a sensitive man because he had chosen this beautiful spot; he would at least be kind. Jerry had told Kaija that Andrew Wyeth and other American artists lived in the area. Jerry's father would introduce her to a community of intellectuals and artists, and she might come to call this place home. She would finally belong somewhere.

"Good, he's here," Jerry said, pointing to an open padlock hanging by the door.

There was no response to his knock. Jerry jiggled the handle and then began pounding on the door, which was evidently bolted from inside.

"Damn it, this *always* happens to me," Jerry said as he struck the door with both fists. "He keeps doing this shit to me." He gave the door a vicious kick.

"Maybe he's asleep or sick or something," Kaija suggested. She wanted Jerry to stop before his father got angry with her.

Jerry glanced up at the windows, which were too high to look through.

"Nah, that's not it, he's doing it on purpose. He's trying to get at Mother through me, damn him," Jerry cursed.

"Let me in, Dad," Jerry pleaded, "please let me in." He began to
slap ineffectually at the door. "It's okay, Dad, I know all about Sophie
Please, just let me in."

There was an unmanly catch in his voice, which Kaija could not stand. But who was Sophie?

"Stop it, Jerry," Kaija ordered, and to her surprise, he did.

"It's hard on Mother, and it's not the first time either. He's never been a good husband to her."

Here Jerry launched into a description of Marge as a young woman: the belle of the ball, the queen of the prom, an F. Scott Fitzgerald heroine in fringed dresses and raccoon coats. But the big tragedy of her life was that she had chosen her most talented suitor instead of the most adoring. She had married Jerry's father, a moody veteran of World War I, and for that she had suffered all her life. Jerry had done what he could to make it up to her.

If that was hardship, Kaija was Marilyn Monroe.

"Who's Sophie?" she asked.

"My father's mistress. Well, not mistress exactly because she used to clean for us. She models for him, but he's screwing her too. She's Jewish," Jerry added darkly.

"So, cleaning ladies can't be mistresses? Not good enough for the lord of the manor?" Kaija was itching for a fight. She filed away the reference to Jewishness for later.

"Don't you start in on me, Kaija, I can't take any more," Jerry snapped.

"Don't you snap at me, Jerry," she shot back. He was so self-absorbed he could not see that being here was awful for her.

Dinner would be a nightmare, Kaija knew. Jerry's father would turn his back on her or ask her unanswerable questions about art theory. Marge would smirk at Kaija and stroke Jerry's hand. Jerry would sulk. The cocktails would be too strong. The food would make her nauseous; the steaks impossible to cut. Kaija would have to switch her fork from hand to hand, instead of eating sensibly European fashion. She would have to fend off ignorant questions, and no one would listen when she said who her parents were. Everyone would notice when she blushed and when her voice trembled. She would cry. She would hate herself.

"I need a nap," Kaija said abruptly and started towards the house, to the tiny room Marge had assigned to her.

Bars guarded the single window; the room had probably been a cage for a crazed relative. A chipped jug jammed full of thistles and other weeds had been set on the night stand to demonstrate that she was unwelcome. But at least she was alone. At least she did not have to pretend to be a self-possessed university student who was above being hurt by rudeness.

Three hours later Kaija held a wet washcloth over her swollen eyelids and then powdered her nose. Wishing she had slices of cucumber to erase all evidence she had been crying, she studied herself in the mirror. A red-eyed insecure young woman looked back at her. But there was no help for it. Kaija shrugged and headed down the stairs.

Jerry did not come forward to welcome her but remained standing between two ancient couples and two young women from the Country Club, who were drinking manhattans and martinis by the fireplace. Marcus, now dressed up as butler, was assiduously refilling glasses before they were drained. Instead of participating in the conversation, Marge kept checking her watch and glancing at the door.

By the time she announced that Mr. Locksmith was unavoidably delayed and that dinner would be served, the peanut bowls were empty and the guests tipsy. Drinking during pregnancy was not thought to be harmful, but had it been, Kaija would have taken huge gulps from her seemingly bottomless manhattan in the hope of "dislodging something." She had taken big mouthfulls as it was.

Murmuring apologies for her husband, Marge seated Kaija as far from Jerry as possible. Ordinarily Kaija sympathized with people in awkward situations, but she was determined not to feel compassion for Marge. Merwin Locksmith was right to stay away. He was roaming the dark woods alone or he was in the tower, entwined with Sophie. He was doing this to spite Marge. He was *not* demonstrating that Kaija was unwelcome.

Jerry flirted mildly with the Country Club girls, whom Marge had seated on both sides of him. Conversation, mostly gossip about people Kaija had never met and jokes she had already heard, swirled around her. She could think of nothing to say. It was an effort just to appear interested.

But she paid attention when Marge, in a voice loud enough for Kaija to overhear, began to confide in the woman next to her.

Evidently Jerry had not been himself after he came back from Korea. He had done nothing but sit around in his pajamas and stare at TV, as if he had been brainwashed. And that was when his fiancée Karen, that unnatural and selfish girl, had decided to break up with him. Marge had almost lost her only son, she said, her voice trembling.

"What he needs is stability and being with his own kind, and I mean to see that he gets that."

Kaija stared down at her plate and tried not to hear more. She did not want to know more about Marge's plans.

The other guests were deploring pregnant women in the slums living off taxes paid by responsible people like themselves and lazy foreigners getting a free ride but still complaining about what had happened to them during the war.

"Those Jews exaggerate so," Marge said wearily, rejoining the general conversation. "Those concentration camps can't have been that bad, just look how many of them are still alive."

No one contradicted her directly, though an elderly man made an attempt to soften the remark. "If only the Jews had left Germany when things started looking bad . . . ."

"Just a minute," Kaija said more loudly than she intended. "That was a vicious and uninformed thing to say, Marge. And as for your point," she said turning to the man, "not everyone can just pick-up and walk away from home. It's more complicated than that."

Conversation stopped.

Everyone looked at Kaija.

Just why was Marge's comment vicious? And how could Kaija make it clear that it was heart-breaking and often impossible to leave one's country? People in danger had old parents, pregnant wives, sick children, impossible-to-abandon lovers, life-long friends, hard-won professions, earned status, clear identity, treasured possessions, and beloved homes. Only those who had done it understood the grief of abandoning a beloved country and a familiar language. In addition, refugees had to have plenty of money in the right currency, documents, knowledge, and connections. But even so, they might not be able to leave because no country would accept them. How could Kaija put this mass into a completely convincing form?

Everyone was waiting for Kaija to say something.

"Six million Jews and gypsies . . . Anne Frank . . . ," Kaija began. No, that was the wrong way to start. Everyone knew that already.

"It's terribly hard to leave. Take my family, for example," she said.

"I didn't know you were Jewish," Marge said.

"I am *not*," Kaija snapped. A blush spread up from her heart, as if she had betrayed someone.

"You and the rest of the Jews . . . ," Marge was saying.

"I am *not* Jewish, I'm Latvian," Kaija said loudly, trying to wrest attention from the personal to something general. "The extermination camps were . . . there are no words adequate to describe . . . "

261

Jerry turned to the girl next to him and boomed, "I'm sorry. I didn't catch what you said about the dues at the Country Club."

"Applications for membership are up this year. . . ," the girl began obligingly.

"That was vicious, Marge," Kaija hissed. "Ignorant and cruel."

She stood up, knocked over her chair, and backed out of the room. She had really done it now. Her relationship with Jerry was finished.

28

Jerry drove in sullen silence, while Kaija sat rigid, staring straight ahead. They had left before Marge was awake, and Kaija was ashamedof herself and still angry at Marge. Instead of delivering a coherent argument or a highly effective sentence, she had been rude, she had made a scene, and she had convinced no one. Jerry could no longer be counted on as a husband of last resort now.

Only Magda could help her. Kaija would talk to her the minute she got back to Bloomington. No longer an expert on America, if she ever had been, Kaija now expected Magda to tell her how to circumvent the law of the United States, which made abortions illegal. Magda's mother must have passed on secret knowledge; otherwise Magda would not take the risks she did.

The friends had seen little of each other lately. Kaija was preoccupied, and Magda was ostracized. Magda slept late, napped through the afternoons, listened to the radio, and chain-smoked. She picked at food she carried openly from the dining room, no longer bothering to smuggle it out. Her knuckles were grubby, her recently fixed teeth stained by cigarettes and coffee, and the skin on her neck was marred by a persistent rash. Musk emanated from her as she pawed through her jumbled belongings. In spite of herself, Kaija saw a cornered animal when she looked at Magda.

Magda lifted the phone suspiciously. Usually she slammed it down without saying a word; sometimes she screamed curses in Hungarian. She had admitted the true pattern of her social life to herself. The fraternity boys sought her out only on week nights, and they no longer went through the pretense of dating by offering meals, hayrides, or movies. They whispered obscenities into her ear and told jokes about traveling salesmen and ignorant farm girls. One had tried to force her into the shrubbery by the Von Lee Theater, no doubt to save the expense of two movie tickets. On weekends these boys took out girls with pronounceable names and simple pasts, girls they could take home to meet their mothers.

Some days Magda did not bother to go to her classes at all, but stayed in bed, moaning to herself. She missed her parents, she was sure terrible things were happening to them in Hungary, and she cried for them and for her country. She was also terrified about her future. She did not have a single relative in America; she had no one to count on for help.

Kaija understood. She, too, wished for relatives; but, fantasies about her mother's dead sister Astra as a sophisticated and understanding aunt got her nowhere. But she did not always rush to comfort Magda. Kaija was not a saint, and the disapproval of the other girls was rubbing off on her. Magda should try harder: she should get up, wash her hair, say "hi" to dorm mates, go to classes, and do her homework. Yet classes felt irrelevant to Kaija too as her mind returned compulsively to her period starting. Some crisis was approaching, which would test their friendship.

In the parking area by the Women's Quad, Kaija declined Jerry's half-hearted offer of help and grabbed her suitcase.

Magda was outside, in the ivied courtyard. She had put on one of her dating outfits, a full-skirted black dress with a scoop neckline and huge white collar, which she and Kaija had found in The Three Sisters, the cheapest of the rundown stores on Illinois Street in Indianapolis. From a distance she looked elegant: the light collar set off her oval face and dark hair, and twilight obscured food stains, scorch marks, and safety pins holding up the loose hem. Magda was beautiful again, an Aphrodite of the early evening, unsoiled by the dirt of Indiana.

Magda's old confidence must have flared briefly too because she was with a fraternity boy. Maybe this nineteen-year-old had bragged he would be elected Bachelor of the Year; maybe he had promised a ride in his convertible in the Homecoming Parade. Magda was no longer likely to fall just for the "crazy about you" line.

The boy leaned closer, put his hand inside Magda's neckline, and began to move the other up under her skirt. Surely Magda did not want that. Kaija took a step toward her, but Magda looked up, met Kaija's eyes, and shrugged. She placed her hand on the boy's and guided it farther under the billowing black material.

Kaija was dismayed but unsurprised. Magda needed that brief moment of triumph, when the boy moaned with desire and when he would fight anyone who tried to pull him away. Afterward he would collapse against her, and she would pat his back as if he were a baby. Where else could women have power like that?

Kaija turned away and dragged her suitcase into the dorm. Magda came in a little later and went to bed without speaking to Kaija.

But the following morning, Magda was shaking Kaija awake.   "Wake up, Kaija, please wake up. You've got to help me, I'm in terrible trouble."

What trouble could be more terrible than Kaija's trouble? Could Magda be pregnant too, in some demonic twist of the pattern that women living in close proximity established identical menstrual cycles?

"They're throwing me out of the University, Kaija. Today, right now, right this minute! We have to hurry."

"Who? what? where?"

Magda thrust forward a letter spelling-out her offenses: she had repeatedly ignored orders to appear before the Student Disciplinary Board and to meet with the Dean of Women. She was therefore ordered to remove herself from the premises by Noon, when the lock on her door would be changed. If she wished to discuss the matter, she could have a brief meeting with the Dean of Women at nine this morning.

Kaija jumped out of bed although it was too late, and she did not want to go. Being identified with Magda, let alone defending her could compromise Kaija's reputation and her place in the University.

But Magda was too energized to notice Kaija's hesitation. Why, those Deans were just like corrupt Russian bureaucrats: they wanted to nationalize her room, they were planning to deport her, they would steal her books and clothes, and they would install their relatives and cronies in her very bed. This was not the time to remind Magda that America was a country governed by laws.

"Oh, Kaija, I am very, very scared of the Big Dean," she cried. "What am I to do? Where can I go if she throws me out?"

"You can stay with me," Kaija offered. "We'll make do with pillows and blankets on the floor." Kaija said reluctantly.

Magda gave her a quick hug. "Thank you, Kaija, you are my very good friend. But they won't let us do that. The Big Dean will deport you too if you take me in. Do I look all right?"

She was wearing an unbecoming orange-pink gingham dress, Capezio flats, and a heart-shaped locket in an attempt to appear Sweet Sixteen. Instead of applying makeup, she was biting her lips to bring out color.

Evidently the Dean of Women did not rate a secretary; she met Magda and Kaija at the door herself.

"You wait outside," she ordered Kaija in a tone that suggested that she knew all about her. Just as Kaija had predicted, accompanying Magda was a mistake. But surely no one could punish her for merely associating with someone declared undesirable, Senator Joe McCarthy to the contrary? Steeling herself, Kaija tiptoed to the door.

As if the all-powerful Dean had arranged for Kaija to watch what happened to bad girls, the door opened an inch. How was that possible? No wiring was visible. Kaija was trembling, and it took her a full minute to realize that the door had simply not latched properly.

The Dean's loud voice started up and went on and on. A book or some other heavy object was being pounded in regular

266

accompaniment. Magda spoke softly at first, but then her voice rose too to create an angry duet.

"Sit down. I order you to sit down," the Dean bellowed. She had probably never confronted someone like Magda, who did not immediately apologize for unnamed offenses. Instead of listing specific violations of the rules, the Dean was flinging one ugly adjective at Magda after another.

"You irresponsible . . . you immoral . . . you dissolute . . . ."

"I am not," Magda interrupted confidently and then named the real issue herself. "I swear to you I am a virgin."

The boldness of it! Was this purity unjustly attacked, extreme courage, amazing deviousness, or the height of folly?

"You are not," the Dean asserted.

"I am. Absolutely. I am a virgin."

"You are not."

"Yes, I am, and I can prove it. I will bring you a certificate. I will let a doctor examine me."

"That's not the point. We know all about you."

"But I swear to you I am a virgin. I will go to a doctor, any doctor, you can choose which one."

The Dean sputtered with frustration as Magda refused to confess and repent. She was too much of a lady to tell Magda to go to hell and too much of a bully to stop. Only the role of an impartial gatherer of facts would have allowed the Dean dignity, but she was beyond that.

"I don't care about any of your certificates, you . . . you . . . baggage. You people may do whatever you like 'over there.' I know Europe is full of immoral . . . but here in the United States of America we . . ."

She paused to search for something definite to distinguish America from other parts of the world. Magda misjudged her silence for weakness and attacked.

"I don't have to listen to **you**, I don't even have to talk to you. You're just an employee, a **woman** employee. I will go to the President of the University."

"Oh, no, you won't. The President won't see you. He would not bother with . . . with a baggage like you."

The Dean took a deep breath and rolled on triumphantly. "Besides, I have a letter from the Board of Trustees. It is my duty to inform you that you are expelled from Indiana University."

No namby-pamby, due-process, innocent-until-proven-guilty here. Administrative decisions were not open to question or legal recourse either.

"Oh, no," Magda's voice wavered. "Please don't do that, please let me . . . ."

"No." The victorious Dean drowned out her pleas. "There is no point in discussing this any further. The University has done everything for you, and this is how you have repaid our sacred trust. You selfish . . . ungrateful. . . ."

"Please . . . ," Magda was crying now.

"I am not going to listen. I don't want to hear another word out of you. But President Wells is such a softie. He told me to give you time to appeal and, if that fails, time to wind up your affairs. So in deference to him, I have postponed changing your locks for a week."

A long silence ensued, followed by rustling and squeaking, and then a horrified intake of breath.

"You ugly old bitch," Magda hissed and slammed the door.

Kaija followed Magda out of the building. They did not speak until they reached the shelter of Dunn's Woods, across from the Library. Magda panted but hurried along efficiently enough.

"Oh, Magda, now what?" Kaija asked when they were safely out of sight of the Dean.

"Oh, I'll leave. I wouldn't stay here if they paid me." She lifted the hem of her full skirt and blew her nose. "They are forcing me to make an action."

"But what will you do? Where will you go? Where will you get the money?"

"I will take up a collection among my Hungarian friends or pass the hat, as you say. And I can always hitchhike."

"Where to?" Kaija asked.

268

"I'm going to Hollywood."

"To see Elvis Presley?"

"To see Elvis."

His name had a magical effect, and Magda burst out laughing.

"Do you know what I did to that old Nazi, the Dean of Women?"

"No."

"Oh, I wish you could've seen it, Kaija," Magda was convulsed with laughter.

"I mooned her," she finally brought out.

"What?"

"I mooned her. I pulled up my skirt, pushed down my panties, and showed her my bare bottom. The look on her face was better than hearing that Stalin was dead."

Why, oh why, had Kaija gone with her?

"Just like the fraternity and farm boys do out on the back roads at night. I learned this was the culture of Indiana while I was here. Teach her to call me a package, I mean a baggage."

By evening Magda was gone, leaving Kaija with a fleeting memory of turning her purse upside down for stray coins and of Magda pressing nylon scarves and jumbled costume jewelry on her to remember her by. Unlike the solid silver teaspoons Alma gave Kaija one by one on birthdays and at Christmas, Magda's gifts eventually flowed out of Kaija's life, joining other lovely insubstantial things in the trash bins of the Midwest.

At the last minute, Magda insisted that Kaija take her sable coat. "You'll need this, Kaija. This is a cold and lonely place, and I'm going where it's warm. But you're happy here. You and I are very different from each other after all," she said, thus closing the door to a final authentic conversation.

There was not enough time for one anyway.

The friends rushed to get ready for the fraternity boy of the night before, who had been persuaded to drive Magda to the Indianapolis train station.

269

They barely had a chance to hug while he revved the engine. Neither Aphrodite nor a monster of ingratitude, Magda looked only like her small, vulnerable self as she vanished.

29

After saying goodbye to Magda, Kaija was overcome by such loneliness and fear that she almost called Jerry. Were she to confide in him, he might offer to do the right thing and marry her, if only to spite his parents. But by now she did not respect or like him, and things would be even worse if she was married to him. She wished fervently that like other girls she had a mother, cousin, aunt, sister, or close friend to advise her. Even dead, desperate Grace had had a boyfriend who loved her and a mother who knew about her transgressions and loved her in spite of them.

Kaija cried because because she was that Alma not a real friend on whom she could rely now. She wished she could go back to the innocent days when Alma and she did their homework together at the round table, walked the twenty blocks from Shortridge to save their bus fare for the movies, and neither of them was pregnant. They had been a great comfort to each other. Alma brought assignments home when Kaija was sick; she assured Kaija that she was smart and would easily catch up with everything she missed. Once Kaija woke from feverish sleep to see Alma setting a vase of red tulips on her windowsill.

But now, Kaija was too ashamed of the disaster she had created.

And Alma was too judgmental to have sympathy. Only Ivars mattered to Alma now. She acted as if Kaija was trying to destroy the institution of marriage if she suggest that the two of them do something together on a weekend night. On the other hand, Alma was hurt if Kaija did not drop everything and rush to Indianapolis on the rare occasions when Ivars was out of town.

Kaija had concluded that friendship with married women was impossible, and Alma was certain that Kaija preferred her books and friends who could talk about what was in them.

Both friends felt abandoned and miserable.

For Kaija everything seemed to be happening behind a pane of glass. She watched as some other girl went through the motions of dressing, sitting in class, and working in the library. Some other girl was terrified and ashamed. Some other girl hoped she would die. Some other girl thought obsessively about ways to kill herself.

But committing suicide was not as simple as Kaija had once imagined. Stepping into the path of a car was no good because she might survive as a helpless cripple. Her parents would go without food themselves to pay for her care, and she would have to wait for others to wash and feed and help her in the toilet. Drowning was out of the question because she would start swimming. Cutting her wrists would inflict a horrible sight on the girls in the dorm. If she hanged herself in the woods of Brown County, someone tough, a hunter or a policeman, might find her, but how was she to get out there without being noticed? The police would scold her for hitch-hiking and bring her back to the dorm. And regardless of the method she chose, an autopsy would reveal she was pregnant, and her parents would die of shame.

It was no use waiting for someone to help her. As always, she had only herself to rely on.

The library was her trusted safe refuge. Most general books about health in the undergraduate reading room made no reference to abortion. The two that did, warned that infection, deformity, sterility, madness, arrest, prison, and death would follow. They like to scare you, Kaija whispered, even as she believed each dire prediction.

A different outcome had to be possible, she reasoned; otherwise the concept of abortion would not exist.

She filled out call slips for six books which were kept in the vast stacks where undergraduates were forbidden to enter, and she was relieved when a perfunctory librarian skewered the slips without glancing at them onto a rusted nail serving as a paper holder.

In the cavernous, cigarette smoke-filled lobby, she paced until the books arrived. She succeeded in smuggling them to her room without meeting anyone she knew.

Only two proved marginally useful. The first, a contemporary anatomy text with crisp diagrams of ovaries and uterus and other organs, bore little resemblance to how she experienced her body. The other was a late 19th century anthology about marriage and motherhood, with delicate endpapers of Madonnas and lilies and a few faded drawings which at least resembled human beings. This book also contained wildly inaccurate information, such as miscalculated fertile periods for women arrived at by analogy to cows, but Kaija did not know that.

With the books propped open on her desk, Kaija examined herself. She easily located her kidneys and liver, and thus encouraged, proceeded by imagination and guesswork to ovaries and uterus. In theory it was simple to dislodge a tiny clump of cells lightly attached to the lining of the womb. But how did one get *in* there? The books did not say.

Kaija had no plan, but she began to assemble supplies anyway: for pain aspirin and a half-empty flask of brandy, which Jerry had pressed on her when she had a bad cold; rubbing alcohol for sterilization; Vaseline for lubrication; a rubber sheet and a dark brown towel for blood; and an extra pillow to muffle moans. She already had sanitary napkins which she would use if she lived.

But she had no tool. Coat hangers were practically synonymous with abortion, but they were stiff and certain to pierce. Crocheting needles were too short and knitting needles too straight. Eventually Kaija's eye fell on the thin wires stretched between wood slats of the folding rack on which she dried her underwear and stockings. Cut and bent into a loop, one of these would have to do. She gave herself three days reprieve to think of alternatives and to steel herself for a level of pain which she could not begin to imagine. Then she would do what she had to, in the middle of the night, when everyone was asleep.

Having made her decision, Kaija fell asleep more easily than she had for weeks, only to wake or seem to, hours later to find

273

Magda by her bed. Magda held out her hand, Kaija grasped it, and the two young women glided out into the hallway. Together they floated down the stairs and through the forbidden door.

Across the narrow parking lot by the old Music Hall, where Grace had swayed with her boyfriend, a country road instead of busy Third Street led out of Bloomington. The two friends followed that until they walked up a long drive in a park of sturdy maples and stately oaks. Kaija recognized where they were the second she saw a gray bench. She was on the grounds of Atminas, Kaija's childhood paradise.

The house revealed itself gradually. First the silvery tiles of the roof, then the verandas shaded by mock orange and lilac, then the large lace-curtained windows. Borders of day lilies, iris, and asters circled the lawn, and a weathered wood fence divided the apple orchard from the meadow. A narrow path led to the pond, where storks waded.

In bomb shelters during air-raids and later in barracks in DP camps, Kaija had obsessively tried to reconstruct this house and its surroundings from memory. And here it was, solid, accessible, and welcoming.

Overjoyed, Kaija started towards the house, only to be blocked by a band of gypsies. Their wagons were pulled up under the sheltering oaks, dark-haired children played quietly in the road, and tethered horses grazed near the frog-filled pond. The scene was peaceful, but the eyes of the gypsies were wary. Homeless and despised for centuries, they were resigned to their fate. Men with swastikas and vicious dogs were on the way. They would mercilessly round up the gypsies, take them to concentration camps, and force them into showers hissing with cyanide. Kaija wanted to warn them but found she could not speak.

The women, dressed in black, drew closer together and turned their backs on Kaija and Magda. Only one weary young woman looked directly at Kaija and nodded in recognition. Speaking urgently in a language that Kaija did not understand, she twisted a thin wire around and around. She made scooping and scraping motions and offered the loop to Kaija.

"Don't," Magda hissed into Kaija's ear. "Don't take it. Don't do it. You will die if you do. You have a long life ahead of you."

Magda's strong fingers fastened on Kaija's wrist, and she half-pulled, half-carried Kaija back through the forbidden door into the dorm, up the stairs, and into her room.

The transition between dream and reality was so seamless that Kaija expected to see Magda next to her when she opened her eyes. But only the wires of the clothes rack thrummed.

Perspiration broke out and gathered under her arms and between her legs. Sweat soaked her bed, but she felt too weak to move the covers. Had she been asleep? Was she awake now? Had she been dreaming, or had she actually been in Latvia? Was the dream a warning or was it a simple result of anxiety? The words, "You will die if you do," was as powerful as her other earlier premonitions.

When Kaija could finally move, she turned on the light. Lifting her hand, she saw that her fingers were covered with blood.

Her period, three months late, had started.

Some mysterious power had warned her and produced a change in her body. This power or Magda had saved her life. Or, had everything happened the other way around? Did her period start first and then her brain provided an explanation by creating the dream of Magda and the gypsies? Here was yet another experience for which Kaija would try and fail to find a satisfactory, logical explanation.

30

Jerry had been right about one thing. The English Department was more welcoming to Kaija and to women students generally than Pre-Med. English professors did not try to keep undergraduates from carnal knowledge. They took pleasure in their ability to shock as they elucidated the mysteries, old and new, or presented as fact research colored by contemporary prejudices.

Emily Dickinson knew nothing about sex because she never married, but Lord Byron had slept with his sister. Dying was a metaphor for orgasm, but sonnet sequences addressed to women were actually about transcending the flesh and merging with God. Furthermore, no great writer had ever put any ideas, political beliefs, or social criticism into his poems or novels. Except for Mary Ann Evans, who would cheerfully have given up writing and her pseudonym George Eliot for the sake of being pretty, and the Bronte sisters, who were writers because they came from a crazed family who happened to get isolated on the moors, women had not written much.

Girls were urged to get Bachelor of Arts degrees in preparation for marriage and volunteer work. They could always teach if they were widowed, the education of children partly dependent on the deaths of husbands. Even so English professors sneered at the very idea of taking the required courses in pedagogy, and they encouraged only the dimmest in that direction. Oh no, not those courses in the School of Education, they cried, where they call each other "Doctor" instead of "Professor" or "Mister" and then are surprised when they get a phone call in the middle of the night to come deliver a baby.

With a B.A. "With Highest Honors" but no courses in the School of Education, Kaija was not qualified to teach. Her only choice was between marriage and graduate school.

Kaija was delighted when professor Hazard admitted her to his graduate Seminar on the Romantic Poets. She had been in his Introduction to Literature class during her freshman year, and she had admired the systematic way he had led the class through Sophocles' Athens and Dante's Hell. She had felt sorry for him when he tried to get students to define the nature of justice or to comment on the symbolic manifestations of sin. Students stared down at their notebooks when he called on them directly, and no one ever raised a hand to volunteer.

Once Kaija was convinced that he really did want someone to speak up, she had taken to answering him every other class period. She enjoyed the dizzying sequence as he followed his original question with others; sometimes he drove her into an unforeseen corner, but more often he confirmed the soundness of her reasoning. He concluded these exchanges by looking into her eyes and murmuring, "That was excellent, Miss Veldre. Thank you very much." He had told one of the English majors in Kaija's dorm that she was his best and most interesting student, which had thrilled her.

His graduate Seminar met in the late afternoon, but Mr. Hazard looked sleepy, as if he had just roused himself to come teach. He stretched and yawned and rubbed his eyes; he loosened his tie and took off his tweed jacket to reveal a clean but rumpled white shirt. A thick gold wedding ring rested comfortably on his finger, but Kaija believed that his wife was a feckless woman. She did not iron his shirts properly or see to it that he got his rest. Why, she probably let sluts' wool collect under his sacred desk.

The English graduate student grapevine, whose information about every detail of the personal lives of professors would have shocked them, reported that Mr. Hazard's wife was pregnant. Kaija decided that a sloppy and fecund woman could not possibly be his intellectual equal. She was only a housewife, a category Kaija had escaped and which she had come to regard as contemptuously as everyone around her. With the callousness typical of young women,

Kaija felt no guilt about Mr. Hazard's wife when she felt his eyes lingering on her slim body and long legs.

Mr. Hazard began each class by reciting some of the assigned poems, his voice manly and melodious, his face alive with the love of words. He was different from other professors who made their graduate students compile bibliographic descriptions, do research on obscure historical figures for the books they were writing themselves, and read literary theories with few references to the novels and poems students had loved as undergraduates.

Listening to Mr. Hazard, Kaija slowly became aware that he had the same beautiful coloring as Maris: gray eyes, blond hair, and smooth skin touched by the sun. Mr. Hazard's eyes were dreamier than Maris' and his mouth more vulnerable, probably because he spoke about poetry rather than surgery and chemical formulas. How had she failed to notice that Mr. Hazard was absolutely gorgeous?

Mr. Hazard had an old-fashioned, almost un-American belief in memorization, and Kaija had had to learn hundreds of Latvian poems by heart in the camps. He recommended that everyone in the Seminar make a practice of committing one poem a day to memory, and Kaija complied happily. Poems in English moved Kaija almost as deeply as those in Latvian. In addition, memorization was practical. Long passages of Keats and Wordsworth as well as her store of Latvian poetry would keep her from going crazy in Siberian wastes, fascist prisons, or South American jails.

It did not take Mr. Hazard long to discover that pressed-for-time graduate students were not following his suggestion to memorize. Love of learning had not triumphed, but at least he could reward the true worshippers at the altar of poetry. Students who could demonstrate knowledge of five hundred lines would be excused from the required term paper. They would simply have to write down what followed several lines he chose at random. What could be easier?

"I am Ozymandias, king of kings. Look on my works, ye mighty, and despair," Kaija declaimed to herself as she walked to the English Department on a foggy afternoon.

"We might as well go into my office, Miss Veldre," Mr. Hazard said when it became obvious no one else would show up. He had given his students the best that had been thought and said, but they had ignored the pearls placed before them.

"The child is father of the man . . ."
"I wandered lonely as a cloud . . ."
"When old age shall this generation waste . . ."
"My love is like a red, red rose . . ."

He supplied a line and Kaija continued, feeling her voice rise and soar. There was an intimacy in this exercise that she had not foreseen. The noises in the hallway subsided as other students and faculty left for the night. Darkness was descending, and drizzle had given way to steady rain.

"Jenny kissed me when we met..." jumping from the chair she sat in Kaija recited, and Mr. Hazard, his voice sounding extraordinarily sexy, joined in at the end.

"Say I'm wear, say I'm sad,
Say that health and wealth have missed me,
Say I'm growing old, but add,
Jenny kissed me."

In the silence that followed, Mr. Hazard reached behind him and adroitly turned down a framed photograph that Kaija wished she had looked at.

"May I?" he said as he looped a strand of hair behind her ear, exactly the way Maris had.

"Yes," Kaija said.

280

He turned off the light and kissed her. Kaija closed her eyes and kissed him back. She believed that the true intimacy of two soulmates was beginning.

Affairs with professors were practically a requirement for women graduate students. Most male students had wives who did the housework, typed their papers, and earned money in clerical jobs at the University and by their ironing skills, which they advertised on bulletin boards, but the relatively few women graduate students were all single. Those foolish enough to fall in love with a professor they had sex with ended up putting up storm windows and babysitting their children while the professors took their wives to the Virgin Islands for "a new start."

Night classes to accommodate students who had to work were unheard of on the Bloomington campus, so Kaija and Mr. Hazard were undisturbed in his office after everyone else left. She tried to use her vivid imagination to lessen the terror of walking back to her dorm alone in the dark. She was on a journey as heroic as Psyche's on behalf of Eros. Like Jane Eyre she was striding away from a man unworthy of her to one who loved her. Why courtly Mr. Hazard did not whisk her away in his hero's phaeton was a trivial question.

In the midst of Kaija's preoccupation with Mr. Hazard, a year after the disastrous trip to meet Jerry's parents, Jerry phoned. As if nothing had changed between them, he asked her for a date. Self-assured and insistent to begin with, he became angry and whining when she refused.

His relentless calls continued, and she grew more and more afraid. But she kept her fear to herself. She tried to confide in her roommates, but they thought Jerry's persistence was romantic. He was carrying the torch for her, she was heartlessly toying with him, and there was no reason whatsoever to be scared.

Jerry waited for her outside the dorm, fell into step, and talked, more incoherently each time. Untreated wounds of soldiers were festering, bodies of his army buddies were rotting, and American women were monsters of selfishness. They did not understand that surrender was the greatest pleasure a woman could experience. They refused to study the works of his master D. H. Lawrence, who explained all this brilliantly. A listening device was planted in Jerry's toilet tank, and a Korean woman with axe raised waited for him behind his red door.

Kaija felt no sympathy. Talk away, she thought, as she tore up his notes and letters. These consisted mostly of lists anyway: numbered names of Korean towns, American military camps, and men who had been on his troop transport. Even when his scrawls became indecipherable, they were still carefully numbered. He tried leaving a blind kitten for her at the English Department, but the secretary made him take it away.

Jerry's craziness seemed fitting to Kaija. He had not noticed that anything was wrong when she was desperate; he had not made that awful visit to his parents easier for her; he had failed to protect her. He was a weakling who could not stand up to his father and mother; he was a whiner who could not deal with wartime memories, as she had. She refused to take his self-pity seriously. Unlike him, she did not have the luxury of going crazy. She had to get an education and a job.

Eventually Jerry disappeared. On one of her Sunday afternoon walks, she saw that the calligraphy by his mailbox had disappeared and the red door was painted dull beige. Jerry was gone, Kaija's past was behind her, and Mr. Hazard dominated the present.

On a little island of light in an empty building, Mr. Hazard and Kaija read hundreds of poems. Kaija relished these sweet hours filled with words; they were a time of intimacy and deep connection. Mr. Hazard looked away from her only when he wrote down a comment she made about a passage which he called brilliant.

Kaija kept her mind blank on her way to the restroom to insert her diaphragm. They made love awkwardly on a church pew, which Mr. Hazard's wife had bought at an auction, stripped, painted, and lined with thin hand-sewn cushions.

Mr. Hazard was an assistant professor of English, in his mid thirties, at a Midwestern University, but Kaija, intoxicated by poetry, assigned to him the power to transform. He was helping her forget Maris and to understand that she had been naïve about Jerry.

Mr. Hazard would play Svengali to her Trilby, he would be Pygmalion to her Galatea, and he would help her enter a normal, happy American life.

Mr. Hazard spoke often about his quintessentially American boyhood in Maine. He had walked in autumn woods with his father and watched wild pink roses emerge from fog along the rocky coast. He did not speak about his wife, and he mentioned their newly arrived twins only in the context of his disrupted nights and unfinished manuscripts. He abhorred departmental politics, and he yearned for a simpler, more authentic life, like Thoreau's. He would find a job near the ocean or lakes eventually. Kaija understood and encouraged his longing. Mr. Hazard was wise to return to the beloved landscapes of his childhood. He would take her with him when he left.

Kaija believed they had perfect intimacy, yet he did not ask, and she did not tell him about the war, camps, or living in exile. She did not mention her parents, Alma, Maris, Jerry, or the mysterious dream that had saved her from an abortion and possible death. She believed him when he said he was in love with her because he saw the wisdom of Europe in her eyes and that he loved her slight accent. She called him Mr. Hazard between kisses.

They met less and less often after the Seminar ended. He had articles to write and courses to prepare. She had tests to study for and a job to find. He was distancing himself from her, but good manners and the fear of being rejected entirely in an embarrassing scene kept her from confronting him. She tried to believe that he avoided meeting because he felt guilty about his wife. He was a nice man. But she was also coming to realize that she was not very important to him. She never had been.

""What are you going to do next, Kaija? Get married?" Mr. Hazard asked her one of the last times they met.

"No, no one's asked me," Kaija said. Mr. Hazard was not going to share his beloved landscapes with her. He would not stand shoulder to shoulder with her as she faced the perils of academe. She was glad she had not told him her daydreams, which seemed pathetically naïve now.

"Don't worry, Kaija, they'll be breaking down the doors for you. But what will you do till then?"

"Get a job in an office, I guess."

"Oh, no, don't do that. You should be at a University while you take your prelims and write your dissertation; you'll never finish otherwise. You're bright enough to get a Ph.D.; you think like a man. I've placed my other students at Yale and the Big Ten schools, but here's a job that's just came in at one of the smaller Minnesota schools. You should apply. I'll write you a recommendation, and you should ask William Riley Parker too. He's the one with real power."

Professor Parker, the great Milton scholar, was the Department star, in spite of the fact that he did not have a Ph.D. He delighted in telling his classes that was because no one was brilliant enough to examine him.

"Of course, Parker's famous, and he's a good man, but he's an anachronism," Mr. Hazard said. "You're dead in academe without a Ph.D."

The end of a love affair, a few off-hand words of advice, a dashed-off recommendation, and Kaija's future was set. On her way to a life of intricate footnotes, Byzantine department politics, and mountains of student papers, she was grateful to Mr. Hazard. He had saved her from being a mere secretary, and he had kept the door open to a life with poems.

31

Shortly after the wedding, Alma discovered she was pregnant. She was embarrassed because two childless years were considered the minimum for educated, respectable couples like Ivars and her. She worried that people would say that she had not been a virgin when she married. She would prove them wrong, of course, when the baby arrived nine months to the day after her wedding. But except for this one concern, Alma was happy.

The baby would make everything perfect. Ivars, carefully polite to Valdis at meals, would begin to show genuine affection to her father. She and Ivars would do things together as a family. For the first time Alma saw that she could have a real life in America rather than merely wait here until she could go back to Latvia. Returning was increasingly unlikely anyway. The Iron Curtain was increasingly impenetrable. But the baby would solidify the happy, safe, and permanent home Alma and Ivars would create in America together.

They named the little boy Janis, in honor of Ivars' father and of *Jani* or Midsummer. Ivars was deeply affected by the birth of his son. The brave little life, his to protect after so many losses, seemed to transform him. Usually undemonstrative, he wiped away tears when the nurse placed his son in his arms.

"Thank you, Alma," he whispered. "Now we have one more reason to celebrate Midsummer."

Joy flooded her. Ivars had actually told her how much he loved her; he had acknowledged that she was the one most important to him. He remembered their first dance together with the same excitement and tenderness as she did; he would be less reserved from now on. She drew her husband to her and locked her arms around him and her little boy. She was strong enough for anything that their marriage and their child required.

Their second child, also a boy, was born two years later and named Valdis, after Alma's father. If the joylessness with which Ivars had married surfaced now and again, Alma told herself she could live with his quirks. If Ivars refused to join a Latvian fraternity, which meant they were not invited to the most prestigious parties, they had more than enough social and cultural events to attend anyway. As it was, she could hardly keep up with the baking and cooking and serving and washing up required for the Latvian Center and the Latvian Lutheran Church. If Ivars arrived home too late to take Janitis to children's folk-dancing, Alma drove him herself.

She sat at the bar in the Latvian Center with fathers who came for the sake of conviviality and beer, while the children learned Latvian songs and simple folk dances. She did not mind, and sometimes the talk about old wiring and new drywall was downright interesting. The men listened respectfully as she described her remodeling projects, and they were transfixed when she talked about bank loans and tax credits.

Late in the evening someone would inevitably remark how lucky their children were. They could sing and dance without fear of bombs and fires; they could fall asleep in their own beds without crying for friends and toys they had had to abandon; they could dream pleasant dreams instead of having nightmares about aunts deported and uncles shot. Regardless of what had happened to their parents and grandparents, these children were untouched by exile and war.

Alma contributed little to this part of the conversation. She kept the turmoil about her mother locked away until she was by herself. Then she wrote hundreds of letters trying to find Velta in Siberia, which had become imperative for her the day Janitis was born. Swallowing her suspicion and dislike of everyone who had access to Soviet authorities, Alma wrote to politicians, government officials, cultural ambassadors, and journalists. She disciplined herself to be patient as she rolled sheets of paper and carbon into her huge Smith-Corona and made painstaking erasures and corrections.

Determined to keep sadness out of her home and away from her children, she carried the addressed envelopes to her car before she went to bed. If one of the little boys turned over and muttered in his sleep when she came in, she froze, her nerves taut. Only when she saw him settled peacefully again did she pour herself a brandy to help her get to sleep.

Ivars and Alma were living in their second house, bought with profits from one already remodeled and sold. Alma had done most of the work because Ivars was kept late at his job. On weekends he still went for the long solitary walks which were a necessity to him. Now and then Valdis emerged from his room to give his daughter a hand, and sometimes he worked at her side for an entire day and evening.

Alma had learned by trial and error, but the work came easily to her, and she was good at it. She enjoyed wielding hammers and paint brushes, and she was thrilled to see dilapidation and chaos give way to order, even beauty. When her father worked next to her and her little boys tumbled about on the lawn, their childish voices self-confident and happy, Alma's heart sang.

She had accomplished a lot, and she would do more. Already she had her eye on another house, run down but statelier than this, among the mansions on North Meridian Street. She was determined to live at one of the most impressive addresses in Indianapolis; that would show her English teacher Miss Donovan, the girls in high school, and all the other Americans who had condescended to her of what she was capable. But she had to be patient. She kept in check her longing to plant apple trees and birches, to start a raspberry patch, to make a bed for perennial flowers. Her father had told her about the harsh frosts which had killed thousands of apple trees in the winter before fifteen thousand Latvians were deported. Planting new trees in America, on property that was truly hers because of her hard work, would show the Godless Russians that they could not break the spirit of Latvians. But she would wait to start a real garden until she was in a place from which she would never have to move again.

The boys needed a permanent place, where they could store their favorite toys, their collections of butterflies and bugs, their photographs, and their school prizes. They must have a home they could always come back to if their lives took a painful turn. Ivars and she would grow old together in this house. Alma pictured herself and Ivars eating lunch in the garden on summer Sundays and sitting across from each other by the fire on bleak winter afternoons.

All her blessings sprang from her marriage: her healthy children, her father drinking less, her energy to work long hours, and her plans for the future. Ivars complained occasionally about his job, but everybody did that. Thank God, he had gotten that Taliesen foolishness out of his head; he never mentioned that Mister Wright who had misled him.

Alma forbade herself to resent it that Ivars did not help her, crazy about buildings though he was. He preferred to spend time alone, and he seldom played with the boys. When she rested after loosening an old pipe or sanding the last bit of woodwork, she found herself thinking that she should not be doing this by herself. Ivars was stronger than she, and this was his home, his family, and his life. How had he claimed the right to remain so aloof?

She took herself firmly in hand then. She had known what he was like before she married him. He was not doing anything different now when he walked alone for miles on sunny days or sat in the Public Library when the weather was foul. She was not a romantic young girl, if she ever had been, who needed constant attention; she did not have to have her husband in her pocket. And Ivars was invariably polite to her. She appreciated his good manners when he thanked her for giving him space, for putting up with his moods, for not nagging him as another wife would. He said he liked their grown-up, calm marriage instead of passionate outbursts, while Alma remembered the fight about Taliesin when she had almost lost him.

The real miracle was that Ivars had returned to her. She still had the roses, carefully dried and wrapped in tissue paper, which he had given her. If doubts continued to trouble her, she scooped up one of her little boys and held his solid body close to hers.

Her marriage *was* all the stronger for not being endlessly discussed, she told herself. When Ivars turned towards her late at night in bed, Alma knew then that he would rather die than be pulled away from her; she understood then that he would never leave her. It would have embarrassed them both to talk about these intimate moments. Only the lower classes and soldiers who had seen all boundaries crumble had words for what happened between them.

And yet, Alma craved words. Not the crude and shameful ones, certainly not. But she wanted Ivars to say something, anything, when their two bodies were one. She wanted him to cry out her name, to whisper that he loved her, to tell her that she meant more to him than Dzintra ever had, and that he lived for the times when their bodies convulsed, and their tears mingled. But he kept his own counsel.

As she poured his coffee and handed him his carefully cooked and beautifully arranged breakfast, a sense of discontinuity struck her. Who was this man, this remote stranger with excellent manners, who bore no resemblance to the passionate man of the night before? Had she imagined everything that happened between them? Why did the two of them not work side by side, why did they not talk about what they had done when they were apart, the way she believed that her parents had?

But there was always a great deal to be done, and she did not allow these musings to get the better of her. Ivars was her husband and she loved him.

Alma and Ivars had agreed that two children were enough for people of their position in Latvian society, and she had silently assumed the responsibility for seeing that was so. But in the tenth year of their marriage, Alma discovered she was pregnant again. She told him as they lay side by side, no longer entwined but still touching. Ivars drew away from her as violently as if she had singed his flesh.

"Damn you, Alma, how could you?" he demanded.

Shame flooded her, as if she had done something crudely lascivious or enticed him into something offensive for her own pleasure.

"Damn you. We were finally getting somewhere, but you've gone and ruined it. I don't expect much, but I do rely on you to count to twenty or twenty-eight or whatever it is you do with the pill."

He had no idea how much his words hurt her. He only knew that Alma was stifling his creativity; she was the one keeping him from the life he wanted. He hated his job with its pencil-pushing and endless boredom. The chance to really live would have been his as soon as they sold this house into which they had moved a couple of years ago. But she had wrecked everything with her fecundity.

Frustration made him savage. "You can't expect to copulate and birth a brood, like some Russian peasant out to overpopulate an occupied country. You're not an animal in heat, Alma. We're civilized people. We're Latvians."

Alma shut her eyes. She congratulated herself for still being alive. He had said the ugliest things possible, and she had not died. That at least was something. But shame for having desired him, shame for having been so open to him sealed her lips. She would lie still so she would not provoke him into saying more.

The winter that Alma was pregnant with her third child was bleaker than all the previous gray winters in Indiana. She hated seeing her half-finished projects, the dirty ice in the streets, her large belly, and the pulse continuing to beat inside her animal self. Her brain told her that she was the person she had always been, but in the smudged light, Russian peasant women, their legs crudely spread, enticed soldiers and copulated with boars. As Ivars' venom coursed through her, she abhorred femaleness itself.

It took all her willpower to get up and see to it that the boys were dressed and fed and off to school. She watched indifferently as her father retreated to his room and Ivars stayed later at work. Because silence could not wound, she spoke only when absolutely necessary, and she listened hardly at all.

"So, where's Ivars this afternoon?" Kaija asked during one of their increasingly rare phone calls. Talking with Alma was terrible these days. Alma answered every question with a monosyllable, and she never brought up a topic herself. Kaija did not know enough about Alma's domestic arrangements to show an intelligent interest or to draw her out. Sometimes, in sheer desperation for something to say, Kaija ended-up giving a convoluted account of some academic controversy, which could not possibly interest Alma.

"Is he home?" Kaija persisted.

"He's at work," Alma said evenly.

"At work? On Sunday afternoon? And you believe him, do you?"

When Alma did not reply, Kaija plunged on recklessly.

"I've not heard of a company requiring engineers to work on Sundays. Only academics stick to it because we have papers to grade and research to do."

Alma's stomach clenched at this piece of snobbishness. She had regularly worked herself into exhaustion, hammering and painting, every Saturday and Sunday afternoon unless she had to go to a Latvian event. But, of course, Kaija never bothered to notice what she did.

"That shows how little you know. Most people have to work on Sundays."

"Of course, Alma, if you say so. All I meant is that Ivars must be getting serious about his job all of a sudden."

How dare Kaija imply that Ivars was lazy and inattentive to his job? He was Alma's husband and his faults were hers alone to know. She was the one who had to make excuses when he did not help out at the Latvian Center, she distracted the boys when they complained that their father never played with them, and she kept people from gossiping. How dare Kaija suggest Ivars was up to something?

After a long pause, Kaija tried again. "So how are you feeling, Alma?"

But this too failed to mollify Alma. Kaija never asked a specific question about Alma's pregnancy. It did not matter that Alma would have been embarrassed had she done so. Kaija had never been pregnant; it was unfair to think Alma was ill-humored because she was. Kaija had no husband either; she had no idea what marriage was like.

"I'm fine, never better," Alma snapped.

"Good. Glad to hear it. Anything else going on?" Kaija asked hopefully.

Alma said nothing.

"I'll be in Indianapolis next weekend. Want me to come over on Sunday afternoon?"

"No, Ivars and I always do things with the boys on Sundays."

"But you just said . . . . Oh well, I'll call you again sometime," Kaija sighed.

Alma sat unmoving after Kaija hung-up. Kaija did not know what Alma suffered, Alma told herself, even as she resented Kaija for coming close and touching the very place that now pulsed painfully. Alma would never tell anyone the ugly things Ivars had said; they would become even more true if she spoke them aloud. Everyone would be revolted when they saw Alma through Ivars' eyes. Kaija would criticize Ivars more than she did already.

But where *was* Ivars? And with whom? He could not possibly be out this Sunday, in the sleet, walking eight hours at a stretch, past the time that libraries and museums closed. Alma would die if he was having an affair. She could see men's eyes twinkling with amusement and envy; she could hear women whispering that she did not know how to hold on to her husband.

Alma stretched out on the couch and put a wet cloth over her eyes. Usually she found the dark empty spaces behind her lids restful, but Kaija had invaded them. Kaija had given a definite shape to her suspicions, and Alma could not rid herself of an image of Ivars whispering "I love you," as he collapsed on the small white breasts of a faceless slender woman.

Alma hardly thought about the coming child as she waited for her pregnancy to end. She pulled the covers around herself more tightly if she woke at dawn and found that Ivars was still not at home. The bursts of energy which had propelled her into cleaning and shopping and contriving before the birth of the boys did not arrive. Without much interest she wondered whether that was normal. Maybe nature would take its course. Nature would have to.

Everything was difficult about this pregnancy. Her body had ballooned, her breasts itched and burned, nausea and heartburn tormented her. Her legs swelled into red mottled logs and threatened to immobilize her completely. She had trouble getting her breath.

She could not stop tormenting herself with the poignancy of making love with Ivars before everything went wrong. If only she had known it was the last time, she would have memorized every movement and touch. But she shamed herself rather than him for his cruel words. She was surprised that her heart continued to beat.

Lost Midsummers

32

Alma went into labor a week before Midsummer, on a clear blue Saturday in June. Ivars happened to be home when a band tightened around her belly, but she was too proud and too bitter to ask him to stay with her. Let him take the boys to the Latvian Center, as he had surprisingly offered to do, let him manage by himself when he returned home with the boys hungry and cranky and no meal in the refrigerator ready to set out. Let him come to the hospital to find out what arrangements she had made for their care. She felt unused muscles in her face stretch as she grinned for the first time in months. She left a note on the cold stove and drove herself to Methodist Hospital.   Alma grinned again at how accurately she had predicted the behavior of doctors and nurses. To start with her satisfaction at being right kept despair away. The nurses mispronounced her last name, not even trying to get it right, and they looked at her dismissively when she corrected them. One of the doctors called her "a naughty girl" because her labor was taking so long, and a vacuous teenage Candy Striper reported that she had not been able to understand the person who answered when she phoned the Latvian Center.

As the pains grew sharper, Alma bit her pillow to keep from screaming. No one cared whether she lived or died. Only at the very end, convinced she was being ripped apart, did she cry out for those who should have been there: her husband; her mother; Mrs. Vilkacis, the kind neighbor who had not escaped from Latvia; a favorite teacher in the DP camps; and, Kaija, her best friend.

Humans had failed her, so she called on Laima the goddess of fate, on Mara the goddess of birth, and all the other female spirits she could think of: the Mother of Roads; the Mother of Woods; the Mother of Winds; and, the Mothers of Fire, Water, and Skies. But they could not cross the ocean from Latvia and the unfamiliar terrain of America and enter the sterile hospital building set in acres of concrete to comfort her.

With terrible clarity Alma saw that Ivars had never allowed her to rest in his love; he had fought constantly against her need to believe that she mattered to him. They had made three children together, yet all that time something inside her had trembled, like a sere leaf about to disintegrate. He had never said that his love for Dzintra was over and done with, that Alma was the only one he loved, and that his marriage was important to him. Instead he had stubbornly maintained his right to remain separate.

His stinginess with himself had kept her from close friendships with women as well. Alma knew every Latvian in Indianapolis, but she had made no real friends after she married. She had even been afraid to have Kaija around too much. Kaija said unforgivable things about Ivars as a husband, but she loved books and poetry and cello music, just as he did. Her body was not marred by bearing and nursing children; she was still lovely. If she set out to do so, she charmed people easily. Alma had been afraid that Ivars would fall in love and go off with Kaija. He had always made it clear that he admired Kaija because she understood him.

But in spite of his withholding, Alma did not pluck Ivars out of her heart. They were married, and she had to hold onto him. She cursed instead the child that would not come and for whose sake she would die in this prison, alone among these strangers. She screamed again for her mother.

"Hush now, behave yourself, Doctor's busy, be a good girl," the nurses shushed. "Upsy daisy, bottoms up," they chirped as they shaved Alma between the legs. Someone started to fit a gas mask over Alma's mouth and nose.

"No!" Alma screamed. She had to fight; she could not let them win. But someone aimed a syringe, the shot found its target, and everything went dark.

Alma dreams she is on a train to Siberia, but she must not struggle or make a scene, or they will beat her again. Sharp metal corners of a heavy suitcase cut into her belly, but she has to hold on to it because the guards have taken every other thing that belongs to her.

The train stops with a jerk, and someone pushes her so violently that she loses her grip. Her legs splay open as she falls on frozen ground. Gray snowflakes, hard as icicles, strike her face and neck. She gropes around until her hands find the entrance to a tunnel cut into ice. She must go into it in spite of her fear. Her mother and warmth and light are at the other end.

Alma has come to help her young mother fell trees, to wave firebrands to frighten off starving wolves, to saw through thick ice for the flesh of living fish. She alone can help her survive winter in Siberia. She must find grasses and leaves to be dried and boiled to prevent scurvy; she must dry mushrooms and store pine bark to be simmered for soup; she must cut sod to patch the roof of her mother's hovel.

The guards rip off Alma's blindfold, and she can finally see. She has arrived at the ruined shack where her mother has sheltered. A massive oven, its fire out, takes up a third of the cramped space. The dirt floor is swept pathetically clean, and bundles piled on a table are neatly covered with a sheet.

Cobwebs cling to Alma's face, and dust clogs her nose. She wets a handkerchief with saliva and tries to rub them away before she lifts the tightly tucked cloth. Her mother's corpse, carefully laid out on the table two decades ago, is perfectly preserved by the cold. Her mother's face is young, but her hands and feet are those of a very old woman, calloused and deformed by punishment and work.

Alma kisses her mother's frozen cheek, covers her face again, lifts her stiff body, and tries to hold it to her heart. She looks around for the infant she knows is somewhere. She can hear it wailing, demanding to be fed. But Alma has nothing to give it, and anyway, her arms are full already with her mother. Better to leave the child here, to die quickly of cold rather than let it live on, unwanted by everyone.

Alma woke dry-eyed and thirsty. Her cheeks were tight with dried tears, her lips swollen, and the incision between her legs pulsed and stung. For the first time she knew with absolute certainty that her mother was dead and had been for twenty years or more. The hundreds of letters trying to find her among the deported which Alma had written after Janitis was born had been futile.

Evidently Alma herself was alive, in a clean bed with curtains drawn closed around it. She concentrated on a point of weak light behind the white material and tried to feel nothing.

She woke again later, this time to the murmur of women's voices, punctuated by laughter and soft cries. The few words she caught were in English; she must be in the United States rather than in Siberia.

But when, the 1950s, or later? Her stomach was more or less flat, the child no longer inside her. For some reason they had put her in a room with women who had given birth to living children instead of allowing her to rest in isolation as befitted a mother whose child was dead. She was not surprised. She had thought all along that the doctors and nurses were callous. She would not tell them that she was glad the child was dead.

The talk of the women grew more distinct. They were all veterans, here for their third or fourth child. Alma knew what they would say before they said it; she had heard it all during her first two confinements. Then, out of loyalty to Ivars, she had condemned the women around her as whiners and hypocrites who showed a weary contempt for men as long as their husbands were absent. But as visiting hours neared, they put on lipstick, teased their hair, and found their breathy little girl voices. They arranged their faces into expressions of sweet suffering before they spoke in gently reproachful tones to their sheepish husbands.

But now Alma listened with interest as the women agreed that no child would ever be born if men had to have the babies and that it was a good thing that this hospital had not started the new practice of allowing husbands to be present during labor and birth. No woman would get any attention then because the doctors would have their hands full with fainting men. It would be worse in here than in the trenches. But what could you expect of men, those large clumsy creatures, incapable of finding their own socks or opening a box of cereal for hungry children?

Alma was shocked to find herself nodding. She would have joined in, were she not afraid that the women would draw together to exclude her as soon as they heard her accent. They would ask her where she was from: Lativa, Lapland, Latvia? Never heard of it, what's the difference, what are you doing here, and when are you going back to your own country?

She envied the women their female visitors, the mothers and sisters and aunts and friends, who tiptoed in two at a time, obedient to hospital policy. Children were not allowed, either because new mothers needed rest or because children had to be protected from the messiness of birth and blood.

Alma tried not to think about Ivars, but her heart jumped each time she heard decisive male steps in the hallway. Visiting hours passed slowly. She had been waiting for months for a reconcilliation; she was beside herself with anxiety and with longing. But Ivars did not come. The other women pretended they did not notice she was alone, either out of embarrassment or pity. Alma hoped they did not think that she was an unwed mother. She had her own husband, of course she did.

A nurse jerked the curtains open, snapped on an overhead light, and set down a pitcher. Behind her was another nurse holding an infant.

"Here's your daughter, Mrs. . . .," the nurse's voice trailed off. "You have a healthy little girl. Six pounds and six ounces."

The nurse thrust the bundle at her. This baby was not hers; it could not be.

"No," Alma managed, "take it away. It's not mine."

"Of course she is," the nurse laughed and pointed to the pink and white beaded bracelet on the tiny wrist. "See your last name? All this baby needs is a first name of her own."

"Take it away, I don't want it," Alma whispered.

The women in the ward were alert, their silence full of condemnation. The nurses looked at each other. Not knowing what else to do, they tried once more to place the baby into Alma's arms.

"Doctor told you in the delivery room you had a girl. You remember that, don't you?"

Doubt flickered. Alma did remember rending pain followed by a bright light splitting her forehead. An infant had been there, wailing and begging to be taken along.

Finally, a nurse said firmly, "Shame on you. This baby needs her mother. Come on, behave yourself."

It was the shaming, her grandmother's favorite method of discipline, which defeated Alma. She did not object when the nurse laid the infant on her bed. She knew she would never feel for this child the fierce protective love she had for her sons. Not curious enough to examine the tiny body and limbs, Alma reluctantly placed a hand on the bundle to keep it from rolling and hitting the floor.

"Well, about time," a nurse said, while another added with more compassion and kindness, "Good girl."

The baby's eyes were shut tight, the little face sharp and red, with no endearing chubbiness.

"You're breast feeding, aren't you? It says on your chart you did last time."

"No. Never. I won't. I refuse," Alma said. They had coerced her into accepting this child, but they need not think they could make her do anything else. It was bad enough that she would have to take care of it for the next eighteen years.

33

Kaija turned off the ignition and sat for a moment. She was not looking forward to the visit. She wished she could keep driving, but Alma would hear that she had been in Indianapolis and she would be hurt that Kaija had not come to see the new baby.

Kaija was no good at baby worship. Maybe Alma would do most of the talking, as she had when the boys were born. She had not taken her eyes from them while she detailed their eating and sleeping habits and cooed and patted and rocked.

Perhaps Alma would also say something authentic about Ivars this time. Usually she bristled if Kaija breathed a single unflattering word about him, but Alma had been more honest at the hospital. She had told Kaija that Ivars had not been to see her, that she was hurt, and that it was not the first time he had failed her.

Alma's house offered no welcome. Paint was peeling off the elaborate trim, one end of the porch sagged, and dirty windows showed between weedy shrubs. Last year's leaves lay rotting in corners of the porch, and the lawn looked as if it had not been cut the entire summer,

Kaija could hardly see Alma's lean and active self inside the slow clumsy woman who opened the door. Ignoring the loud voices of the boys arguing in the back of the house, Alma slumped down on a pile of tangled blankets at the end of the couch. A white bassinet stood in the far corner.

"She's just like other babies," Alma replied to Kaija's awkward questions. She took Kaija's gift-wrapped package containing a tiny dress embroidered with butterflies and set it down unopened.

"So, how's Ivars? Did he ever show up at the hospital?" Kaija asked after she had run out of questions about the baby.

301

"He's fine. Of course he came to the hospital."

"But you said . . . ."

"Oh, that," Alma laughed dismissively. "Forget about that. He came right after I talked to you."

Intimacy with married women was impossible. One minute they hinted at betrayals so huge and pain so excruciating that they could not put them into words, or they complained about the irritating petty habits of their husbands, only to freeze you with an uncomprehending stare if you referred later to what they had said. When their husbands showed up, they made a display of such marital coziness and wifely compliance that it left you doubting your sanity. Kaija had been a fool to expect the kind of honesty from Alma that she got from her single friends.

"Well, where did Mister Ivars say he'd been?" Kaija said, not bothering to hide her disapproval.

"At home."

"Doing what? You said you had arranged for Mrs. Kalnins to take care of the boys."

"Oh . . . he was . . . sketching. He had an idea for a building to commemorate the birth of his sons."

"Oh, Lord, of all the narcissistic, self-indulgent, phony . . . ."

"You don't understand, Kaija. His creativity is very important to him. He has to have his privacy, and he's grateful to me for giving him space."

"Who says so? Ivars?"

"Yes, of course, Ivars."

"And did he show you his drawings? Were they so brilliant that they made up for the way he hurt you?"

"I wasn't hurt, I was just . . . . Anyway, Kaija, I wish you wouldn't pry. You know nothing about being married."

"Thank goodness for that," Kaija laughed. Feminist writers were informing women that they themselves could become the men they had wanted to marry and that a woman without a man was like a fish without a bicycle. Kaija agreed with the feminists and at the same time longed for a man whom she could love. Most of the men on the Minnesota campus where she taught were married, and it was glaringly obvious why no one had married the single ones. Whenever Kaija spent time with Alma, she was reminded that marriage did not automatically equal happiness.

Alma glared, and Kaija swallowed her laughter.

The fan whirred slowly, stirring air thick with humidity. It was oppressive as only an overcast August afternoon in Indiana can be. The silence between the two women lengthened.

Kaija walked slowly to the bassinette. As if on cue, the baby began to whimper. Alma sat unmoving, staring straight ahead. Should Alma not pick her up and rock her or something?

Finally, unable to stand it, Kaija said, "The baby is crying." She felt like a fool.

"I can hear."

"Well, shouldn't you do something?"

Alma heaved herself up, and without glancing at the baby, lumbered into the kitchen.

"Let me give you a hand with these dishes," Kaija offered as Alma set a bottle to warm. Glad of something to do, Kaija gathered dirty glasses and plates from the living and dining room and added them to those already stacked in the chaotic kitchen. She turned the water on full force, trying to shut out the small, increasingly hopeless cries. Short of letting the baby invade her heart, she would do anything to lighten Alma's misery, she thought as she plunged her hands into hot water.

When Kaija returned to the living room, the baby was still in the bassinet, a bottle propped in its mouth.

"Isn't she a little young . . . ," Kaija began, then thought better of it. "What's her name?"

"Jautrite. After one of the young women who worked at Stabules."

"Jautrite," Kaija repeated blankly. "Jautrite" meant someone merry and playful, while Alma must have been at her most despairing when, alone in the hospital and miserable about Ivars, she had to pick a name. Perhaps she had wished for a sunny temperament for her daughter, but Kaija heard only bitter irony in her voice now. Difficult to pronounce for Americans, the name would mark the little girl as different from the very beginning. That Alma had chosen it without thinking it would make Jautrite's childhood difficult was saddest of all.

The baby sucked hungrily. Her eyelids, blue and almost transparent, slid closed, then snapped warily open. The perfect little hands, not adroit enough to hold on to the bottle, flailed in the air and dislodged it. A vein began to throb in the baby's temple. Kaija turned away, unable to watch. A hopeless little monkey face, she told herself, trying to push away pity.

Kaija did not know the latest gossip in Indianapolis, and her job kept her too busy to read the Latvian newspaper <u>Laiks</u>, which would have provided a topic. American academic politics and scholarly controversies were difficult to explain to outsiders, but maybe she and Alma could talk about practical matters in teaching.

"It's hard for us women professors to convince our students that we know what we're talking about," Kaija said. "Students expect us to mother them, and they complain about their grades the way they wouldn't dare to a man. My male colleagues can say something completely cock-eyed, and students will write it down and memorize it. But when I lecture about recent research on women, students say that's just my opinion and that they have plenty of opinions of their own."

Alma looked blank, but Kaija pushed on. "Actually I think I don't know how to teach because I had no role models. I didn't have a single woman professor at Indiana University. Should I be sweet or harsh to my students? What do you think? I refuse to flirt with my male students the way some women do."

"I don't get it," Alma said. "What's so hard about waltzing into a classroom and chattering about a book for forty minutes? You have the rest of the time to yourself. Ivars would love a schedule like that. He could work on his poetry."

"Ivars is writing poetry again?" Kaija asked, surprised and a little envious. She had thrown away her poems about kisses in the rain and green ivy against gray stone walls as soon as she learned about the rigors of literary criticism and of life in academe. But had her poems really been as naive and clumsy as she had thought? She had enjoyed writing them far more than the academic articles required for promotion which she worked on now. Graduate school had a lot to answer for.

Decisive steps on the stairs from the second floor made Kaija turn.

"Well, if it isn't Kaija. Good to see you," Ivars greeted her as he strode into the kitchen. "I was in my room writing, but I heard your voice, and I just had to come down."

"Good to see you, too," Kaija said sincerely. He would help with the conversation, and she was genuinely curious about his writing.

"I'm working on a poetic drama about orphans, based on themes from the *dainas*."

He gestured excitedly as he quoted lines, explained allusions, and summarized a scene.

Suddenly he stopped mid-sentence. "But you don't care about that old Latvian stuff. I apologize for boring the American professor."

"I'm not bored, I'm not. I am interested in things Latvian," Kaija cried.

But Ivars had already closed the door to his real self.

"Very humid today, isn't it? But I'm afraid that's normal for this time of year," he observed.

After a few perfunctory comments on the weather, he bowed ironically to Kaija and disappeared up the stairs. Alma looked relieved to see him go.

"I'm sorry he didn't stay," Kaija said.

"He's busy," Alma murmured.

"I better get going too," Kaija said. "The baby is sweet."

"Yes. You always have important things to do," Alma said dully as she ushered Kaija out.

Lost Midsummers

34

Kaija noticed Roger Spear, a colleague from a neighboring Minnesota campus as soon as she walked into the lobby of the St. Francis Hotel for the annual meeting of the Modern Language Association.

"Welcome to San Francisco," he said as he sprang up from a love seat and opened his arms in welcome. "Glad you're staying in this hotel, Kaija. It looks like an excellent program. I see you're giving a paper tomorrow. Here, let me help you with your bag," he offered.

"I hope we can spend some time together, Kaija. We Midwesterners have to stick to each other." He smiled, showing off dimples.

After that Kaija ran into him everywhere: in the coffee shop, at the session where she gave her paper, and at four others she only attended. That they have dinner together on the last night seemed inevitable.

A tennis-playing, bird-watching, physical-fitness extolling professor of American Studies, Roger had read enough reviews of books about feminism and women writers to be an agreeable dinner companion. It would be all right with Kaija if their evening ended with companionable sex and vague promises about getting together again. They both drank a lot of expensive red wine, which would see them through any awkwardness.

While Roger settled the bill, which he insisted on paying, a headache announced itself in Kaija's temple. She wished she was going back to her room instead of accompanying Roger to his.

Like many other women of her generation who were pioneers in their professions, Kaija had not found true love with an equal. She could have with Maris, but Jerry and Mr. Hazard had disappointed her, and a few brief affairs after they had come to nothing. She gave herself sexual latitude like men, which would have been unthinkable in the 1950s. Sex was pleasurable but could be dangerous to the naïve. In any case, she expected nothing from it. It was neither romantic, nor mysterious.

Waiting for Roger to unlock his door, Kaija thought with longing of her luxurious room and comfortable bed. Two academic journals and a new novel by Fay Weldon were on her nightstand; it was more likely she would enjoy them rather than Roger. But it seemed childish to back out now.

"I want you to understand this doesn't mean anything," Roger said as he slid deftly between the sheets. "My wife and I have an agreement."

Whatever enthusiasm Kaija had mustered vanished, and her temple began to throb in earnest. Dislike for herself and for him washed over her. What was she doing here, with a man to whom she meant nothing? And he was almost certainly lying about his wife. She probably had no idea what he was up to, which was not much.

Kaija yawned, and Roger let out a discouraged sigh. He must have skimmed a current best seller about women's sexuality and paid particular attention to paragraphs about foreplay because he began to move systematically from Kaija's eyebrows to the soles of her feet. He bypassed Doctor Payne's spot but paused every twelve inches or so elsewhere to plant a loose dry kiss.

An image of an old-fashioned vacuum-cleaner picking up popcorn in a movie theater lobby formed in Kaija's mind, only to give way to an anteater snuffling through dry grass. She opened her eyes to get rid of the images, but the anteater positioned himself at the foot of the bed, snorting and sneezing. She burst out laughing.

Roger's responding chuckle sounded artificial. "What's so funny?"

She was laughing, then howling. Afraid to edge into tears, she buried her face in a pillow and pounded on the mattress.

Roger sat up. "What's this about? Tell me."

Kaija swung her legs to the floor and groped for her clothes. "I'm sorry, Roger," she gasped, "but I have to go."

"What's going on? You have to tell me."

"It's nothing really," she lied. The habit of being polite ran deep.

"Out with it, Kaija. It's only fair you tell me. I need to know for next time."

His motive for wanting to know set her off again.

"Actually, it's partly you, and partly me," she brought out. Her laughter subsided, and she could hardly keep back tears.

"I want to love the man I make love with, and I want him to love me. I don't want to have sex with someone to whom it means nothing. I've never felt so diminished as a woman in my life."

"But I said that for your sake, Kaija, so you wouldn't fall in love with me. I don't want you to get hurt. One would think you'd appreciate that."

Fall in love? With him? Kaija sucked in her cheeks and pressed her lips together, trying to imitate Virginia Woolf at her most ladylike, but the anteater snorted, raised a paw, and waved.

"Thank you for a very good dinner, Roger," Kaija said when she could speak without laughing or crying. "It's just that I want to feel something when I make love."

"Such as?"

"Friendship for starters."

Dammed-up words burst from her. "But what I really want is love. Love, intimacy, passion, even transcendence. I want a soul mate. I want a man whose energy is equal to mine, a man who is as smart as I am, a man who too has overcome hard things in his life. But if I can't have that, I'm much better off alone. I am not going to sleep with married men at conferences ever again. It's too depressing. And too, too funny."

"So, I gathered," Roger said stiffly and then slammed one at her.

"As for the rest of it, honey," he said in an easy glide from collegiality to condescension, "three cheers for you, but life isn't like that."

"I hope you're wrong," Kaija said as Roger locked the door behind her.

Back in her room, Kaija stepped out on the balcony. The lights of San Francisco twinkled below, and a familiar solitude enveloped her.

Maris had promised that he would always be with her. In an effusive moment he had said he would be her eyes if she went blind, he would be her limbs if she were crippled, he would be her ears if she went deaf. He would hold her when she cried.

Had he meant it even then? Or were they only words, like those in the sophomoric conversations she remembered from the 1950s? If you had to lose one of your senses, which one would you choose to give up? Does a tree falling in the forest make a sound if no one is there to hear? Is reason more important than emotion? They had talked seriously about these old chestnuts because they did not believe that the world would change or that they would grow old.

She felt only tenderness for Maris now. Her anger at him had long since evaporated. She wished she could see him, just to tell him she thought about him sometimes. That alone would be enough; nothing more would need to come of it. She expected they could not kiss like that again.

She let loneliness take hold of her completely. Her mother's health was failing, and her father was frailer every time she saw him; her parents would not be here forever. She longed to be back at Atminas, the Summer House, where every nook comforted her and every flower cheered her.

Her friendship with Alma, once very significant for itself and also as her connection to Latvians, was dissolving for lack of attention.

But she could at least change that. She made up her mind to see Alma more regularly. She would do everything she could to make their friendship flourish again.

35

Alma and Kaija were spending more time together. Their routine was similar to the one they had had in the 1950s: they met at 10 o'clock sharp on Saturday morning, and they shopped into the afternoon, when they were hungry and thirsty. But now, Kaija's shoulders ached, and Alma's hip was killing her. Everything else was different from the 1950s as well, when passing a day together did not require an effort.

Kaija's parents were upset when she set-out for Alma's house. Her visits from Minnesota were too short already, so why did she have to see other people? Kaija apologized and made promises, which were hard to keep. She was tense when she arrived at the ivy-covered Indiana limestone mansion set far back in the deep, maple-shaded lot on North Meridian Street.

Alma was nervous too, but she was good at hiding it. She grinned, slid behind the wheel of her silver Saab, squared her shoulders, and revved up the engine. She handed Kaija a precisely folded map of Indianapolis and told her to keep her finger on the X marking her house.

Indianapolis had grown a great deal since they were in high school, when the nickname of Naptown actually fit, but Alma never got lost. She just liked to be prepared for every emergency. She was proud of the secure life she had created, but no disaster would surprise her.

"In what other country could a girl like me arrive at age fourteen and end-up owning blocks of property on the 'north side,' and acres of woods near Lake Lemon?" she asked. Kaija relaxed, glad that Alma was taking the lead.

Until they got to the actual shopping, it was hard for Kaija to think of subjects to talk about, but the opportunity to speak and hear Latvian was precious, no matter what the subject.

They were on safe ground for now because Alma loved telling Kaija about old schools and warehouses she was turning into condominiums. She was shoring up foundations, knocking down walls, opening up ceilings for light, reinvesting profits, and planning her next projects.

"I'll make at least $120,000 on this one building alone," Alma boasted. "Not bad for part-time work. And all I did was manage, none of the actual grubbing around."

For that Alma hired Mexicans. She housed them in one of her less sumptuous properties and paid them minimum wage. They were badly underpaid compared to American construction workers, but Alma justified it because they would not make a fraction of the money in their own country. She taught them plumbing and wiring, so that they returned trained for good jobs, and she bought their bus tickets back to Mexico. Alma believed that people from foreign countries would turn to crime if not supervised by someone like her.

Kaija was determined not to argue. She swallowed statistics and logical comebacks about exploitation of workers and excessive profits for employers, about the vast difference between the rich and the poor. She forbade herself to point out that Alma was an immigrant too.

Everything Alma did was legal. It would not occur to her to knowingly violate the law of the United States, which she considered as reprehensible as spitting on the American flag. A small replica of the Stars and Stripes was glued to the right-hand window of her Saab, and a larger one flew in front of her house, on sunny days only, please. She had recurring conflicts with Takesha, her African American housekeeper, over the respectful raising and proper lowering of this flag. Takesha, who had been born in this country, had nevertheless been known to leave it drooping in the rain or flapping around helplessly after midnight.

Censoring what she said was Kaija's method for getting along; flattery was Alma's.

"I don't understand, little Kaijin, why you say that Latvians are among the invisible immigrants. Everyone can see us. Plus, you look fabulous. People can't take their eyes off you."

Kaija did not allow herself to be lulled. "Little Kaijin" and "fabulous," for goodness sake, all six feet and more than five decades of her.

"You're brilliant, Kaijin, I always said you were. Just think of the thousands of students you've taught spelling and grammar." That was as far as Alma's understanding of Kaija's work went. Kaija had long ago given up trying to explain what she actually did.

Once Alma had detailed her sons' successes, Kaija asked, "And how is Jautrite?"

"All right," Alma said shortly.

Kaija did not persist. She wanted to believe that Alma's daughter really *was* all right.

Alma broke the ensuing silence.

"What are you thinking, Kaijin?" she asked as she made a decisive turn into a parking lot.

About passionate kisses at midnight, a blood-red cashmere sweater, or an almost do-it-yourself abortion, Kaija might have said to an American friend. Indianapolis always flooded her with nostalgia and tormented her with painful memories. From there they might go on to deplore hypocrisy regarding sex in the 1950s; they would trade stories about the ignorance and death that resulted; they would mention that foreigners and everyone else who was different were despised. But Maris and Jerry and sex were secrets Kaija had kept too long; she had no right to dump them on Alma now. Alma would only be hurt that Kaija had not told her earlier.

"I'm trying to remember your favorite departments in L.S. Ayres," Kaija said. This pleased Alma, and she counted them off on her fingers—domestics, china, linens, jewelry—until they were safely inside Nordstrom's, heading towards the paisley Ralph Lauren sheets on the sales rack.

313

In the late afternoon Alma and Kaija returned to North Meridian Street for a real meal, instead of washing down marshmallow sundaes with cokes on East Washington Street, as they once had. Ivars was actually home, and he joined them for a quick glass of wine before heading out to an unnamed destination.

In Alma's dark red velvet TV room, Ivars gave Kaija a subtly conspiratorial look. What would her life have been like had she married him, Kaija wondered, and not for the first time. Tall and fit, he was all the more handsome for the silver streak in his dark hair and the deepening lines near his mouth. She knew now that she criticized him in order to rein in her attraction to him.

Alma poured out generous amounts of red wine in heavy crystal goblets, and the substantial sandwiches and creamy casserole her housekeeper had left would serve as lunch and dinner both. But Alma was subdued in her husband's presence, and Kaija gave-up trying to talk to Ivars. His customary irony, playful rather than cutting tonight, made real conversation impossible. Both women relaxed when he left.

After dinner, the two friends were too tired to go out again, to a movie or concert. Alma flicked on the TV, and Kaija headed upstairs to the newly remodeled guest suite.

She stretched-out in scented water in the hand-painted porcelain tub and dabbed gently at her face with a warm washcloth. Surrounded by mirrors, orchids, and ferns, she soaked for a long time, hoping water would dissolve her disappointment. She had tried her best, and Alma had too, but they had been on edge with each other and had once again failed to feel close.

Kaija dried slowly, sniffing at lotions and perfumes, which were more luxurious than she bought for herself. Alma no longer went in for romantic names like L'Air du Temps, Shalimar, or Crystal. The bathroom was stocked with cosmetics that sounded like medical regimens—H2O Plus and Prescriptives—but their fragrances were wonderful. The scents could take Kaija right back to the pond filled with water lilies and reeds behind the Summer House, bringing nostalgia to disturb her sleep.

By the time she pulled on her pale peach silk nightgown and read a few pages in a novel by Pat Barker, she could hardly hold open her eyes. She felt as if she had been drugged or had pricked her finger on a magic spindle. She fell into sleep, heavier in Alma's house than anywhere else, until vivid dreams of screaming horses or wandering lost and homeless in a foreign city woke her at three in the morning.

Alma stayed awake longer. She sipped Benedictine, rubbed rose-scented lotion into her hands and feet, and watched a little TV, the Golden Girls and a rerun of Lawrence Welk. Without looking at the titles, she popped in and yanked out documentary videos. Skeletal victims greeted American soldiers in concentration camps, women wreathed with flowers lined up at a Latvian Song Festival, and relatives separated by the Berlin Wall moved before her eyes. Nothing was arresting enough to blot out her disappointment about the day.

She sighed, turned off the TV, and looked at her purchases. Where was she going to put all this stuff, which she did not need and did not want? Her closets and drawers were too full already, but she could not bring herself to throw out anything that might be useful someday. Americans had no idea that when another war came, consumer goods would not be available. She would be grateful then she had her stretched out polyester slacks, to wear when she scavenged for food and scraps of wood.

In her bedroom she jammed a set of new sheets and two packets of cotton underwear into a laundry hamper which held other unopened packages. She would deal with everything in the basket later, when bad dreams woke her. In her canopied bed, she turned her back on a stuck drawer stuffed with expensive new bras and badly worn slips and rearranged the pillows to cushion her aching hip. If she was lucky, she would have four hours of uninterrupted sleep. She had trained herself not to listen for Ivars, but she still woke at regular intervals during the night.

315

In the morning Kaija was eager to leave. She had a whole month before another visit, which this friendship required. Saying goodbye to Alma was easy this time; they would meet again in the afternoon.

Men in expensive suits and women in pretty dresses and with strings of amber beads were taking their seats for the concert at the Latvian Center, but Alma and Ivars were not among them. What on earth was keeping them, Kaija fretted. They should be in the front row with other successful exiles, this model minority. Jautrite's parents should be on hand to encourage and to congratulate their daughter. Kaija felt resentful, as if they had dumped the entire responsibility for Jautrite on her.

Lights dimmed, the audience quieted, and seventeen-year-old Jautrite walked out onto the bare stage. She seemed vulnerable, probably because no accompanist entered with her.

Jautrite's thin white shoulders jutted out of a stiff strapless dress. Gray taffeta, an odd choice for a young girl, the dress fit snugly over her breasts, which were as full and round as a mourning dove's. But Jautrite had none of the peaceful self-possession of that bird. Kaija thought she could see her hands shake. Jautrite's dark hair, pulled tight across her scalp, fell in thick loose waves around her neck. Her hair reminded Kaija of Ivars, but otherwise she did not resemble either of her parents. Kaija caught her eye, smiled encouragingly, and focused her whole self on Jautrite doing well.

Jautrite bowed, took a deep breath, and began. Her pure soprano split the air, then lilted and soared, taking the audience with it. Proprietary pride surged in Kaija, as it did when she succeeded in getting a shy student to speak up in class. But she knew this feeling was unearned now. She had done nothing to raise this lovely half-woman, half-child.

After singing a poignant prayer for Latvia, Jautrite began a series of folk songs about orphans, and Kaija thoughts turned briefly to history. Latvian women had died young in childbirth and from

316

overwork, leaving their children in the hands of cruel stepmothers. Many, although strongly attached to the soil and the natural world, had been serfs not allowed to own land until reforms in the 1860s. Like orphans, they had been denied warmth and rest by cruel task masters.

Kaija's compassion surged toward Jautrite. Jautrite had hardly been mothered herself, and she was trying so hard to please her parents now. Ivars should be especially moved by her efforts because he worked with orphan songs too in his poetic drama. Sometimes, however, he talked with pride about wealthy defiant Latvians who had retained their independence during centuries of German oppression. Not every Latvian was descended from serfs.

Kaija brought her attention firmly back to Jautrite and another song in which an orphan tried to catch the setting sun as she yearned for her mother's love.

Loud sustained applause following Jautrite's performance continued until four young men with guitars and a *kokle* jumped onto the stage. They were greeted with laughter and friendly applause, but their music could not touch people's hearts the way Jautrite had.

At intermission Kaija found Alma in the back of the hall, calmly receiving congratulations for her daughter's performance. Ivars was nowhere to be seen.

"Was she really that good?" Alma asked as soon as Kaija and she were alone. "I only heard the last song."

"Yes, she was. She was wonderful. Oh, Alma, how could you miss it?"

"I had trouble getting my father settled. He was much too sick today, but he wanted to come with us, but what would people say? It's ridiculous how he dotes on that girl. The two of them are like vines, tangling and twining around each other. Ivars is looking for a place to park. They should resurface that lot, I've said so for years."

"For goodness sake, Alma, there's a whole empty meadow out there. Ivars should have...you should have...someone could have...."

"Never mind, Kaija. We've heard Jautrite before. She's been driving us crazy, practicing day and night."

"Well, well, if it isn't Professor Veldre honoring us with her presence again," Ivars greeted Kaija with practiced insincerity. It was as if he and Kaija had never exchanged a single authentic word.

"Have you congratulated Jautrite?" Kaija demanded.

"We're on our way now, esteemed Professor. But will you do us the honor and join us later? We're hosting a party in honor of creative expression."

Kaija wanted to slap him. Instead of distancing himself in this ridiculous way, he, of all people, should have listened to his daughter sing. Jautrite's whole performance had been a plea for her parents' love.

"I hate that damn facetiousness," Kaija snapped, as Ivars wandered off.

"Don't scold, Kaija. And do come to the party. You can praise Jautrite, you can give a speech if you like. Ivars says he'll go to your parents' place and bring you in his arms if you don't come of your own free will."

The party was at a Turkish restaurant in Broad Ripple rather than in Alma's house, probably because Ivars liked defying Latvian convention in small ways. Kaija doubted that he had wanted to spare Alma the trouble. Like other Latvian men of his generation, he believed that women who worked full-time nevertheless had time and energy to entertain elaborately.

Kaija was confused about what the party was supposed to celebrate. Jautrite was not present; she would never have picked this restaurant. No teenager would choose to spend an evening with balding men, glittery overdressed women, and belly dancers gyratig in a way meant to be provocative. Kaija hoped that Jautrite was with others her age, laughing and whispering with her girlfriends, though no such promising group of friends had surrounded her after the performance.

Platters of food and carafes of water and wine were circulating at a table crowded with Latvians Ivars' age and older, many of whom Kaija did not know. Ivars was dancing with a pretty red-haired American woman in a skimpy vivid green dress. Her slightly condescending expression resembled Ivars.' The two could be high school sweethearts whose faces had grown similar during a long marriage. They swiveled their hips in parody of the belly dancers, burst out laughing, and fell into each other's arms. Kaija felt Alma tense.

The belly dancers descended from the low stage, wove around Ivars and the woman, and began circling the room. Stomachs rolled, and hips undulated; diaphanous gold and magenta veils swirled. A dancer stopped in front of a prosperous-looking red-faced man and stared at him until he placed his hand on her quivering belly and stuffed dollar bills into her billowing orange pants with the other. Men clutching money reached for other dancers.

"Those women are disgraceful," Alma muttered. "But that's the Turks for you."

"Try blaming the men instead of the women for once, Alma, and quit stereotyping the Turks," Kaija snapped. She felt like a traitor at this party from which the guest of honor was excluded.

"I am not stereotyping, Kaija," Alma said calmly. "I judge people by what they do. But you can't deny that the Turks and the Hungarians are . . ."

"Listen to yourself, Alma. You're doing it right now. You talk as if all Americans are alike, all Russians, all Germans, all Jews. And now, God help us, you're after the Turks. Being prejudiced is bad enough but denying that you are is worse."

"Don't you tell me about the Russians and the Germans, Kaija. After what they did to Latvia, I don't care about their books and their music. You can point all you want to your Emerson and your Dickinson, but I watch TV and I see what Americans are like. But, of course, you wouldn't know because you've abandoned the Latvians and gone over..." Alma stopped mid-sentence. Ivars had

319

his arms around the redhead and was nuzzling her neck. It was an eternity before he let her go. A group of tipsy American women, glasses raised, saluted her as she returned to their table.

Ivars jumped-up on the small stage and began to dance by himself. At first, he ground his hips in a driving rhythm, like a bad impersonator of a frenzied Elvis Presley, but gradually his movements slowed and became graceful and fluid. His usual reserve and self-protective irony melted away. He was one with the music, his entire body suffused with motion and light.

People stopped talking and turned to watch. He took off his jacket, flung it into outstretched hands, loosened his tie and then let go of that as well. He pushed up the sleeves of his white shirt, and a strand of his dark and silver hair fell over his forehead.

Kaija could not take her eyes from him. No wonder he had been called the handsomest of the Three Handsome Brothers. She had renounced him for Alma's sake, she was alert for anything about him to criticize, but she *was* attracted to him. Desire and embarrassment brought blood to her face. She hoped she was not bright red as she pressed a water glass to her cheek to cool it.

Neither cheerfully vigorous like Latvian folk-dancers nor blatantly sexual like American rock stars, Ivars was dancing in a way uniquely his own. It was more erotic than anything Kaija had seen.

Latvian men gave themselves body and soul like this only when they sang, and not always then. Instead of being an embittered engineer relying on flattery from a series of women, Ivars could have done anything and been anyone if he had put his whole self into it like this. Tears of compassion rose to Kaija's eyes for his unexpressed creativity, for the superficial affairs with which he diverted himself, for his unhappiness. She saw exactly why Alma loved him while receiving so little in return and why she clung so stubbornly to the belief that only a man could make a woman happy.

Ivars paused to accept a drink, and cheers, whoops, and applause erupted. The redhead, arms outstretched, started towards him, and two other women jumped on to the stage and began jerking back and forth. Ivars ignored them, and the three retreated awkwardly. He moved toward the tables crowded with diners. Women reached for him, stuffing money into his pockets and waistband. He nodded coolly after each offering and, without missing a beat, danced away.

Ivars stopped in front of Alma and held out his hand. She was dying to join him, but she shook her head. She had felt graceful and competent in his arms decades ago, but now she was tense on the rare occasions when they danced together. And that was when she knew the dance steps. There was no way she could improvise. She would be a public spectacle if she swished her bottom around like that, and Ivars might laugh at her later.

Ivars shrugged, pulled ten- and twenty-dollar bills from his waistband and pockets, and dumped them into Alma's lap. He bowed politely, retreated, and danced toward Kaija.

Her feet were tapping already when Ivars held out both hands. An image of Alma's hurt face when Kaija had danced with him in the old Latvian Community House flashed by, but she and Alma had been teenagers then. They were adults now, weren't they? Nothing had ever happened between Ivars and her, and this was only a dance.

The beat of music was insistent, and Kaija began to match her movements to his. At first, they danced without touching, but when the music slowed, Ivars pulled her to him. He took her in his arms and brushed her cheek with his lips.

"Run away with me, beautiful Kaija," he whispered. "We should have done it years ago."

When the music came to an end, they stood close to each other; he held her as if she belonged to him. Kaija shut her eyes and swayed with him.

She was exhilarated when the music started again, although Ivars' breath no longer caressed her neck. This dance ended too, and another began. She wanted to dance with him out into the night, to run to his car hand in hand, kiss fiercely, make love, drive away, leave everything behind. Two misfits in Latvian society, they would wander the world together. They might return as a respectably married couple; they might be even be forgiven eventually if they were humble enough. Such things did happen. A Lutheran minister in another Midwestern city had been harshly condemned when he ran off with his choir director, but now he was a pillar of that community and a leader in the Latvian Lutheran Church Association. But if they were never accepted, he would be her Latvia and she his.

"Come," Ivars said, pointing to the door. "It's not too late."

"Actually, it is," Kaija whispered. "My love," she added awkwardly.

Esteemed professor, Ivars would tease her. He would mock her before too long. He would not be faithful even to her.

"I think you're wrong," he said, "but we'll see about that later."

Perfectly in step, they circled the dance floor again.

Ivars stopped in front of the band leader.

"Play September Song," he ordered.

The bandleader shook his head. "Not my kind of music."

Really, this was too much: too much nostalgia, too much sentimentality, too much grasping at fleeting romance. It was ridiculous and over-dramatic, Kaija told herself, but her body vibrated.

"Forgive me," she said. She squeezed Ivars' hand and putting her other hand against her flaming cheek, she headed for the restroom.

When Kaija had collected herself enough to return, Ivars was dancing with the redhead again. Kaija gulped down a glass of ice water and muttered a quick apology to Alma for snapping at her about the Turks.

Alma nodded absently. She was often short like that. Kaija would try to explain and apologize better for being rude the next time she saw her. Right now, she could not stand seeing Ivars dance with anyone but her. If she stayed she would make snide remarks born of jealousy about the redhead. She would not criticize Ivars himself.

She thanked Alma and left without saying goodbye to Ivars.

Although it was only eleven o'clock, the lights in Kaija's parents' rooms upstairs were out when she tiptoed into their townhouse apartment. She arranged sheets and pillows on the living room couch, lay down, snapped off the light, and waited impatiently for sleep. She wished that she was at home; she could calm herself more easily in her own bed.

She needed to get some sleep because she would leave Indianapolis at dawn, but it refused to come. The anger, excitement, desire, and regret of a single afternoon and evening would keep her unsettled for days to come as well. A colleague was teaching her Monday morning class, but she had to be back in Minnesota for her afternoon seminar. The tiring day ahead was fine with her; she liked that she was vigorous and could work hard after a long drive. The drive would be pleasant. Kaija had a novel by Penelope Lively on tape, a story about the professional life of an unmarried historian and her poignant love affair in Egypt during the war. Kaija expected she would be tired enough to sleep the following night.

After counting back from one hundred to one, Kaija was still awake. She congratulated herself for keeping her ten-year-old resolution, even when it came to Ivars, not to make love with married men to whom she meant nothing. To do otherwise wronged other women. It violated feminism and women's solidarity, which Kaija took seriously. She was proud that she had stayed true to herself. She had not left the restaurant hand and hand with Ivars, but she knew she had wounded Alma, her oldest friend, by dancing so long and so intimately. Outward appearances mattered to Alma.

Kaija was honest enough to admit that she had not abandoned Ivars on the dance floor out of loyalty to her friend. She had in fact been aware only of Ivars, not Alma. She had walked away from him because, as she had laughingly said to her women friends, at her age it was too much trouble to take off her clothes for anyone.

She did not want to find out that her body would not welcome a lover with warmth and moistness as eagerly once.

"I've never seen anything as beautiful in my life," Mr. Hazard had whispered when he unbuttoned her blouse and reverently kissed her small firm breasts, her smooth tan skin a contrast to the white lace of her bra. She had felt beautiful and powerful. His words and the poetry they read together convinced her that he loved her.

That's just sex, people said to denigrate foolish decisions and fleeting experiences. Kaija's mind had said no to Jerry, but her body had responded otherwise. Someone might say the opposite as well: that's just a glance, a dance, a line from a song, a kiss in the dark. Nothing happened, no real sex, no self-revelation, no affair—nothing. Yet romantic moments without "real sex" were powerful. Kaija knew she was not the only woman to feel this way. An American friend had told her that the surreptitious kisses and cautious petting in the 1950s had been a hundred times more exciting than nightly intercourse with her kind and enlightened husband.

Kaija's parents' living room was chilly. This late in September everything seemed more distinct during the day, but evenings came too soon and darkness went on too long. Against her will, the words to September Song began to repeat in her head; Ivars flung down money and backed away from Alma; he danced towards Kaija; his lips brushed her cheek; his hands took possession of her. Damn it, she muttered, pounded her pillow, and turned her back to the room.

Latvians were sensible and cheerful on the outside so that it was easy to miss inner turmoil of romantic yearning and regret. Many believed in first love, fated love, eternal love, to love was to suffer, to giving all for love was commonplace. All that was nonsense. Kaija was a rational person, she reminded herself. She pulled her sheet and duvet over her head.

She heard the muffled taps anyway. She knew she would see Ivars before she put her eye to the peephole in the front door.

"Let me in, Kaija," he mouthed. "Please, Kaija."

324

His tie draped loosely around his neck and his white shirt open almost to his waist, he carried his shoes in one hand. He looked sure of his welcome.

"Is the party over?" Kaija whispered as she undid the locks and chain.

"Not yet," he said.

"Where is Alma? Is she still at the restaurant?"

He lifted Kaija's chin and kissed her. His hand glided confidently over her breasts, down her back, and up her thigh, crushing the white gauze of her nightgown.

For a few seconds she was nineteen years old, in Maris' parents' living room, terrified of being discovered but kissing wildly.

"No," Kaija whispered, grasped Ivars' hand and kept it from moving. "We can't. We're in my parents' house."

"Think they'll spank us?" Ivars laughed. His lips rested on her neck.

"No, really, we can not," Kaija said a little more loudly. "I mean, I won't. Alma is my friend. Please, Ivar, you have to go."

She began moving him gently toward the door. More than anything she wanted to embrace and hold on to him; at the same time, she was glad that he allowed himself to be maneuvered to leave.

"Alma . . . my friendship with her . . . I'm sorry . . . you have to go," she said. Making love with him would change her life. And Alma's.

"I'm sorry too."

And sooner than it seemed possible, he was back on the front steps and she was locking the door behind him.

The floor creaked above. One of her parents was on the way to the bathroom.

"Are you all right, Kaija?" Judge Veldre called out. "Did anything happen? Is someone else down there?"

"No. I am alone." Kaija said and leaned against the door to barricade it.

"No. Nothing happened. Nothing at all," she added.

Lost Midsummers

Part Four

Separate Lives

1980s

Lost Midsummers

36

On the way to a morning session of a conference at Indiana University, Kaija almost collided with a disheveled man in front of the Student Union. He looked at her without recognition, but there was something familiar about him. He reminded Kaija of Jerry. She had been angry and afraid when he stalked her in graduate school, but she had not thought of him for years.

If that *was* Jerry, he had aged and shrunk a lot, and he had shaved off his handsome beard. But his walk was the worst part. He shuffled along stiffly, like homeless people, Viet Nam vets, the mentally ill, and other survivors who stay alive because they are full of courage or drink and drugs.

Kaija's heart contracted with pity, but she did not try to catch up with him. She was glad he had not recognized her. She had no wish to show Jerry that her life had turned out better than his.

During the lunch hour, driven by curiosity, she walked to the Lilly Library of rare books. If Jerry had succeeded even briefly as an artist in Indiana, she might find something about him there. But the only item under the name of Locksmith was a limited edition of reproductions of his father's paintings.

Most of these were of a grave dark-haired woman, whom Kaija assumed to be Sophie. Kaija liked the painter's frank appreciation of her fleshiness: Sophie's solid body blazed against a background of tangled woodbines or sparsely furnished interiors. She wished she could see the actual paintings to study a small imperfection near Sophie's wrist. Was that a scratch made by careless love or a partially obliterated number from a concentration camp?

Jerry had implied that Sophie was unsuitable as his father's lover because she was a maid and Jewish, but Kaija's anger did not return even as she remembered her youthful outrage. She was glad she could think of him with indifference and a little compassion.

Nostalgia took hold, and Kaija drove into Indianapolis rather than bypassing it on the way home, as she had planned. Should stop and see Alma? Maybe Alma missed her. Maybe their friendship could once again be resurrected. But Kaija was afraid of Alma's anger; their meeting would only be painful.

In the weeks following the party in Broad Ripple, Alma had made excuses about getting together, and Kaija had felt too guilty to insist. The friends had drifted apart once more.

Kaija drove past upscale specialty shops and malls with names which celebrated a vaguely heroic, largely fictitious British past: Castleton Square, Keystone at the Crossing, Pendleton Pike, and Lafayette Square, as a nod to Revolutionary America rather than a tribute to French culture. Alma's cruel English teacher, Miss Donovan, had maintained that only English pilgrims and other respectable British citizens, craftsmen and honest merchants, had settled in Indianapolis. Latvians, Estonians, and Hungarians, reminders of destructive wars and messy European politics, did not fit her version of history.

Heralded by espresso machines and Mexican restaurants, ethnic diversity had arrived in Indianapolis. More African Americans were visible downtown rather than confined to the near North Side, though relatively few names of streets and parks honored their culture. Kaija hoped that would change for them, but Latvian—with its strange proper names ending in s's and a's, and its diacritical marks above and below letters—would never enter the vocabulary of the city.

The old L.S. Ayres Building no longer housed a department store, though its famous clock, the designated meeting place of thousands of girlfriends, was still in place. Kaija continued walking towards the Circle Monument. It seemed unsurprising that on this trip of nostalgia awakened by a coincidence, Kaija should come face to face with Jautrite. They met in the very heart of Indianapolis, in front of what had once been the Circle movie theater.

Jautrite was almost unrecognizable as the pretty girl singing three years ago. She had chopped off her wavy dark hair, and the remaining stubble was streaked with bright blue. Dark circles under her eyes showed up unhealthily pale skin, and a rash marred her chin. Leather straps and metal chains circled her wrists and cinched her waist. Kaija tried not to stare at a large bruise on Jautrite's neck, which was impossible to dismiss as a mere hickey caused by clumsy teenage sexual exuberance. Vampires and fanged animals came to mind.

They stood looking at each other awkwardly until Kaija took Jautrite by the hand. She regretted it instantly. Stale sweat and something else, repulsive and decaying, hit her. Damn Alma for not taking care of her daughter, and damn Ivars too. What did they expect Kaija to do?

Kaija knew nothing about children. She had determinedly not paid attention when other women went on and on about theirs. If there was something more boring than a group of women talking endlessly about their grandchildren, Kaija did not know what that was. She had not even skimmed Doctor Spock in the 1960s when conservative commentators laid all rebellious behavior by college students at his door. Jautrite was supposed to turn out all right. Lots of children whose mothers did not love them did.

Kaija wanted to murmur some pleasantry and extricate herself when a line of poetry, "How do you like your Blue-Haired Girl now, Mr. Death?" began to swirl in her head. It took Kaija a moment to realize she was tormented by a misquoted line from a poem by e. e. cummings. Jautrite was not dead, but she was in desperate need of help.

A hesitant half-smile flickered on Jautrite's face.

"Hello . . . Miss . . . Professor . . . Mrs. Veldre," Jautrite said. Like other Latvians, she rapidly discarded references to Kaija's single status and professional achievements in favor of a totally fictional "Mrs.," an honorific supposedly flattering to every woman over twenty-five.

"Jautrite, it's nice to see you," Kaija said, glad to have a conventional phrase to fall back on. She hoped Jautrite could not tell how much her appearance had shocked her.

Jautrite looked at Kaija expectantly.

"Come, have lunch with me," Kaija offered, though part of her hoped Jautrite would refuse. This mutilated child needed more than a meal. What was she going to do if Jautrite told her the truth about her life? Kaija cursed herself as she steered Jautrite to a booth in the back of a restaurant.

"I haven't seen her, if that's what you want to know," Jautrite said abruptly. "She's mad at you too." They both knew who "she" was.

"Actually, I was going to ask about you," Kaija said.

She stifled her impulse to blurt, "Who bit you, why are you in chains, where did you get those awful clothes, and stop ruining your life."

"Where are you living?" she managed instead.

"Not on Meridian Street, that's for sure. There's no one there who cares about me. You know that Grandfather Valdis died, don't you? But where did she say I was?" Jautrite's eager question belied her indifference.

"Well, let me see." Kaija searched her excellent memory for anything Alma might have said but found nothing. Since the party at the Turkish restaurant, Alma's chilliness and Kaija's awkwardness had kept the two friends apart. Kaija had called Alma at Christmas and a few other times when she thought she would go mad if she did not speak in Latvian. But they lapsed into English anyway.

"I knew it, she *didn't* tell you where I was," Jautrite said triumphantly, "Did she say *anything* about me?"

"I don't believe so," Kaija admitted.

Jautrite's hopeful expression collapsed.

"Maybe I just don't remember," Kaija offered.

"Oh, don't bother protecting her. I know she didn't. She doesn't care what happens to me. It's all the same to her whether I live or die. Admit it."

"She didn't say anything, but I . . . ."

"Look, let's cut that polite Latvian crap, with everything orderly and clean and smiling on the surface but scarred and damaged underneath. Like those linen cloths with neat geometric patterns Latvians spread over every bureau and table, and the green ceramic vases they set on top, so no one can see the gouges and burns."

"Jautrite, your mother has had a lot to . . . ."

"See, you're doing it right now. You don't like me saying that my mother does not care if I die, so you'd rather tell me how much Latvians have been through and how hard they've had to work."

"Your mother and I . . ."

Jautrite set down her spoon. "You're so into the Latvian thing that you don't remember what you asked me."

"I do, actually. I asked you where you were living."

"Very good," Jautrite nodded. "Excellent. Give yourself an A, Professor."

Stung by Jautrite's hostility, Kaija nevertheless almost laughed at the perfect mimicry of Ivars.

"All right, Jautrite. Let's start all over. Where *are* you living?"

"On the south side, as far away from North Meridian as possible."

"Which street?" Kaija could recall only defeated-looking bungalows from years ago, but perhaps urban renewal had changed the area.

"I'd rather not say. You'll tell her, and she'll force me to go home."

"But you just said that she doesn't care."

"Very good, Professor, another A for you. Excellent logic and recall, but you just don't get it. She doesn't want me at home because she loves me. She's worried that some Latvian will see me and tell every other Latvian in Indianapolis that I wasn't wearing a freshly ironed summer dress. You remember their crazy phone system, with everyone knowing everything ten minutes after it happens. I could ruin her precious reputation."

There was no point trying to defend Alma. Jautrite would not listen; she might refuse to talk altogether.

"Please, let me help this angry, hurt child somehow," Kaija prayed silently to herself. "Please, help me put aside my irritation and concentrate on her." She hoped the right words would come, the way they did when she was with a troubled student.

"So, Jautrite, is your place nice? Do you have space to practice your music? Is there a piano?"

Jautrite relaxed slightly. "Pastor Saulcere asked me about my music too. I ran into him a couple of weeks ago. Do you know that you two are a lot alike? Different from other Latvians. The first thing others want to know is what fraternity your father or grandfather belonged to in Latvia decades ago, what's your profession, what honors, what salary, what house, what neighborhood, what everything."

Determined not to get side-tracked into her practice of correcting stereotypes, Kaija countered with a question.

"Do you have a room of your own?"

"I live in a house and, yes, my room is in the basement. I live with my family."

Kaija's eyes were drawn to the bruise on Jautrite's neck again. A family of drug addicts, sadists, and perverts.

"It's a nice family, big, eight of us altogether." Jautrite had finished her minestrone and was digging into lasagna.

"That must be lively."

"It's very quiet actually. Doctor . . . the Dad . . . he believes in discipline. Oh, it isn't like that," Jautrite said as if she too could see the whips and handcuffs Kaija imagined. "It's not a cult or anything. We love each other . . . we live together in love."

"So, there's a Dad," Kaija prompted. "And is there a Mom?"

"Of course, there's a Mother," Jautrite said scornfully. "It's a real family. I take care of the youngest kids, and I help her with everything. She couldn't manage without me, especially when Doctor . . . . That's why I can't have a job right now."

"But what about school? What about your education? What about your music and your singing?"

334

"I just told you. I take care of everything, the cleaning and the house and Doctor . . . . "

Jautrite stopped herself again from saying his name, as if the mere mention of it would cause him to materialize. "It's my decision. I am free to choose. I chose my new family. We'll always be together, the Family that Prays Together Stays Together," Jautrite recited in a monotone. "And they love me, they really do, they wouldn't know what to do without me. They're totally perfect."

When Kaija said nothing, Jautrite continued.

"When you call her . . . oh, don't bother to say you won't, you can hardly wait. Anyway, tell her I'm living with my family, tell her that my family loves me, tell her that I love them. I love them more than I do her, tell her. I'm going to live with them until I die."

Kaija shivered involuntarily at Jautrite's reference to death.

"So, what's the name of this new mother you've found?" she asked, trying to sound matter of fact.

"Ha! Very good, very clever, Professor, but I can't tell you that."

"Is your new family nice?"

"Of course, they're nice. I told you, we live together in love. Doctor . . . anyway, he's very educated, he has all kinds of degrees."

"A doctor, is he? A medical doctor or a professor of some kind?"

"He's not at a hospital or a school or anything. He could be if he wanted to. He's totally brilliant. He's taught at lots of famous universities, they're all begging for him to come back. But he's the one who says no. He wouldn't go, not if they got down on their hands and knees. He's finished with elitist secular institutions."

"So, what's his specialty?"

"He's got degrees, in psychology and things, he has every specialty there is."

"Dessert?" Kaija offered.

Jautrite wiped her plate with the last of her bread and pushed it aside. "No, thanks. I shouldn't have eaten this as it is, it's got meat in it. Doctor Eden won't like it. He can tell when people have eaten flesh, they smell different."

Finally, Doctor Eden. What a stupid, ridiculous name, just right for a perverted, manipulative, sadistic phony. Kaija wanted to shake him till his eyes rattled. He should be in prison for Jautrite's bruises, visible and invisible.

Instead she said, "That's unusual, to have such a keen sense of smell, I mean."

"Yes, isn't it?" Jautrite beamed. "And you know what else? He can bend spoons from five feet away and he can shatter glass just by looking. He can tell exactly in what part of your body you're resisting him. He can open doors, read minds, see through walls. He's totally powerful."

Parlor tricks discredited a century ago, Kaija told herself, but she was afraid nevertheless. She forced herself to say, "I'd like to meet him. Come, Jautrite, I'll give you a ride."

"Oh no, please don't. No, please. I'm not supposed to . . . he'll know . . . I shouldn't . . . I . . . ."

"Be talking to me?"

"Yes."

"It's all right, Jautrite, it's natural you would. I've known you since you were a baby." Kaija wished she could say that she had looked out for Jautrite since then too.

"But that's just it, that's worse actually. I'm not supposed to talk to anyone I know, I mean, people I used to know. It's not good for me, it sets back my program. He'll be mad at me for ruining his work."

"I'll come with you and I'll explain. My car is just down the street, by the City Market."

"No, please, please, no," Jautrite said desperately and bolted for the door.

"Thanks, Kaija," she threw over her shoulder. "You're very kind."

"You deserve better than this, Jautrite. Phone me. Please. I want to help you," Kaija called after her. She dropped a few bills on the table and followed the blue hair. But Jautrite wove through a group of school children and disappeared into a crowd of adults.

"So Jautrite is in trouble again, and you're trying to find her," Alma said flatly. "So what else is new?"

"There's no Doctor Eden in the phone book or in the city directory. I suspect that's not his real name anyway. But I bet we could find him if you and I put our heads together."

"She's gotten herself mixed up with a criminal degenerate."

"It might even be fun, Alma, the two of us searching for her, like detectives."

"She's gotten herself mixed up with a criminal degenerate," Alma repeated stubbornly. "And now I'm supposed to tell Ivars and get him riled up too. After everything we've done for her. Good schools, nice clothes, a house in the best neighborhood, two parents, and not a worry in the world. No bombs, no looting, no shooting, no nothing. I'd give my right hand to have the life she's had."

Alma paused to pick up steam. "And what has she given me? Shame and more shame. People ask me about her, and what can I say? Thank God, the boys are doing well, so I can change the subject. First there was that business with Melody. I would have kissed the ground in gratitude if my mother was alive and my father paid for Indiana University, free and clear. But not Jautrite, oh no. She's no sooner unpacked than she calls to say that she's moving out of her dorm and into some dump with Melody, a woman who looks like a Russian tank, with combat boots and everything. 'But I love her, Mother,' Jautrite had the nerve to say to me. To me, her mother. I raised my children to be normal. But after all the sacrifices I've made, and with my father hardly underground, Jautrite announces that she wants to live 'an authentic life' and that Melody is the only one left alive who cares what happens to her. Money doesn't fall from the sky, I said, and Latvians don't do such things. She's spoiled, just like the rest of her generation."

"Maybe Jautrite was upset about her Grandfather dying. You told me they were very close. Maybe this woman knew how to comfort her, maybe they loved each other."

"I won't listen to filth about love, Kaija, not from you."

"It's not filth, Alma. Love isn't only for husbands and wives."

"I don't want to hear this, Kaija. You'll tell me next about all the men you've rolled around in bed with. Everything goes with you Americans and academics and leftists—men with men, women with women, single women with married men, cows with horses, sheep with goats. Any immorality is fine with you."

"Now just a minute, Alma. That is going too far."

"Yes, immorality. Sleeping with anyone you want, trying to seduce Ivars."

"Ivars? . . . . I am not interested in Ivars," Kaija said.

"Yes, you are. He's always talking about you, telling me that you understand him, and his poems and I don't know what all else."

"Oh, Alma . . . . I haven't read a single line he's written since he was in his twenties. The last time I saw Ivars was three years ago," she said, firmly tamping down guilt and the delight of hearing what Ivars said about her. "Nothing happened," she added.

"Oh yes? You were practically having sex with him on the dance floor, Kaija. Everyone saw you."

"That is not true, Alma. I only danced with him. And anyway, Jautrite . . . "

"Don't bother me about Jautrite, Kaija. I know where he went when he disappeared from the party. I had to invent lies and say goodnight to everyone by myself, as usual. He didn't go off with the other . . . slut . . . because that redhead was looking for him too."

"Don't call me a slut, Alma," Kaija said. They had left Jautrite far behind.

"I'll say what I want, and you . . . you stay away from my husband," Alma hissed. Stored rage and pain, which might have been better directed at Ivars, erupted and burned Kaija.

"Please, Alma, let's not fight. This is ridiculous. I didn't sleep with Ivars. You're my oldest friend . . . ."

"Friend? Go and run to your Hungarians and Americans, to that Midge or Magda. You always do exactly what you want, Kaija. You're the most immoral . . . ."

A string of epithets followed. Their ugliness shocked Kaija into silence. Kaija experienced each one as a searing injustice: she *had* made mistakes, but she had also learned, defined her own moral code, and tried to follow it.

Damn Alma. Kaija was tired of overlooking the unforgivable things Alma said just because she had no mother and because Ivars made her unhappy. I didn't get much love from my mother either, Kaija wanted to shout.

"At least I don't attack my friends, Alma, while you let fly with anything that comes to hand. I'm sick of the things you say to me. And you expect me to understand and to forgive everything."

"I haven't even started on you," Alma shouted and slammed down the phone.

Kaija sat in the gathering dusk, breathing in the bitter scent of white and dark red chrysanthemums on her desk. This friendship would have died years ago, she told herself, if she had not kept it alive. But this time she was done with Alma; she really was. She could get along without Alma; she had plenty of practice of being alone. She had loved and lost before. Tears of grief stung her eyes, but she was too defiant and angry to notice.

Lost Midsummers

37

Ingrida Veldre—Professor of Art History, daughter of a general, wife of a judge, mother of a professor, scrubwoman of insurance offices, a displaced person, and an exile—died as quietly as she had lived the last part of her life. Always remote from others, she gradually stopped going out altogether and retreated to bed, surrounded by her beloved books. Only Pastor Saulcere remained her friend and constant visitor. He was with her, reciting her favorite Psalms and Karlis Skalbe's poems, as she died.

Pastor Saulcere did his best to comfort Kaija. Her mother's death had been peaceful, and she had been ready for it, he told her. Ingrida was now free of memories she could not bear; God had received her tenderly and was comforting her.

Kaija tried to be glad her mother had not suffered, but she was desolate for herself. Her mother had not addressed any last words to her; she had left no messages.

Kaija resolved to make her way through grief by concentrating on her work. She had done so after Maris and Mr. Hazard; she had gotten over the lost friendship with Alma in the same way. She made lists of things to accomplish, and she tried to feel satisfaction as she crossed them off, one by one. But she lost interest in the tasks before she finished them; she slept restlessly if at all; and she was too tired to get out of bed when she woke. Mornings were grey and hopeless, and evenings were worse. There was no real point to anything.

Kaija felt her heart was growing hard. She had always loved teaching Shakespeare's tragedies: explicating difficult passages, getting students to understand the characters, encouraging them to ask questions, and slowly leading them to appreciate the beauty and absolute rightness of the language. But now she found even this burdensome. She was annoyed with Romeo and Juliet for being so impulsive and by young lovers in general. Two kids like them would get over each other in a matter of days now or they would be marched off to a therapist, she observed grumpily. She was not moved when King Lear was reunited with Cordelia; she skipped part of her lecture about forgiveness and reconciliation at the end of the *Winter's Tale*, which had always touched her. Instead of writing notes of encouragement, she scrawled "C's" on papers she would have given a B- before.

She considered aimlessly wandering by herself in malls and sitting in coffee houses a waste of time, but she sought them out now in order to distract herself. She zoomed into parking places, cutting off doddery old men and overburdened young mothers. If a waitress in a restaurant was only momentarily inattentive, she did not leave her usual twenty-percent tip in cash, which she believed every minimum wage worker deserved. Feeling hounded by charities and political organizations to which she had cheerfully written checks before, she threw away fund-raising letters unopened.

Kaija resented her women friends for complaining that their mothers visited too often, asked too many questions, and interfered in their kitchens and in their parenting. Her friends did not know how lucky they were. They were foolish to be embarrassed when their mothers boasted about their successes or tried to match them up with unsuitable men.

She disliked herself more each day.

Systematic as always, she wrote down methods that her friends had mentioned as useful after break-ups and divorces. She avoided negative people, saw her friends, went for long walks, did yoga, took warm baths, wrote down reasons to be grateful, and tried anti-depressants.

But her desolation remained unchanged by pills and by a brief foray into therapy. Kaija listened politely when the intelligent young therapist told her not to blame herself for her mother's unhappiness but to get angry instead. It was her mother who had failed her by withdrawing; she had abandoned Kaija entirely by dying. The words made logical sense, but Kaija could not feel their truth. The therapist's suggestions seemed foolishly naïve because Kaija told her nothing about her childhood and adolescence.

One bitterly cold evening in February, when every cell in Kaija's body rebelled against going out, she nevertheless kept to her resolution to see her friends regularly. She forced herself to take a shower, wash her hair, put on her black velvet pants and white silk blouse, and wrap a long string of black beads around her neck. Bundled up in her heaviest coat and scarves and shawls, she drove across town on the icy deserted streets.

A favorite colleague who managed to retain his good humor through the long Minnesota winters excelled at cheering up his friends. This night there was tender beef, glazed winter vegetables, and plenty of red wine. After-dinner entertainment consisted of a spirited competition to see who had failed to read the largest number of Great Books, and should that prove disquieting, a mini-massage for each guest.

Seafoam Rising Light, a large solemn-looking woman with muscular tattooed arms, welcomed Kaija into the study. The utilitarian space had been transformed into a cozy retreat. Dozens of candles provided light, a space heater hummed, and a humidifier dispensed mist and the scent of lavender.

"I am a massage therapist and a spirit-guide, Kaija. I can answer all questions important to you while I work on your body," Seafoam announced.

Kaija turned away to hide her skeptical smile. She removed her blouse and bra as instructed and lay face down on the warm padded table. Seafoam produced a large crystal on an almost invisible string.

"We have to consult the crystal to see whether it's good for us to be working together tonight," she explained. "Let's ask him."

The crystal took its time deciding.

"No? Maybe? Don't know? Yes? Oh, good, the crystal says yes," Seafoam finally said.

She placed her warm hands on Kaija's temples and held them there. Very slowly she started massaging her scalp. It had been a long time since anyone had touched Kaija so intimately.

"You are a very spiritual woman," Seafoam intoned. "You have the gift of intuition, but you do not use it. In fact, you do not value it as you should. You discount your insights and you try to dismiss your feelings; you do not ask the spirits to guide you. You do not pay attention to your body. You live only in your head. You worship logic."

Enjoying Seafoam's firm yet gentle touch, Kaija tried to hide her skeptical smile. What a lot of hocus-pocus, all of a piece with a crystal who made decisions and with Seafoam's incantatory manner of speaking, like that of a Druid priestess in a bad movie.

But by the time Seafoam began to knead Kaija's feet, Kaija was leaving logic behind. Did not Yeats, Kaija's favorite poet, abandon skepticism about mysterious other realities when he saw a bird come out of a clock without hands and cuckoo at him in spiritualist Madame Blavatsky's salon? Later he went on to marry a woman one-third his age because she could do automatic writing and bring him messages from the spirit world. Other writers had dabbled in spiritualism too. Even intellectuals rigidly trained in theology and philosophy had been seduced by mysticism.

The puzzling intuitions which Kaija had tried to ignore came back to her vividly: her foreknowledge that she would see the severed arm and screaming horses during the war, her certainty that Stella's was going to die, and her dream of Magda warning her not to try an abortion. Her strong response to Ivars was irrational too, though she had fooled herself that it was only logical because they both spoke Latvian. Some unknown power had guided her with the dream about Magda and the gypsies and had kept her alive and safe from harm.

Like many academics, Kaija believed in a clear-cut division between reason and mere feelings. Sound logical or clear physical evidence was one thing, and superstition, intuition, and alternate realities something else entirely. But with Seafoam's warm hands releasing tight knots in her neck and shoulders, Kaija understood this was a false dilemma. She could think, *and* she could feel. There was nothing wrong with using both abilities.

"And another thing," Seafoam was saying. "You should wear red underwear. It will help you out of depression and lighten your grief."

Startled by Seafoam's descent to this bit of trivial advice, Kaija opened her eyes. A graceful bird skimming over waves capped with foam was tattooed on Seafoam's forearm.

"A seagull," Seafoam said before Kaija could ask. "A *kaija.* Just like you. We were destined to meet."

Kaija's colleague must have told Seafoam that Kaija's name meant *seagull,* and Seafoam's observation that Kaija was depressed and grieving did not require extrasensory perception. Everyone was depressed in February in Minnesota; most people in their fifties had experienced grief. Yet although Kaija tried to dismiss the seagull as mere coincidence, it felt numinous.

The following morning, Kaija's car took her straight to Nordstrom's, and her feet carried her up to the lingerie department. She was seen carrying a package of red underwear when she came out.

"I feel very alone, Doctor Juang." Kaija moaned in reply to Lee Juang's polite question of how she was.

The acupuncturist took Kaija's wrists and concentrated on her pulses. She peered into Kaija's mouth, lifted her tongue, and studied it.

"But *are* you alone?" Lee Juang asked.

"Of course, I am," Kaija bristled. "I'm more alone than anyone I know. I don't have a single friend whom I have known since my childhood. My friends have mothers, fathers, brothers, sisters, husbands, children, grandchildren, nephews, nieces, uncles, aunts, childhood friends, ex-husbands, wives of ex-husbands . . . ." Kaija's voice trailed off.

345

The acupuncturist inserted a slender needle into Kaija's earlobe. Her hands hovered an inch above Kaija's chest.

"Any pain here?"

Kaija winced.

"Heart ache," Lee Juang nodded. "Great sadness lives in the heart, and unresolved grief settles in the lungs."

Kaija could not have predicted three months ago that she would be lying on an acupuncturist's table. But Seafoam had aroused her curiosity about mind/body connections, spirituality, life after death, and other matters too embarrassing for an academically trained person to believe in. Chinese medicine, of course, rested on thousands of years of empirical observation. She had not Imagined, however, that she would let someone put needles into her body, never mind that Chinese doctors removed brain tumors and Chinese dentists had extracted millions of teeth without anesthesia.

Kaija felt the loss of her mother more acutely than ever. Lee Juang seemed to understand her isolation.

"We'll talk later about how alone you are. But first you must rest. Then we will ask the Great Spirit for help," Lee Juang promised.

Kaija's prohibitions against stereotyping did not stop her now. Lee Juang was Chinese, so she had direct access to the Mysterious Wisdom of the East. Lee Juang was happily married and therefore the very person to advise her. At the center of a large close-knit group of relatives, she understood Kaija's longing for relatives and for a man who would surround her with love.

Lee Juang guided a final needle into Kaija's big toe and disappeared behind a beaded curtain. Music like distant birdsong filled the lightly shaded room. Tinkling glass and the rhythmic grinding of a pestle assured Kaija as she drifted off to sleep that Lee Juang was nearby, mixing her herbs and preparing her foul-tasting tonics.

"Feeling better?" Lee Juang asked when Kaija woke. "I've been meditating on your question. We *could* ask the Great Spirit to bring you a man."

Yes. That's it. *Go on, ask.* Kaija was ready to light incense, bow in four directions, make offerings, walk backwards, tap her forehead to the floor, do whatever it took.

"But the trouble with men," said Lee Juang, the happily married woman, "is that they never grow up. So, for you, a little dog."

Kaija's body filled with delight at the absurdity of the solution. For the first time since her mother's death, she burst into whole-hearted laughter.

Having followed intuitions and coincidences, Kaija found herself in an unfamiliar Minneapolis suburb on a rainy evening. The split-level house next to which she parked was unremarkable except for two ugly cement lions flanking the front door. A garish painting of a leopard covered the entire wall of the foyer.

Kaija was disappointed. She had come to consult a woman who was wiser than herself, and she expected such a person to have good taste. But this leopard could have come from a truck in a K-Mart parking lot which sold bullfighters, flamenco dancers with teeth clamped on stems of orange roses, and angry roosters poised for attack on black velvet.

"Go on down," Gabriella said, pointing to the basement. "I'll get my son to knock it off." She took the stairs two steps at a time.

Loud thrumming alternated with shouts in another part of the house. Did wise women and "spiritual intuitives," as Gabriella called herself, yell at their teenagers just like ordinary people?

Gabriella did not look like an ancient crone ready to dispense other-worldly wisdom either. Skinny as a pre-adolescent, she wore gold tights and a tight purple tube top, which must have been as difficult to crawl into as a garden hose. Only small wrinkles near her green eyes suggested that she was in her forties.

Gabriella led Kaija into a tiny windowless room and lit a fat candle on a scuffed plywood bureau. Purple and gold paper streamers from the ceiling moved back and forth.

"Did you like my painting?" Gabriella asked.

"Which one?"

"The one in the foyer, right where you came in. Like it?"

Kaija was determined to tell the truth. Gabriella had probably intuited anyway that Kaija thought the leopard and the two lions guarding the front door were tacky. Could Gabriella also tell that Kaija had consumed more wine and ice-cream since her mother's death than she liked? Kaija crossed her arms and grasped her elbows to prevent Gabriella from peering farther into her and finding something more embarrassing,

"I didn't care for the leopard," Kaija admitted. "I'm sorry. That's just me."

"Good. I can see we'll get along because you're not afraid of the truth," Gabriella said. "It doesn't matter about the painting, but I do want you to know that leopards are my source of power. I was a leopard in one of my former lives. After I was the Angel Gabriel, of   course."

Gabriella pulled down her tights and pointed to her naked left buttock. A tattoo of a leopard with Gabriella's big eyes and sharp little cat face gazed up at Kaija.

Kaija managed an uneasy smile. It was ridiculous that she was in this place, with this person. She would leave if she had any sense. But maybe the stagy details were only an indication that Gabriella was from California? Maybe this was Gabriella's way of shocking Kaija out of the safe visual references of the academic world? Kaija's curiosity kept her riveted.

"Relax, Kaija," Gabriella said kindly. "I work only for the good of Spirit and for the happiness and welfare of all people. I will not hurt you or trick you."

She took Kaija's hands in hers, studied the palms, and pressed them against her heart. The gentle warmth flowing from Gabriella reminded Kaija of Seafoam and Lee Juang. But the skills of those two women were based on detailed knowledge of human bodies. It was murky at best where Gabriella's insights came from. For all Kaija knew, they might originate in Hell, if such a place existed.

In the 1950s, when Kaija attended Latvian Lutheran church services, she had memorized a passage which forbade worshipping false gods. Pastor Saulcere had explained that meant one should not love wealth and fame more than God, but he also said it was a warning against fortune tellers, mediums, spiritualists, and gurus. They might pretend to have divine knowledge, but it was more likely they were in touch with forces of darkness. A visiting minister had been much harsher. He had condemned all pretenders to extraordinary spiritual powers as worshippers of the Devil, who tricked innocent souls into eternal suffering. Pastor Saulcere would urge Kaija to leave and stay away from Gabriella.

Kaija did not want to imagine what her former professors—rational and scientific-minded everyone—would say if they saw her looking to Gabriella, an uneducated woman with a poor vocabulary and a taste for kitsch, for advice.

"Your shoulders hurt from carrying someone," Gabriella said. "This dead person is very heavy. She is crushing your lungs."

Maybe Gabriella studied obituaries in newspapers and then waited for the bereaved to show up. Maybe she called the university and pried out information from an inexperienced employee in the personnel office. But Kaija was beyond searching for a logical explanation for Gabriella's intuitions. She wanted only an end to her sadness, and she hung onto Gabriella's every word.

"I see a woman in a garden. It's autumn, but it's pretty nice outside. It's far away and long ago. Not quite in the Olden Times when they wore long gowns and stuff, but more like black and white movies, slinky dresses and all. Everyone's dressed up. Wait. The woman is bending over an old guy in a bed. Does that mean anything to you?"

"I'm not sure," Kaija said.

"A house in the country . . . late roses in a garden . . . no, other dark flowers, more puffy . . . daffs? . . . dahlias? . . . she is upstairs, looking down . . . a hospital . . . a sick-room . . . her husband wants her . . . but that old guy is holding on . . . he's a mean old bastard . . . she'll have to chop off her hand to get free. . . he won't let her go . . . "

Gabriella looked intently at Kaija. "You getting this? Want me to go on?"

Kaija nodded.

"All right then," Gabriella sat up straighter and closed her eyes.

"The old guy says . . . please, don't . . . no, he's not the kind who says please . . . don't you dare leave me . . . that's it, he's threatening her . . . I order you . . . a skeleton talking . . . he's alive but he's a skeleton . . . I order you not to leave. . . she tries pulling away her hand . . . oh no, he's really mad now. . . he's shouting . . . don't you dare leave . . . I did everything for you . . . you owe me . . . bad daughter . . . ungrateful girl. . . selfish woman . . . don't listen to your husband . . . you stay . . .you . . . no, you come with me. . . you're my wife . . . you're a mother . . . you're my daughter . . . hurry . . . shots in the garden . . . the two men will tear her in half. . . don't leave me . . . the soldiers will beat me. . . my wrists tied . . . bad daughter . . . bad wife . . . soldiers in the garden . . . dahlias . . . red mums . . . blood on the grass . . . "

Gabriella stopped talking and let out a long shuddering sigh.

"Go on," Kaija whispered. She knew that garden and that house. She had been there. She had heard those words. She had seen her mother's indecision and her father's fury.

She knew for certain now that her Grandfather had not died before they left. He had been alive. They had had to leave him behind.

Her father had dragged her mother to the car. He shoved and pushed and cursed. The car doors slammed; he held her arms to her side to keep her from flailing and from jumping out. He shouted at her to be quiet. She screamed and clawed at the door. She pounded on the back window as the Summer House disappeared behind oaks lining the long drive.

"No," Gabriella moaned. Her normal voice was gone. Coarse guttural noises, something between groans and barks, issued from her throat. It was an ugly male voice, like that of the Devil in *The Exorcist*, too rough and too powerful for Gabriella's slender throat and small frame.

Gradually Kaija became aware that words were interspersed with grunts. Her linguistics courses in graduate school were no help in identifying the language. It was not a Romance language; it was neither Germanic nor Slavic. The words belonged to a violent, pestilence-ridden Europe of centuries ago, and yet they were exactly right for the horrors of the Twentieth Century.

Gabriella's head rolled side to side; her hands raked the air.

The terrifying voice stopped as suddenly as it had started.

"Soldiers . . . tanks . . . they beat him . . . guilt . . . silence. . . shame . . . ."

Gabriella sat up and looked around, as if her attention had wandered and she had dozed-off.

"Go on, tell me more," Kaija cried, every reservation about mediums and parlor tricks forgotten.

She was back in the garden where her mother had struggled; she was in the car where her father had tried to restrain her. Her calm and reliable parents had changed into strangers. She had tried to forget their terrifying transformation as well as Grandfather left behind.

In the DP camps she had asked, "Where is Grandfather? When will he come?"

Her mother looked away and did not speak, so her father was the one who answered. The General was safe. He had died before they left Latvia; he was buried in a deep grave near the Summer house; he was at peace; soldiers with guns could not harm him. He was safe as houses.

But houses were not safe. Kaija's parents' flat in Riga was probably dust and ashes; the Summer House must be an uncared-for ruin. Dust to dust, and ashes to ashes, Pastor Saulcere had said at her mother's funeral.

But the tragedy of Ingrida forced to abandon her father had a stubborn life. It took Ingrida over for the second time, after her friend Alexandra was abducted. Torture of the General and then of Alexandra was too much for Ingrida to intergrate.

"Did the soldiers really torture my Grandfather? Did my mother say anything, Gabriella? Did my father hit her? Did he tie her hands? What did she say? Tell me."

Gabriella shook her head. "That's all. Enough. Don't ask me. I shouldn't have told you what I did. You're not ready."

"I have to know," Kaija cried. She leaned forward, so that her face was an inch from Gabriella's. She would force the truth from Gabriella if she had to squeeze her throat and push the words out one by one.

"Tell me," Kaija commanded. She remembered her radiant and loving mother; she had lost a great treasure when her mother changed. She willed Gabriella to speak.

"Forget about the soldiers," Gabriella said. "Stay with your mother. No, your father did not hit her. He shouted that it was her duty to leave; she was his wife and your mother. She screamed she didn't care what happened to you, Kaija."

"I know," Kaija whispered. "I've always known that she did not care about me."

Kaija had said the painful truth out loud.

Violent anger at the soldiers rather than her mother seized her. She raged at them for crushing the saplings of birches, for killing dahlias and roses. She cursed them for her Grandfather's suffering. She wanted to hurt them. She threatened them until she could no more.

But slowly tears of compassion replaced her rage. Her mother, like other women in wartime, had been forced to make a choice, which was really no choice at all. Like other men, her father had been pushed from gentle respect to fury. Kaija's beloved parents, those two thoroughly civilized people, had been wrenched from their real selves. They had lived with guilt and shame. Her father had tried his best to make amends and to live a normal life.

Kaija cried first for her mother and her father, and then for Alma, for Alma's parents Valdis and Velta, and for Jautrite. All had been wounded by the ever-expanding circles of violence and madness war left behind. Her compassion touched the bitter men drunk on Park Avenue, Ivars unable to commit himself to creativity or to his marriage, and to damaged veterans living on the streets and on Park Avenue. She cried for overpowered women, humiliated men, and terrified children.

Her tears gave out eventually. But then, like water gathering in dry ruts in a river for the second time, compassion rose in her heart for herself, for the child trying and failing to win her mother's attention, for the girl wanting to make her mother happy with straight As, and for the mature woman she was now, still yearning for her mother's love.

Gabriella cleared her throat. "Are you all right?" she asked.

Kaija nodded. Her eyes burned.

"Your mother is here," Gabriella said softly. "She wants to say something."

Kaija looked up, fully expecting to see her mother next to Gabriella. But she saw only Gabriella's kind smile.

"Your mother says, 'I love you, Kaijin, I've always loved you. I am ashamed that I screamed I didn't care what happened to you. I wished I could unsay it. I hoped you did not remember. But I am glad that I went with you and your father. I love you, Kaijin.'"

"I love you too, *mila mmmin*," Kaija whispered as her mother's image faded.

Gabriella handed Kaija, dehydrated and exhausted, a glass of water.

The water tasted good. After a while Kaija heard to the steady beating of her heart, which was vulnerable and sore, but open and full of love. She wrote a check for $100 for Gabriella, money which did not seem adequate recompense for what she had learned.

Kaija was ready to drive home on the well-lit street of a modern city. War raged in many parts of the world, but this night Kaija was in a peaceful place.

Lost Midsummers

38

Jautrite settled into Kaija's apartment as easily as if she were returning home from a short trip. Kaija could not say exactly how this had come about. She had invited Jautrite to stay for a couple of days, so she could visit the university, fill out applications, and find a job and a place to live. But that had been weeks ago.

Jautrite had been heroic to escape from Doctor Eden; she had found the strength to act in spite of severe brainwashing. She had planned and packed and watched and then, while the Edens were preoccupied with allaying the suspicions of a social worker, she had slid out the back door, with fewer than twenty dollars in her pocket. She had slept in cars and abandoned buses, stood in line in churches for free food, and mowed lawns and cleaned houses. Eventually, she had made friends with a series of single women, stayed rent-free in their homes, and saved money from menial jobs. She was now ready to apply to college.

Kaija was full of admiration. Jautrite's escape was as brave as Latvians sailing at midnight across a stormy Baltic Sea to Sweden, Latvians surviving Nazi Germany, and Latvians tiptoeing past sleeping plantation owners to escape slavery in Mississippi. Many young Americans without family support took to drink and drugs or ended up on the streets. Some such damaged souls showed up in Kaija's classes, where they spoke of themselves as perpetual victims, tried to secure special privileges, and got angry when they failed to do so. But other unloved children, Kaija and Alma and Jautrite among them, found the willpower and courage to shape their lives. Everyone who did so was a small miracle.

Jautrite looked different from the exploited young woman Kaija had seen in Indianapolis a year ago. Her skin was clear, her clothes immaculate, and her hair, though chopped off and shapeless, was its normal color. Not a bruise, bite, or chain in sight. Her few possessions—bleached plain white t-shirts, faded jeans, a shapeless gray sweater which had belonged to her grandfather Valdis, and a stack of sheet music—fit neatly into a large backpack, which she stored in the closet of Kaija's study. The thin mat on which she slept, did yoga, and meditated did not take up much room, and neither did Jautrite.

Understanding and forgiving her mother had given Kaija immense energy. She had enough love for the whole world. To help Jautrite fill out applications for scholarships and jobs was the least she could do. She would be Jautrite's mentor in a successful academic career. She would show Jautrite that being unmothered need not stand in the way of a successful life. She would give Jautrite the benefit of her own hard-earned experience of love affairs and men. Eventually Jautrite would come to feel safe and talk about Alma; Kaija would encourage, soothe, and advise. Finding words for painful events had healed Kaija and helped her forgive her mother, and it would do the same for Jautrite.

Kaija took Jautrite to have her hair cut and shaped, so that dark waves instead of spiky clumps framed her regular features and large eyes. As a private tribute to Magda, Kaija drove Jautrite to a dentist to have her teeth cleaned and cavities filled. Jautrite's frequent and severe headaches vanished after Kaija surmised that she needed glasses and ordered them. Kaija was delighted as Jautrite exclaimed over each leaf and flower that she could distinguish, and every street sign she could read through her fashionable purple frames. To bring color and pleasure into Jautrite's life, Kaija took her shopping for cosmetics and clothes.

Kaija was happy to pay for everything. She kept her own possessions to a minimum so that she could pack quickly. Her two excesses—books and clothes—were neatly stowed in bookcases and closets, organized according to priority what to grab if she had to flee from soldiers or a Midwestern tornado. But Kaija felt more fully at home now. In her new expansive mood, she added comforts and small luxuries: a cover with a blue Japanese iris on it for Jautrite's mat, full spectrum lights against winter depression, a silk pillow emblazoned with entwined poppies, a pizza stone, and a stack of wood for the fireplace, which Kaija had never bothered to use, but which Jautrite was eager to try.

Jautrite—bright, avid for knowledge, and touchingly grateful—reminded Kaija of her younger self. Three women— Seafoam, Lee Juang, and Gabriella—had led her out of the bleak landscape she had inhabited after her mother's death.

Kaija felt fortunate she could express her gratitude by helping someone else. And there was also the small, secret satisfaction of getting along better with Jautrite than Alma had.

Speaking in Latvian and playing with the language was a big part of the pleasure. Kaija and Jautrite delighted in collecting phrases that could not be translated, such as ""Kur tu vazajies?" "Where have you been?" did not come close to conveying that one had been wasting time, moving aimlessly from place to place like an old rag over a dirty floor. Metaphors, allusions, and slang—as in "health nut," "social animal" or "you rock"—became delightfully absurd when translated literally into Latvian. Prefixes could change the meaning of a single verb into dozens of distinct meanings, and Jautrite and Kaija competed to come up with as many of these as they could. Or they picked a favorite subject—ecological awareness, strong women, spirituality, nature, gender equality, the pleasure of hard work —and recited *dainas*. Ancient Latvians had been startlingly wise and enlightened centuries ago. Jautrite, while often critical of Latvians themselves, maintained that Latvian language and culture were superior to all others.

Jautrite's opinions amused and flattered Kaija. "You really get it how hard it is to be a woman on your own, Kaija; *no one* else has a clue." "You're *so* different, Kaija, you don't have *anything* in common with Latvians. You're *always* kind and generous, they're *always* judgmental." "I'm going to live exactly like you." "I want to be like you." "I wish I *were* you, Kaija."

Jautrite talked endlessly about her future plans, as only the young can. She seemed less mature than twenty-three, but Kaija ascribed that to early emotional neglect and recent terrifying experiences. Jautrite would grow up under Kaija's tactful guidance.

Jautrite promised she would make Kaija proud. She would study hard, she would graduate from college with high honors, and she would get a Ph. D. in music theory. She would not waste time on men; she would devote herself to learning only. Well, maybe she would have an affair, so she could have a baby to whom she would give the love that she had failed to get herself. No, she would not have children, but she and a totally perfect man would travel all over the world together. Or she would have a succession of lovers who would die of heartbreak when she discarded them. No, she would remain celibate, join a cloistered community of intelligent and creative women, rely on their friendship and support, write music by herself all day long and sing with them every night. Kaija laughed at these contradictions even as Jautrite's excess of youthful energy made her feel young again.

Jautrite was curious about Kaija's past, and Kaija planned to tell her about her love life. Kaija had not met a man who knew and loved her real self, but she was glad she had not settled for less. She liked living alone; she did not feel lonely. She enjoyed reading and teaching and writing, and she loved her friends.

Kaija wished she could make up for what the younger woman had suffered. Jautrite had been a virgin when Doctor Eden raped her. His wife had known but had not interfered as he forced himself on Jautrite again and again. Jautrite had been too terrified to object when he assaulted a thirteen-year-old runaway he had ensnared at the Greyhound bus station. She still felt guilty, but at least this event had propelled her out of the house of the Edens.

Kaija expected that it would be as difficult for Jautrite to speak authentically about her mother as it had been for her. But after recounting her experiences with Doctor Eden, Jautrite went on easily to Alma.

"I loved my mother so much, but she didn't love me. She hates me. I did everything for her, but she never noticed. She hated to have me around. 'What are you doing here?' she'd say if I sat down next to her. 'Go to your room, I'm tired of you.'"

"She criticized women who had careers, but all she did was work: scrounging for materials, balancing books, learning Spanish so she could order her Mexicans around. She'd be up on the roof hammering and she wouldn't hear a word I said.

"But she did everything for my brothers. They got their clothes from L. S. Ayres, while I had to make do with a worn jacket she picked up at a garage sale. She pretended not to see when they twisted my arm and pulled my hair. My father just turned up the TV or went up to his study. Well, sometimes she did tell my brothers to cut it out, but that was because she didn't want me to have bruises for the Latvians to gossip about. 'Good,' is all she'd say if I got straight A's, but she'd call everyone in Indianapolis if one of my brothers had a decent report card. My mother hates me. She wishes I was dead."

"You were such a bright and beautiful little girl, Jautrite. I would love to have a daughter like you," Kaija said, surprised at the depth of her regret that she did not have children.

"Your mother was a little girl too when she lost her mother for good. Imagine how hard that must have been for her," Kaija remarked.

Jautrite listened dry-eyed as Kaija wiped away tears.

"Don't you feel any sympathy for her?" Kaija asked.

"No, I do not," Jautrite shouted. She ran into the bathroom and slammed the door. Jautrite had lashed out at Kaija in the restaurant in Indianapolis for defending Alma, and a small warning bell about her sudden rages went off in Kaija's head. But Kaija wanted to keep her talking. She knew it was possible to reconcile with a dead parent, but she wished Jautrite and Alma would make up while they were both still alive.

Everyone else had failed Jautrite too. "I loved Doctor Eden, Kaija, I really did. I did everything for him, but his family always came first. Bloody Blood Family; I was nothing next to them. Take Georgina, the music teacher. I worshipped the ground she walked on, but she treated me like a servant. 'Did you do the laundry?' she demanded the minute she walked in the door. She never noticed how happy I was to see her. When her daughter came to visit she made me sleep on the couch. She said her daughter had back trouble and needed a firm bed. As if that was the real reason . . . . "

359

Jautrite would get it all out and then she would stop, Kaija told herself. Jautrite was very intuitive and academically smart. If I. Q. scores were still held in the high regard they had been in the 1950s, Jautrite would have a "genius level" score, just like Kaija. Her intelligence would help her see that recounting past failures of other people was unproductive. Kaija told herself to be patient.

The two women settled into a pleasant routine. A movie, a concert of classical music, or a play at the Guthrie Theater on the weekend. Singing songs together from the hundreds of Latvian songs they knew by heart on the drive home. A cozy cup of coffee and a bowl of oatmeal in the morning, a glass of wine while Kaija made dinner. Kaija had not cooked much except on visits to her parents, but she started doing it again. Jautrite praised and ate and praised some more.

Jautrite was terrified if Kaija asked for help in the kitchen. She asked dozens of questions about how to stir a pot of simmering soup, and it took her ten minutes to wash and slice five radishes for salad. Kaija found it easier to do everything herself. Cooking was not necessary for intelligent women anyway. Thousands, probably millions of women had gotten stuck in kitchens when they would have been better off developing their minds and doing socially useful work. It was only natural that Jautrite felt incompetent after Alma's exacting standards.

"I love you so much, Kaija. I'll do anything for you. I'll even learn to cook. Soon," she added.

Jautrite was on her way to becoming Kaija's family. Their relationship would be starkly different from what Kaija had imagined with Maris and Mr. Hazard and Jerry and Ivars, but it would be nurturing and permanent. Jautrite would be the daughter Kaija had never had. Jautrite would reconcile with Alma, and Kaija and Alma would be reunited through her. Kaija would not be solitary in her old age.

As if reading Kaija's mind, Jautrite said, "Of course, you'll live with me when you're old, when it's too hard for you to be alone. I'll do everything for you. I took great care of my grandfather Valdis, and I'll take even better care of you."

Kaija was touched, although sometimes Jautrite's devotion seemed excessive.

"I'll always love you best, Kaija, much more than I will my husband and children. I'll die if anything happens to you."

Kaija tried not to mind when Jautrite interrupted her work or her sleep because someone had hurt her feelings at one of her temporary office jobs or when the cute guy she had met at Starbucks did not call.

After Kaija had had an especially hard day, Jautrite insisted on massaging Kaija's feet and rubbing her back. She had acquired these skills during a stint as an assistant to a yoga instructor, and she was eager to keep them up. Jautrite's large hands and firm touch made Kaija wince, but she was determined not to show her discomfort because Jautrite so badly wanted to please her. Instead of the little dog Juang Lee had recommended to Kaija for companionship, Jautrite wriggled with pleasure and bounded around the apartment like a Golden Retriever whenever Kaija praised her.

Jautrite curled up at the end of Kaija's bed, in a position she said was best for giving a massage. Increasingly often she dozed off.

"Jautrite? Are you asleep, Jautrite? Wake up, Jautrite." Kaija shook her.

"Please let me sleep here," Jautrite muttered sleepily. "It's so warm, and I feel so safe with you. I've never felt safe with anyone, not ever."

"Wake up, Jautrite," Kaija repeated. "You have to sleep between your own sheets."

Jautrite sat-up looking dazed. She recounted one more time the latest crisis at work and every nuance of her reaction while Kaija pulled her to her feet. She repeated how hurt she had been when Alma had failed to send her so much as a card for her birthday and how grateful she was that Kaija had made a real Christmas for her. No one else had ever been good to her.

It took all of Kaija's willpower and strength to maneuver Jautrite into the study and to settle her down on the new futon.

As the school year went on, Kaija felt less energetic. Her legs trembled, her neck muscles were permanently clenched, and her shoulders hurt so much that she cried out when Jautrite hugged her. She felt depleted after every class, even when a lecture or a discussion had gone especially well. When she stretched out in front of the fireplace in the evening, she needed Jautrite's help to get up.

One Sunday morning in early spring, Kaija took Jautrite along to a small café and bakery she had been going to for years.

"Is this your daughter?" Sheryl, the waitress newly renamed barista, asked.

"No," Kaija said.

"Yes," Jautrite said simultaneously.

"No, she's not my daughter." Then, feeling irrationally guilty, Kaija quickly added, "But she's a good friend."

"Why couldn't you just say I'm your daughter? Why did you have to contradict me? Why did you disown me? Why didn't you let her think we're family?" Jautrite demanded as soon as they left the bakery.

"I didn't disown you, Jautrite, but you already have a mother."

Kaija set morning buns, cups, coffee, cream, and three oranges on a tray and asked Jautrite to carry them out to the tiny balcony. The outdoor furniture was still in winter storage, so the two women settled down on a blanket on the floor. The sun felt good on their legs, bare for the first time since the autumn. They sat in companionable silence, reading the New York Times.

Jautrite could be difficult, but then no one was perfect, Kaija told herself. Jautrite was almost her family, and one had to accept the quirks of family members, even more than those of friends. Jautrite's talents and promise far outweighed her flaws.

With the sun warming her and Jautrite next to her, Kaija daydreamed. She would have a house on the edge of woods when she was old. A stand of white birches would give way to solid oaks, then to soft darkness under pines. Yellow leaves would settle on blood-red dahlias and white chrysanthemums near the front door. A pale late rose scented the air. Kaija would stand up to social workers and other well-meaning busy bodies who wanted to put her in an institution for the sake of regular meals and stupefying pills. She would meet death in this house.

Kaija would be retired from teaching, Alma would have cut back on remodeling, and the two friends would spend time together, as they had in their adolescence. They would reread cozy stories set on Latvian farms, read aloud passionate lyric poems by Aspazija, and search for copies of classics about Latvian girlhood on the internet. Their white hair flying, they would scold Aspazija's husband Rainis, the great Latvian poet and dramatist, for his selfishness and infidelities. They would walk in the woods, make *piragi,* and recount happy memories. They would be attentive and gentle with each other.

As if intuiting Kaija's fantasies, Jautrite said, "I'd give anything for my mother to pay attention to me, but she never had time."

When Kaija did not respond, Jautrite demanded, "Are you listening to me, Kaija?"

And then, like an actress in a well-rehearsed performance, Jautrite hurled herself into a soliloquy about Alma's failures.

"Wait," Kaija interrupted. "I know all that, Jautrite. It would be good if you tried to let some things go. Maybe you could start by intending to forgive. Maybe if you admitted that your mother did not intend to hurt you every time she . . . ."

"No, I can't. I won't," Jautrite cried.

"Listen, Jautrite, it may sound simple-minded, but it works. My mother wasn't there for me, but the relief was immense when I finally put everything together about her and forgave her. Don't wait until your mother dies . . . . "

"No, no, no, a thousand times no," Jautrite shouted. "I don't care what happened to you. You just don't get it, Kaija, what it's like for me. Listen, I'm telling you . . . ."

Kaija could not get a word in as Jautrite nailed Alma to the wall, word by furious word. Jautrite's black anger scalded Kaija's skin and settled in her chest.

"All right, Jautrite. I agree it *was* awful. But what do you expect me to do about it?" Kaija interrupted.

"I expect you to listen to me, that's what," Jautrite blazed.

"But I have. I have spent hours listening to you. Repeating the same old stories doesn't solve anything and it certainly does not help you. Try to forgive just one thing, try to remember your mother has suffered too. You cannot change the past, but you can do something about the future. Decide on one thing you can do now. But do not ask me to listen again."

"But you have to. We're really close, we're like husband and wife. We share everything."

"No, we are not like husband and wife. Our friendship isn't a marriage." Kaija stopped herself from digressing into a disquisition on the shortcomings of marriage. "What happens is that you talk and I listen. I don't make you sit still while I go on and on about all the bad stuff that's happened to me since the day I was born."

"But it's your duty," Jautrite shouted.

Kaija sighed, and with an effort got to her feet. Jautrite did not move her extended legs to make progress easier.

"I'm going to lie down," Kaija said, steadying herself against the glass door of the balcony. "Please bring in the cups and the tray when you're done."

Jautrite's hand shot out and grasped the tray, ready to send it crashing over the railing of the balcony. "You are so selfish, Kaija. I do everything for you, but you never notice. I was the one who brought this tray out here in the first place. I wait on you hand and foot. I would have done all the cooking too, but I didn't because you damaged my self-esteem, you explained things I already knew. You treated me like an idiot. You're *ordering* me to carry your stuff . . . ."

Jautrite looked poised to lunge.

"Don't think I liked the Latvian food you cooked either, chicken and fish and other flesh. I prefer vegan or at least vegetarian. I don't even like living here. I only do it for you. I don't have my own room, I don't have a piano, and you shut your door whenever

you feel like it. I don't have five minutes to myself. You're just like
. . . "

"Stop it, Jautrite. Just stop. Don't end our friendship the way
you've ended others. I tried . . ."

"No, you didn't try. You exploited me. Didn't you just order
me to pick up your dirty dishes? Admit it. Didn't you? I won't be
your slave. I will not. I refuse."

Jautrite's large hands reached towards Kaija.

"Don't you dare leave, Kaija, I'm not finished with you," she
screamed.

Not taking her eyes from Jautrite, Kaija backed away.

Perched on the edge of her bed, Kaija wished she could lock
the door. She kept her eyes on the handle, as if that could keep
Jautrite out.

Slowly, tremulously, she came to a decision. She would tell
Jautrite to leave. She would help her find another place to live; she
would help her pack and move. She would lend, no, she would give
Jautrite money if necessary. But no matter how guilty she felt, she
would not let Jautrite stay.

Kaija had been wrong to believe that she and Jautrite were
alike. They were both intelligent and ambitious, loved Latvian songs
and language, and had mothers who were damaged by war, but they
were not identical.

Kaija had been naïve to ignore Jautrite's practice of using
and then blaming older women. Jautrite's barely contained rage
erupted eventually against everyone who helped her. Kaija's
generosity and patience could not change another person. In order
to find peace, Jautrite herself would have to do the hard work of
learning to forgive.

39

"You got family back there?" Ivars' colleague asked Alma at a Republican fundraiser.

Right on schedule, Alma noted with satisfaction. Americans said that the minute they learned of an upcoming trip to Latvia. Hordes of starving refugees trooped across their TV screens every night, but they assumed that the travelers they were speaking to would find homes and relatives untouched by war and occupation.

"No, I do not," Alma snapped.

"Why are you going then?" the man asked.

When Alma did not answer, he said "You'll have a great time," and began naming nephews who had taken him pub-crawling in Dublin.

It was a disgrace that a well-educated man, one who handled contracts with foreign companies, did not know any history or politics, Alma fumed to herself. Travel to countries occupied by Russians did not resemble comfortable jaunts elsewhere.

"I'm not going to have *a great time,*" Alma grasped the man's sleeve. "My relatives died in Siberian labor camps. The few who survived and returned to Latvia went mad, or committed suicide. The Russians forbid anyone who returned from Siberia to practice their professions and to live in Riga. So if any of my relatives are still alive, I will not be able to see them."

"I'm sorry," the man said.

So he should be. Let him be sorry that he had raised a subject painful to her. She would not tell him that things were not quite so bleak. Alma had recently received a reply to a carefully worded letter of introduction she had written to a distant cousin named Dalija, whose address she had found among her father's papers.

367

Irisa, her cousin's thirty-three-year-old daughter, had written back. Cousin Dalija, Irisa, and Irisa's three daughters were going to meet Alma at the airport in Riga.

Two letters had traveled thousands of miles over land and sea, and suddenly, just like that, Alma had relatives. In a tiny country cut-off from the rest of the world for almost half a century, she had family waiting for her. Isolation and loneliness were the curse of exile, but Alma was no longer alone.

Cousin Dalija was seven years older than Alma, so she would remember Alma's mother. She would tell stories about Velta and about Alma herself as a toddler. The instant Alma and Dalija hugged, Alma would have family solidarity and motherly affection, just like everyone else.

Alma was pleased to learn that Irisa was a medical doctor; her relative had achieved what Kaija had failed to do. Irisa wrote that she was currently unemployed, however; things were too chaotic and salaries too low to bother going out to work. She lived on a small state subsidy for her daughters and whatever else she could scrape together. The three girls were looking forward to the visit of their rich aunt from America.

But something about Irisa's letter nagged at Alma. It was too abrupt, too matter-of-fact. Irisa had not said that she was delighted to learn that Alma existed; she had not thanked Alma for making the effort to find her; she had not praised Alma for persistence and ingenuity. And why had Dalija not written herself? Alma would never leave such an important task to her daughter. But she squashed her premonitions, if that is what they were.

"What will you take for presents?" Mrs. Lapsa asked Alma as they were shaping *piragi* in the Latvian Community Center kitchen.

Mrs. Lapsa wiped her hands on her apron and sighed. "Those people don't have a thing over there. 'Deficits' of everything, as their bureaucrats like to say. I took three suitcases, each one stuffed to bursting with presents for my relatives. I left all my own good shoes and clothes there for them too. My son Ojars didn't have a belt to hold up his pants, and I was stark naked under my dress when we

368

got on the plane back to America. We gave them everything because of those damn deficits."

Deficits. Alma fastened on the word. What a stupid piece of jargon, what an outrageous lie to cover up the fact that all the best goods produced in Latvia went straight to Moscow. That's the Russians and their ridiculous Three- and Five-Year Plans for you! Deficits wasn't even a Latvian word. The Russians stole it from upstanding American businessmen and accountants to cover up their own laziness and corruption.

Irisa had used the word too when she asked Alma to bring a winter coat for her twelve-year-old daughter "because currently we have a deficit of those." *Deficit.* The three syllables drummed in Alma's head as she moved around in the Latvian Community House kitchen, slamming cupboards and clattering pans.

Of course, she would bring the coat and other gifts. She could afford to be generous to her relatives. It was terrible that a mother, who was also a doctor, had to ask someone she had never met for essential clothing for her child. Alma remembered having to wear ugly hand-me-downs. But she had made up her mind not to care how she looked; she had never asked anyone for anything. She had kept her pride.

Alma would bring coats for all of Irisa's daughters; she would bring a dozen coats. That would show the Russians. She would clothe every Latvian who had starved and suffered in the inhuman cold of Siberia.

That was impossible, but at least she could make sure that her relatives were warm and snug while the Russians shivered bare-assed in the snow. She would bring fleece hats, flannel nightgowns, lambswool sweaters, moisture-wicking underwear, good socks, sturdy shoes, and fur-lined boots. She would personally eradicate every shortage her relatives had had to endure.

Russians had forced Latvian women to wear men's underpants and drive tractors, but Alma would demonstrate that coercion could not change the fact that men were men, and women were women. She would bring lace slips and sleek pantyhose and expensive perfume. Alma's three suitcases, the most that regulations permitted, would prove that American democracy was superior to Russian totalitarianism and that capitalism would triumph over communism in every part of the globe.

Alma shopped like a crazy woman. She bought everything she heard was in short supply: material by the yard for dresses and suits; zippers and buttons and linings and thread; spices enough for three restaurants; radios, videos, cameras, lights; crayons and notebooks and ballpoint pens; batteries, vitamins, aspirins, pills; tampons and condoms; diapers and toys.

Too excited to sleep, she made lists and plotted strategies. If only she could smuggle in a computer so that her cousin Dalija and her husband could rejoin the world. Irisa had not mentioned a husband, but she had three daughters, so she must have one. If Alma disassembled a bicycle and packed the parts into separate suitcases, would that fool the customs inspectors? And was a small washing machine taken apart really out of the question?

Alma was avid for stories of Latvians circumventing Soviet regulations. An elderly woman had bribed an Aeroflot pilot for ten gallons of gasoline, which she had proudly hand-carried in buckets as a present to her son-in-law.

A pious widow had smuggled in Bibles and hymn books by smearing sanitary napkins with red nail-polish and arranging them as the top layer of her suitcase. The young man at customs had slammed the lid down so fast he had almost crushed his fingers.

Alma ignored complaints about ungrateful and greedy relatives. "May your relatives from Latvia come to visit," was fast becoming a standard curse among some American Latvians, even as they tried to meet demands for trips to Disney World, Hollywood, Fifth Avenue, the Mall of America, and every mall in between.

Alma's relatives were going to be different. They would love and respect her; they would appreciate whatever gifts she chose to give them. When she paid for them to visit her in the United States, as she intended to do, they would come because they wanted to spend time with her, not to get a lot of stuff that she paid for.

Alma lost her composure when a clerk at the Post Office handed her an eight-page pamphlet of regulations Soviet authorities had imposed on packages sent to countries they occupied. "Cautionary Recommendations," "Prohibited Items," and "Restricted Articles" danced before her eyes.

"Here are the rules dreamed up and enforced by the Godless Russian Communists," she started to mutter to strangers waiting to buy stamps.

"Here are just a few examples of the things they've forbidden to people whose countries they stole in World War II: fashion magazines, seed catalogs, religious articles, manuscripts, photographs, maps, musical greeting cards, vitamins, used clothing, cloth by the yard..."

Her voice picked up volume as she continued. "And no more than one of these: coats, suits, skirts, shirts, blouses, shawls, handbags, gloves, eyeglasses. Let's hope that's a pair of gloves and two lenses in one frame for the glasses. Only one musical instrument, one hearing aid, one medical thermometer, one book, and that one to be inspected and approved. No more than seven ounces of tea, three and a half of spices, two children's toys, and too bad if your relatives have three children. No more than ten cards, ten labels, and three sets of new underwear."

"'Niet, niet, comrade, you're under arrest,' she mimiced. 'A bra and a slip and a pair of panties constitute more than one set of underwear. Three items are a set and a half. Off to Siberia with you because you brought a bra.'"

"Millions of Russians don't do any useful work at all. They get paid for arresting people who violate these restrictions. They appropriate whatever they want for themselves, and they have the nerve to call their stealing confiscation. But Russians stole from their own people too, from packages sent by grieving relatives to Siberia, so what can you expect? Stalin and the Russians and the Godless . . . ."

People flattened themselves against walls; some tiptoed out. The woman who had tried to give Alma a pamphlet about Jehovah's Witnesses in concentration camps held up her package like a shield. The man in a camouflage jacket, probably a Viet Nam vet, waved his crutch and shouted, "Right on, lady!"

371

Gone postal, needs counseling, victim of sexual abuse, and nut case, people whispered.

Kaija knew how to get students to pay attention even to dusty old plays, Alma thought bitterly, while her own attempts to educate Americans about important international matters had ended in chaos.

She had converted no one.

She pushed away the memory of Kaija.

Growing increasingly agitated and breathless, she repeated her speech all the way home.

40

Latvia looked breath-taking from above, its dark green forests bordered by white sand and sparkling blue sea. A pearl in the ocean. But decades of neglect, evident in crumbling plaster and unpainted woodwork, greeted Alma at the Riga Airport. An old man descended the steps of the plane ahead of her and with some difficulty knelt on the ground. He kissed the earth and rested his cheek against it. A guard yanked him to his feet and shoved him toward the terminal.

"Don't obey him, he's a Russian," one of the returning exiles advised in Latvian.

"Isn't that terrible? So young and a communist already! Anyone can see that guard is still wet behind the ears."

"He hasn't learned how to spit over his lip."

"He should rub duck shit on his chin to make his beard grow."

The young guard flushed a furious red. He hated these exiles returning from America, who acted as if they had every right to be here. Although even children were required to speak Russian in schools, these American Latvians spoke Latvian loudly at every opportunity, pretended not to understand Russian, laughed at regulations, and did not quake at the sight of his uniform. Travelers in earlier years had been quiet and respectful because they knew they could be arrested otherwise. But now there were too many of these Americans to put in prison.

"Missing the good old days when you tortured people?" an elderly woman taunted.

The guard grabbed her camera, unfurled the film, and stepped on it. Then, as if the obliterated images could still spring to life, he ground the black ribbon into asphalt with the heel of his boot.

"It is strictly forbidden to take photographs," he warned. "These are highly important military installations."

Someone pointed to a rusting luggage cart abandoned in a patch of exuberant weeds, and everyone laughed.

"Go to Liepaja, you silly capon," a man sneered. "The Russians are guarding their stupid statue of Lenin there for twenty-four hours a day. But the old crook will get toppled anyway."

Reinforcements, in the form of other grim-faced guards, arrived. Soon the American Latvians found themselves in a windowless room with the door locked.

"Ladies and gentlemen, here you see the best accommodations the Soviet Union has to offer. No air, no water, no chairs, and no toilets," a man declaimed.

"Like the Russian trains to Siberia."

"Shame on you. Don't trivialize what the deported suffered," a woman scolded.

"I wouldn't dream of it. What I meant was . . . ."

Mild bickering mixed with bravado continued. Alma retreated into terrified silence. Her father had been convinced that people who had escaped in 1944 would be arrested, bludgeoned, deported, or shot the minute they set foot on Latvian soil. Valdis dead was safely beyond the reach of the Soviet secret police, but they could throw Alma in prison and keep her there. The United States government was not going to create an international incident by trying to rescue her.

After an hour the guards unlocked the door and herded the Latvians towards Customs. Relieved, Alma joined the chorus of criticism of the upswept floor and unwashed windows. The moving baggage belt, arranged for maximum inconvenience so that travelers with suitcases had to squeeze through a tight line of others still waiting to retrieve their possessions, was repeatedly pointed to as confirmation of Russian stupidity.

Alma staggered into the lobby with her three suitcases. Reunited relatives were embracing and kissing, laughing and crying, giving and receiving flowers. The fragrance of carnations, roses, and sweet peas wafted around her as she moved her bags forward, one by one.

No one looked like her relative, though in the absence of photographs she had only her imagination to guide her. Alma sat down on her suitcase. She was ashamed that she was the only one without a welcome.

Someone tapped her on the shoulder, and she looked up to see two stocky women. Russians. Kaija used to scold her for stereotyping, but Alma was sure that she could unfailingly distinguish by a single glance Russians from Latvians.

"You're Alma," the older woman said without a trace of a Russian accent. Her intonation was different from that of American Latvians, but she was clearly a native speaker of Latvian.

"Dalija." Alma opened her arms to hug her.

Dalija grasped her elbows as if to protect herself and took a step back. Her daughter Irisa smiled and nodded but did not extend her hand.

"You certainly took your time," Dalija said. "The others are a lot smarter than you. It didn't take *them* forever to get through Customs."

Dalija sounded so accusatory that Alma almost apologized for the guards locking everyone up.

"It was a long trip," she said.

"What do you mean, long trip? What kind of traveling is that? What kind of traveler are you? I would have been here hours ago," Dalija huffed.

"These are for you, Aunt Alma," the youngest of three dark-haired girls held out white daisies tied with a red ribbon. Alma inspected the complexions of the three girls to make sure they were not the descendants of Mongolians. Their eyes were not slanted, and their smiles were sweet and shy. Irisa's husband must be a Latvian; in the worst case he was a German or a Finn. The ribbon around the flowers was red, that vulgar color communists adored. But the slightly bitter scent of the drooping blossoms and the girl's shy courtesy brought unexpected tears to Alma's eyes. These girls were

Alma's relatives, and these wilting daisies were flowers from a Latvian meadow. This was what Alma had come for.

"I need something to drink," Dalija announced. "I almost died of thirst waiting for you."

Alma glanced around for a snack bar or a dispenser of cold drinks.

"Well, if you aren't going to treat us to a drink, Alma, I have to have something to read. We're all great readers in our family. Give me money for the newspapers, Alma. We must read the papers immediately."

Dazed from her long flight, sleepless night, and fear-filled past hour, Alma handed Dalija several five-dollar bills. Dalija disappeared before Alma could ask whether American currency would do.

"Thank you for the flowers," Alma said, and Irisa smiled shyly, just like her girls. They stood in awkward silence while Alma dismissed questions about prices and exchange rates as impolite and politics as too risky. She was determined to get along with her relatives.

"What are your daughters doing this summer, Irisa?" Alma ventured.

"Not much. They're only seven, nine, and twelve," Irisa sighed and relapsed into silence.

Getting to know Irisa was not going to be easy.

Dalija returned empty-handed and smiling, but she looked glum again as soon as they were in a taxi.

The airport was still in possession of Soviet authorities, but change was evident elsewhere on the streets of Riga. Men on ladders were removing signs for "Soviet Boulevard" and replacing them with "Aspazija Boulevard." People dressed in colorful folk costumes unique to each district were singing on a corner near Brivibas Piemineklis., the Monument to Freedom. Subject of dreams and memories of every exiled Latvian, the monument had miraculously survived Soviet occupation. Even the massive statue of Lenin nearby could not diminish its simple power.

Thousands of flowers had been laid below the gray stone figures of men breaking chains and a woman holding up three gold stars. Someone had arranged the individual bouquets to form a harmonious, ever expanding design, and the fragrance of lilies and roses, punctuated by the sharp clove-like scent of carnations, floated in through the open windows of the taxi.

"Let's stop," Alma said impulsively, "I want to lay down flowers too."

The driver ignored her. He had spoken in Russian when Dalija negotiated the price of the ride, so perhaps he did not understand Latvian.

Alma leaned forward and tapped him on the shoulder.

"Let's stop. Halt," she added for good measure.

The driver swore and slammed on the brakes. The taxi came to a screeching stop in a lane of fast moving traffic. The women and girls were flung forward, tires squealed, horns blared, and metal crumpled. Four drivers were out on the pavement before the debris had settled. Shouting in languages Alma could not identify, they shook their fists and shoved each other.

Suddenly Alma was in a terrifying and unfamiliar Latvia, where anger swirled, violence threatened, no one spoke Latvian, and the only language she could identify was Russian. This was not the intimately familiar lovely Latvia, neglected and exploited during Soviet occupation, yet still beautiful and magical. This was an alien place in the possession of harsh and unjust people who could punish Alma for breaking their arbitrary rules.

"See what you've done, Alma," Dalija scolded. She picked up the largest suitcase and made her way adroitly to the sidewalk. "Don't just stand there and roll your eyes. Get that suitcase and come on."

"But we can't just leave. We have to wait for the police, we're witnesses to an accident."

"You foreigners, you're all alike," Dalija laughed. "Dumb as suckling babes. Law Number One in the Soviet Union: never, ever get involved with the police."

377

Blood was trickling down Alma's leg from a cut made by a door handle with a knob missing. But the pain was nothing compared to being called a foreigner. A foreigner in her own country. A stranger in the land where she belonged.

"May I?" Irisa said in a half-whisper. Her firm hand grasped Alma's elbow and guided her safely to the sidewalk.

All the jokes about Soviet architecture—wobbly cement boxes designed by committees of factory workers and street sweepers-- had not prepared Alma for the soul-destroying ugliness of Dalija's and Irisa's five story apartment building. Not a single flower or blade of grass pushed through the packed-down dirt in the trash-strewn yard. Children fighting and women scolding in foreign languages crowded the sidewalk. Caked mud, dried patches of urine and vomit, and the stench of boiled cabbage filled the stairwell.

Dalija unbarred the double-locked door of the apartment, which she shared with Irisa and the three girls. The living room was small, but other people evidently lived here too because Alma could hear whispering and surreptitious movements in the kitchen. Dalija kicked off her high heels and collapsed on the short couch.

Irisa brought in platters of white bread covered with a gray fish paste and an overly sweet, artificially yellow cake and set them on a crate serving as a coffee table.

"Please," she said and dropped her eyes.

Alma forced herself to smile and chew and swallow. She had been unrealistic to expect relatives like Mrs.Veldre's friends in faded photographs taken half a century ago. Alma had imagined an elegant cousin leading her into a blossoming orchard. The table would be set with good china, which had somehow escaped the vandalism of Russian soldiers and the greed of Soviet bureaucrats. She would be offered slices of raspberry mocha torte and cups of exquisitely delicious coffee. Or a wise elderly woman who resembled Alma's grandmother would pull out a chair at a round oak table in a cool farm house kitchen. Bowls of sour cream, dark bread, fried herring, and potatoes seasoned with butter and dill would taste exactly the way they had in Alma's childhood.

Alma told herself sternly that Dalija and Irisa were doing the best they could. Shelves in shops were empty, and the women had gone to some trouble to feed her. They had also put on their best summer dresses, never mind that the huge flowers on the black background of Dalija's dress were red, while white daisies were scattered on Irisa's dark blue material. They had walked long distances in spike heels, bought the bouquet of daisies, and ridden to the airport in buses packed with smelly Russians. They had done the best they could.

The three girls--Vijolite, Margrietina, and Rozite--all diminutive names of flowers—finished off the sandwiches and cake as soon as Alma declined seconds. Irisa began pouring out brandy which Alma had brought.

Dalija took a sip and frowned. "So, this is what your American brandy tastes like. I wouldn't want to comment in any detail. Myself, I drink only French cognac. Only the best for me. But we'll make do. I hope you had plenty to eat. I don't want you to go back to America and complain that Irisa didn't feed you."

Irisa's face was bright red, Alma noted, either from embarrassment or from the unfamiliar brandy.

"Thank you for the meal," Alma said. Her resolution to be polite to Dalija was fraying.

The three girls began to drift towards the kitchen.

"Sit down," Dalija ordered. "Let's see what your rich aunt from America has brought for you."

Rich aunt. Here was that phrase again. Alma was proud that she had plenty of money, which she had earned by her own hard work. She had made a point to show off her wealth by wearing three gold necklaces, a gold bracelet, a gold watch, and a heavy necklace with chunks of amber embedded in silver. Let the Russians see that they had failed to make her into a homeless beggar. But Dalija made it sound as if Alma was rich through no effort of her own, as if she had never had to scrub a stranger's toilet, take abuse from an angry customer at the bank, or drag home salvaged pieces of lumber for the sake of saving a quarter.

Dalija set the largest suitcase at Alma's feet and lined up the girls according to height. Their faces turned expectantly toward Alma as she began distributing scented soaps, rich lotions, and glossy lipsticks as well as chocolates, notebooks, and pens.

Gradually Alma became aware of silence. Why did no one speak? Why did no one say, "This is nice," or "I like this" or just plain "Thank you"? That must the fault of communism, which taught that what is mine is mine and what is yours is mine too. But Alma was hurt that her effort and care were not recognized immediately. Of course, the girls were shy. On the other hand, that bully Dalia had probably ordered them to say nothing.

Dalija looked at her new lipstick in the mirror of the silver compact Alma handed her and sucked in on her teeth.

"Oh, this really is too bad, Alma," she sighed. "This is Revlon lipstick, but I only use Christian Dior. And this one is beet-colored, but I only use clear red. She dropped the offending lipstick into her pocket and held her hand out her hand for another.

"You must wear a lot of make-up, Alma," Dalija continued conversationally, "because you don't look your age. But then all of you Americans look young because you've had such easy lives, not like us who stayed in Latvia, where we belong, doing our sacred duty to our homeland. Me, I'm too honest to cover myself with paint. Life is easy for American women," Dalija continued. "Nothing to do except worry about what to wear, while men do all the cooking."

"Where, for heaven's sake, did you hear that?" Alma outraged forgot her determination to get along with every one of her relatives. She was no feminist, but this really was giving men too much credit.

"On television. The men stir the Campbell's soup, and the women put their feet on the table and chatter on the phone."

"I have, I mean I had a friend who teaches Women's Studies, and she says that American women do most of the housework even when they have full-time jobs."

"Women's Studies? What's that? My special friend has a big couch in his office; he'll show you how to study women," Dalija chuckled.

Rozite, Dalija's youngest grand-daughter, touched Alma's hand. "I'd like to taste that Campbell's soup someday, Aunt Almina."

Aunt Almina. Alma resolved to ignore Dalija. She turned her attention to the girls and Irisa. She groped under the half-raised lid of her second suitcase for the winter coats she had rolled into tight bundles.

She had been flushed with success when she found coats in the off-season, and she had cheerfully paid for quality that most American children could only dream of. Her own boys had worn heavy wool jackets, and in the 1950s they too would have found these light weight coats amazing. Magic coats from the moon, Alma had called them as she squeezed out air and rolled and taped them to fit more into her suitcase. The material was said to be a by-product of the American walk on the moon, and the colors were glorious: the silver of stars, the green of lush shade-loving plants, the purple of twilight, and the red of raspberries and good wine.

Dalija sighed as she slipped on a full-length midnight blue coat. "Oh, it's too bad, but this doesn't go with the rest of my wardrobe, Alma! A coat like this must be worn with pants only and never with skirts. Now I'll have to go to the expense of buying slacks. And you, Rozite, don't even think about wearing that little silver coat to school. Someone will steal it. Tell your mother she'll have to find something else for you when it gets cold."

Seven-year old Rozite patted the pockets and grinned.

"Silver," she said. She twirled around with the coat flying.

"Silver is for princesses," she said and threw her arms around Alma's neck. "Thank you, dear Aunt Almina, thank you very, very much."

Rozite leaned into Alma's side while the Dalija inspected the other coats and found wanting them wanting: there were too many pockets or too few, the collars lay too flat or stood up too high, zippers were faddish, buttons were out of date, and Velcro would never hold together through more than one wearing. And who would have thought that Alma would bring coats filled with the feathers of dead ducks and farmyard chickens? If she had gone to a good shop, she would have found something modern.

Dalija's words, sharp as sandpaper, made Alma want to slap her. She glanced at Irisa, who had tears in her eyes. She mouthed "Thank you," in Alma's direction, not speaking up either because Dalija had intimidated or for the sake of sweet peace. The faces of the girls radiated curiosity and pleasure.

Alma must not ascribe Dalija's nastiness to the others. She had thought that she was not listening but Kaija's pleas not to stereotype floated into Alma's consciousness. Let's try to be kind, Kaija used to say. Alma knew Dalija was mean and greedy, but she might only be trying to hold onto her pride. She was just one person while Latvia was full of generous, intelligent, and polite people.

Compassion for Dalija beckoned to Alma one final time. Dalija must have been about fourteen when Russian soldiers occupied Riga for the second time during World War II, barged into homes, and seized whatever and whomever they wanted. God only knew what they had done to Dalija then. Dalija had endured humiliations and injustice and fear during the half a century of occupation which followed.

But Alma could not overcome her competitiveness and pride in how perfectly she had met her own hard experiences. Like Dalija, she too had experienced war and its aftermath, but she had not turned into a monster. She had achieved success without the advantages Dalija had: Dalija and Irisa were mother and daughter, they were in their own country, they knew the customs and the legal system, they spoke in their own language, and they lived together. Irisa had helped and cheered and comforted her mother.

"I have to start to my hotel," Alma announced.

"What hotel? Which hotel? Why a hotel?" Dalija demanded. "Why do you want to give money to the Hotel Riga when your relatives don't have two rubles to rub together? You must be a millionaire, throwing your money around like that. How many dollars do you get paid each month anyway? Americans, they never want to tell how much the state gives them, but me, I'm honest enough to ask. You must stay here, with us, Alma. You must give your American dollars to Irisa; she'll exchange them for you. She'll give you an allowance every morning, and she'll pick out the presents you should buy to take home. She'll let you have whatever money is left over at the end, but you'll want to leave that as her tip."

Irisa had turned her back while Dalija spoke, but she turned directly to Alma now. "We have a few small gifts for you too, Aunt Almina."

"Yes, yes, we must give you something," Dalija chimed in.

Her eyes came to rest on the stuffed moose head above the tiny TV.

Alarmed, Alma stood up, then sat back down.

Each of the girls hid something behind her back. They asked Alma in which hand they were holding a gift. Then without making Alma guess more than once, one after another they came up, curtsied, and handed her something.

Every object was carefully wrapped in brown paper decorated with flowers and birds the girls had drawn. And the gifts themselves could not have been chosen more perfectly.

Tears spilled unbidden from Alma's eyes.

A *vadzele*, a small, beautifully carved round wood box with white sand mixed with tiny beads and slim shards of amber in it. Alma would treasure it for now, and she would leave directions to have the contents scattered over her coffin when she was buried in America, which right now seemed to be a totally foreign land.

Irisa and the girls must have spent hours trying to find the little pearls of amber in the white sand on the shore of the Baltic.

A *prievite,* a bookmark with the word Alma hand-woven in it surrounded by symbols of suns and pine branches in yellow, green, and dark red.

And a small Latvian flag, set in a wood stand carved in the shape of Latvia and decorated with a piece of amber.

Irisa and the girls had understood that Alma, the exile, needed these symbols of her beloved Latvia. And they had spent time and money they could not easily spare. They had given Alma what she neeed

Picking up her precious gifts, Alma insisted on taking the wilted daisies to the Hotel Riga as well. The painful place deep in Alma's hear was gently touches and soothed. She would never abandon Irisa and her daughters; she would even try to be tactful so as not to bring Dalija's wrath down on them.

In a taxi on the way to her hotel, she remembered a *daina,* one of the ancient four-line verses.

Dod, Dievini, kalna kapt,
Ne no kalna lejina.
Dod, Dievini, otram dot,
Ne no otra mili lugt.

Dear God, let me climb uphill,
Rather than walk down.
Dear God, let me give,
Rather than have to beg.

She relaxed back into her seat. It was late, and the streets of Riga were empty. Only a few cars passed, their headlights dimmed to save irreplaceable bulbs. The old loneliness threatened her once more; Alma was familiar with such gloomy moments. But then she thought of the girls and their plans to go to Brivdabas Museum the day after tomorrow. And Irisa, what would Irisa like? Opera? Concerts? Shopping? Alma knew nothing about opera except for a few solo arias from concerts sin the Latvian Community House. But secure in her sense of Irisa's kindness and intelligence, she relaxed. She would ask Irisa teach her about music and the rest of Latvia.

41

Instead of strolling on a well-kept drive winding through a familiar park and past an established orchard, Kaija fought her way between brambles and weeds, over slabs of broken concrete, and around piles of trash until she found a path leading to the Summer House. Gone were the lilacs and mock orange; in their place a huge windowless shed blocked the view to the road. No trace remained of the flower beds filled with tiny spring ephemerals followed by irises and lilies; only rotting stumps marked the place of the birch grove. The pond, where storks used to wade, was dry.

Mismatched small panes of glass held in by cement and rotting boards had replaced the large sparkling windows so that the front of the house looked mutilated. It reminded Kaija of the blinded, bleeding horses which haunted her dreams. The roof over the main entrance sagged, threatening to collapse on anyone wishing only to touch it. Gone was the wide veranda and with it the long summer afternoons of lemonade, books, and leisurely talk. The stylized bronze sculpture of Aspazija, superb lyric poet and revolutionary dramatist, courageous Latvian woman, and Kaija's role model, had disappeared from its niche near the front door.

Kaija's shoes squelched with dew, and her ankles itched with mosquito bites, which were impossible to scratch satisfactorily. But at least the three doors in the back of the house, although missing their sturdy steps, looked usable. Vegetables, snapdragons, and asters flourished on a small square of ground cleared of weeds and overgrown grass. Kaija's spirits lifted: the dedicated gardener might speak Latvian.

Rags and torn curtains fluttered almost imperceptibly in the windows, and Kaija could feel rather than see people moving around inside. Her father been afraid that she would be arrested if she merely attended the 1991 First International Conference of Latvian Scholars in Riga; he was convinced that if she went into the country side, she would be imprisoned by the authorities or beaten by Russian settlers. She had not told him she would venture to the Summer House. She wished Alma were at her side to protect and embolden her. Kaija told herself she would be all right; she had been alone during the crises in her life.

The people in the Summer House were probably descendants of Nurse Jelums, furious now that the daughter of the Judge had come to reclaim his property and terrified that they would be put out on the street. Or they might be Russian laborers brought in to replace the Latvian farmers who were deported, as individual farms were turned into collectives. Ostensibly here to do the work of those in Siberia, their real purpose was to dilute Latvian culture and language. They would regard the Summer House as rightfully theirs after forty years of residence; they would consider her a shameless thief, who had arrived in broad daylight. But instead of taking possession Kaija wanted only see the house; she believed that would heal the wound deep in her heart.

A dog started barking when Kaija knocked. The growls and barks grew louder when she knocked again. Only the rotting doors, clumsily reinforced here and there with strips of plywood, kept the furious animal from her. Wishing she had brought along her umbrella for a makeshift weapon, Kaija tried to take large steady steps on her trembling legs.

Under an ancient oak, the only one of dozens remaining, Kaija stopped, placed her hand on the trunk, and waited for strength to flow from it into her. Fears and doubts jabbed at her. The inhabitants would refuse to talk to her even if she waited forever. They would scream and curse her if they came out. They would attack her with cudgels and rakes. The raging dog would savage her. Kaija had heard tales of inhospitality and worse from present occupiers to returning owners at the conference.

The barks rose in volume as the door jerked open. A burly bald man in a dirty t-shirt used both of his hands and his large body to restrain a huge mongrel with muscles so massive he seemed to have no neck.

"Go away!" the man shouted in Russian-accented Latvian.

"Good morning," Kaija said.

"Go away!"

"Excuse me, please," Kaija brought out. "I only want to talk."

"You! Go! Dog bites."

"Please I only want to talk to you. Five minutes only. Please," Kaija held up five fingers.

"Go!"

"Please."

"Go!"

Kaija reached into her jacket and pulled out a small canvas bag.

"Only talk," she repeated and waived her tourist billfold.

After a moment of glaring at her silently, the man produced a surly, "Okay." He seemed to know the myth that the small bags hidden and hanging from the necks of American Latvians were stuffed with dollars.

He spat on the ground, the saliva narrowly missing his boots. With one hand grasping the dog's fur, he started toward Kaija.

"No," Kaija shouted, "no dog." She dropped her money and passport back inside her blouse and held up both palms as if to that could block the animal.

"No dog," she repeated.

The man jerked the dog into what had once been the Summer House kitchen and kicked the door closed behind him.

"Shut up, Shostakovich," he shouted.

The dog quieted, and Kaija had another flash of foolish hope. The Russians living here had named their dog after a composer; maybe they were cultured people, willing to talk to strangers.

Snarls and barks erupted again.

The man shouted towards the house, "Shut up, you son of a whore."

The man had probably named the dog after a beloved tractor or his wife's ex-husband.

"You want my house," the man said with steely anger.

Kaija sighed and continued the tedious process of trying to understand and be understood.

Only well into the exchange did Kaija say she wanted to see the inside.

"I love this house. I lived here when I was little," she said, hoping to soften him.

She had felt as safe nowhere else as in her mother's study and Annina's kitchen. With her mother's arms around her, she had looked at colorful pictures, listened to enthralling stories, and played simple melodies on the piano. Annina, the cook, had allowed her to water the asparagus fern in the morning-facing windows of the kitchen and to arrange dried maple leaves under loaves of bread ready to be baked. But Kaija had loved her own room best of all.

She pointed and gestured to indicate the room was on the second floor; it had wide windowsills and a tall tiled oven reaching almost to the ceiling. She formed a square with her fingers to suggest the tiles; she made circles with her hand for the windmills painted on them.

The man stared, and the dog growled.

Kaija plodded on. She refused to be diverted by gratitude that the man was listening to her at all or by fear that he would attack her the minute she stepped inside.

"Blue tiles with windmills. Blue." She pointed in the direction of her room.

Blue. The man's face lit up with understanding.

But the closed-off look returned almost immediately. "No. Police say no."

The excruciatingly slow game of charades continued. The man mimed pulling down and carrying someone heavy, pressing eyelids closed, making a sign of the cross over a corpse. With an effort Kaija understood that the police had forbidden entry because someone had died in the room. *Her room.*

But who and when? Was a corpse lying in her bed?

The man's scarred hands sketched a noose. Whether murder or suicide, the only certainty was that the death of a woman had not been natural or peaceful. It was impossible to learn more, but the death in her room would continue to haunt Kaija. She realized that to plead more with the man would prove fruitless.

Kaija handed the man $20.

"Thank you," she said.

The man took the money, held out his hand for more, and shrugged when she did not add another bill. He embarked on a harsh monologue of either orders or curses.

The mutilated windows of the Summer House were the last thing Kaija saw as she walked away.

Later, standing alone on the road to Riga, as she waited for the driver and the car she had hired, Kaija tried to contain her disappointment. The landscape was familiar and deeply comforting, but the house and the garden did not resemble the Latvia she remembered. It was too long ago and too late to make them flourish again. Her childhood paradise would have to live only in her mind.

But the real Latvia must exist somewhere. Kaija refused to let the disappointment about the dilapidated house and the horror of a desperate woman hanging in her room define Latvia for her. If she could only stay open to experience, something else would happen. Some coincidence, event, or person would help her. She would grieve for her irretrievable childhood, but she would not give in to despair. She would not live in bitterness. She would search for the real Latvia instead.

Unable to sleep after returning to the Hotel Riga from the Summer House, Kaija got out of bed at four a.m. She turned over her room key to one of the Russian women stationed at the end of every corridor, who recorded all comings and goings. When the woman asked for her destination, Kaija pretended not to understand.

It was almost light outside; nights were transparent this far north, so close to Midsummer. The pre-adolescent boys who begged from and harrassed tourists during the day near Brivibas Piemineklis had collapsed in a sleeping heap and did not accost her. Their working hours were over or she was not worth the trouble.

An old woman was sweeping the pavement; another was arranging flowers people had left at the foot of the monument into an ever-expanding design. Kaija wondered whether the women were street sweepers employed by the city or courageous freedom loving Latvians risking imprisonment and beatings for tending to the beloved symbol of independence on their own initiative. The woman holding up three gold stars at the top of the monument glowed. Kaija kept her eyes on the statue for a long time, until she too felt brave.

The streets behind her were filling up with people in drab coats and jackets hurrying to work. They disappeared down dark basement steps or into large buildings without a single light showing. Kaija followed a few, hoping to come to a stand or a restaurant serving coffee; she asked for directions from two or three passers by. After a dozen blocks she gave up. Under Soviet rule, buying a cup of coffee in the center of a large European city was impossible in 1991. We have a deficit, a man said to Kaija.

How did people get to work on the long dark mornings this far north without coffee? No wonder Nescafe was a much-requested item in packages from relatives. Caffeine consumed on rare occasions could have a powerful effect, so coffee had also gained a reputation as an aphrodisiac.

Trying to find her way back to the Hotel Riga, where generous amounts of coffee were being poured for tourists to demonstrate that shortages did not exist in the Soviet Union, Kaija stumbled into an alley cut-off from light by squat trees with dense branches. The ground was muddy and the air damp, although it had not rained recently. Busts on stone pedestals closed in around her. It was probably light elsewhere by now, but Kaija could hardly read the identifying inscriptions in this dim area dedicated to preserving one version of history.

Implacable faces of generals, colonels, and bureaucrats regarded her. Described as heroes in the fight against fascism, these were the men who had ruled Latvia; they had shipped to Moscow food Latvians raised for themselves; they had condemned Latvians to imprisonment and death. But they were not beloved. No one had laid flowers at their feet; no one was in the alley to pay respects.

Had Kaija and her parents not escaped in 1944, these were the men who would have judged and comdemned them. Kaija felt the pure terror of others had lived with under their rule; it went far beyond shortages and humiliations. Her body thrummed with the horror of Velta, Alma's mother, being deported. Kaija wished she had had the knowledge and wisdom to comfort Alma when they were still friends. She wished Alma was with her now.

Kaija hurried towards a thin shaft of light splitting the darkness at the farthest end of the alley. It would occur to her later that the alley and forbidding stone figures had been a hallucination. She had not slept, eaten, or drunk water for twenty-four hours or more; she had experienced shock, fear, and immense grief at the Summer House. But she no longer ascribed her experiences to some commonplace physical conditions only.

Kaija had not found the authentic Latvia she longed for at her childhood home, nor did she encounter it in the few distant relatives she eventually sought out and met. She found the real Latvia elsewhere.

She was in touch with something intimate and precious whenever she was surrounded by Latvian language. Though frequently interrupted by Russian, Latvian could still be heard on the streets of Riga. A menu was surprisingly delightful when it was in Latvian; TV commercials were funny and more absurd in Latvian than in their English originals. Kaija was thrilled to hear words and phrases of half-forgotten songs and poems and to memorize them anew. She was deeply touched to visit places where Aspazija had lived and worked. She laid down dark red and creamy white roses at Aspazija's statues and former residences. She sang, "Dievs sveti Latviju," God Bless Latvia, the national anthem, together with thousands at a Song Festival.

Kaija fell into easy conversation with Latvian women working as maids in hotels, selling flowers and amber on the streets of the Old City, or sitting next to her in churches and concerts. She spoke with young men browsing in bookstores or smoking at nearby tables in an amusing cafe which had just opened on an otherwise dismal block. Latvians were inevitably polite and welcoming; only Russians pushed ahead in lines and forced her off the narrow, cobbled sidewalks. Kaija tried to stay true to her life-long campaign against stereotyping by reminding herself, though sometimes forgetting, to say "some Russians."

Despite vastly different experiences from her in the last half century, many people she met by chance seemed intimately familiar, as if *they* were her relatives—as recognizable as the landscape near the Summer House, yet as unique as the traditional folk costumes of each district and village.

At a roadside stand selling raspberries and heirloom tomatoes rarely found in the Unites States, Kaija asked the woman weighing her purchases about the history of the farmhouse and the fortuitous survival of the birch grove during collectivization.

"Please, go see for yourself. Please look at the orchard and garden especially," the young woman kindly offered.

Several varieties of berries were ripening near the farmhouse. Kaija remembered from childhood some of the names and the tastes—*janogas, erksogas, upenes*—but she was not sure of the English equivalents. She had not searched them out or planted them in the United States, as some exiles did.

A strong voice called out to her. "Please gather and taste. Please. You are welcome. You have not eaten berries like these since you were a girl. I have chamomile inside for you to take home. Pick three blue bell-flowers to press in a book for remembrance."

The unexpected generosity and the familiarity of everything offered brought tears to Kaija's eyes.

"I can see you are a displaced person," the voice continued. "I believe you need to hear me reciting."

A sturdy small person, no more than five feet tall, took Kaija by the hand and led her toward the dappled shade of an apple tree. For a moment, Kaija was confulsed. The person in front of her seemed a man and a woman both, yet neither.

But then she noticed gray braids secured at the nape of the neck, a long skirt with a finely embroidered border, and an amber pin holding together a shawl. Judged by such externals, this person was clearly a woman. But being certain of gender was less important than usual. Kaija felt that though fully awake, she had fallen into a dream.

The woman was much older than Kaija had first judged by her decisive movements. Hundreds of tiny lines marked her face, dozens of white hairs grew on her chin, but her blue eyes were merry and knowing.

"Listen," the woman said, "this is the poem for you."

She let go of Kaija's hand, lifted her face to the sky, and began.

All Kaija's doubts about her being a woman vanished. Her voice was melodious and nuanced, in a word, womanly.

She had chosen, "Sauciens Tale," A Call into the Distance, a long poem of eight elaborate stanzas. Kaija remembered that she, too, had memorized it once, in the displaced persons' camps, when she was about ten. But that had been decades ago, so that now she could only feel the absolute rightness of each line, without being able to produce the next.

"Sauciens Tale" was written by Fricis Barda for the Latvians who were driven into exile in 1905. Directly addressing the wanderer who has lost his country and everything else, the poet speaks of the pain of separation and the anguish of exile. He urges the wanderer not to forget Latvia and promises a final homecoming. On that distant joyous day of new freedom, trumpets will sound, flags and blossoms will lie on rooftops like snowdrifts, but the wanderer will bring with him the suffering of his long years of exile. He will ask what he can accomplish in the ashes and ruins of his country; he will be uncertain whether he has the strength to do anything at all. But return he must. He can at least offer to Latvia his heart which has endured so much.

The literature professor inside Kaija began noting the rhyme scheme and other formal elements, classifying the poem as romantic and nationalistic, and filing away words and metaphors. But by the second stanza none of that mattered.

The old woman had *recognized* Kaija. She was speaking directly to her about her experience. She understood that although Kaija lived a comfortable and privileged life in the United States, she had suffered because she had had to leave home and live in exile. Returning at the beginning of new independence was more complicated than simply joyous.

By the time the woman finished reciting, Kaija was crying freely. Her alienation and all the critical comments she had made about Latvians were dissolving and flowing away, taking with them the pain of exile. She was known and accepted. She was home. She was one with every tree and cloud and blade of grass.

The woman waited until Kaija had finished crying.

"Good," the woman said. "Crying is healing."

The feeling of being in a dream, the sense that the odd and unusual was unsurprising and even fitting, persisted. Kaija drew herself up straight and rubbed her eyes, but the strangeness did not dissipate.

They stood looking at each other, not quite willing to part. And then suddenly Kaija thought of it, a question she could ask, almost a test that she could give. It would bring this significant exchanged to a close, and it would return Kaija to the everyday world.

"Tell me," Kaija said, "do you happen to know a poem which contains the line 'the riches of the heart cannot be destroyed?'" Kaija had been searching for this poem which her teachers in the displaced persons' camps had quoted endlessly to encourage students to study and thus accumulate the only riches available. She had not seen the line among poems by Karlis Skalbe, which she had hunted for in anthologies, and no one in her acquaintance could identify it. She was no longer certain if Skalbe *was* the author or whether she was quoting accurately. She should have included this line in the Latvian Mantra, the rules of behavior she had once isolated and used to torment Alma.

"What were the words again?' the old woman asked.

"The riches of the heart cannot be destroyed."

"Oh yes," she murmured, "that *is* the last line in 'For Friends' by Karlis Skalbe. But it's a little different. 'The riches of the heart do not rust,' is how it goes."

And Kaija knew that was so as soon as she heard it. The riches of the heart were safe. They could not be destroyed by war and exile. They had guided Kaija and they had given meaning to her life.

> Es nezinu kas vakar bija,
> Es nezinu kas ritu bus,
> Tik ausis salc ka melodija:
> Sirds bagatiba nesarus.

> I do not know what's past,
> I do not know what now will be,
> I only hear as a melody,
> The riches of the heart do not rust.

The riches of the heart survived when everything was lost and even when the heart was ravaged. Here was part of the faith she had once despaired of finding.

Like so much else in Latvia, Kaija's encounter with the old woman was–and was not–magical. But one thing was certain: the old woman had given Kaija what she needed and had completed her return home.

Finding relatives had been most important to Alma.

Finding soulmates as well as Latvian language, literature, culture, and natural world had been essential to Kaija, and she had found them all.

Lost Midsummers

Part Five

Midsummer

1990s

Lost Midsummers

42

On her way to Floral Park Cemetery, Alma stopped at the flower shop across from the Methodist Hospital where Ivars had bought red roses for her half a century ago. She selected one bunch of white carnations and two in bright red, to approximate the colors of the Latvian flag. The bouquet was for her father's grave. The flowers were expensive, but then everything cost money in America, and Alma was too much in a hurry to drive around seeking a bargain. In Latvia, blue bachelors' buttons, orange-red poppies, and white daisies flourished along roadsides and in fields of wheat, and farmers were glad if anyone picked them.

The elderly shopkeeper took his time wrapping the flowers and dealing with Alma's credit card. He kept his eyes on the TV, where a local newscaster was interviewing a heavily made-up old woman in a red suit who claimed to have been Stalin's secretary. Alma wanted to take the young newscaster by the scruff of the neck and march him to Siberia to be confronted by Stalin's victims. That would teach him to fawn over that old tart who behaved as if she were a celebrity.

Americans would slam Hitler's personal secretary into prison as a Nazi war criminal, so why not Stalin's?

But that was the Americans for you, foolishly sentimental about all things Russian. But Russians would turn their backs on democracy soon enough. They would think nothing of invading peace-loving countries like Georgia, Ukraine, and the Baltic States to reestablish their empire.

Alma did not explain this to the shopkeeper only because her attempts to educate Americans inevitably failed.

Like other Latvians, Alma regularly visited the dead. She tended her father's grave every Saturday so that it would look good when people stopped by after church on Sundays. Her hip screamed in pain when she knelt down to pull weeds and wipe bird droppings from Valdis' headstone. She scrubbed the brass vase, filled it with fresh water, and sat back on the grass to arrange the costly blossoms. She hummed her favorite hymn, "Augsa aiz zvaigznem," Beyond the Stars, which promised that people who were estranged on the earth would meet lovingly and see deeply into each other's souls; all earthly hatreds would disappear. Alma's mother and her father were waiting to embrace her, while Stalin jumped around in pain down below, as small spiteful devils pricked his trousers with their red-hot pitchforks.

It was hot and humid, and Alma was glad of the shade of the birch she had planted, against cemetery regulations, by the plots she owned in the Latvian section. A few elderly Latvians were also tending graves near the simple gray granite monument dedicated, "To the exiles who lost their beloved Latvia during World War II." Alma heaved herself up and walked over to give them her observations about Stalin's secretary. With satisfying vehemence, the small group went on to deplore the newscaster, TV programming in general, Russian immigrants settling in Indianapolis, the sloppily mown grass, and the lazy manager of the cemetery. It was a scandal that he failed to keep out men from the adjacent housing project who stole flowers from the dead to further their flamboyant sex lives.

Alma would be buried next to her father, where her mother Velta should be. At first Alma's sons would pay some elderly widow to tend her grave, but that would not go on forever. Ivars would be buried at her side, but only if he happened to die before she did and only if she was the one making the arrangements. He shrugged whenever she asked where he wanted to be when he was dead, and who knew about her children? Young Latvians left Indianapolis, settled hundreds of miles away, and claimed they did not care what happened to their bodies.

Jautrite would not even know that her mother was dead.

And Kaija would not care, Alma thought bitterly. Kaija had her academic honors, she knew famous writers, musicians, and professors in Latvia, and she traveled God knows where in addition to her homeland. According to the Latvian grapevine, she had gotten herself all the way to Nepal last summer. If Kaija had stayed in Indianapolis, which was the closest place to home they both had, they would still be friends. But Kaija maintained that there was nothing for her to do here because there were no job openings in her academic specialty in the whole State of Indiana. Alma doubted that very much. Kaija wanted to chatter about her Renaissance, but she could have had a good job years ago, teaching composition at the Indiana University Extension in Indianapolis. English was English.

A powerful lassitude, exhaustion really, overtook Alma as soon as she got back into her Saab. She did not ascribe this feeling to the tight control she exercised over her pain and rage. She allowed herself to remember only the times when her father was sober and kind, and she forbade herself to speculate about Ivars' late hours, the exact whereabouts of Jautrite, and Kaija's absence.

She tried to feel satisfaction about things she accomplished, and she recited her blessings: a handsome husband, successful sons, a better house and a bigger bank account than any other Latvian in Indianapolis. And she had done her duty to Latvian society in America and in Latvia too by attending political demonstrations, signing petitions, and giving generous monetary donations. The Russian military were mostly out of Latvia; she and other Latvians had accomplished at least that. Russians did not leave Latvia only because President Regan, that dear man, said, "Mr. Gorbachev, tear down this wall."

Stabules belonged to Alma too, though it had taken a lot of money for legal battles and bribes to get aged Russians out of her house. Restoring the buildings fully would take more money and effort, but she was determined to do it. Alma hoped one of her sons would move to Latvia or at least take his children to spend summers there, though so far neither had shown any interest in doing so. Her sons lived on the two coasts, as far away as possible from her, but at least one had married a Latvian.

And Alma had her work. She knew she was brilliant at bringing neglected, vandalized, filth-strewn buildings back to their former glory and beyond. She worked long hours now only when she wanted to. When she felt especially low, she drove by the houses she had restored. She wished she could show Kaija everything she had done to rescue each house.

Alma blew her nose and told herself to stop thinking about Kaija. But a familiar spiteful voice started up in her head right away. Alma had taken excellent care of her father all his life, but should it not have been the other way around? She had lavished love and care on her sons and on the Latvian community, but she was often alone on weekends and long winter evenings. She loved Irisa and her three girls, but they made no difference in her daily life and loneliness. No one called, no one dropped in to see her. Kaija had friends everywhere while Alma had no one to whom she could speak the truth about her life. Yet she had done nothing to deserve such loneliness.

In the evening Alma, straight-backed and determined to have a good time, pulled up to a farmhouse at the edge of the woods. She knew right away that she should not have come. A dozen separate groups of Midsummer Eve celebrants had positioned themselves beneath gloomy oaks. But there was no focal point for the festivities, and no one was in charge of welcoming new arrivals. The detached clusters of people reminded Alma of Americans picnicking in city parks on weekday nights, with individual families eating their separate sad little meals.

The earlier Latvian practice of placing planks on sawhorses to form one common table in the shape of a huge "U" was nowhere in sight. A lot of the food looked American too: rotisserie-roasted chickens from grocery stores, sliced ham, and even potato chips. Only the tiny pretty sandwiches topped with salmon and dill or with fancy cold cuts decorated with thin slices of pickle met with Alma's approval.

It was a disgrace that the common bonfire had not been built. Were Alma in charge, she would have seen to that first. She would have told her sons to get it blazing on the pretext that it kept away mosquitoes, but really so that the young men could show-off by jumping over it, while women and girls watched, neither applauding nor cheering, but noticing.

Maleness still thrilled Alma, as it had that enchanted Midsummer's Eve when she had danced with Ivars and in the early years of their marriage, before Jautrite came along and ruined everything.

One of the few times Alma had visited Kaija in Minnesota, they had watched fleet-footed young men, handsome as gods, at the head of a Syttende Mai Run. She had tried to explain how exciting that was, but Kaija had laughed and said, "Women and men belong side by side, shoulder to shoulder, not with women bringing up the rear."

Alma jerked her mind away from Kaija once more.

The farmhouse itself was padlocked against visitors who might only wish to use the bathroom. The Latvian cellist whose country house this was had explicitly rejected the role of host when giving his permission for the gathering. People need not think that he would playact as the owner of an ancient farm and stand around all night, wearing a huge oak wreath, groping for half-remembered words to Midsummer *dainas*, and refilling beer mugs.

Nor would the merry-makers who demanded beer and cheese by singing centuries' old verses be met by Tiffany, his fourth wife. She was American and very young, and she could hardly be expected to bake *piragi* and to make *Janusiers,* the traditional caraway cheese for Midsummer.

Alma wished she had made up a party of acquaintances and that she had brought food instead of starting out so impulsively. Then they could all look for enchantment together. But real magic was possible only in Latvia.

She had never seen the fabled ferns bloom in deep woods at midnight, not even when she was passionately in love with Ivars. Nevertheless, she longed to see, just once before she died, silver and white blossoms explode above dark soft mounds of foliage. That was as near as she could come to describing her aching need for a connection.

Nostalgia for the 1950s, when as newly arrived immigrants she and Kaija went everywhere together, flooded her. They had all lived close to each other. Everyone had been poor, but meals had just materialized in those first years, and there was always plenty for the young women and the somewhat fewer young men who had not lifted a finger to help with the cooking. All the women had married anyway, in spite of the relative scarcity of men. With the exception of Kaija, of course.

Alma was certain that everyone had felt treasured in that distant, enchanted time when exiles clung together for companionship and for safety. Then anyone who spoke Latvian was welcomed with astonished delight, like a long lost relative. Older women and married couples had rallied around her after Kaija abandoned her for Indiana University. That Alma's parents had not graduated from the University of Latvia had not counted against her then. Later, of course, it had started to matter, as did her Indiana Business College certificate instead of a University degree. Ivars could have changed all that by joining a Latvian fraternity, but he had refused to do that and a lot else that would have made her life easier.

Alma understood the social code prevailing among American Latvians so intimately that she hated to hear it put into words. It had pained her when Kaija insisted on articulating "the Rules" and mocking their absurdities. Kaija called Latvians pro-education but anti-intellectual, and she refused to overlook a single instance of conformity, snobbery, anti-Semitism, or right-wing paranoia if a Latvian was guilty of it. Of course, she could snipe at Latvians from a safe distance because she would always be welcome. Kaija's father was a member of the most prestigious fraternity, and Kaija was a professor.

Latvians held academic titles in high regard, but Kaija laughed at that too, saying they were stuck in the nineteenth century, when professors were exalted because they lived in "ivory towers" and medical doctors, said to be "in trade," were looked down upon by so-called aristocrats, that is, those living on inherited wealth. She repeatedly pointed out, to everyone's irritation, that Latvians were sexist because they called men with the most peripheral connections to universities "Professor" and women scholars of distinction "Mrs." She maintained they had been disrespectful when they called her mother Mrs. Veldre instead of Professor Veldre.

Remarks like that had kept Kaija from getting a good husband. What other explanation could there be since Kaija worked in a university chock-full of men, leftists and socialists though they were? Kaija called herself a feminist and said nasty things about marriage, giving no consideration to Alma, who had been married all of her life. Feminism was not even a Latvian word. They had had to import it from somewhere, probably from Godless Russia, where Lenin's wife had thought it up in order to destroy the family. She would like to see Kaija's face when she told her that.

Alma hated the way her mind kept returning to Kaija.

Brooding about her estranged friend made her color with anger and hurt.

People would see her red face and say that she was having hot flushes. Alma refused to give the younger generation any reason to snicker privately at the eccentricities of their elders or to abandon Latvian society for American. As it was, there were not enough people under fifty here now.

Alma caught a glimpse of Kaija's father at a table reserved for fraternity members. Judge Veldre was still going strong in spite of the death of Mrs. Veldre ten-years-ago. He must be near ninety, but he stood ramrod straight, with his head proudly lifted, as if he were the very pinnacle of manhood. The fraternity members were wearing crowns of oak leaves instead of their usual visored caps and colorful ribbons, but they would stick together like burrs in a mongrel's coat and talk only to each other anyway. The ladies, as they referred to their wives, were in floating dresses and foolish shoes more suitable for tea on manicured lawns than on rough ground marked by bird droppings and gnarled roots.

A sharp sense of loss made Alma's eyes sting. Really, really, she should not have come. Nor would she have, but for the intense yearning which had seized her that afternoon for an embrace from Ivars, for the time when her sons were little, and her father worked by her side, for the fragrance of damp woods, wilting flowers, blazing fires, and for people who knew who she was.

Alma's thumb, which she had cut as she braided stiff stems of Sweet William, daisies, and evening-scented stock into her Midsummer's wreath, began to throb. She had used dental floss, a decidedly American material, to bind them. The flowers from her garden had little scent because she had put the wreath in a beer cooler to keep it fresh. But flowers were really fragrant only in Latvia. Maybe she should have worn a scarf, as was traditional for married women, instead of a wreath.

Standing alone, Alma felt as alienated as she had from her American co-workers in the 1960s, bubble-headed young women who had not believed her when she tried to tell them that her mother had been deported to Siberia because of no fault of her own. To her dying day Alma would not forgive the one who had said, "But she must have done *something.*" They did not understand why Alma did not simply send bus and airline tickets for her mother to come from Siberia to the United States, and they went blank and scuttled away when she tried to explain. The memory of their hopeless ignorance made the skin on her neck prickle.

Swallowing tears, Alma veered around and started back the way she had come, towards the empty farmhouse she had passed earlier. Her injured thumb pulsed and stung.

Something glimmered between the dark trunks of trees, and Alma stopped. Anything was possible at Midsummer, of course, but she knew that even her desperate longing could not make ferns bloom at twilight, on the edge of the woods, in America, and for her alone.

A woman stepped out of the shadows and into the path. With the setting sun behind her, the woman's features were shadowy. She was tall and though more solid than a mere girl, she too wore a wreath of some kind of large white blossoms. The play of shadow and light made her appear other-worldly, and for an instant Alma thought it was her own mother, miraculously resurrected.

Alma searched in her purse for her glasses as the woman opened her arms in welcome. Mist and twilight had misled her. It was only Kaija, inappropriately dressed for a Latvian event as usual, in tight jeans and a loose white man's shirt. Kaija had gained weight, Alma noted with satisfaction. She was not so likely to appeal to Ivars now.

"Almin, my dear friend," Kaija said. She spoke as if they had never been estranged.

Alma had vowed that if she ever came face to face with Kaija, she would lift her head proudly, turn on her heel, and stride away, leaving Kaija exposed and looking foolish.

But instead of that Alma heard herself speaking endearments. "Kaijin, dear little heart, my sweet small bird."

Kaija too spoke in Latvian as well. "Almin, my beloved sweet friend, I'm overjoyed to see you. Can you come and sit with my father and me? Or have you promised to spend the evening with others?"

Kaija did not demand, as another Latvian might, "What are you doing here by yourself? Where is your husband? Why didn't he come with you?"

"Actually, I was just leaving."

"Oh, please don't go." Close-up and smiling entreatingly, Kaija looked like the girl she had once been. Alma caught a whiff of fragrance of white roses entwined with mock orange, which Kaija wore in her short grey hair.

"We need you, Almin, we cannot possibly do without you. Please, you have to help us sing," Kaija motioned to the fraternity table. She made it sound as if Alma would confer a great favor by staying.

Alma's heart, which she had kept closed for so long, opened.

Being with Kaija again was better than having Ivars at her side for the sake of appearances; it was more magical than seeing ferns burst into bloom and drop white petals over dark mounds of foliage. People would remark that Alma had been seen at the table of the best fraternity, but that mattered to her less than it would have another time. Holding hands, the two women walked over wild wet grasses, towards the table at the edge of the woods.

Kaija had been right; the singing did need help. Alma had a good memory, she knew hundreds of stanzas and half a dozen different melodies for Midsummer instead of the one sung most frequently, and her voice was still lovely. After these came self-confident drinking songs, better remembered because more frequently sung. Later the songs of longing for the trees and hills and rivers of Latvia lead inevitably to the laments of orphans and serfs. Punished by cruel stepmothers and harsh overlords, denied rest and warmth, the orphans yearned for their mothers. But to reach them was as impossible as catching the sun.

Jautrite had loved those orphan songs, Alma remembered. Alma wiped her eyes, reminded herself to go easy on the beer, and started to recite her private mantra: husband, house, money, sons, and rescued buildings.

"You're crying, Almin," Kaija whispered.

"Oh, it's nothing. I'm just being silly. Must be those orphan songs," Alma said, trying to swallow tears.

Very gently Kaija brushed a strand of hair from Alma's eyes and took her hand in hers. She did not shush Alma or tell her to cheer up; she did not produce a logical argument that Alma had many reasons to be happy or that others had it much worse. She was simply with her.

"My father . . . no, my mother . . . my relatives in Latvia . . . Stabules . . . Jautrite . . . I won't be able to stop once I start."

"Go ahead, Almin, tell me. Pretend I don't know anything, and please tell me. No matter what you say, I will always be your friend."

A stream strained against bracken, crushed cement, barbed wire, and hacked down trees. And then it broke through. Alma was powerless to stop as she named her losses: dreams and longing for her mother, love and hurt from her father, disappointment with her relatives, the remoteness of her husband, long distances from her sons, and the loss of her daughter from her life. She was shocked that she could find the words. She wanted to get it all out, in front of her, instead of holding it jammed inside, secured by the tangle of barbed wire around her heart. She had to speak now, while Kaija listened. She knew she would never trust anyone else enough to to do that again.

The stream widened, gathered strength, and swept away debris and dried mud and rotting weeds. Eventually it slowed and ran clear.

"And Jautrite . . . she's like an orphan," Alma concluded. The last sentence tore out of her.

Kaija squeezed Alma's hand. "And you too, Almin. You're an orphan too. What, with your mother dead in Siberia, and your father as good as dead towards you for all those years."

It was up to Kaija, who had received so much generosity and love from others, to understand and to forgive. "It's all right, Almin, it is all right. You have been through a lot. And look at all you've accomplished."

"Thank you. You've been through a lot too, Kaijin," Alma whispered. "Too much suffering and loneliness for both of us."

Her weeping had left her fragile. She would not cry like this again.

"I promise you will see Jautrite again," Kaija said. "She's a survivor, like you. She's a Latvian woman, for goodness sake. She will be all right."

Far away, on the edge of the meadow, strong young voices were taking up a faltering Midsummer song.

"Listen," Kaija said, delighted. "Those singers know the words."

"Maybe they're Latvians recently arrived from Latvia."

"And young people from here too. They're all singing together."

More than a dozen people were walking across the meadow.

Kaija was as impulsive and as curious as ever. "That's great, I'm so glad they're here, let's go talk with them. What do the Latvian Latvians think of American Latvians, what is America like for newcomers now, where are they living, do they have a Park Avenue

409

of their own, is being an immigrant different from being a refugee living in enforced exile like us, do they have better jobs, is outright discrimination less, is condescension the same . . . ."

She stopped herself and turned her attention back to Alma. "But not now. Tell me about Midsummer in Latvia, Almin. Please. I was too young to remember much."

Alma thought of sitting alone on the white stone by the kitchen in Stabules, with all the celebrants gone, and of her father turned away from her, his face to the wall. She remembered singing with women and girls in the camps, she felt Ivars' arms around her as they danced, and she saw her oldest son leap over a bonfire.

But then an entirely different scene—remembered, imagined, or dreamt—came to her.

Alma is in the kitchen of Stabules. Velta is bending over a white enamel tub on the kitchen floor, which she has lined with fragrant fleshy plants that grow on the edge of the pond. They are called *kalmes* in Latvian, and Alma does not know their name in English. She has never seen them growing in America, but that does not make them less real.

The fragrance of birch branches, which Valdis has cut and carried indoors, mingles with that of *kalmes* as Alma's mother pours warm water from a jug.

Tenderly, tenderly she sets Alma on the smooth green leaves and brushes a strand of hair away from her eyes. Tenderly, tenderly Velta washes Alma's face and shoulders and the rest of her body.

The rising steam obscures her mother's face, and the old despair threatens Alma as she tries to catch her hand and hold-on.

But then she feels a gentle touch, and hears Kaija's voice:

"Viss ir labi, Almin, es esmu šeit."
"It's all right, Almin, I'm right here."

And the fragrant, green mist enfolds them both.

A Novel of Exile and Friendship

THE END

Lost Midsummers

Acknowledgements

I began writing this novel more than twelve years ago when the phrase "shopping for relatives" and its double meaning would give me no peace.

Many friends have been kind enough to read the manuscript in its many versions, and without their suggestions and encouragement I would not have arrived at completion: Dwight Allen, Rose Ann Findlen, Jean Lind, Dale Kushner, Kirin Narayan, Ray Olderman, Star Olderman Lisa Ruffolo, Sam Savage, and Ann Shaffer.

Because of the span of years, I may have inadvertently overlooked someone, and I heartily apologize.

I am especially grateful to my editor, David W. Jackson, for his patience, excellent advice, and meticulous attention to the text. He also designed the cover and interior layout of *Lost Midsummers*.

And, to the American Latvian Association Cultural Fund for generous financial support so that this book, my gift to Latvia, could appear in 2018, for the Centennial Celebration of the Republic of Latvia.

Lost Midsummers

About the Author

Agate Nesaule, born in Latvia in 1938, experienced the turmoil of war and of displaced persons' camps in Germany in the 1940s. She came to the United States in 1950, where she taught herself English by translating *Gone with the Wind*.

Educated at Indiana University and the University of Wisconsin-Madison, she was Professor of English and Women's Studies.

She has published academic articles, literary essays, and an award-winning memoir *A Woman in Amber: Healing the Trauma of War and Exile* (Soho Press, 1995; Penguin, 1996), that has been translated into six languages.

Agate lives, writes, and gardens in Madison, Wisconsin, and is currently working on *Coming Home: A Memoir*, about her father, spirituality, and Latvians in exile.

Bobbi Harte Photography

Lost Midsummers

Made in the USA
Lexington, KY
25 April 2019